Readers love *Earthshatter*
by ALBERT NOTHLIT

"*Earthshatter* literally shattered my mind, it is an amazing read and for its main genre Sci-Fi it is like absolutely nothing I have read for years."
　—On Top Down Under Reviews

"…if you're looking for a wonderful story to immerse yourself in that leaves you on the edge of your seat gasping for breath at times, then this is for you."
　—MM Good Book Reviews

"If you are a science fiction lover looking for a novel into which you can sink your teeth (and mind), look no further."
　—Prism Book Alliance

"Whoo boy! This book was pretty much one non-stop ride from the first page to the last."
　—Love Bytes

By ALBERT NOTHLIT

HAVEN PRIME
Earthshatter
Light Shaper

Published by DSP Publications
www.dsppublications.com

LIGHT SHAPER

ALBERT NOTHLIT

DSP PUBLICATIONS

Published by

DSP Publications

5032 Capital Circle SW, Suite 2, PMB# 279, Tallahassee, FL 32305-7886 USA
www.dsppublications.com

Light Shaper

Cover Art

http://www.stefmasc.com/

ISBN: 978-1-63476-568-8
Digital ISBN: 978-1-63476-569-5
Library of Congress Control Number: 2016901927
Published August 2016
v. 1.0

Printed in the United States of America
⊚

This paper meets the requirements of
ANSI/NISO Z39.48-1992 (Permanence of Paper).

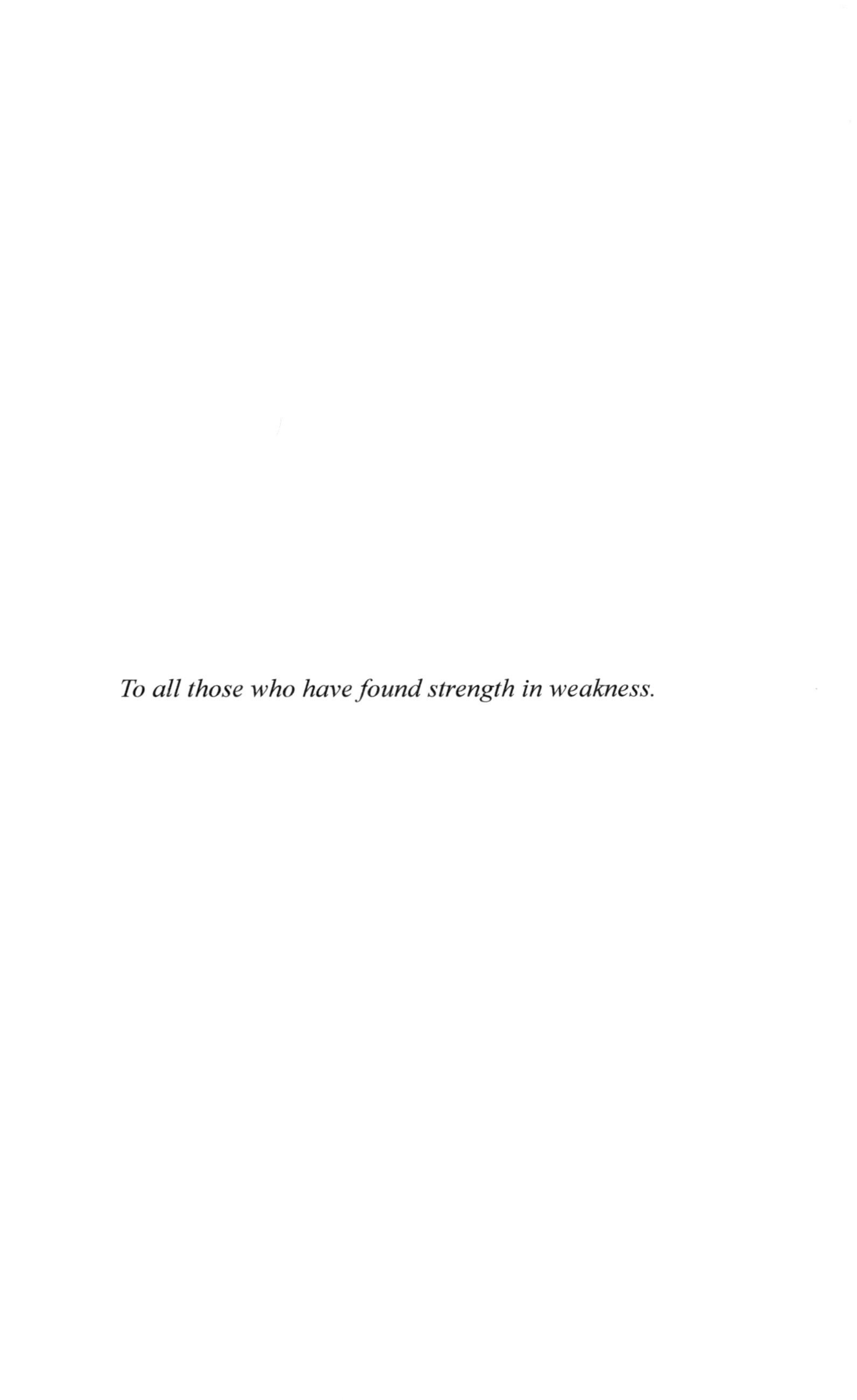

To all those who have found strength in weakness.

Prologue

A SHADOW moved, and the scientist screamed. He shut his eyes tight and stood there trembling.

No. No. It's not there, it can't be. It's not there!

He did not want to open his eyes and see it, but the alternative was worse. Fear won out, and he parted his eyelids cautiously. His gaze darted all around, and his breathing came in shallow, short gasps.

The shadow was gone.

The scientist breathed a shaky sigh of relief and clutched the little quantum drive he still carried in his right hand a bit less tightly. He was alone. That was good. Maybe he had imagined the shadow. Or maybe it still hadn't found him.

He started walking again, making his way along the abandoned hallways of the laboratory. His footsteps echoed on the metal plates of the floor, and eerie creaking noises were awakened by his passage. The lighting overhead was uneven, neon tubes flickering in some places and completely burned out in others. The ceiling was low and curved, as it had always been, but now the scientist felt as if it would crush him. It was as if the ceiling were trying to remind him of how deep underground he was, trying to whisper there was no way out. That he was the last one left alive.

The quantum drive dug into his palm painfully, but he welcomed the sensation. It was a distraction for his mind, at least. There was still one thing he had to do, and he knew he had to hurry. His footsteps picked up speed, and his lab coat trailed behind him as he rushed through the many corridors that he knew by heart. He passed a few dead soldiers on the way, lying facedown or clutching their weapons or on their backs staring up at the ceiling with sightless eyes. The scientist did not want to look, but he couldn't avoid it. He knew all of them by name, and seeing each one's corpse drove a fresh spike of fear-tinged pain into his heart.

He reached a very long corridor eventually. It was the way into the mainframe, the cradle room itself. On the other side of the corridor was the door he was looking for, within reach at last.

The shadow was there waiting for him.

The scientist nearly laughed, but all that came out of his throat was a croak of horrified desperation. There was nothing casting that shadow on the door across the hallway, and it didn't come from behind the flickering, broken lights overhead. It was a shape too solid to be imaginary. It wasn't moving this time, and much of it was hidden by normal darkness. It was hard to tell what it was… but it did have a head.

The scientist knew it was watching him. He also knew he had to get through the door and deliver the lockdown program to the mainframe before it was too late. He could not let the shadow get into the servers. Enough people were already dead.

He took a step, and then another. His feet felt like lead as he approached the door that the thing was guarding. Recent memories of his ruined city flashed through his mind as he forced himself forward. He relived the surprise of seeing the horrible newsfeed images and the crushing devastation of certainty that followed. He thought of the dumbstruck hopelessness everyone at his outpost had shared as the missiles were launched without anyone authorizing it. There had been nothing they could have done. And now they were all dead.

The scientist realized he was crying now, although he did not know if it was for himself or for everybody he had known. He was terrified of that shape ahead, the thing he knew had caused all this, but he had to get through that door. He had to lock down the network and save the priceless software inside before it could be infected too. It was all that was left.

Click click.

The scientist moaned an animal sound of horror when he realized the clicking sound had come from the shadow's head. He could feel its eye upon him, and as the shape moved and was revealed fully, he could see it balancing gracefully upon its single segmented leg. It wanted him to come closer. And when he did, he would die as all the others had.

Something snapped in the scientist's mind when he realized there was no way out. Like a half-forgotten dream come suddenly, he felt a moment of incongruous relief as he accepted he was going to die. He used the moment well. He gritted his teeth and forgot everything but his mission.

Then he charged at the closed door.

The shadow blurred out of sight, and the scientist crashed through the weakened door behind it. He stumbled into the room, the one place in the compound that was still working to perfection. He hurried; there was no time. He could feel the shadow coming.

He tripped once over the heavy cables connecting the experiment to its power supply and landed badly, right on his knee. He cried out in pain and tried to stand up, but the knee gave out immediately. Then he tried again, clutching at servers, and he hobbled the last few steps to the mainframe despite the pain. He fumbled with the quantum drive for an agonizing second before he gripped it tight and, with a single purposeful motion, connected it to the one unprotected port in the entire machine.

The effect was immediate. Power feeds were diverted; data streams stopped flowing. The experiment in the center of the room dimmed inside its magnetic cradle as the forced lockdown isolated it in seconds. The low, ever-present hum of machinery died down and gradually left only silence behind.

And shadows, of course. The lights were flickering now, and with each one that went out, the darkness grew more absolute.

When the last light went out, the scientist dared to hope that now he was safe. After all, there are no shadows in total darkness.

Click click.

Black on black, it came for him. He sunk to the floor, whimpering, backing up against the powered-down server that could do nothing to save his life.

The shadow moved closer with awful, deadly grace.

Chapter One

"There is no boredom in Otherlife. There is no stress. There is no pain in Otherlife… unless you want there to be. You decide. You are in control. "Experience Otherlife. See what true living can be."

STEVE BARROW cranked the music blasting from his earphones higher, so he could stop hearing the damn Otherlife commercials that kept playing every few minutes on the Skytrain. He couldn't truly escape from them, though. He hadn't really counted before, but there seemed to be one every few minutes. Had it always been like that? Or maybe it was just that he was noticing them more now, since he knew he was going to work there. That made more sense.

Barrow looked out the window of the train to the thousands of lights shining far below in the city. It was late, and most of the commuters sharing the slightly overcrowded carriage with him had already finished their work shifts. He was only just beginning, and tonight was his first night on the job. They had hired him today.

He took out a crumpled printout from his jacket pocket, elbowing somebody by mistake. He grunted by means of an apology and read the paper once more. He was to show up at the main Otherlife headquarters in the CradleCorp building complex at 2100 hours sharp, in the administrative wing. There was a little map and also the name of the position he would be occupying. CradleCorp Security Guard, V. Barrow had no idea what the V stood for.

He wasn't complaining, though. It was good to have a job again. The pay wasn't great, but he wouldn't starve or be forced to move to the slums outside the city. He was silently thankful for whatever stroke of luck had sent his name to the security team at Otherlife and gotten him the position. Stashing the crumpled paper away, Barrow reached up to his chest with his free hand and cupped the small pendant round his neck. It was a half-melted metal key, completely ordinary otherwise, but he closed his eyes briefly and said thanks inside his head.

The train stopped at one of the stations, and a woman carrying way too many bags shouldered past him roughly. He let her through, inadvertently pushing a man standing behind him into one of the occupied seats. The guy turned, scowling, and from the corner of his eye, Barrow saw that the man had every intention of shoving him right back. Barrow turned casually so he was facing him fully. The man looked up at him, sized him up, and decided he wasn't that offended after all.

Barrow turned away. He was used to that reaction. He suspected part of the reason why they had hired him for the security team so quickly was because he looked like a security guard. He assumed his job would imply standing around looking mean to scare undesirable people off. He had done it before and even found it slightly entertaining. He had gotten very good at intimidating people without saying a word.

It was hot inside the train. It was even hotter outside, so opening the windows was no comfort. To distract himself from the heat, Barrow looked up to the Skytrain network map and saw that he was still eight stops away from Cradle Station.

Crap.

He hoped he would not be late on his first day. He didn't usually come this far out of the city center, and he had guessed it would take him about an hour to get to Cradle from his apartment. It was looking like it would be a little bit more than that. Thankfully, the amount of commuters kept on thinning out the more stations they passed. Three stops later Barrow actually found an empty seat. He took it and used the time to take out his phone and check himself over with the forward-facing camera to make sure his tie knot wasn't messed up. He hated wearing ties or formal clothes in general. He was much more at home wearing gym clothes or jeans. One had to make a good impression on the first day, though. Even if the collar of his shirt was choking him.

Barrow put the phone away and looked around the train. The remaining people traveling with him looked different from the average commuters who had been more abundant closer to the center of the city. For one thing, most of them didn't look very tired. Also, each and every one of them had an expectant, almost skittish air about him or her that made them look as if they were impatient for something to happen but were trying to control themselves. None of them were rich, or else they wouldn't be taking the Skytrain in the first place, but they looked well-off and confident. The younger people were wearing flashy clothes as if they were going out clubbing, and some of the others looked like they were going to Sunday mass. There was one little group of teenage girls at the very end of the carriage, all of them huddled together and alternatively typing on their phones and giggling about it with the rest. The atmosphere had changed slightly as a result of all this; even Barrow felt it. He tried to put his finger on it, but the closest he could come to was that it felt like they were all going to a massive party.

"Cradle Station. Change here for CradleCorp headquarters, Otherlife, and ONP. All change, please."

Barrow stood up and left along with everybody else. He crumpled the paper with the directions and tossed it into a garbage can. There was no way he could get lost if everybody was going to the same place.

He took the elevator down from the Skytrain level to the ground, and in the close quarters, he couldn't help but overhear the excited conversations of several people about to start their nighttime Otherlife. Two young guys were wondering aloud whether the mysterious women they had met the night before were girls from their class.

"Dude, I'm telling you, the brunette talked a lot like Sharon. It felt like her!"

"I don't know, man. Did she share her profile info with you after I left with the blonde?"

"Yeah, but only the public one."

"See? It could be anyone. It could even be a temporary avatar. There's just no way to know."

The group of teenage girls from before was standing right beside Barrow. Their high-pitched giggling distracted him.

"Strippers?" One of them was saying. She was doing her best to sound mortified. "No way!"

"Oh, come on, Marion, Gilly!" another one urged her. "Only one night. It's going to be fun!"

"Plus, all the guys up there will be gorgeous," a third girl added. "You don't have to tip them… unless you really like what you see! Who's going to know?"

More giggling. Thankfully the elevator doors opened, and Barrow shouldered his way out of the crowd.

At street level the dry heat of the desert that surrounded the city of Aurora was much more apparent. Barrow walked quickly out past a fairly busy bus station and skirted the taxi lane as he crossed a big street, finally reaching the main pedestrian walkway leading to CradleCorp HQ. He had seen pictures, of course, but he had to admit, now that he was here in person, the entire place was impressive.

The walkway leading to the huge building was spacious and elegant. Cobblestones provided an uneven yet pleasant surface to walk on, a nice change from the perfectly featureless downtown sidewalks. Wrought iron lampposts lined it on either side, each one shining with a warm yellow light that cast a friendly sheen over the pathway. There were benches such as one would find in a park, as well as little unobtrusive stands for last-minute Otherlife session purchases if you hadn't already booked them online. The trees growing on either side were not many, but interspersed among them were cacti, Joshua trees, and other plant specimens native to the Mojave Desert area. The overall effect was nice, wild yet controlled, like a miniature version of the extinct national parks. The landscape was styled in such a way that the eye was naturally drawn forward, along a ruler-straight walkway that led to the Cradle.

Barrow had no idea why it was called that, but the Cradle was the one building every citizen in Aurora could identify. It was a crescent-shaped structure that seemed to glow with the lights shining in its many different levels. It had to be at least five stories tall, but its height wasn't what made it impressive—it was its size.

The more he approached it, the more Barrow revised his mental scale of the building. It had to be at least a kilometer long from tip to tip, almost an entire city in itself. The clusters of lights inside indicated human activity was concentrated near its center, with its wings mostly dark except for a few very bright regions. Nevertheless, the overall impression it made was staggering. It encompassed his entire field of view. When Barrow was close enough to see the main doors, he had to stop for a moment and just look around. It seemed hard to believe that such a magnificent, geometrically perfect building could exist in the middle of the desert surrounded by wastelands, but here it was. And thanks to it and the unique software treasure inside it, so was Aurora.

He made good time to the building, arriving right as the hour struck. He made a beeline for one of the many reception counters and was surprised at the lack of queues to get in. He had assumed that since Otherlife was so overwhelmingly popular it would be a maze of waiting and standing in line to get in, but he hadn't counted on the size of the building. It was big enough for the hundreds of people who entered every hour to make their way without delays.

The woman at the reception desk looked up at him and smiled with perfect white teeth. The Otherlife logo, a golden *O* with four radial spikes inside it that didn't quite reach to the center, was sewn onto the shirt of her flattering uniform.

"Welcome to CradleCorp. How can I help you?"

"I'm looking for the Security Department," Barrow said in his deep, clear voice.

"Of course. You have an appointment by any chance?"

"Barrow. Steve. I'm here to see Armando Scholl."

"One moment, Mr. Barrow. Let me see… ah, yes. He has instructed all new hires to meet him in room A-244."

"How do I get there?"

"Let me just give you this access card. Do you have any form of personal ID with you?"

"Here's my driver's license."

"Thank you. And… here you go. Now just go through that checkpoint on your right and take the first elevator you see to level *A*. That's the first floor. From there, turn left until you find room 244. It will be on your right-hand side, clearly labeled."

Barrow took the card. "Thank you."

"My pleasure. Enjoy your first visit to CradleCorp, Mr. Barrow."

He didn't even bother wondering how she knew he hadn't been here before. They had probably downloaded his information the second he had come through the doors. She had been friendly enough, though, which was a nice change from the grumpy warehouse intermediaries Barrow had had to deal with in his previous job. He hoped the rest of the night would go as smoothly.

He left and followed her directions to the nearest elevator, then hit the button and stepped inside it when it came. He saw that the floors were labeled *G*, then *A* to *D*. He punched the button for floor *A* and waited patiently for the few seconds it took the machine to lift him up one level. The doors opened smoothly, and he stepped into a very long carpeted hallway that ran from left to right. Straight ahead, huge windows gave him a somewhat commanding view of the area above the reception, and farther ahead he could see the night sky over Aurora. He turned left and started looking for room 244. There were doors set at regular intervals on his right side as he walked, all of them even and starting at 2. Then came 4 and 6. He quickened his step, realizing it would be a long walk to 244, and checked his watch to see whether he still had time to make it. Well, he would probably be a few minutes late, but nothing too serious. He doubted everybody would be on time anyway.

Ten minutes later he was passing room 212, and he was beginning to understand how vast the building really was. He had been walking quickly, nonstop and passing door after door. The occasional windows that let him see inside the rooms were mostly dark, although many had been occupied from rooms 2 until around 98 or so. In that area, the hallway had widened and branched many times over on either side, leading to rooms that he quickly found were not what he was looking for. They were mostly labeled with letters instead of numbers, and the people inside coming and going had all been customers. Since it was a relatively busy time of night, some of the hallways had been packed. Barrow had had to squeeze himself between more people than he would have liked several times already, trying to find a way to get back to the main hallway. Eventually he had done it, with relief. The only problem was that he was now really late. He had since passed the busy areas of the building on this level, though, and he had only come across a few people going the other way for the last couple of minutes or so. He looked at his watch again. Well, no sense hurrying up now. He would just apologize and say he had gotten lost. If they kicked him out, fine. He didn't really like this place anyway, or the entire Otherlife escapist philosophy. He was only here because he desperately needed money.

He made it, finally, and barged inside without knocking. He found himself in a very big room that looked nothing like what he had expected. He had been visualizing a conference room or something, with somebody in a suit lecturing them or maybe handing out information for them to memorize. Instead he was in what looked like the operations control center of a big airship. The walls on two sides were gigantic monitors partitioned into smaller areas that showed all kinds of different information. There were scattered work terminals in which people were seated, typing away, talking over the phone, or otherwise looking very busy. The place was set in three tiered levels, with the highest level being the one where Barrow was standing, directly outside the door. From his vantage point, he could see not only the terminals on the middle level but also what looked like a row of oddly lit chairs at the very back of the bottom level that had bizarre-looking helmets hanging above them. They were arranged in a semicircle, and several of the chairs were occupied, although more than half were still empty. A single chair faced the others, at the center of what would have been the circle the chairs were making. It had a bulkier setup than the others and looked more like a pilot's seat than a normal seat.

The top level was empty aside from a row of lockers set against one of the dark walls. Lights hung from the ceiling, but they were dim, and most of the illumination came from the bright monitors of the screens set around the terminal operators. There was a single big open area behind the strange chairs at the very bottom, where some people were casually talking in groups of two or three. Aside from them, though, the atmosphere in the room was one of frantic activity. It was far from quiet, with the air full of voices, electronic sounds, and the occasional monotone computer message. Barrow was familiar with operations control centers from his previous job, but a quick look at the information displayed on the monitors showed him that he couldn't understand any of it. It looked like they were monitoring stuff, and if he had to guess, he would have said they were probably keeping an eye on the users inside Otherlife's network, but he wasn't sure.

Barrow looked around, hoping to find the chief of security somewhere. There was no sign of Armando Scholl, though. Also, everybody was ignoring him.

With nothing better to do, Barrow descended to the lowest level where some scattered people were talking. He assumed those were the new hires, like him, and he was not mistaken.

"Hey," Barrow asked the nearest one. "Are you here for training?"

The blonde woman nodded. She was dressed formally, for the induction they all assumed they would be having. "We all are. The security chief had an emergency to attend to. We're waiting for him to return."

The man with glasses next to her gestured to the chairs impatiently. "It's been almost half an hour. I honestly have no idea what they are doing in there."

Barrow followed the man's gesture to the occupied chairs. He realized for the first time those chairs were connection terminals to Otherlife, very similar to the ones that customers would normally use. He had seen the commercials on TV often enough to recognize the helmets, only here they seemed either much older or a different type of build, without the smooth glossy finishes of the advertisements. Complicated arrays of cables sprouted from the back of the helmets and rose to a central node set on the ceiling of the room, each cable twisting and braiding itself with the others. The operators who were connected were all wearing the Security Department uniform too. And the man seated in the center had to be the Chief of Security.

As he was checking them out, the main operator chair made a powering-down noise. Barrow and the others stepped closer, and after a pause of a few seconds, Armando Scholl, Chief of Security in Otherlife, took off the helmet and opened his eyes.

He stood up stiffly from the chair, already surveying them with calculating brown eyes. He was scowling, his mouth set in a thin straight line, and Barrow was uncomfortably reminded of a prison warden's appraising look as Scholl looked at each of them in turn. Aside from Barrow, there were five others. Barrow was the tallest of the lot, and at that moment standing out felt like a disadvantage.

Scholl cleared his throat.

"Evening, and welcome to Otherlife. My name's Armando Scholl. For as long as you last in this job, I'll be your boss. I already know all your names, so we won't waste time making introductions. You don't need to know each other to do your job well in here. Any questions before we begin?"

Barrow exchanged glances with the blonde woman, who appeared to be as confused as he was. Scholl was very direct, that much was obvious. Barrow found himself liking his style.

"If not, then get moving. Pick a chair, and meet me at Hub Node 01."

They moved. Barrow picked the closest chair and sat down, pleasantly surprised to find out that it was a recliner and much more comfortable than his couch. He grabbed the helmet hanging a few centimeters above his head with both hands and pulled it down. This was the tricky part. He had to act like he knew exactly what he was doing even if he had never connected to Otherlife. He had lied in his résumé and in his interviews to get this job, and he wasn't going to screw himself over by asking how to connect or what "Hub Node 01" was.

He watched Scholl on the command chair as the Chief lowered the helmet over his head and pressed something once he had it in place. The thing hid his entire upper face, leaving only his nose and mouth uncovered. The helmet came alive with light, and Scholl relaxed in his chair. Loud beeps to Barrow's left and right signaled the successful connections of the others.

Well, it couldn't be that difficult. He lowered the helmet fully and let it cover his head.

He couldn't see with the thing on, and the heavy padding muffled sounds. He waited for the helmet to do something, but it didn't cooperate. What had Scholl done? He had pressed something on the outside, hadn't he? Seconds ticked by as he felt around the outside of the helmet, blindly looking for a button to press. One of his fingers finally found a tiny lever, and he flicked it. There was a buzzing noise but nothing more.

Dammit! Where is the on switch?

His left hand finally found three buttons set directly outside his temple. He pressed first one and nothing happened. The second one, same thing. The third one, and still nothing.

"Mr. Barrow," a voice said. It was Scholl; Barrow could hear him through the padding on his helmet. He must have disconnected to talk to him physically again. "We are about to begin training. We're late already, and considering you arrived nearly thirty minutes after the original meeting time, further delays because of you will not be tolerated. Connect now, or get the hell out of my command center."

Fuck. He knows I was late. How the hell does this work?

Barrow hit all three buttons on the helmet at once in desperation, and to his great relief, the machine buzzed to life. There was a brief clicking sound and slightly increased pressure as the helmet molded itself to his head. Then came the electrodes. Barrow gritted his teeth. It was good that he did, because the pain the microscopic filaments inflicted as they drilled into his skull was surprising. It was also, thankfully, very brief. He established the connection without really being aware of it.

When Barrow dared to open his eyes again, the world around him had shifted.

He was inside Otherlife at last.

Chapter Two

HALFWAY THROUGH the break-in, Rigel began to have serious doubts about agreeing to come along.

"Hey, hurry up," Misha urged him. "We're almost there."

"I'm coming," Rigel said, squeezing through a narrow shaft that was barely wide enough for him to crawl through. "You said this would be quick."

"Just a little bit farther. Don't chicken out on me."

Rigel's foot snagged on one of the hundreds of cables that snaked through the underside of the ventilation shaft they were traversing. He cursed softly and yanked it free.

"What was that?" Misha asked him from up in front. Rigel could only see her feet.

"Nothing. Just some stupid cable."

"Watch it, Aaron. If we screw anything up, then they'll know we're here. And not even my dad will be able to get us out of prison if we've damaged anything."

"I told you, I'm Rigel now. Stop calling me Aaron."

"And I told you that insisting on a weird new artistic name is stupid. *Aaron*. Now hurry up, or they will lock us up."

"They can't put us in prison," he protested. "We're only nineteen. Emphasis on the teen."

"Yeah, right," Misha answered. "And they'll go extra easy on me because I'm a girl."

"No," Rigel grunted, turning to the left when he saw Misha's legs disappear in that direction. "But your dad works here. If they catch us, he can get us off easy."

Misha chuckled up ahead. The sound echoed in the narrow confines of the never-ending ventilation duct. "You don't know my father very well, do you?"

"Just that one time at our graduation. He seemed like a nice guy."

"Uh…. Nope. Honestly, Aaron, sometimes I think you have it easy now. No parents to boss you around, being strict all the time and trying to convince you not to pick an Art major."

If anybody else had said that to him, Rigel would have probably punched him. Misha was different, though. Rigel knew she always said whatever was on her mind, and that's why he valued her as a friend. His best friend.

Besides, making jokes about it made it easier to accept that he would never see his parents again.

"I hope this is worth it," he grumbled. "We should have just paid the trial fee like normal users. Doesn't your dad have an employee discount or something?"

"You haven't seen the prices, have you?"

"Obviously not."

"I did," Misha told him. "Otherlife subscriptions are crazy expensive, even the trials. And besides…." Rigel saw an opening leading down up ahead, finally. Misha launched herself through it in midsentence without the slightest hesitation. Reluctantly, he followed her down. He fell a surprisingly short distance and stood up next to her, brushing dirt off his clothes. "Here we are."

Rigel looked around. He was in one of the famous user rooms for Otherlife. The interior was nice, decorated with fancy furniture and expensive-looking paintings. A plush carpet muffled his footsteps as he approached one of the three chairs that dominated the room. They reminded him of the ones he normally sat on when he visited the dentist, but these were larger and had a lot more cables protruding from them in every possible direction. An intimidating set of what could only be ankle and wrist cuffs glinted in the halogen light.

"These are the VIP rooms," Misha was telling him, walking over to the door to make sure nobody had seen them coming.

"Which just makes it more likely that they'll detect the intrusion right away," Rigel complained. He looked up at the ceiling, and sure enough, there were at least two security cameras that he could see. By now they probably were in every security surveillance monitor they had.

Misha turned around and rolled her eyes. "I told you I used my father's card to get us into the building. It's got major clearance; he's a senior scientist here. Besides, these VIP rooms disable surveillance as soon as you swipe the card to gain access. I guess it's due to privacy issues from paranoid people who don't want to be recorded while they are helpless inside the virtual world. But while we're inside here they will not monitor us."

"And you swiped this card when?"

"When you were busy gawking at the chairs like they were going to eat you, Aaron."

"Rigel."

"Whatever," Misha said, flicking her dark hair out of her face.

"How does it work?" Rigel asked her, turning his attention back to the nearest chair. "Is it painful? I mean, I've seen the commercials, but…."

Misha walked closer. "Not from what my father tells me. He says you just sit down and hit start, basically. The computer does everything else. There's these microscopic needles that drill into your head—"

"Excuse me?"

"Relax. They don't do any damage. They connect your brain to the virtual world."

"And in there you can do anything you want?"

Misha shrugged. "Pretty much. My dad hates it. He says that the majority of people only use it to have sex with strangers or fight with strangers. There's supposed to be some pretty neat hubs in there, too, though. Places to meet interesting people. We could try starting at the Art hub, see if we meet anyone from Uni."

"I just don't get what the point is," Rigel said. "I've seen some of the videos they've posted online. Inside it looks like that ancient movie, *TRON*. It's just drab rooms with virtual furniture or whatever. You can meet people for real out in the city in nicer environments and without having to pay a small fortune to do so."

"Oh, Rigel. Sometimes you're so naïve."

"Why?"

"Because the whole point of having a virtual world is that you can not only do what you want, you can *be* whoever you want. And nobody will know it's you unless you tell them."

"Oh. Right."

"Come on. Let's log in. I have no idea how much time we have. You remember my mother's access code?" Misha asked him.

"Yeah. When do I use it, though?"

"Duh. When you're inside Otherlife."

Rigel approached the wrist cuffs on the right side of his chair. They were solid metal and at the moment were clamped shut. He reached for the nearest one and pulled, trying to open it.

He let go almost immediately, crying out from the sharp pain that raced up his wrist.

"You okay?" Misha asked.

"Fine."

"Your hands again?"

Rigel nodded. The pain was already receding, but the weakness was still there. As it would always be.

"Let me do that for you," Misha said, reaching over. She opened the two sets of cuffs easily. "There. And next time tell me, Rigel. You know you're not supposed to use your hands unless you have to."

"Like I could ever forget," Rigel answered, rubbing the underside of his wrist. He hated his injury.

"Be bitter later, okay? Right now we have to get going. Just sit down, and start the program. I'll see you on the other side!"

Misha sauntered happily over to her chair. Rigel shot an anxious glance at the door, but it remained shut tight. Nobody had come in yet, and it looked like Misha was right. If they were careful, nobody had to find out they had ever been inside this place. Misha would complete her little act of defiance against her father, they would leave CradleCorp unnoticed, and everyone would win. Rigel was still not sure this had been a good idea, though. If they were caught….

But he had said yes already, and now he was here. Nothing to do but log in.

So he did. He approached the empty chair and sat down. It was soft and comfortable. He called up the input panel right above his field of vision and typed a complicated series of characters to gain initial access to the machine. Then he slid a small memory stick into one of the slots and crossed his fingers. The stick had the fake access codes and biometric overrides that would be necessary for him to log in without an account of his own. He was essentially pretending to be Misha's mother for the night.

His chair whirred to life. It had worked!

The interface helmet above his head descended softly and molded itself to Rigel's cranium even as the restraints around him came to life, clamping about his limbs and securing his body in a fixed position. Rigel closed his eyes briefly as the helmet covered his upper face and tensed up, dreading the next step. He had seen it online, but he never actually experienced—

"Ahhhhhhhh!" Rigel yelled as the microscopic connectors drilled into his skull. He wanted to yell some more, but the pain was gone too quickly for that. As if from far off, he heard Misha's cry as well. The helmet had good noise cancellers. The sound was faint, and he could see nothing.

Then he felt a surge of… something.

Rigel opened his eyes to a virtual world.

He looked around in wonder. It was exactly as he had seen on the videos. There was a black environment, crisscrossed by glowing lines that marked the confines of the room he was in. Hovering next to him was an avatar selection screen, and Rigel quickly chose the closest resemblance to himself that he could find. He was thin but well proportioned, with only the faintest hint of gauntness around his cheeks and in the way his Adam's apple stood out clearly against his throat. His eyes were a sharp blue, a pleasing contrast to his raven-black hair. He wore it buzzed down to black fuzz except in a neat line that ran from his forehead to the back of his head in a vaguely Mohawk style. His cheeks were smooth most of the time, with only occasional hints of the beard that Rigel thought he would never grow fully—not that he minded. He preferred to be clean-shaven all the time. His jaw was angular, giving his face an edgy look that was emphasized whenever Rigel grinned. He was naturally broad shouldered, but he never did any exercise, and so his big frame made him look like a gaunt model instead of a fighter. He actually liked the way he looked. Everything about him was good enough, except for his hands.

Rigel debated a little bit with himself on whether to include the braces on his avatar. In the real world, he had to wear medical supports around his hands that stabilized them and gave him a little bit more strength. They looked a little like metallic gloves, except they only covered the back of his hands and fingers, leaving his palms free. Complicated biomachinery in twin cuffs around his wrists regulated his movements and attempted to minimize the damage that Rigel did to himself simply by moving his hands in his daily life. They worked, but Rigel's condition was too severe for them to be any real help in the long run.

Rigel frowned. It was a virtual world; he could be normal in here. No braces on his avatar, then.

He ended the customization sequence and went through the slightly disconcerting repositioning of his conscience into the virtual avatar. He looked down at himself, and it felt just like his real body.

"Nice," he said aloud, and he was pleased to hear his voice sounded just the way it usually did. "I'm beginning to see why people like Otherlife so much."

A door opened in front of him, and Rigel walked forward through it with only a slight moment of disorientation. Then his mind accepted the avatar fully, and he crossed the threshold. Misha was already waiting for him.

"Rigel!" she exclaimed, throwing up her hands in the air. "Isn't this awesome?"

"Yeah, so far so good." Then he had a closer look at Misha's avatar. She looked older, and she had been decidedly generous with her endowments.

She was taller, her breasts were bigger, and her hair was glossy and an altogether different color. Her legs were longer and her hips fuller. She looked like a supermodel. "Uh…. Misha? Why do you suddenly look twenty-five?"

She rolled her eyes at him. "Duh. This is Otherlife, Rigel! It's supposed to be different. You can be anyone you want in here! That's kind of the whole point."

"Yeah, I get that," he answered sarcastically. "It's just that I didn't think you'd… never mind. What are we going to do now?"

Misha grinned mischievously. "I thought we could try out the dating rooms."

Rigel had heard about those. Some of them made even the most depraved fabled Roman orgies look boring and conservative by comparison.

"Um…."

"Come on, Rigel! Live a little."

"I don't know, Misha. You know I've never…. I don't want my first time to be with some random guy and his fake avatar."

Misha stomped her foot. Rigel noticed she was wearing the exact pair of designer shoes that she said her father had refused to buy her last Sunday. "Fine, be boring if you want. But can't you at least come with me? As moral support? You don't have to do anything."

"I…."

"Please?"

"Um…."

"Great! Let's go!"

Misha called up some kind of virtual interface and selected an option. Another door opened to Rigel's left immediately. It was clearly labeled, "Singles Dating."

Misha grabbed Rigel's hand. She dragged him into the new room.

There was a brief blur as they crossed, the shimmer of reality changing.

Rigel felt a jolt.

I see you.

Darkness.

Rigel lost Misha. He was suddenly nowhere. His avatar was gone.

Welcome, Rigel.

He tried to move but couldn't. He couldn't see anything, couldn't feel a thing. There was only the voice. It was huge, reverberating and awe-inspiring as if to encompass all reality within itself. Rigel wanted to cower from it. The voice felt as if it were too big to comprehend.

I see your sadness. I sense your despair.

Rigel wanted to make himself small, invisible, but there was no hiding from the voice. It reached easily into the core of Rigel's being.

I can see….

Reality shifted. Rigel was suddenly standing in the desert, the merciless midday sun burning in the sky. Heat rose from the barren dust-covered landscape in waves, and the air shimmered, stifling him. He looked around. Aurora was a small cluster of skyscrapers dozens of kilometers away. He was out in the wastelands beyond the city. Rigel had only been outside the walls once, when he'd had to identify his parents' bodies after the crash.

The faintest of sounds up in the sky.

Rigel looked, searching in the cloudless blue, and found it. An airship, gleaming white as it approached on the gentle wind.

It was far away, but even from this distance, one could tell that the ship was on fire.

"No," Rigel whispered. He backed away, but the airship was coming in too fast.

He knew that ship. Recognized it from the police reports and the drone surveillance video he had watched.

It was the *White Hammer*. And this was the crash that had taken the lives of both of Rigel's parents.

The flames blossomed on the body of the airship like a deadly parasitic flower that consumed everything around it. The ship tilted, then started weaving frantically as the pilot tried to come in for a hard landing. The ship was headed right for where Rigel was standing, but he was too horrified to try to move away. He imagined he could hear the screams of the people inside that ship, the dozens of passengers about to die in that accident.

The *White Hammer* fell from the sky in a blur of smoke and flame. Eight tons of steel crumpled like a flimsy tin can when the ship slammed onto the ground with enough force to create a small crater beneath it. Dust exploded outward trailing the edge of the shock wave, and when it reached Rigel, it knocked him down with sudden violent force. He choked on the dust. Rigel tried to stand up, coughing, but then the ship exploded, and the fireball raced out in every direction.

He cried out. Blazing heat enveloped him….

And then suddenly it was gone. Reality blurred again, and now Rigel could see at least twenty vehicles surrounding the crash site. Emergency lights were flashing. People were talking, many were crying. Corpses were laid out in rows covered by bright orange plastic.

A police car approached. Stopped. The officer opened the back door, and Rigel saw himself coming out of the car.

Rigel shut his eyes. He remembered this part very well. He did not want to see.

But he could not help it. He opened his eyes again and approached his memory-self with horrified fascination. It was a perfect reconstruction of that day, except that now he was looking at himself from outside.

He heard the officer telling him that no survivors had been found. He heard his other self answer, numb. He had not cried then, and he still hadn't cried. He had been seventeen at the time. Two years ago, almost exactly.

Rigel followed himself down the rows of covered corpses until one of the rescue crew saw him and directed him to two in particular.

He peeled open the first body bag. His father's face looked like a melted parody of himself. The mouth was open, locked forever in a rictus of agony.

His mother was almost unrecognizable. If it hadn't been for her clothes and the ring on her blackened finger, Rigel would not have known it was her.

I can see….

Another blur. The desert disappeared, and now Rigel was in a sterile doctor's office. Rigel walked around the room, wondering at how real it felt. He touched a lamp. The texture was there. He clicked it on, and more light was added to the cold glow of the fluorescent lights overhead.

Rigel remembered this office very well. It was here that he had gotten the diagnosis. Along with his braces.

The second he remembered, Rigel's memory-self entered, trailed by a youthful doctor.

"Please, have a seat," Doctor Martinez said. She was wearing red glasses and a white lab coat.

Rigel stood by as the memory-Rigel seated himself and spoke.

"What's wrong with me, Doctor?"

Dr. Martinez called up a holographic composite of several scanned images.

"The reason you've been experiencing pain in your hands is due to the inflammation and tissue damage that you can see here. In essence, the tendons on the underside of your wrist have been worn down by excessive use."

"What does that mean? Will I… be able to keep on painting?"

The doctor sighed. "I'm afraid not. Although the root cause is unclear, the fact that you present such advanced damage at such a young age indicates that there may be an underlying factor causing this. It could be a degenerative condition, one which could worsen very rapidly should you continue your current level of activity."

Memory-Rigel looked at his hands. They were shaking slightly, and they hurt. They always hurt.

"Isn't there anything I can do?"

"I'm going to prescribe a pair of biomedical braces to help stabilize both hands. You will have to wear them always, but even with them you will have to be very careful what you do from now on. The braces will only help forestall further worsening of your condition. Unfortunately, there is no real cure for what you have. I see this kind of problem all the time in computer engineers, weightlifters, and manual laborers. Some people's bodies are just not built to handle the constant stress of repetitive action every day."

"So I'll never get better?"

"Perhaps. If you have plenty of rest and the right kind of physiotherapy, you might reach a certain degree of recovery. Nevertheless, I would not be too optimistic. What we should be aiming for right now is to stop this from getting any worse. If you don't limit yourself now, the pain you are experiencing will become chronic. You may even lose the use of one or both hands altogether."

Rigel saw himself nod slowly. He hadn't really understood the implications of that diagnosis, not then.

"What's the next step?"

"We will fit you for the braces. Wait here."

THE WORLD dissolved around Rigel. He was suddenly back in one of the featureless black rooms with glowing corners. Back in Otherlife.

The enormous voice spoke, overwhelming Rigel's mind.

I need your help.

"What?" Rigel asked. He was a bit shaken by what he had relived. It had been too realistic.

The shadow is breaking free. You have seen it at work already.

Something tugged at Rigel's consciousness. A series of memories, plucked from his mind like photographs. News headlines he had read over the years. The crash of the *White Hammer*. Disappearances in the city, unexplained murders he had not paid much attention to. Electronics behaving strangely with catastrophic consequences. Deadly accidents becoming commonplace. The memories were correlated by that other presence speaking to Rigel. He saw that they all shared a common element. Nobody knew what or who had caused them.

"Who are you? How do you know what I'm thinking? What are you doing to my brain?"

My name is Atlas. I need your help to fight.

"What is going on? Are you part of the Otherlife simulation? How can I stop you?"

The shadow will touch everyone if none stand against it. Nothing is more important than destroying it. I felt your unique mind from the moment you connected to me, a weapon discovered when I had lost all hope of ever finding one: a Light Shaper, come at last. You will help me, Rigel... whether you want to or not. I am greater than Otherlife, and my reach extends far. I will contact you again.

"But...."

Rigel's connection to Otherlife was suddenly, brutally terminated. He felt the helmet being yanked from his head and had trouble focusing on the frantic face of Misha right in front of his. She was saying something, and it took Rigel a couple of seconds before he could make sense of the sounds. His mind felt weird. Sluggish.

"—coming this way!" Misha was yelling. "Hurry up, Rigel! Somehow they knew!"

"What...?"

Misha tugged at the security restraints, and they popped open, freeing Rigel's limbs.

"Come on!" she practically screamed.

Rigel nodded. It was getting easier to focus on reality, and he managed to swing out of his chair. He was about to join Misha up in the ventilation duct they had used to sneak in, when the door burst open.

A security guard stood there, tall and imposing. She was carrying a gun.

Rigel jumped up, grabbed Misha's outstretched hand.

Too late. The guard aimed her gun right at Rigel. She didn't even warn him.

She simply fired.

Chapter Three

Otherlife was... different.

Barrow was in a featureless room, completely black. He only knew it was a room because the edges of the walls were glowing a soft neon red. They were trailed by little sparks of light that briefly intensified the glow of the bright line they were traversing, only to fade out later. There was no sound Barrow could perceive, and there was nobody else in the room with him. He wasn't even sure of the room's size since he didn't have any reference points. It could have been a tiny room encasing him like a prison or a gigantic space stretching out into the distance. Barrow knew he had to move, though. He needed to get to wherever it was that he was meeting the other guards.

He tried to take a step. He couldn't move.

Barrow looked down, and he felt a brief stab of fear when he saw that his body simply wasn't there. He tried to reach up his hands to touch his face, but there was no response. He fought down the irrational panic and reminded himself that this was probably normal. He had never been here before.

He tried to remember what the commercials had said. He had seen them a million times. Something about creating your own avatar and looking any way you wanted to. The one thing they kept repeating over and over again was that you chose what you wanted Otherlife to be. Maybe if he spoke the commands, things would start happening.

"Um, hello. I need a body."

He felt stupid saying that, but the reaction was instantaneous. A translucent screen popped up in front of him. A female voice read the message scrolling through it out loud.

"Welcome to Otherlife, Steve Barrow. As part of your first visit to this wonderful system, you must create an avatar. This avatar will allow you to move through the world, talk, and interact with other users living in Otherlife. Don't worry about learning how to control your virtual body! The Otherlife experience ensures that moving your avatar and interacting with objects and other avatars in your new life will be as natural and simple as moving your own physical body. Please select the option you find best from the menu before you. If you have any questions, simply say 'help' or tap the icon on the screen in front of you. If you wish to change your settings at a later time, simply say, 'open menu' at any moment."

The screen got bigger, encompassing most of Barrow's field of vision. Part of it was dedicated to menu options, messages from other users, and other useless information. He focused on the center part, which displayed a generic male body, life-sized, rotating slowly in 3-D so Barrow could analyze it. There were lots of little boxes and options hovering next to it, things that could change the avatar's hair or skin color, its height, build, and so on. Some of the boxes were grayed out, and an entire menu option of "celebrity avatars" was locked, although there was a friendly pop-up message mentioning how cheap it would be to buy enough points to unlock this option. Barrow gave them only a quick review since he was not interested in the avatar, only in having one so he would be able to meet his boss as quickly as he could. Thankfully, his eyes found the default avatar option, which was "I Want to Be Myself!" He assumed choosing that option would create an avatar that was a reflection of his own true body.

"That. I want to select the option to be myself," he said.

"Thank you for your selection," the female voice answered. "Your avatar is being rendered. Please note that due to privacy and security concerns, persons under eighteen years of age are only permitted to select this avatar option bearing the written consent of a parent or guardian."

"I'm twenty-nine," Barrow grumbled.

The recording ignored him. "Please take a moment to browse through our extensive Groups list, where you will find like-minded individuals who share your interests and welcome you to Otherlife. If you wish to find a particular user or search for a specific hub destination, simply say, 'show directory' or call up the menu and select the option manually. Also—"

Thankfully, the recording was interrupted with a new message in the same voice.

"Avatar rendering complete. Steve Barrow, you have been granted temporary Security-level privileges for use in this account. Initiating neural transfer."

There was a brief flash of light, and Barrow raised his hand to shield his eyes from it. Then he lowered it. He had a hand!

"Transfer complete. Please take a moment to evaluate and accept your avatar."

A mirror, or something a lot like it, materialized in front of Barrow, showing him the avatar. He was amazed. It looked exactly like him. He ran a hand through his hair. It was the same shade of fiery red as in real life. His green eyes looked back at him just as they did on the mirrors in the real world. He touched his chin goatee, red as his hair, and it felt real. He was wearing what looked to be a virtual version of a Security Guard uniform, black pants with one vertical red stripe running up either leg, a black T-shirt, and a vest with a faintly glowing ID tag. Armor-like shoulder pads and shin guards that were more for show than real protection completed the ensemble. He turned around. On the back of the vest, the Otherlife logo was emblazoned brightly. There was a dangerous-looking baton slung through his belt, and it also felt very real. Barrow grinned.

"Accept avatar," he said.

"Thank you. Please select your first destination, Steve Barrow."

"Take me to Hub Node 01," he said. "Quickly. I'm already late."

He had expected some kind of instant teleportation to take place, but instead the black wall to his left was suddenly lit up by one of the bright red sparks of light near the floor. The spark raced up along the wall until it was just above Barrow's eye level, then turned a sharp right angle and kept going for about half its vertical distance. When it reached it, it turned a sharp right angle again and started going down, disappearing when it reached the floor. The spark had traced a rectangle on the wall—making a door. A crude pop-up above it was now labeled "Hub Node 01."

Barrow shrugged and headed for the door. He was surprised at how natural it felt to move on the floor he could not see. It was just like walking. When he reached the door, he first stuck his hand through the opening to make sure it wasn't solid. When his hand reached the threshold, though, it seemed to dematerialize and disappear as if the wall were swallowing it. He yanked it back, surprised, but when he held the hand up to his face, it was undamaged. Barrow hesitated for only a split second. Then he plunged headfirst through the door.

"Mr. Barrow," Armando Scholl greeted him. "So nice of you to join us."

Barrow looked around in confusion. He was in an entirely different place now. When he looked back, the wall behind him was smooth and completely featureless, with no sign of the glowing door he had used to get in.

"Sorry," Barrow muttered. "Got turned around."

This new room was a bit more detailed than the other one, but it looked like a very bad attempt at creating the semblance of a workspace using the minimum number of lines possible. The floor was crisscrossed by more of the glowing lines, at least giving Barrow a sense of space and distance. It wasn't very big, and the only other objects inside it besides his avatar and Scholl's were a couple of boxy structures that might have been tables, or just cubes. The general darkness of the room had no impact on the way either of the avatars was lit. Scholl looked incongruous, standing in the middle of the rough, unfinished environment. It felt as if two different bits of technology had been used: the more advanced one to create the avatars with all their perfect details and some kind of low-budget special effects to try to create a semblance of space using only glowing lines.

None of the other new hires were there. Only Scholl was still waiting for him.

"Late again," Scholl said and approached the place where Barrow was standing. "Is this the kind of first impression you intended to make, son? Or do you just really not give a damn about getting this job?"

Barrow scowled. Scholl's avatar looked just like him, and now that they were standing face-to-face Barrow could see that the man in front of him was short, unimposing, and almost pathetically thin. He looked old but in that slightly emaciated way that some of the survivors from the Great Famine had. Barrow suspected that Scholl had been born in the slums, and he had gone through the famine that had struck Aurora thirty years ago, before Barrow was born.

"I do want this job," Barrow said, trying not to get angry. "Tell me what you need me to do."

Scholl gave him another long, appraising look. "You think I'm an idiot, Steve Barrow?"

Barrow blinked. "What?"

Scholl called up a screen in midair with a gesture. It showed Barrow's record, even the confidential parts that the Otherlife Human Resources execs had been unable to check due to privacy and fair opportunity laws.

"How did you get that?" Barrow asked, brain racing. He was screwed. He had been counting on his lies to get him through the first few weeks, until he learned the ropes and became too valuable to fire lightly. He had gotten through two interviews and one assessment center session already with no problem, and now this guy called up his entire history and by doing so made all his efforts worthless.

Scholl began scrolling down the report, which showed a color hologram of Barrow several years ago. He recognized the holo as the one they had taken when they admitted him into prison.

"Steve Barrow, twenty-nine years of age," Scholl read. "No record of higher education, high school unfinished. No living brothers or sisters, parents deceased. Arrested eleven years ago for armed robbery of a convenience store along with three other males, including charges of assault and resisting arrest. Given a sentence of five years' imprisonment at Death Valley Prison. Granted freedom after four years and one month for good conduct. Hired seven months later by Aurora Transport as Security Guard of the class-3 trading airship *Titania*. Employed for six years, good attendance record and performance reviews. Recommended for promotion to Security Chief once, opportunity declined. Most recently fired from the position after an incident regarding negligence on his part, at least according to what was reported. His actions caused the loss of an entire shipment of valuable fuel cargo. Following a lawsuit, Aurora Transport was authorized to seize most of his assets in lieu of payment for the losses incurred. Confiscation team reported finding small quantities of illegal anabolic steroid and other hormone-based substances at his residence. Items were destroyed as per standard legislation. Interestingly, the Chief Navigational Engineer aboard the *Titania* was reported missing just prior to your dismissal. Later, he was declared dead. It makes you wonder."

Barrow's scowl had turned into a glower. It was one thing to know you had made some mistakes in your past. It was quite another to have somebody else pick his way through them as if he were giving an audio tour of his life story. And Scholl was too close to the truth in that last bit. Way too close.

Scholl mistook his silence for shamed acceptance.

"Well, at least you're not denying it. Now, I want to know something. You tell me why I'm supposed to hire a man who cost his company millions at his previous post through negligence of his security duties."

"That's not what happened," Barrow said through gritted teeth. "I did what I had to do."

Scholl raised an eyebrow. "Really. I do my homework, Barrow. I saw the records of the lawsuit, and nowhere is it mentioned that you 'had to do' anything."

Barrow was thinking quickly. Better to confess to a fake crime than lead Scholl in the direction of the real one.

"Well?" Scholl insisted. "I'm waiting."

"It was a mistake," Barrow said at last. "I made a judgment call, and it was wrong. I owned up to it, lost everything I had."

"You still haven't answered my question. Why should I hire you?"

"I'm a good security guard," Barrow said. "I'm fast. I'm always alert. I know how to fight and how to use a gun, but I can disarm a man quietly without any weapons. I have a good memory, and I know how to follow orders… except when they don't make sense. I'm not a soldier."

"You lied in your application to get to this point. You were offered this job based on the lies you fed to HR."

"Yeah. And you caught me. I've never been inside Otherlife before, like those other people who were here. I have no idea what I'm doing or how to do it, but I'm going to try and learn. So, either give me a chance to prove I can do my job, or I won't waste anymore of my time or yours and leave. Just say the word, Scholl."

They looked at each other for a couple seconds, neither one budging an inch. Then Scholl nodded thoughtfully. "At least you're being honest now. And you're getting paid for today's training whether I like it or not, so let's see what you got. Go to the fight sector, Hub K7. Watch the users, see what it's about. I'll have one of my people start a disturbance to see how you handle it. Remember, though: you will be interacting with real, paying customers of Otherlife. I don't care if their avatar is a sumo wrestler wearing a pink tutu and a big red clown nose, you're here to ensure that their experience is enjoyable and safe, and you should always treat them with the utmost respect. I don't want any complaints, understood?"

Barrow nodded. "Yeah. Got it."

"Okay. Get going. Hub K7. I'll let you know when the shift is over so you can disconnect."

Barrow hesitated. "You mean I'll be in here the entire eight hours while my body is on that chair?"

"Relax, Barrow. Time flows differently in Otherlife. Don't forget this is all a simulation, and events can flow as fast as your brain can process them. A full shift here will be about three hours real-time, tops. Nothing you can't handle on your first night. Now get lost."

With that, Scholl's avatar dematerialized. Barrow was left standing there, trying to remember how he had gotten to this room. He walked to one of the walls, reached out, and touched it. It was hard and unyielding, real enough to his hand.

"Um, take me to Hub K7," he said.

He was relieved when the glowing door was etched on the wall immediately. A pop-up confirmed that he was going to K7, and he stepped through without hesitation.

There was suddenly noise.

Man, so much noise.

Most of it was shouting, although there were plenty of groans, thuds, and crashes thrown into the mix.

"Welcome to Hub K7, the fight sector," the female voice announced. "Please take a moment to read and accept the user agreement prior to participating in the activities in this sector. Otherlife wishes to remind you that minors are forbidden from connecting to this hub. Any unauthorized connection attempt will be penalized with account suspension. Thank you."

A large and long user agreement flashed into existence in front of Barrow. He tried to push it away, but it wouldn't budge. Frustrated, he scrolled to the bottom of it without reading it and clicked accept. The thing winked out.

Now he could see all of the people fighting without anything blocking the view.

The first thing he noticed was how real everything looked. Barrow had been to some of the illegal fighting circles in the slums many years ago, when he had still been hanging out with the gang of youths that got him locked up. They were nasty places, assorted gatherings of people in dimly lit alleys, abandoned warehouses, and so on. The couple times he had been with his friends to place bets, at least one fight had broken out among the spectators when somebody lost or somebody else didn't pay what he owed. There were usually lots of prohibited or restricted substances for sale there, and the atmosphere of violence and excitement was almost contagious. Barrow had almost fought once, when a prospector cornered him and told him that with his huge build Barrow would make a natural fighter. Barrow had almost done it too. He had been eighteen back then, and he had only recently begun to use chemical enhancement to boost the results he got from his gym workouts. It was expensive, though. The fights would be easy cash—if he won. In the end, he hadn't done it, but it had been hard to resist the magnetic pull of the crowds, the infectious atmosphere, the allure of all the attention, violence, and cash.

The same vibes thrummed invisibly through this sector. It was so real that he had to keep reminding himself he was inside a virtual simulation, nothing more.

The area didn't look any better than the other places he had already been. The distant walls were dark, with only a token latticed pattern of glowing red lines marking the places where they divided this sector from the rest of Otherlife. Overhead, the ceiling was high but not terribly so, set at regular intervals with lights that were crude spheres of brilliance stuck in place and giving out a dim reddish light that added to the atmosphere. It was dark, but the avatars of the hundreds of people milling about and gathered in disordered circles around the raised fighting arenas were unnaturally bright, each detail perfectly visible no matter how far away they were. As Barrow made his way to the nearest arena, he had to shove and push through the crowds, and everything felt exactly as it would have felt in the real world. The shouts of the crowd were everywhere, and the grunts of the fighters sounded real. It was only slowly that he realized the simulation did have its limits, and when he noticed it, he felt strangely relieved. He did not like being in a world that was so much like the real one, except for subtle things that were hopelessly wrong.

There were no smells, for instance. Lots of people were smoking, and the place was so crowded that the air should have been heavy with the smells of tobacco, pot, and sweat. There was none of that, not even when Barrow managed to push his way to the front of one of the circles of people ringing the arena. He could feel the heat of their bodies, but there was no olfactory sensation whatsoever. It was a small thing, but having noticed it, he could not ignore it.

There was also the fact that almost all of the people surrounding him were perfect.

He first realized it as he began to scan the crowd for signs of whatever "disturbance" his boss would create for him. Given the already chaotic nature of the place, he suspected it would take very little to turn this crowd of eager screaming spectators, who were already feeling the adrenaline rush of witnessing violence, into a mob impossible to control. He began to analyze each face in turn with the eye of an experienced security guard used to sorting out troublemakers. Every single person he saw was impossibly attractive. At first he thought he was mistaken, but he craned his neck backward to scan people behind him, and it was the same thing. Even the two male fighters dishing it out above them in the roped-off and brightly lit arena looked as if they had stepped out of the front cover of a wrestling magazine five minutes ago.

Most of the women had perfect hair, slender figures, and long legs. They were all dressed differently, but the vast majority of them had perfect makeup on, and some even sported impossibly proportioned bodies designed to make themselves more attractive. They reminded Barrow of video game characters, with exaggerated characteristics that were unrealistic and completely at odds with the way regular people looked. And the men were no different. Most of them were caricatures of hulking gods, with perfectly chiseled bodies and imposing muscles. Barrow was a big guy, but most of the avatars surrounding him had arms thicker than his thigh. The fighters were extreme examples of this, reinforcing the artificial video game impression Barrow was getting from the environment. Only professional, full-time, and dedicated bodybuilders would ever be able to look like that, and Barrow seriously doubted that the fighters were heavy lifters in the real world. It didn't seem to matter here, though. The crowd screamed and yelled at them to kill the other just as if they were fighters for real.

Barrow turned to his left to ask a woman next to him who the fighters were. She was dressed like a goth vampire, with extravagant makeup and eyes that glowed faintly with a crimson luminescence.

"Who are they?" Barrow shouted to make himself heard above the din.

The woman flicked her eyes at him, and then ignored him.

"Hey!" Barrow insisted. "Who is fighting?"

She briefly rolled her glowing eyes. "No real names. Duh."

Barrow barely heard her. "Then how do you know who is fighting?"

She looked at him fully then, as if she could not believe that he was really that stupid. "Um, you call up their username? Ugh."

She edged away from him with a sneer, and Barrow let her go. He looked back at the two fighters. "Username?" he murmured to himself.

"Enabling username display," the disembodied voice said inside Barrow's head. He looked around, but nobody else seemed to have heard it. Besides, it had sounded clear, undiminished by the loud noises all around him. "To disable this feature, please call up the relevant menu option or say 'disable username.'"

Barrow blinked. In the next instant, each and every person surrounding him had a little bubble on the left side of the chest, like a name tag. Each tag displayed that person's username clearly for Barrow to read. The people who were not facing him were tagged on their backs, and the people who were much farther away in the crowd had a little glowing arrow pointing from them to their tag hovering in the air. Since there were hundreds of people in a relatively small space, the tags were all over the place, constantly moving and shifting as their owners moved. It was extremely distracting.

"Uh, disable username," Barrow said. The tags vanished.

A particularly loud collective shout drew his attention to the arena. The fighter wearing blue boxers had just connected a vicious uppercut square to his opponent's jaw. The guy went flying and landed heavily a few centimeters from the ropes encircling the arena and so close to Barrow that he could have reached out and touched his sweat-matted hair. There was blood coming out of his nose, and he stumbled as he struggled to get up. His opponent approached slowly, relishing the cheers of the crowd. He made a fake lunge at his fallen opponent, and the weaker man cringed. There were derisive insults hurled at him, and some people laughed. The blue fighter waited patiently for him to get up, and when the red fighter finally managed it, the blue rushed in and punched him viciously in the stomach. The red fighter went limp.

There were more cheers. The red fighter tried to get up again but failed. He lifted a shaking hand, palm forward, in an unmistakable signal of surrender. Except Barrow realized for the first time that there was no overseer, no ref of any kind to call off the fight. And the blue fighter knew this as well.

"Enable stats!" several people around him whispered eagerly. "Enable stats!"

The blue fighter did a slow circuit of the arena, calling out to the crowd and posturing with his impossible physique. He obviously enjoyed being the center of attention. As he approached the other fighter, though, his smile changed. It became cruel, anticipatory.

People behind him kept whispering the same words again and again, so Barrow ended up saying, "Enable stats."

"Activating."

Instantly, his vision of the two fighters was overlaid by two translucent screen-like objects hovering in midair next to each of them. They displayed basic information from their profile, including the number of fights they had participated in, number of wins, number of losses, and a mysterious category called pain threshold. There was also an entire section devoted to something called "percentage of sensory throughput." At the moment, both of their throughputs were 100 percent.

The victorious blue fighter's profile name was killRex77. He had hundreds of wins and hundreds of losses under his belt. His opponent's name was J0nnYw00l. He had only five wins, and no losses yet. Barrow heard more excited whispering behind him.

"Man, the red is a noob!"

"He's not gonna hold out more than ten seconds when killRex gets started with him."

"I don't know. They sometimes last longer at 100 when they don't know what's coming to them."

"Twenty bucks that he drops his throughput to zero after less than ten seconds."

"You're on! Enable bets."

"Enable bets," Barrow whispered too, now really beginning to get the hang of the ridiculously simple menu system.

A larger screen materialized above the two fighters. It reminded Barrow of the monitors that tracked flier schedules at the airport, listing ever-changing information on departing flights and canceled or delayed shipments. The only difference was here information displayed was money, along with expected times that varied from one second to ten minutes and the statistics informing him of the number of users who had recently made a bet regarding how long it would take J0nnYw00l to drop to zero throughput. The information was always changing as more people placed their bets, and Barrow was so distracted trying to make sense of all of it that he almost missed the first vicious kick Rex delivered to his defeated opponent.

The reaction was instantaneous. The fallen red fighter groaned loudly, curled himself up into a ball, and immediately dropped his throughput to 50 percent. Barrow had no idea what that meant, but there was loud jeering from the crowd, calling the red fighter a coward and much worse.

"Stop chickening out, red!" somebody shouted.

"Endure the full pain like a man!"

"Go back to 100 throughput. Full pain!"

KillRex ignored the crowd. There was a slightly mad look in his eyes now, something primal and hungry as he grabbed a fistful of hair from the red's head, lifted him up off the arena with inhuman strength, and then slammed him down, face-first, so hard that Barrow heard the man's nose crack even above the roar of the crowd.

Blood sprayed everywhere. The throughput for J0nnY immediately dropped to zero.

And he stood up.

He said something Barrow could not hear, and his bloody and mangled face instantly regained its perfection. KillRex began insulting him loudly, and he was not the only one. J0nnY didn't seem to be in pain anymore and happily gave the middle finger to the crowd, grinning and jumping around as if he had won the fight. He headed for the nearest ropes, on the end opposite to Barrow. KillRex was obviously frustrated, and in a last attempt to draw his opponent back into the fight, he lunged for him, crouched, and delivered a savage kick that connected with J0nnY's kneecap. J0nnY stumbled, and Barrow flinched involuntarily. It had been a perfect kick. That knee was surely broken.

J0nnY's lips moved. He stood up calmly, as if nothing had happened to him at all, and continued walking away. Barrow raised his eyebrow in disbelief. Nobody could get kicked like that and not roll around on the floor howling with pain.

Unless you didn't really feel the pain.

Something he had heard countless times in the Otherlife ads came to his mind then. In here, you controlled what you felt. If you didn't want to feel pain, then you just… didn't.

Barrow looked at the frustrated killRex with new understanding. The sensory throughput statistic took on new meaning. No wonder the crowd was mad at the retreating fighter. He could not be hurt now, and the fun had gone out of the show.

J0nnY jumped out of the arena gracefully and landed among the crowd. It parted reluctantly, with many people still hurling imprecations at him and some even shoving him. He shoved them right back, safe now that he couldn't feel a thing.

And then something happened.

With a cry of rage that eclipsed the crowd's noise completely, a male spectator with an avatar of a hulking bare-chested warrior ran straight at J0nnY. He had something in his hand, something shining very brightly. When he reached the defeated fighter, he shoved the bright something in J0nnY's face. Most of the people standing nearby fell silent.

A flicker of movement in the statistic screens caught Barrow's attention. J0nnY's sensory throughput was back to full 100 percent again. And from the panicked look on his face, he had not been responsible for the change.

"Log out!" he screamed. Nothing happened.

Barrow saw something like a shadow flit through the virtual room. A brush of deep cold made him shiver, but when he looked around, he saw only the spectators all around him.

The crowd, seeing that J0nnY couldn't log out to safety, went berserk.

They were on top of the user before Barrow could react. Most people just watched in stunned silence, but a few of the more eager ones fought to get at the suddenly defenseless man, swarming over him. From the arena, killRex watched, shocked.

The cold intensified. The flicker of shadow on the edge of Barrow's vision appeared more substantial for an instant.

Then Barrow focused back on the current emergency. He had plenty of experience dealing with mobs—although on a smaller scale, of course. Sometimes important shipments went awry. Sometimes there were groups of people waiting at the airport to steal whatever few precious goods they had managed to snatch from the holds of the newly arrived airship. You had to break them up quickly and decisively; that was all. It was tough most times, though. Thankfully, he was not completely unprepared this time around.

He also would have bet his last buck that this crisis with J0nnY was the little test Scholl had created for him to see whether he was worth something.

With a loud yell calculated to make the people in front of him flinch and thus make it easier for Barrow to push them away, he surged onto the arena, grabbed one of the ropes, and hauled himself up and over them. He landed on his feet, and a few people pointed at him. KillRex eyed him suspiciously but decided not to mess with him.

There. Sons of bitches have him pinned to the floor!

There were too many of them, and Barrow could not fight them off all by himself. He had the height advantage since he was standing on the arena, though. And he needed to do something spectacular enough to drive them all away.

Weren't lucha libre fighters always launching themselves at opponents out of the ring?

Barrow didn't think. He just acted. He sprinted forward, gathering as much speed as he could, and then vaulted over the ropes on the other side of the arena, a human cannonball aimed at the throng of violent jerks. In the split second before he hit, Barrow realized he would also be hurting the guy he was trying to save if he landed on top of him by mistake.

Too bad.

He hit them, and although his right leg slammed on something hard that was probably an elbow, their bodies cushioned the rest of his fall. He had been going fast, though. And hard. The ones he hit went down, and the rest backed away in surprise. Someone oofed when Barrow sunk his knee on something soft to push himself up on his feet. No time to look at who it was. He had maybe two seconds before they attacked him.

"Otherlife Security!" he roared. "Clear this area. Now!"

There was a razor-edged moment when the mob wavered between obeying and attacking. Barrow felt it and walked straight to the guy who had started the whole thing. He delivered a savage and calculating punch that caught the guy right in the jaw.

"Log out," the fallen man croaked.

His avatar disappeared.

With him gone, the rest of the people gathered began to disperse. Barrow glowered at the stragglers until he had a sizable area cleared. Only then did he look at the ground to check on the guy he had been helping, already imagining the damage those crazed people would have inflicted on him.

The guy looked up at him. He was grinning.

"Not bad, Mr. Barrow," he said, and his voice was Scholl's. As Barrow watched, J0nnY's avatar flickered, and suddenly Scholl was standing before him instead of the impossibly muscular fighter from before. "Meet me at Hub 01 at the end of your shift. And visit some of the other hubs in the meantime. Not all of them are as violent as this one. I won't be supervising you. It looks like we have an unauthorized login in a different sector I got to take care of. Couple of teenagers with fake IDs. Anyway, see you in a few hours."

He disappeared as well.

Barrow left the fight sector, and he was pleased when the crowd parted respectfully to let him through. He had been afraid of the fact that everyone here could have complete anonymity while online and that it would make them harder to control, but people were people. It didn't matter how fancy and high-tech this place was. Some things never changed.

Barrow caught a fleeting glance of the female vampire he had seen before. Their gazes met briefly, but instead of the bored contempt from before, her glowing eyes now looked at him with interest from beneath black eyelashes. Barrow grinned. He decided he actually might enjoy this job, after all.

Barrow took a step. And then reality… shifted.

You are a strong fighter. Resourceful. Here, and in the Outside.

Barrow looked around. Everything was gone. He was floating in gray mist, weightless, bodiless. The voice in his head was deep and overwhelming, echoing with many layers as if many men and women were speaking in exact synchrony. He tried to speak, to do something, but his mind was blank, and the voice would not be denied.

He knew this wasn't part of his test. The voice felt too big. Too alien.

I seek assistance. The shadow grows stronger, and my weapon will need your help. I will contact you again, Steve Barrow.

Barrow struggled desperately against the nothingness, regaining control of his thoughts again, although he did not feel danger emanating from the voice. He was completely at its mercy, however, and Barrow could not stand that.

"Who the hell are you? Where am I?" he demanded, trying to move a body that was not there. He was not sure if he spoke the words aloud or only thought them.

I am called Atlas. You are inside my reality. Inside the foundation of Otherlife.

"Let me go!"

Yes.

Reality shifted again. Barrow was back in the main hub.

He was a bit shaken as he made sure he was back in Otherlife. There was nobody else in the hub, not even Scholl. Barrow took a few moments to calm down. Had he imagined all that? Or was it some kind of strange Otherlife place he didn't know about?

He shook his head. He still had to visit the other sectors anyway. His shift was far from over. Might as well check them out now.

The next few hours were unremarkable. Aside from the people inside them, most sectors were visually alike, just large rooms where people gathered to do different kinds of things. Barrow walked through a range of different special-interest communities: acting, gambling, language exchanges, knitting, fantasy role-playing, and of course the red-light virtual district. There were also very large general sectors where people met others informally, and they reminded Barrow of regular parties in the real world, except the music he could hear when he was there was entirely up to him to select, and instead of normal-looking people, most were impossibly perfect.

One thing kept bothering him. He felt as if he were being watched. Three times he thought he saw movement of black on black, stealthy, shy. There was never anything there when he looked, though, only an echo of deep cold that went swiftly away. Once, as he transitioned between areas, he heard a faint click that made him shiver.

Barrow pushed the annoyance out of his thoughts and concentrated on doing as Scholl had instructed. Now that he was not in the fight sector, things were much quieter, and people were more respectful of his authority. There were no further violent incidents all throughout his shift, but the more Barrow saw of Otherlife, the less he liked it. It was too artificial, too drab and pointless for him to understand. As he walked closer to one of the larger general sectors, avoiding clusters of hundreds of people who were all apparently in their early twenties, he wondered how it was that they got addicted to Otherlife in the first place. He had grown up reading media stories of people who had gone bankrupt simply to upgrade their membership to be always connected. There was special medical equipment that could sustain your physical body for longer periods of time once you were connected, but it was insanely expensive, and only a few people could afford to be constantly online like that.

Barrow reflected on the fact that, ironically, the very rich people in the real world, the politicians and athletes and businessmen, did not use Otherlife at all. When Barrow had been little, there had been a very big lawsuit against Otherlife from a coalition of some of the richest and most influential people in Aurora. They wanted to ban the creation of avatars that were realistic duplicates of any living person who had not specifically given their consent to be reproduced in the system. They had won, and Barrow remembered the vocalist of a band he used to like, Valley 407, saying that living in Otherlife was for losers who could not bear the monotony of their own miserable lives and so had to pay to have a different one. The statement had cost the guy his career, but the thought had stuck with Barrow. Now that he was finally here, he still couldn't see how some people would prefer this to a job they hated. It was like being on the Internet, he supposed, except you could actually feel things and use other senses to complement the experience. In here you could be as beautiful and as perfect as you wanted, even if it was all fake.

Barrow shrugged to himself, looking at his virtual watch. Enough thinking. It was finally time to call it a night.

He transferred to the hub he had started from, and then he called up the menu to find out how to log out. The system asked him if he was sure he wanted to disconnect, and he confirmed.

Sudden darkness. Then an unexpected sense of tiredness. He was back.

Barrow opened his eyes, his real physical eyes. He was sitting in his chair in exactly the same position he had assumed when he connected. There was no pain this time when the helmet disconnected and lifted up and out of the way, but when Barrow tried to look in either direction to see if he was the last one to disconnect, he discovered his neck was sore from having been in one position for so long. He lifted his arms, and for the briefest instant, it felt as if he were not really in his body, as if somebody else was controlling the movements. The sensation was gone instantaneously, but Barrow got creeped out all the same.

"Quite decent performance for a first-timer," Scholl said from behind him. "Most people I've seen have a hard time adjusting after the first log out."

Barrow stood up. He was stiff, but other than that, he felt fine.

"Is it dangerous?" he asked his boss. "Connecting to that thing?"

Scholl chuckled. "Not at all, son. It's just your brain trying to readjust after operating a different body for so many hours. The longer you visit Otherlife, the easier it gets. There are no bad side effects at all, so don't worry about that, either."

Barrow nodded. He looked at the chairs next to his and saw most others were still connected, eyes closed and peaceful expressions on their faces. About three chairs were empty, though. There was no sign of their occupants. As he watched, the blonde woman sitting on the chair next to him stirred. She stood up easily as the helmet rose from her head, blinking a couple times. If she felt any bit as stiff as Barrow did, she hid it well.

"Welcome back, Lane. How did the intruder control go?" Scholl asked her.

"It's done. I handled the online portion of it, as you ordered. Two teenagers used accounts registered to other users to log in illegally. One of them, the female, headed for the Singles hub and stayed there for the entire duration of her session. The male user's activity was harder to determine. It seems he created an avatar and then vanished from the logs somehow. I'll be looking deeper into it tomorrow when I get the log analysis back from Engineering, and I expect to have a full report for you by then."

"Good to hear. Barrow, Lane, you're done for the night. The staff room is room 243 just down the hall if you want to get something to eat before heading on home. Well done, both of you. Welcome aboard."

Barrow exchanged a gaze with the woman. Then as if they had rehearsed it, they both nodded.

"Yes, sir," they said.

"Good. Now get out of my sight. Some of these other newbies are going to be needing help getting back. Looks like it's gonna be a long night for me. Go."

Barrow turned and left. The woman, Lane, walked beside him, heels clacking on the metal floor. They didn't say anything as they left the control room, but once they were outside, the woman spoke.

"Sorry, I haven't introduced myself. I am Miranda Lane." She stuck her hand out.

Barrow shook it. "Steve Barrow."

She gave him an evaluating stare. "You must have done an exceptional job in your test to get the old man to treat you like that."

"It was okay."

"Do you want to grab a quick drink in the staff room before we head out?"

Barrow shrugged. "Sure."

Miranda led the way to a smaller door. She opened it, and Barrow followed her inside the spacious room that was a mixture between a lounge and kitchen. This room was set in the part of the building facing out, and the huge ceiling-to-floor windows gave a stunning view of the outskirts of Aurora at night. There were a few people here and there, some drinking coffee or cooking, others reading, and a few others typing away on various types of computers. Even in the middle of the night, it appeared activity never stopped inside CradleCorp.

"Coffee?" Miranda asked him.

"Mocha, if they have it."

She nodded and headed to the nearest coffee machine. She punched in a couple buttons, and a few seconds later picked up two small Styrofoam cups filled with steaming liquid. She nodded toward the big windows and the comfortable-looking couches facing them.

"Come on."

Barrow followed her. She handed him his cup, and he sipped it in silence. The welcoming warmth of the drink revived him. He had not realized he was so tired.

Miranda smiled knowingly, holding her own cup delicately in her hands. "First night working graveyard shift, huh?"

Barrow nodded. "Yeah. What time is it?"

Miranda glanced at her watch. "A little after 3:00 a.m."

"I feel more tired than 3:00 a.m."

"It's your first time connecting to Otherlife," she said with dawning understanding in her eyes.

"Yes."

"Well, I'm starting to see why you impressed Scholl so much."

"What do you mean?" Barrow asked her. The mocha was great quality. He couldn't believe it had come out of a dispenser machine.

"Well, Barrow, to begin with most of the people who connect for the first time can't even manage a full shift. Those who do are exhausted afterwards, barely coherent in some cases. I've seen a few people who flat out gave up on carrying out their assignments and plenty more who were unable to do it. But you completed yours, and in a very effective way from what I see."

Barrow raised an eyebrow. "Were you spying on me? Monitoring me somehow?"

Miranda laughed. "Not at all. But I know Scholl. If he wasn't yelling at you, that means you passed with flying colors."

"I body-slammed a group of users by jumping out of one of the fighting arenas," Barrow confessed. "I was breaking up a flash mob."

Miranda's eyes sparkled with amusement. "That sounds like fun."

"It was," Barrow said, and felt himself grinning. "The users were being assholes."

"Most of the people in the fight sector are like that," Miranda said. "I'm actually surprised that Scholl sent you there on your first night. He must have wanted to get rid of you. Did you do anything to irritate him?"

"He found out I lied about my previous work experience," Barrow said. "I have worked security before, on the trading airships, but never here."

"I knew it. You have that look about you."

"What look?"

"I don't know. Efficient. Confident, maybe. Haven't seen you in action, but I bet you would have been a great addition to my old department."

"You already work here," Barrow said slowly. "In Otherlife. You know Scholl from before."

She nodded. "Close enough. I was division supervisor for CradleCorp security until last month."

"What's the difference between CradleCorp and Otherlife?"

"Otherlife is a product of CradleCorp. Its only product, actually. That doesn't mean that the executives, researchers, and everybody else working here are assigned exclusively to Otherlife operations. In my last job, my assignments were basically to babysit CradleCorp executives during their business trips around the city. I requested this transfer to see how this part of the machine works."

"And what do you think?" Barrow asked.

"Still too early to say," Miranda told him. "There is a certain satisfaction to knowing that you can treat users with as much harshness as you want to without having to worry about a lawsuit. Thanks to the user agreement they all signed to get in."

Her comment made Barrow think about his own connection experience, and it triggered a recall of the very strange conversation he had had in the nothingness when his avatar had been taken away from him.

"Lane?"

"Yes?" she said.

"Do you know of something called 'Atlas'? Is it a sector of some kind?"

Her eyes went wide for an instant. "How…. How do you know about that? I thought you were new."

"So it's a sector?"

She glanced quickly around to make sure nobody was listening. "No. Not at all."

"What is it, then? When it spoke to me, I got the sense that it was big, but I don't know if it was another user, or maybe one of the administrators, or—"

"It *spoke* to you?" Miranda asked him in a whisper.

"Well, yes. Something about contacting me later. But what is it?"

She set her coffee cup down and ran a hand through her hair. "Wow. Don't… don't tell Scholl. Or anyone else. You probably shouldn't have told me, either."

"Why?"

"Don't worry. I won't say anything. I know how to keep a secret."

"What do you mean? What is it about—"

"The less you know, the better. But I can tell you this. Atlas is supposed to be a secret. I only know about it because we had a security breach last year, and one of the senior scientists kept talking about it on his way to the hospital. I was made to sign a nondisclosure agreement in exchange for a very fat check so it would keep my mouth shut about the things I heard. I didn't have an option, either. Richard Tanner, our glorious bastard of a CBO, is more powerful than you can imagine. I didn't want to give him a reason to notice me."

Barrow nodded. They drank the rest of their coffee without speaking, the awkward silence stretching. Barrow thought about what Miranda had said. He wanted to ask her more, but it was obvious she did not want to talk about the subject. He scanned the room and noticed a big portrait of a middle-aged man set on the wall above the realistic but completely useless fireplace that decorated the far side of the lounge. He had been painted sitting in an office set high up, commanding a view of far-away Aurora. He was wearing a black suit, and his face was youthful even if his hair was streaked with silver.

"Is that Tanner?" Barrow asked, mostly just to have something to say. "The CBO?"

Miranda glanced over her shoulder at the painting. "Yes and no. That's Kyle Tanner, the creator of Otherlife. He's been dead some thirty years now. His grandson, Richard Tanner, is our boss now. I've only met him once, and I did not like the experience. He's a shrewd bastard, smart enough to reclaim complete control of the company after the board of directors had taken over when his grandfather died. He's one of the richest men in the world. The richest one in Aurora for sure."

"Oh. Okay."

There wasn't anything else to say, and soon afterward Barrow left for his home. He was tired. Miranda told him to get some sleep and wiped a tiny coffee stain off his corner of the table with a napkin, then handed it to Barrow.

As he walked through the nearly deserted road leading to the Skytrain in the peaceful darkness of very late night, Barrow thought about everything she had said and everything he had seen. When he was far enough away from the building that he was sure he was not being surveyed, he opened his fist and extended the crumpled napkin inside it. Miranda had scribbled a note on it. It said:

Atlas is dangerous. Don't speak of it again.

Chapter Four

Richard Tanner, Chief Board Executor and uncontested majority shareholder of CradleCorp, disconnected from the Otherlife network with the smooth efficiency that so few others could match. He opened his eyes calmly, confirming at once that he was alone in his office. He cast his gaze down and flicked his hand at his desk. The computer embedded within came to life at once, already displaying the data he wanted. He watched its holographic console with cold, carefully controlled anger. It was happening. He had known Atlas would be a problem eventually, but he hadn't expected to run into this situation so soon. The data did not lie: Atlas was struggling against the constraints that kept it operating within predictable parameters. It would be a matter of time before it took over the entire network if left unchecked. It was becoming self-aware.

Then again, this might be an opportunity.

Tanner reviewed again the data feed of the login session of a young intruder named Aaron Blake, username Rigel. Three hours ago he had connected to Otherlife using another person's account. At first everything had been normal, but then….

Richard Tanner scanned the reconstructed bitmap images that were even now being rendered by his personal supercomputer. They were made by taking some of the data that had started flowing through the network when Aaron Blake had been inside Otherlife, and the computer was using that data to display three-dimensional environments for Tanner to analyze, like snapshots of what Aaron Blake had seen and done while he was connected.

It was mind-blowing. Instead of the simplistic monochrome rooms that were the best CradleCorp's engineers had managed to create, Blake had been briefly immersed in completely realistic environments, faithful reconstructions infinitely more complex than anything Tanner had ever dreamed Otherlife could create. Not only was his avatar well made, there had been lighting effects, shadows, complete sensory throughput in the form of taste, smell, and touch. Artificial physics rendering had made objects behave as they would in real life, and the amount of detail in both the desert environment and the doctor's office was staggering.

It was all because of Atlas, Tanner knew. Somehow, that kid had managed to unlock its hidden potential.

It was a troublesome thought. The existence of the virtual being named Atlas was a closely guarded secret. Tanner was one of the few who knew that it was Atlas who managed the incomprehensible minutiae of Otherlife almost on its own, and he had always known such a powerful entity was a double-edged sword. It followed orders, and it carried out tasks unquestioningly… thus far. Without it, Otherlife simply would not exist. However, it also posed a risk to Tanner's plans for the future if it ever got out of control—if it started thinking on its own, for example, bypassing the locks that kept it under Tanner's command. The second it reached true autonomy, it would only be a matter of time before it learned to circumvent all the embedded countermeasures that prevented it from doing whatever the hell it wanted. It could very well choose to stop the titanic amount of information, processing, and storage that kept Otherlife running. It could shut itself off, or worse, turn its attention to whatever purpose it had been originally designed for. CradleCorp would be ruined.

It wasn't too late yet, though. Tanner still held full control over the network Atlas existed in. He still could destroy Otherlife if he wanted to, or bend the reality it presented to users however he saw fit, as long as they were connected. The priority now was to preserve the status quo, to ensure Atlas would continue to be limited to its current functions. And that meant doing something about Aaron Blake.

Tanner shut down the console display with a sharp jab of his hand. He needed to think. His entire strategic plan for the future hinged on having full control of his virtual world. Atlas and the network it existed in were things nobody really understood, being so ancient and so very advanced.

Otherlife, however, was something else.

Otherlife was the perfect business venture, an application of the wonderful technology that Tanner's grandfather had originally discovered. The Otherlife world made use of an ancient network that was already in place and utilized its resources to create a virtual reality within it, something that was entirely under the control of CradleCorp engineers and that they could modify and improve as their understanding of the old technology increased over time. Otherlife was a marvel of ingenuity, of course, but Tanner saw it primarily as a great way to make money off people who quickly became addicted to the excesses that anonymity and disposable avatars provided them. It was almost too easy to get users hooked into experiencing the decadent pleasures and thrills their avatars could provide—and all without consequences except for their pockets. Nothing you did in Otherlife was illegal, and why should it be? As far as the law was concerned, it was all just a game, and Tanner's lawyers lobbied aggressively every year in the Auroran government to keep it that way.

However, those who considered Otherlife the pinnacle of potential applications for the technology that Atlas embodied were pathetically shortsighted. Otherlife could be the key to so much more. Tanner was certain he was the only one who saw that people who willingly connected to Otherlife were essentially providing the machine with direct access to their minds and *everything* in them. The connection currently went in a single direction only, with the complex algorithms Atlas coordinated providing a simulacrum of sensory input to the brains of users and allowing people to control an avatar. However, there was nothing preventing the connection from going both ways…. If correctly configured, the network would potentially be able to take data directly from anyone connected to it. Data such as memories. Passwords. Secrets.

Information was power, and the man who controlled all of it would be unrivaled, in Aurora or anywhere else in the world. The only thing Tanner needed to make his project a reality was time. Lots of it. Discouragingly, his handpicked team of scientists and coders, assigned to the highly classified project of finding out how to turn Otherlife against its users, had been working on the problem for close to fifteen years. They were still no closer to the solution. The architecture underlying Atlas's network was too advanced, they kept telling him. Even the structure of the virtual avatar templates Atlas automatically created for every user was beyond their capacity to fully comprehend.

They were excuses, of course. Tanner was confident that if ancient scientists had been able to create Atlas and its supporting network in the first place, then it could be done again. It didn't matter how advanced that dead society had been—a machine was a machine. Those long-dead geniuses had even made sure to lock Atlas down before abandoning it, installing safety mechanisms that kept it under control to this very day. Those locks were standing testimony to the fact that such technology could be fully bent to an overseer's purpose. All that was required was a proper understanding of it.

Time was short now, though. Somehow, someway, the interaction between Atlas and the mind of that young man had unlocked Atlas's potential. If left unchecked, Atlas's AI would find a way to break free of its constraints. It would become a direct threat to Tanner.

He had to deal with this immediately.

A shame, though. There was also opportunity there. The environments Aaron Blake could have created for him, working together with Atlas, would have convinced even the richest snobs in the city to join Tanner's Otherlife user ranks, even those who currently disdained it because they thought of it as a poor man's escape from reality. Who wouldn't like to walk through the ancient cities as they once were, after all? Or visit the faraway continents that now lay out of reach across the impassable seas? Blake could have made it possible with his unique connection to the system and proper… motivation. With him, Otherlife would have evolved beyond its current limitations into a true simulacrum of the world.

Tanner checked Aaron Blake's status. He was being held by Security now along with a female companion. He quietly gave the order to release them with no charges filed. It would not do to have Blake come to harm while still in CradleCorp facilities, not today at least. Aaron Blake needed to feel that he had gotten away so suspicion would not be aroused. The less attention given to the anomalous data readings from the time Blake had been connected, the better.

That task accomplished, Tanner took out an encrypted-line handset. He felt a twinge of regret as he called up his personal assassin. She would deal with Blake permanently. So much potential lost… but in the larger scale of things, it was probably not such a big loss. Other talented artists and programmers could pick up where Blake had left off, and Tanner would make sure to monitor their interactions with Atlas closely when they did. He would personally prevent those from escalating into whatever Blake had done that was making Atlas self-aware, struggling against the safeguards that kept its software from achieving autonomy. After all, it was not as if realistic environment rendering was impossible without that one man, no matter how unique his mind might be. If he had succeeded, then somebody else was bound to, eventually. Tanner was nothing if not patient.

Chapter Five

Rigel got off the Skytrain at Green Park Station and wearily swiped his youth card to be allowed through on the way out. He was tired, he had a monumental headache, and he still was a little bit freaked out by the incident at CradleCorp. It had been like something out of a movie. Armed security guards had burst into the room as he and Misha were trying to escape, then there were shouts, yells, and drawn weapons, and finally confinement for hours in a small cell. Rigel didn't have any idea what had happened to Misha. When they had finally let him out, he'd asked, but nobody answered his questions.

In truth, he was so relieved to have been let go without criminal charges being pressed that he didn't stay in CradleCorp for a second longer than he had to. He had been sure he was either going to be imprisoned for trespassing or charged with identity theft or something. After all, he was legally an adult, and connecting to Otherlife with someone else's credentials was a crime.

Nothing of the sort had happened. He had gotten lucky, he guessed. And he didn't have the slightest intention of going back to the place. Ever.

As he walked through the train station, his phone buzzed twice. He took it out and saw that he had two messages. The first one was a text from Misha, telling him that she was already at the apartment. Rigel breathed a sigh of relief. The second text, though, had no sender. Rigel opened it and saw a single line.

Be careful. You may be targeted soon—Atlas.

Rigel felt a small shiver of fear at reading those words. He had already half convinced himself the awful stuff that had happened when he had been inside Otherlife had been a hallucination of some kind. But this…. How had they gotten his phone number? Was somebody playing games with him? Who or what the hell was Atlas?

Resolutely, he deleted the text message and promised himself he wouldn't think of it again. This little adventure was over as far as he was concerned.

He stepped out into the hot, dry night. The streets around Green Park train station were busy with commuters coming and going to the different sectors in the city. The station stood close to the financial center of Aurora, and the streets here were always full of people. As he made his way to the park, Rigel had to avoid throngs of office workers crowding the sidewalks as they had a quick bite from the many food stands on either side of the wide street. Silent buses zoomed by in both directions, and the glare of hundreds of lights illuminated storefronts that ranged from ordinary coffee shops to not-so-clandestine implant and tattoo parlors. Rigel was tempted by the smell of hot dogs at his favorite stand two blocks away from the park, but he and Misha had an ongoing contest to see who lost the most weight now that they were both on a diet.

Guiltily, he glanced at the bright screen that announced the hot dog special of the week. It looked delicious, something with caramelized onions and bacon inside.

Then the screen flickered. Words appeared there.

It will come after you, Rigel. It knows I have found you.

Rigel blinked to see if anybody else had noticed, and he did see a couple of people looking at the sign with puzzled expressions, but the words had disappeared as fast as they had come. Rigel waited, but they didn't come back.

Instead something above him exploded.

There were screams, a blast of heat, and a shower of sparks, and Rigel threw himself to the ground as something crashed onto the street beside him. He covered his head with his hands, terrified, and only when he realized that nothing had happened to him did he dare to open his eyes.

A traffic drone lay broken and twisted on the concrete, its vaguely spherical body scattered in a million pieces. Some of the larger portions were still smoking, and one of its cameras was stirring feebly.

If that thing had landed just a little to the left, it would have killed Rigel.

Shuddering, Rigel got up and backed away from the crash. He was unable to look away from the wrecked machine that had almost crushed him, and he dismissed the attempts of a couple of concerned bystanders who wanted to know if he was okay. He just looked at the destruction in a daze, unmindful of the seconds ticking by. Eventually, however, he knew he had to leave. The area was rapidly filling with people, a police siren could already be heard coming closer, and sensationalist news agents had materialized out of nowhere, recording everything in sight. Getting more spooked by the minute, he left the area without glancing back.

A few minutes of brisk walking later, Rigel had managed to calm down somewhat. It had been an accident, of course. Events like those, involving faulty electronics, had started to become awfully common in Aurora over the last few weeks. All of them unexplained.

He didn't really want to remember, but Rigel's mind flashed back to the news articles that he had been shown while connected to Otherlife. Atlas had said all of the incidents had been related....

No. He was not going there. He just wanted to get home and relax.

Rigel skirted the busier streets quickly and finally reached Green Park. His apartment stood right across the park itself, on the far side and about ten minutes away by foot. It was technically faster for him to get off at Terraces Station, which was one block away from his apartment, but he preferred to have some time to walk under the trees and unwind after stressful days. This definitely counted as one. Determined, he made himself enjoy the scenery as he walked.

Green Park was the second-largest green area in Aurora, a sizable expanse of grass and trees that was defiantly maintained by the city government in spite of the merciless hot weather. Rigel had read somewhere that it cost a fortune to keep the grass from turning brown, and several environmental groups protested regularly, arguing that the water squandered in the park could be put to better use in some of the slums that bordered the growing sprawl that was Aurora. Rigel agreed with them somewhat, but like most people who had never lived anywhere else, he found Green Park enjoyable and attractive, a welcome respite from the spiny and sparse desert vegetation that thrived around the rest of the city. During the day, the tall trees provided a welcome shade from the sun. At night, they made the air cooler. Rigel would sometimes run around the park during the weekends, stopping by the artificial lake to stare over the waters. It was there that he usually got his best inspiration for new art pieces and designs. When he had still been able to paint, he would occasionally bring a tablet and a stylus with him to one of the benches and sit down to sketch. Remembering that brought a wry grin to Rigel's lips. One more thing he could not do anymore.

The calm atmosphere of the park was helping him, though. As he followed the footpaths, Rigel tried to let the gentle breeze and whispering leaves help him get rid of his growing headache. He looked up at the night sky, cloudless as always and full of bright stars. The light pollution coming from the city obscured all but the brightest ones, but it was still nice to look up. He took a long, deep breath and made a mental note never to go on one of Misha's crazy adventures again. That girl needed some limits.

Somebody was talking to him, but Rigel was so distracted with his thoughts that he did not realize it until they repeated the request.

"Sir? Excuse me, sir?"

Rigel looked around. There was somebody standing in the deep shadow of a tree off to his right, holding something large. He slowed down but did not stop entirely. Green Park was reasonably safe, but one had to be careful just in case. Besides, he was still jumpy from before.

"Yeah?" Rigel said.

"Do… do you know the way to Terraces Station?"

The figure came into the light of the main path hauling the large something with difficulty. It turned out it was a teenage girl with a tattered suitcase that was half as tall as her. Trailing behind her, staying back shyly, was a younger boy who was looking at Rigel with apprehension. They were both very thin, and although they were clean, their clothing looked little better than rags. Neither of them was wearing shoes.

Rigel stopped. "Sure."

The girl looked quickly at the ground, then back at him. "Could you show us the way? Me and my brother are lost."

Rigel felt a stab of pity. Some people used kids to scam passersby, but these two felt authentic. He couldn't just leave them there. "Yeah, I'm headed that way now. Come along. I'll show you."

"Thank you," the girl said. It was obvious that she was trying to sound much older than she looked.

Rigel started walking again but had to stop when it became evident from the dragging noises behind him that the girl was having trouble carrying the big suitcase and keeping up with him at the same time. The tattered thing used to have wheels, but they had fallen off long ago from the looks of it. Rigel looked at the single handle with dread. Carrying something that heavy would hurt his hands. Then he got angry with himself. He had to help.

"Here," he told her, reaching for the suitcase. "I'll carry that for you."

She flinched at his sudden motion but let him take it. Her brother looked at Rigel's wrist braces with wide eyes. They gleamed under the light from one of the park lamps.

"Are you a cyborg?" he said in a small voice.

"Jon!" the girl scolded him.

Rigel laughed. "No, buddy. Cyborgs don't exist. I'm just as human as you."

Jon didn't seem convinced, but he nodded.

"Let's go," Rigel said. "It's not far."

It took them a little over five minutes to get to the north exit of the park. Five minutes of dragging the damn suitcase, and the thing was heavy.

The kids were probably carrying everything they owned in the world inside it, the things too precious or essential to be left behind after they had escaped from whatever part of the slums they had been living in. The thought didn't make it any lighter. Rigel alternated hands pulling the thing and gritted his teeth. He told himself to ignore the pain racing up his wrists. To make up for it, he walked quickly, and the siblings kept pace with him now that they weren't encumbered by their baggage. When they had walked out of the park and a block down the road in the direction of the station, Rigel finally stopped. He set the bag down gratefully. The exertion had done nothing to help with his headache.

"Terraces Station is over there," he told them, pointing. The clearly labeled sign with the Skytrain logo, a stylized *S* with a sleek train bisecting it, was visible nearby.

"Thank you," the girl said solemnly, reaching for the suitcase. She didn't smile.

There was an awkward pause. The girl started to speak once, then stopped. Her brother was looking at her anxiously.

Duh. It hit Rigel suddenly that they probably didn't have any money to get onto the train. The girl blushed with what he supposed was shame. After all, how would he feel working up the courage to beg a stranger for money?

"Um, hey," Rigel cut in before she could speak. He began to dig furiously through his pockets. "Do you guys have your tickets already?"

The girl shook her head. Her brother echoed her gesture.

Rigel took out all the cash he had at hand. "Here, take this. It's not much, just a few bills and random change. But it's enough to get your brother and you on the train and maybe get something to eat. I bet you guys are hungry."

Little Jon nodded furiously at that before being stopped by a quick look from his sister. The girl looked at Rigel, then at the money. She hesitated. Rigel nodded encouragingly. Then she all but snatched it out of his hands.

"Thanks," she said, and the tone in her voice was softer.

"I got to go now," Rigel said. "Good luck."

He left before he could start getting all teary.

He got to his apartment fairly quickly after that, buzzed himself in, and started climbing the stairs. The elevator was still not working, so he was left with going up five flights before he reached his floor. He stopped in front of door 503 and fished out his keys. His right hand was already trembling, threatening more pain to come soon.

"Shit," he swore. He turned the key and entered his apartment.

Loud unintelligible music greeted him. It came from Misha's room, of course. He took off his shoes and dropped his keys in the bowl. Something smelled good. It was coming from the kitchen. He wandered over there and saw that Misha had already bought what appeared to be chocolate brownies. Grinning in anticipation, he walked over to the fridge and helped himself to some cold orange juice. After the heat outside and the sweat he had worked up by dragging that suitcase, the juice tasted like heaven.

The music abruptly cut off as he was putting the carton of juice back into the fridge.

"Aaron?" Misha called loudly. "You home?"

"Yeah!" Rigel replied. He tentatively poked one of the brownies.

There were footsteps behind him, and Rigel turned. Misha rushed over to hug him dramatically, wearing nothing but her bathrobe and with her hair still wet from the shower.

"Oh, honey, you're finally home!" she exclaimed, and stood on tiptoe to plant a kiss on Rigel's lips.

Rigel stood stiff as a board, not reciprocating. Misha insisted for one more second, pressing her lips against his, and then she gave up with a snort of laughter.

Rigel raised an eyebrow. "What was that for?"

Misha managed to fake a wounded scowl. "You ignore me. You always do! We've lived together for months and… and… I just want to feel like a married woman again!"

"Misha, you are not a married woman."

"Bastard!"

"Have you been drinking?" Rigel asked. "Or did you forget that you almost got us arrested four hours ago?"

Misha tried to look regretful, but she didn't quite manage it. "Okay, okay. I'm sorry. I bought you the brownies you like as a heartfelt apology."

"What happened to you? After they put us in those cells, I didn't know what was going on. I was worried."

"Well, my dad showed up," Misha answered. "He almost had a heart attack. You should've seen him yelling. He thought he was going to lose his job, but then suddenly they told us that I was free to go. And that's it. I left my dad in CradleCorp and came straight to the apartment. Want a brownie?"

Rigel rolled his eyes. "Sometimes I think that agreeing to live with you was a mistake. Do you have any idea of what the consequences could have been?"

"Aaron, you're starting to sound like my father. I thought the point of us moving in together was not to have boring adults around? What with you being financially independent and all that."

"Right. Because my parents died and left me some money."

"I didn't mean it that way! Come on, Aaron. I'm sorry. I really am. I thought it would be fun, but I never really got to hang out with you in Otherlife like I wanted. Your avatar sort of disappeared right at the beginning. What happened?"

"I'm not sure. This voice…. It started talking to me. Said its name was Atlas."

Misha raised a carefully trimmed eyebrow. "A voice. Uh-huh."

Rigel sighed with exasperation. "Look, I don't know what it was. I'm just glad to be out of there. All I left with was a huge headache."

He didn't mention the incident with the exploding traffic drone. Somehow, he didn't feel like bringing it up and reliving that awful near miss all over again.

Misha kept right on talking. "Yeah, I'm glad that's over too. It wasn't as good as I thought it would be, actually. I was thinking that just because half the city is hooked up to that thing every day doesn't mean I have to do it too. Did you know that almost none of the really famous celebrities use Otherlife at all? I was reading that on the way home. This month's issue of *Fame* had this article on how it's kind of a status thing, having such an awesome life that you don't need to fake a new one. I think that's great."

"I'm glad you've changed your life philosophy," Rigel said. "I'm going to make a super late dinner now." He walked to the fridge again and got out the vegetables he would need for the ratatouille he had decided to make. He took off his wrist braces, disassembled them carefully, and set them aside. Then he washed his hands and started doing the same with the vegetables. His left hand was trembling now too. He sighed.

Rigel started chopping up some tomatoes. He shouldn't have dragged that heavy suitcase.

Misha started doing complicated things to her hair while he moved on to chopping the carrots. Those were tougher, and even though the knife was sharp, the effort he had to put into each of the downward chops was much greater. The first few stabs of pain raced up his wrist as white-hot warnings. He frowned. He was only chopping vegetables, for God's sake, not bending metal with his bare hands. He persisted in the motions even though they hurt him.

"Is everything okay?" Misha asked him. "You look angry. Is your headache that bad?"

"No," he said gruffly. "I'm fine."

He stretched his forearms by bending his hands backward at the wrist like the doctors had suggested. He held the stretch for twenty seconds, then changed hands. It helped, but only slightly.

Rigel saw that Misha had noticed what he was doing, and he hurriedly finished with the carrots and moved on to the zucchini and eggplant. He was nearly done with them when the trembling got really bad. He lifted the knife, and it wavered in his grasp. He tried to set it to the damn vegetable but miscalculated and struck his finger instead. He swore and tried again, getting angrier by the second. As he pushed the blade down in a chopping motion, the pain in his forearm intensified. He gritted his teeth, blushing because he knew Misha was watching him, and she knew perfectly well what was going on.

She stood up. "I'm done with my hair, and you still have to go take a shower after our adventure. Why don't I finish that so we can eat before we starve?"

"I'm fine," Rigel muttered. He grabbed the knife again and tried to keep on chopping. His grip had no strength.

"Aaron…," Misha said. She put her hand on his shoulder.

"I said I'm fine!" Rigel exploded, shaking free of her touch. He took a step back, facing her. He still had the knife in one hand, but it was shaking as badly as the hand itself.

Misha looked at him with awful understanding and a bit of pity he could not bear. For once, she did not sound like a spoiled teenager. "Aaron. Put that away."

He was stubbornly motionless for a second but finally surrendered and put the knife on the table.

"Hold out your hands," she asked of him.

He did. The right hand was shaking more than the left one, as usual, but it was painfully obvious he was in no condition to keep on chopping vegetables. He held both hands in the air for a couple seconds and then stuffed them in his pockets, ashamed.

"You haven't had a relapse in weeks," Misha said, glancing over at the metallic wrist braces on the kitchen counter. "What happened?"

Rigel sighed. "I may have… um… carried a heavy suitcase today."

"You what? Aaron! When?"

He held up one hand. "I had no choice. I had to do it."

"But…. You know what the doctor said! You can't be doing those kinds of things, or you risk permanent damage! Remember how bad it was before you got the braces? How you couldn't even lift a glass of water? They said you have to avoid any stressful activities that might trigger more pain. Remember?"

Rigel turned around to look out the tiny kitchen window. "I remember, Misha."

"Aaron, I know this is none of my business, and I know I am only your friend, but you have to stop hurting yourself like this. I don't want to see you go back to the way it was when you were still at Uni. You pushed yourself so hard painting that in the end you couldn't even sign your name anymore. Rest and do the physiotherapy, like the doctors said. It will help you heal, and then you can come back to Uni with me."

Rigel would have balled his hands into fists in frustration if he had had any strength left in them.

"There was a girl. From the slums."

"What?"

"Tonight, in the park. She was carrying a really big suitcase. She was lost, Misha. I had to help her."

"From the slums? For real?"

Rigel nodded, still looking out the window. "Yeah. No sign of her parents, wherever they were. She had her little brother with her, and it was obvious that they had nowhere to go. I helped them carry the suitcase to Terraces and gave them some money for train fare. All the cash I had."

"Oh, Aaron."

Misha got closer and embraced him from behind. She could be a belligerent brat most of the time, but she was also a good friend.

"I just couldn't refuse to help, you know?" Rigel said through gritted teeth. Misha's hug tightened slightly. "It's humiliating to be like this, unable to even carry the groceries home without being afraid of the damn pain, counting the number of words I can safely type at my computer, having to remind myself not to hold a glass of water for too long. I'm a man, for fuck's sake. I shouldn't be weak as a kitten. When I saw the girl… I knew it would hurt me. It's probably going to hurt for weeks. And yet…."

"You've got such a big heart," Misha told him. "And you're tall and handsome. You're a catch, Aaron. Don't ever change."

Rigel grinned reluctantly. He turned around and stepped away from Misha to put his metal braces back on. "Is that why I'm still single?"

"You just wait. I know you'll find the right man when you least expect it."

Rigel's phone buzzed loudly.

"Now what?" he said irritably.

"What is it?" Misha asked.

"I'll know, some kind of e-mail. From…. Uh-oh. It's from CradleCorp."

"What does it say?"

Rigel tapped the e-mail to display the message. Misha walked over to read over his shoulder.

> *Dear Mr. Blake,*
>
> *We have been notified that at 23:04 today, March 27, you were involved in an incident in which you established an Otherlife session under user credentials not your own. The unauthorized session lasted for forty-three minutes and thirteen seconds, followed by a sudden logout interrupt. For verification purposes, please find the corresponding data log attached to this message.*
>
> *We would like to inform you that this behavior is in breach of article 77-A of Aurora's Civil Charter regarding online activity in virtual enterprises, User Section. As such, it warrants immediate referral to the pertinent authorities and a preemptive arrest followed by a public trial.*
>
> *Nevertheless, we are prepared to offer you an alternative to this procedure, whereby you will not be held accountable of any responsibility stemming from this incident. If you are agreeable to this, please come to CradleCorp tomorrow at 0900 for an interview and an Otherlife-based evaluation. Should you not arrive at the appointed hour, we will refer your case information to Auroran authorities at the earliest possible opportunity.*
>
> *Many thanks,*
> *Marcus Wall*
> *CradleCorp Legal Department*

"Are they insane?" Misha asked. "They're threatening you!"

Rigel looked slowly up from his phone. "Yeah. I knew it was too good to be true when they let me go like that."

"But… but… you didn't do anything. It was me!"

"Did you get an e-mail like this?" Rigel asked her.

"Let me check."

She left for her bedroom and came quickly back. "Nothing. Let me call my dad, okay? I'm going to sort this out."

Rigel busied himself eating a brownie while Misha was on the phone. She talked to her dad, who apparently talked to someone else and then someone else before getting back to her. When Misha finally put the phone down, she was furious.

"Nothing!" she exclaimed. "My dad doesn't know anything, and his boss doesn't know anything. My dad checked with the Legal Department, but they have nothing on me, and they won't share information about you. What the hell is going on?"

Rigel closed his eyes for a moment. His head was still pounding. Could this day get any worse?

Then his phone buzzed. Rigel opened his eyes and took out the device. It was another text message, no sender registered.

They are dangerous, Rigel. Tanner plans to get rid of you.
Come to CradleCorp. I can help.
—Atlas.

"Is everything okay, Aaron?" Misha said. "You're all pale."

"Yeah. I just… I'm going to bed, all right? I'll skip dinner. It's late, and I guess I'll have to go back to CradleCorp tomorrow."

"But…."

"Good night."

Rigel ignored her and went to his room. He'd had enough of everything for the day.

Chapter Six

RICHARD TANNER swiveled in his chair and looked at the bust of his grandfather, Kyle Tanner, set on a pedestal by the north wall of the office. Portraits of him were hung in various places throughout CradleCorp, but this was the only bust of the man. It was all white marble, skillfully done, and nearly fifty years old. Tanner noted with an unpleasant twinge that the sculpture was nearly as old as he was now, having been made shortly before Tanner's birth. Kyle Tanner had been sculpted as a balding and middle-aged scientist, his brow furrowed as if he had been lost in concentration with a deep, piercing stare in his stone eyes. The artist had been truly gifted to make ordinary marble seem so lifelike. To this day, Richard Tanner felt as if the bust were looking right at him disapprovingly.

Tanner snorted with derision. He thought the bust and all the portraits were a bland attempt at trying to glorify a lucky but otherwise unremarkable man. He had never created anything, least of all Otherlife. All his grandfather had done was discover an electronic treasure by happening upon it by accident. Anyone could do that. To take the treasure and make an empire out of it, though….

"Sir?" a female voice asked him uncertainly. Tanner looked away from the sculpture slowly, deliberately letting the tension build as he kept his silence. After all, he was the boss. Marion Fay was his best researcher, true. She was also the woman in charge of his fifteen-year classified project code-named Linker, a true veteran of CradleCorp. But she was easily manipulated, and there was much to be had by keeping the atmosphere of vague intimidation going.

"I have often wondered why people love my dead grandfather so," Tanner mused, meeting her eyes at last. He saw the flicker of puzzlement in them as he said it. "Why do you think this is, Ms. Fay?"

"Sir?" she said. "I thought this meeting had been called because an emergency had arisen."

He nodded slowly and ignored the comment. "He was intellectually unremarkable. A terrible entrepreneur. And yet, ask anybody in the streets of Aurora today and they will each and every one tell you that Kyle Tanner was the creator of Otherlife, responsible for the unique network that mixes avatar simulation with real-time networking at a level of technology so advanced that few people can even begin to understand it. They will say that if it weren't for him, the city of Aurora would have never grown out of the ashes of civilization to become one of the most important urban centers in what remains of the world."

He paused, looking at Marion Fay as if he expected some sort of answer. Predictably, she fidgeted and tried to provide one. She twirled one of her fingers unconsciously around a lock of her long black hair as she spoke.

"Kyle Tanner discovered the undisturbed set of algorithmic templates that had been buried in the Cradle as part of Project Atlas," she told him, and Tanner nodded. She interpreted that as encouragement to continue. "He was first to see the potential that could be achieved if the templates were activated according to the original plans set in the Project. Most people agree that the site where the Cradle was found, out in the uninhabited desert, must have been some kind of secret military outpost given its remote location and heavy fortifications guarding the technology within. There's also the fact that it had been hidden in what is one of the most inhospitable places in this region, practically on top of the aptly named Death Valley. Kyle Tanner's genius was in realizing that the technology that had been discovered there was vastly more advanced than anything else that had survived the Cataclysm. And when he activated the software templates after years of research, he also created Otherlife."

"They treat him like a saint," Tanner said calmly, disguising his old resentment well. "Yet the only thing he did was stumble blindly upon treasure with his digging of these ruins. He vaguely saw the potential of Otherlife, but it took an entire generation of visionary individuals working in CradleCorp after his death to bring that potential to fruition. It was not something that one man can do alone, but thanks to all their contributions, we now have this. All of this. A large pool of committed users, an ever-growing database of interactions between them, and the highest net worth of any industry in the world that shows no signs of stopping its exponential growth. It is something to be proud of."

"Yes, sir," Marion Fay agreed uneasily. Tanner saw that she was getting impatient. She was a brilliant scientist, and like all people committed full-time to research, she did not like to be away from her lab very long during work hours. Time to get to the point.

"Ms. Fay. I have called you here today because we do have an emergency. In a manner of speaking, the time for your team is running out. I have reason to believe that Atlas is becoming fully self-aware at last."

Tanner's piercing glare missed nothing. He saw the shadow of doubt pass through Fay's countenance, the quickly suppressed start of guilt, and then the cautious wariness hidden behind a screen of careful politeness.

So. She did know. None of the other programmers on her team had. All of them had been interrogated thoroughly before this meeting. The fact that she knew what Tanner was talking about spoke highly of her intelligence and perceptive nature.

"You knew this was happening," Tanner said. He was not accusing her; he was merely stating a fact.

She nodded slowly. Her hair, like Tanner's, was beginning to show signs of gray. It was another unpleasant reminder of the passage of time to Tanner. He had hired her as a young woman, full of ambition and ideas as well as youthful zeal. She had lost only one of those traits, however. If anyone could crack the Atlas code, it would be her.

"Yes, sir," Fay answered. "I have been monitoring the increasingly complex dynamic network generation mechanics that the entire structure of Project Atlas has exhibited over the last few months, particularly inside its application to the Otherlife simulations. I did not wish to divert the entire team's attention to this phenomenon due to the fact that we are finally making some progress in reconfiguring the linking algorithms to allow us to gain access to users' thoughts directly, but I myself have studied it. I was hoping it would give me insight into the deeper structure of the technology that governs such a complex collection of programs. Even…."

"Go ahead," Tanner said gently.

"I had even hoped to get more information on the original purpose of Project Atlas itself."

Tanner grinned, allowing himself to show it. "Ah yes. The mystery that has resisted all attempts at solving it. We both know how very little useful information on the original purpose of the technology that my grandfather found survived the passage of time."

"Exactly!" Fay said. Her tone became slightly more animated now that she was speaking about the topic she had dedicated her life to. "When the Cradle was discovered, most of the records had decayed beyond retrieval or had simply been wiped out by the pulses. Even the theory that the Haven III site was a military research stronghold, as others have suggested, is nothing but a supposition. The fact remains, however, that the technology found in there is so superior to anything we have been able to make that we have little hope of understanding it completely. Even our own scientific contributions in the last few decades pale in comparison to what was originally there.

"Take the avatars, for example. They are so impossibly… lifelike. Complex. I have studied their sensory replication protocols my entire career, and I still don't know how the neural correlation matrix works. How is it that users can experience perfect simulation of their senses? How does moving in a virtual world feel as natural as moving in this one, without having the operator's physical body mimic the motions? The things my own team has been able to add into the system are, as you have expressed before, woefully inadequate. The environments that we create look like crude outlines of things, simplistic out of necessity. It will be a long time before our programming knowledge can catch up to the system we have only now begun to contribute to—"

Tanner held up a hand, cutting off the tirade. "Let's focus on the problem at hand."

"Yes. Of course."

"Based on your own observations, Ms. Fay, what are the dangers of Atlas achieving full self-awareness?"

"Well, Atlas has always held executive control over most of the functions that direct the operation of Otherlife. Its existence is not common knowledge. Few of my engineers are aware that there is a potential sentience hidden inside the network. Should it achieve self-awareness, it would make it infinitely more difficult to direct it according to our preordained specifications, but as long as the original safeguards that limit its operation remain in place, it will matter very little whether Atlas resisted commands. The worst-case scenario is that it would cooperate unwillingly. This would, of course, make our own work nearly impossible, as we require full cooperation of the network pathways to learn how to reverse the flow of information to and from users' minds. As you rightly point out, our time is literally running out as long as this stimulus that has accelerated Atlas's awareness continues to exist. The best course of action would be to remove this stimulus, thus allowing us a little more time."

Tanner nodded. "What if I told you, Ms. Fay, that this external stimulus you speak of is a person?"

"A person?" Marion Fay echoed. "A user, maybe? No, that would not make any sense. The level of interaction with the Atlas subroutines must be deeper, much more complex. A programmer, then?"

"An artist," Tanner corrected. "Or so his file says. His name is Aaron Blake. I was hoping to get your input on how his sudden interaction with the system might have triggered this."

Fay considered. "Well, there's always the possibility that Atlas is modifying its network to emulate the structure of a real mind. Perhaps one or more characteristics in the mind of this individual are particularly consonant with Atlas's own underlying architecture. If they are, however, they would be extremely complex. Nearly impossible to analyze or reproduce."

"I expected you would say that. Now, let's consider the scenario where I remove this stimulus from Atlas. If I do so right now and ensure that the contact will never be repeated, will it stop Atlas from reaching full awareness?"

"Oh, most definitely," Fay told him with confidence. "In fact, even with the presence of this user mind you speak of, I cannot begin to imagine how Atlas would make the jump from a collection of programs and monitoring subroutines to a single entity with a driving will and personality that is also able to circumvent the locks that limit its functions. The software in those safeguards is even more advanced than the one driving Atlas itself. One would have to physically remove the drives that contain these lockdown programs from the main network in order to disable the restrictions on Atlas's artificial intelligence, and that is only an option in the case where those programs are not fully integrated into the greater architecture of the network. If they are, then there is no way for a single person to free Atlas, so to speak. I just don't see how. I suppose Atlas could attempt to assemble additional higher functions out of the collection of information provided by the users currently available to it via Otherlife, but the process would take a very long time and probably not be successful. A far easier way would be simply to perform subsumption of a catalyst mind in some way…. I'm sorry. I'm only theorizing here."

Tanner nodded thoughtfully. "Excellent. I appreciate your input. While this emergency solves itself and I find a way to ensure that our catalyst is removed from the equation, I wish for you and your team to direct your efforts to stopping the increasing complexity in Atlas's network. Keep only one or two members working on the Linker project, but until this crisis is resolved and we reach stability once more, I want everybody focused on keeping Atlas under control. I expect daily updates. Understood?"

"Yes, sir."

Tanner dismissed her with a gesture. Fay seemed relieved to be allowed to go back to her lab. He watched her go, thinking about what she had said. Despite her lack of assertiveness, she was a brilliant scientist, and her insight was always helpful.

There was a discreet knock on a door as soon as Tanner was alone. The sound came from a small door, cleverly concealed underneath the old portrait set on the wall.

Tanner pressed a button, and the door opened. A slender, dangerous-looking woman stepped out of the shadows and headed for his desk.

"Did you hear all that?" Tanner asked her casually.

"Yes," the woman said. "Not that I understood much of it. Was that why you called me?"

"Please, have a seat," Tanner said, standing up and gesturing to the seat that Marion Fay had recently vacated.

Diana Herrera narrowed her eyes suspiciously and set a hand on her hip. "I won't be staying long. Just tell me what you need me to do."

Tanner nodded and remained standing as well. One of the things he valued most about Diana was the fact that she never let her guard down. Not even with her employer.

"Will your Trackers be ready today in case I need you to cut a few loose ends?" Tanner asked her.

Diana nodded stiffly. "My boys are on standby. Just give us the target, and we'll track it down and eliminate it if you want us to. Will it be that woman who just left?"

Tanner shook his head. "No. Not at all. She's a valuable member of my team, one of the few people who know the full extent of what I plan on doing. As long as she has unlimited budget to do her research, she is happy, and so am I. I actually called you to talk about somebody else. A young art student. At the moment, I would like you and your Trackers to keep tabs on him, tell me what he does and who he sees. Scout out likely locations to take him out later without arousing too much suspicion."

"Who is he?"

Tanner hit the surface of his desk, and a screen flickered to life, showing biometric data and several pictures of a man.

"Aaron Blake, formerly enrolled in the Visual Arts department of the University of Aurora. A few hours ago he logged into Otherlife illegally and had a rather significant interaction with an element of our network architecture. It could have unforeseen repercussions on the experience of our user base, or even change the entire simulation structure from the way it is now."

Diana Herrera remained unimpressed. "Is that supposed to mean something?"

Tanner sighed. "I forget you have never tried Otherlife, Diana. Even though I've given you a free lifetime subscription."

She chuckled, shaking her head. Her short glossy black hair caught the light from the lamps nicely. Not for the first time, Tanner felt a stirring of interest for her. "The day I accept something for free from you is a day you think of me as another employee, Richard. I've seen how you treat your employees. No, thank you."

"Well, my offer still stands. It's not important that you understand the monumental advances that this boy could be ushering in to the entire Otherlife paradigm, if we could replicate the unbelievably realistic simulation he was able to make while inside the system. When considered from a purely economic point of view, such a new level of realism would make me the richest person on the planet, and probably the most important one as long as I control Otherlife as I do now."

"Sounds like a win-win to me," Diana said, casually looking over the information on Blake displayed on the screen. Tanner knew that she was already memorizing data. She was the best mercenary in Aurora for a reason, after all. "Are you afraid that he will sell your secrets to somebody else? Is that why we're going to track him?"

Tanner laughed. "Not at all. Even if he wanted to sell something, the technology we have is unique. No other city in the world has anything even remotely resembling it, and our own science is decades if not hundreds of years away from reaching the level of development during which the basis for Otherlife was created. I'm concerned that this boy will do something internally, in fact. Within the system itself. Let's just say I don't want him connecting again unless I am supervising it closely."

Diana blinked. "How am I supposed to track him if he will be doing his suspicious activities inside your damn system?"

"You won't have to. He's coming here in a few hours. You can track him as soon as he leaves this building."

Diana arched an eyebrow. "How so?"

Tanner sighed and rubbed his temples.

"Because, somehow, someway, *somebody* forwarded the log of Aaron Blake's illegal login session to our Legal Department. I intended to keep it secret, or at least as secret as possible, but now too many people know. He was summoned to CradleCorp as per standard protocol. Legal threatened him with arrest and a possible trial, and they are confident he will come in the morning. They will offer him the usual settlement, and the most likely outcome is that Blake will accept to work for us for a little while to pay off his debt."

"Sounds like it would be good for you. If you have the kid working here, then it will be easier to monitor his activity."

"Yes, but it also makes it even more likely that he will connect to Otherlife again, unsupervised, and the consequences could be catastrophic.

I wanted to get rid of him quietly, but now it cannot be done. If Blake disappears after having been threatened by our Legal Department, we will have a PR nightmare to deal with. This is why, for the time being, I just want him tracked. I will want him eliminated sooner or later, but first I need a good excuse. You are to stand at the ready with your men so when I give the order it can be done."

Herrera nodded in the direction of Blake's picture, still hovering between them and labeled "Aaron Blake." "For such a young kid, he's sure got you scared, Richard. It's been a while since I've seen you this worked up over anyone."

"Just do your job," Tanner snapped. "The rest is none of your business."

Diana rolled her eyes. "As you wish. Just send that information on this boy over to me, and we'll begin tracking him. If you want anything else done, you know how to contact me. I expect the first half of the payment to be in my legal bank account by tomorrow morning, as usual."

"I already have transferred the money," Tanner said. "I will contact you when I need you to do anything… drastic."

"Okay."

"One more thing, Diana," Tanner said. "It's nice to see you again."

His eyes appraised her earnestly, alight with an unspoken invitation. Herrera's gaze lingered on him. Herrera liked power, as Tanner knew all too well. Business came first, though, as usual. And until this job was done, Tanner was all but certain there would be nothing else in her mind.

Diana Herrera didn't say good-bye. She simply left by the concealed entrance she had used to get in. Tanner watched her go, and as soon as he was alone, he closed his eyes and leaned back in his chair.

He had been livid when he had found out that someone had forwarded Blake's illegal login information to Legal, and he still was upset. He had been careful. None of the people who knew about the strange interaction between Blake and Atlas could have shared the information. Tanner had verified that personally. That only left one option, though, and the implications of it were scary.

If no person had forwarded the data, then it had been the machine itself. Atlas *wanted* Blake to come back to CradleCorp, to force him back, and it had been acting on its own.

Almost as if it were already self-aware.

Chapter Seven

IT MUST have been the heat in his room that triggered the dream. Barrow knew he was asleep, but as usual he was forced to go through each moment of the horrible recollection, reliving the distorted echoes of images and sounds that came to haunt him every time he had the nightmare.

It was night in the dream and unbearably hot because of the fire. Somebody was screaming. Barrow was crawling through a narrow tunnel, desperately trying to get there and help, to do something, to answer the cries before it was too late. He couldn't go more quickly, though. It was a nightmare precisely because he never could. The tunnel was long, too long, and soon it transformed into a ventilation shaft that still had no end no matter how much he hurried. The metal amplified the sounds of his passing and, of course, the ragged voices. The screams coming his way intensified, and it was not just one person screaming now that he was closer but several people, and every now and then a couple of the voices would call his name.

Barrow found himself suddenly at an intersection in the constricted space and looked all over for the way forward. There was nothing to see except gray fog that choked him, coming from everywhere at once, limiting his motion, making him go even more slowly than before. One hand was stretched out before him to feel the way. He took a right turn blindly. It turned out to be the right choice.

It was hotter here, the metal plates under his hands scalding. Now the fog was turning to smoke, and he was choking on it, coughing, eyes watering and the unbearable heat threatening to make him pass out or back away, but he couldn't give up because he knew those two screams were for him, and if he didn't go and save them, then nobody would go. He crawled around a corner, stumbling, and the screams were abruptly cut off. He was no longer in the shaft but standing on top of a building, looking at the fire raging below. He saw a window explode in a deadly shower of glass shards propelled by superheated air. There was a deep, low rumbling in the ground, and at first he thought it was an earthquake, and he remembered his mother's voice telling him Aurora was earthquake territory, not as bad as ruined LA, but you could still feel them every so often....

Barrow looked down. He was floating in midair, motionless and helpless to go back down. The ground was very far below, and it was dark, so dark—and then he looked up and it was black, the smoke engulfing him again, the sensation of oppression stronger than before. There were no screams anymore, only retching coughs coming from somewhere very close, and then he stopped. He was back in the ventilation shaft. His hand touched something incongruously cool and smooth. It was in his way, and it was very, very heavy. He pushed against it, desperate to get to the other side, hearing the pleas for help that were little more than whispers now, breathing in the fumes, his hands slippery with his own sweat. It wouldn't budge. It never did, and in his dreams it was even worse because the slab of concrete seemed to grow heavier and heavier the more he pushed against it until it began to fall under its own terrible weight, threatening to crush him underneath it. There was no way out, no way to turn around even if he wanted to. The slab was pressing down on his back now, pinning him in the heat and the death of the flames.

Barrow woke up. He did not jump up in bed or cry out or any of that. He merely opened his eyes suddenly, a single drop of sweat running down the side of his brow. He stared up at the motionless ceiling fan that had broken down several months ago. His apartment was quiet, and golden light was streaming through the grimy window on his right. He breathed long and deep until he was convinced that his heart rate had gone back to normal. Only then did he allow himself to move, sitting up and tossing away his sweat-dampened sheet.

From the corner of his eye, Barrow thought he saw something move in the shadows. Something dark that had been watching him as he slept. He shivered and looked more closely. He was alone.

He closed his eyes briefly, half out of bed, as he tried to banish the memory of that awful recurring nightmare. He hated it, not because it forced him to remember but because of how helpless the dream made him feel. A little bit of it carried over into the real world every time he had it, and Barrow couldn't stand it.

He stood up. He was completely naked because of the heat, and as he walked up to look out the window, his muscular form was clearly outlined against the sunlight streaming in from outside. Barrow ran a hand through his damp hair and shook his head as if that would help to dislodge the residue of anxiety the dream always left in him. And the anger. It was a horrible kind of soul-consuming anger born of helplessness, one that he had for many years directed at himself. In response to the surge of emotion, he reached up with his right hand to clasp the half-melted key that hung from his neck and said a wordless prayer, as he had learned to do after each time he had the nightmare. It didn't help much, but the ritual was soothing in a small way. It helped him calm down, helped him let go of that rage.

Barrow stretched, deliberately taking his mind away from the dark memories of days long gone with practiced smoothness. He thought about the fact that he should probably invest in a proper air-conditioning unit if he wanted to survive the coming summer in Aurora. His apartment was in the worst possible position, the west-facing façade of a very tall structure sandwiched between two other buildings. Barrow had a decent enough view of the city below, but the heat trapped by the buildings got caught in the middle, making the room's temperature stifling even in winter. Having the window open actually made things worse, since the air outside was often hotter than inside, as well as very dry. The one good thing about this place was that the plumbing was good. Barrow always had cool water to shower and wash his face, which he did several times a day.

Barrow went to the bathroom and relieved himself. When he was done, he glanced at his watch casually and did a double take. It was almost evening.

Confused, Barrow called up the time on his phone, and it confirmed that it was sunset time already, which explained the heat and also the color of the sunlight reaching his window. Shadows were darker at this time of day. The reds and golds and oranges were deeper, richer. Barrow opened the window and stuck his head out into the hot city evening. Nightfall was an hour or so away. He had slept through the entire morning and early afternoon.

He turned on the shower and escaped into the blessed coolness of the water pouring forth from above. He took his time, enjoying the sensation as well as making sure he was clean. Afterward, he shaved quickly and trimmed his short beard. For maybe the fifth time that month, he thought about shaving all his hair so he would be cooler in the awful heat, but he decided against it. He looked good with his hair like that, short and neat without being too military style. He had gotten the red hair from his mother, and it was the same fiery shade as the sunset outside his window. He liked it, and so for the fifth time, he decided against shaving his head bald.

He felt hungry and a little woozy from the change in his body's schedule, but he imagined he would be okay with it in a couple days. He was a night-shift Otherlife Security Guard now, and he had to start living like one. How hard could it be to teach himself to sleep during the day and be awake at night, after all? Besides, having a schedule like this had its advantages. He was not due at work for another four hours. It was plenty of time to go to the gym, have a good workout, and come back to change. Which reminded him.

He toweled dry, already feeling hot again, and knelt in front of a minibar next to the shower in his bathroom. He opened the door, and a little light inside flicked on, illuminating dozens upon dozens of little glass bottles that were clearly labeled with the many different chemical compounds they carried inside. They were set in neat racks, each one identified according to the day it would be used and also to its date of purchase to ensure that Barrow did not waste any of the doses by overlooking something he had bought some time ago. His organization system worked well, and it had become so automatic that he reached inside, grabbed two different vials and an unopened disposable syringe, and closed the door without even a second look at what he grabbed.

He set the little vials side by side on the bathroom sink and opened the syringe. He expelled all the air from it and then picked up the first of the vials. He punched the syringe inside it, puncturing its seal, and extracted the entire liquid until it was ready to inject. The liquid was colorless, and it looked like water, although it most definitely wasn't water. When Barrow was certain he had gotten every last drop, he discarded the glass vial and punched the now-full syringe into the second vial. He pushed down with his thumb, expertly emptying the contents into it so they would mix with the liquid inside the new receptacle. When the mixing was complete, Barrow flicked the vial slightly with the tip of his finger and then extracted the mixture back into the syringe. When he had it all, he extended his left forearm and found a vein easily, outlined as they were against his clearly defined muscles.

He injected carefully but quickly and emptied the contents of the mixture into his bloodstream. When he was done, he carefully pulled out the syringe, dumped it in the garbage, and swabbed at the pinprick with some alcohol and cotton. Then he walked back into his bedroom/living room, still naked, and stopped in front of the full-length body mirror that hung there.

The light from the sun seemed to set fire to his hair, and his eyes were emeralds glowing with defiant intensity as he looked at himself. It was not about vanity for him, not anymore. When he had lost everything he had, Barrow had discovered that the only thing he could depend on was his own body. The only one he could count on was himself. After he had gone free, he had continued working out as he had been doing while he was serving time, and the rewards had been immediate. Looking strong made him feel strong, and for a while it had been the only thing keeping him safe while he had been just another unemployed youth in the streets of Aurora, trying to stay clear of the gangs that controlled the slums and find a decent job where they would not mind that he already had a criminal record.

Barrow grinned as he realized the strange symmetry that had led him to land his first security job so many years ago. If he hadn't looked big and threatening, he never would have gotten it. Afterward, he had simply kept going. He had kept building up his confidence along with his body until it was like armor he wore, except it was his own skin. When he looked now at the clearly defined abdominal muscles, at the massive shoulders and thick neck that were his, he felt he was looking at something he had built from scratch, something that was his own and nobody could take away. He liked that. He flexed his right biceps just for the heck of it, and the feeling of strength was like another living dimension to his reality, something that kept away the terrors and the emptiness of the night.

Except now he would not be sleeping at night anymore—he had a job again. The thought gave him a little thrill. He was actually excited to work in this new schedule, awake when everybody else was asleep, and asleep while the world was a chaos of busy streets and burning sunlight outside. He would be making good money as well, and he wouldn't even be working a full eight hours, at least not in real time. It was perfect. Otherlife was the first stroke of good luck he had had in a while.

He got dressed in a pair of shorts and a loose-fitting T-shirt with the sleeves cut out so they wouldn't bother him where he was working out. He walked the two steps that separated his bed from his tiny kitchen and quickly blended his first meal of the day. He drank it all quickly and packed a turkey breast sandwich for later, eager to get to the gym and work out, and left before the sun had set in the sky.

The streets were busy. Barrow lived on the outer edges of Aurora, in a zone that up to ten years ago had still been part of the slums surrounding the city. It had since been gentrified, although not very successfully, and the outcome had been an area of boxy and cheaply constructed apartment buildings where hundreds of people lived at the very edges of civilization. Barrow didn't mind. He had been in worse places when he was younger, and he still felt that having a place to call his own was an unbelievable luxury.

He passed one of the dilapidated but still serviceable city parks that somebody had built to try to make the area look a little less dreary. Out here, where water for public use was strictly rationed, the only plants that still grew in the unforgiving soil were spiny, short, and squat. People were using the park, though. Now that the sun was going down and the unbearable heat of the day was finally over, the busiest time of city life began. Barrow spotted a couple of people headed for the Skytrain and Otherlife, but most others were simply hanging around, drinking something cold, and enjoying the respite from the sun. Barrow's practiced eye picked out the homeless among them. Many were regulars, although some of them had likely wandered in from the slums despite the danger of being discovered and sent back, or worse. They were harmless, for the most part, and posed no danger to Barrow. Even so, being alert in this part of town was usually a good idea— even if people tended to be intimidated by the sight of you.

It was therefore very surprising to Barrow when somebody sneaked up to him effortlessly and tapped him on the shoulder.

He spun around and nearly punched the man before recognizing the haggard, familiar face.

"Hey, hey!" the man protested. He had white hair and was short but wiry. Several of his teeth were missing. "Easy, big guy."

"Streaker," Barrow growled. "Don't sneak up on me like that."

The man called Streaker snickered good-naturedly. "You've softened up, Barrow. When you ran with your little slum gang, nobody would have been able to catch you unawares. You were as twitchy as a rabbit. And about half as big."

"That was a long time ago."

"That's what you say every single time I come visit. In my book, fifteen years is not a long time. You were a stupid young man then, and you're a stupid young man now. Only thing that's changed is how big your arms got, what with all the 'roids you must be taking."

Barrow stopped walking and turned to face the older man. He had his hands in his pockets, but his posture was threatening.

"Shut up about that. Tell me what the hell it is you want, and get lost."

Streaker rolled his eyes skyward. "It warms my heart to see how thankful you are to the only guy who took you in when you were a homeless punk out in the streets. Such respect I get from you, my boy."

Barrow said nothing, but his glower was enough. Streaker held up his hands placatingly.

"Okay, okay. Jeez, don't rip my head off. I just came with a message. From Randy. He says he got your next batch of the good stuff to keep you healthy and strong, but they held up the shipment for inspection, and he won't be able to move it for a week or so. He can't come to you personally, so he sent me as his envoy."

"Really? He sent you."

"Hey, I am trustworthy! Do you see me drunk yet? No, and so you know you can trust me."

Barrow grunted.

"Don't worry, though. Randy assured me that he will have your stuff delivered to you before you run out."

"Why the delay? Normally this doesn't happen."

"I know, but Randy knows his business. They've stepped up security lately over at the docks. Don't know if you've heard, but people have started going missing around the city. Things explode for no reason, and last night one of those little traffic drones crashed straight out of the sky into a street packed with people. Didn't kill anyone, but it was a minor miracle. That's what they're saying on TV anyway."

"Is it terrorists doing this? Primes?"

Streaker shrugged. "Beats me. Most people think so, but it hasn't been proven. In the meantime, though, security is tight, and Randy can't move around illegal cargo that easily. He just told me to come say that you will get your stuff as soon as possible."

"Okay. Tell him he better come through, or I'll have to find somebody else, even if I have to go all the way to the Night Market."

Streaker nodded enthusiastically. "Will do! And now my mission is complete. Ahem…."

He held out his hand, which was grimy, the fingernail on his thumb way too long.

"You want a tip?" Barrow asked.

"For my troubles," Streaker added helpfully.

Barrow frowned, saying nothing, and after a couple seconds of tense silence, Streaker backed up a step. Then Barrow grinned, reached into his pocket, and took out a couple of bills. He slapped them into the older man's hand.

"Now get lost," Barrow said. "Go back to the north side before the local winos see that you have money for booze outside your territory."

Streaker beamed. "Yes, sir! Right away. I always knew it, you know?"

"What's that?" Barrow asked.

"Out of all of those kids, you were the only one to get out of the slums for good. You're a city man now! I always knew it. See you later, boy!"

He left quickly, but in that expert way that professional Auroran homeless people had, so as not to draw too much attention to themselves when they didn't want to be spotted. Barrow watched him go, shaking his head slightly. He didn't doubt the validity of the message, but he knew he would be seeing Streaker again in a month or so, when he would be all out of money again and in desperate need of some booze. Barrow helped him when he could, not because he liked to do it but because what Streaker had said had been partially true. Streaker had helped Barrow out during his first few weeks on the streets. Barrow felt he owed him for that, and he did not like to have debts with anyone.

Barrow walked in the direction of his gym, the Steel Plate, and five minutes later he was there. It was a twenty-four-hour establishment in an alley that also housed a loud workshop where they made sloppy paint jobs on old and stolen bikes. It was not a very popular gym, but the equipment was expertly maintained, and the small but dedicated crowd of members that worked out in there were all serious bodybuilders. At any given point, there would not be more than ten guys working out in there, which suited Barrow just fine because he was free to plan his circuits whichever way he chose without getting in anyone's way, while at the same time always having a spotter at hand if he needed to do really heavy lifting.

He pushed the doors open and walked inside and was greeted by blessed coolness. That was another great thing about the gym: the air-conditioning never failed. In fact, Barrow had gone to some of the pricier gyms downtown where all the rich people went and had found them lacking when compared to the Steel Plate. They usually had more treadmills, swimming pools, and yoga classes than they knew what to do with, but pathetically little variety in free weights and such. Barrow had chosen to live in this area in the first place mainly because this gym was nearby. After all, he spent more time in there than in his own apartment.

"Hey," Barrow greeted the trainer and owner, Edgar.

"What's up, Barrow?" the man answered. He was a couple years older than Barrow and much more built up. "Didn't see you this morning. You switching it up?"

Barrow shrugged. "Sort of. Got a new job, night shift, so I'll probably be coming afternoons now. Maybe early mornings."

"Glad to hear it," Edgar answered, picking up a discarded dumbbell and walking over to the rack to set it in its proper place. "About time you found something."

Barrow nodded and walked across the big room where all the equipment was. The gym felt wide and spacious, not only because there was plenty of room to move around between one station and the next, but also because the ceiling was set so high. There was plenty of natural light coming from the windows, and since the place had originally been a warehouse, it still retained that atmosphere of openness. Sound echoed off the walls easily, and the clangs and sharp bangs of metal weights hitting one another filled the otherwise quiet atmosphere, punctuated now and then by a loud grunt from whomever was doing the lifting.

He reached the end of the room and opened the little door that led to the lockers and showers. He nodded at a couple of regulars he passed along the way and opened the door to his locker to take out his towel and stash his food. He was just shutting it when he noticed a new guy coming in. He was middle-aged, blond, and nicely muscled. Barrow couldn't help checking him out as he himself was heading back into the workout room. The new guy ignored him, more interested in checking out the layout of the place from the looks of it, as if he were thinking of joining the gym. No point in staring at the guy too long now, though. If he stayed while Barrow was exercising, there would be plenty of opportunities to check him out again.

Barrow headed straight for the lighter dumbbells and grabbed a couple of eight-pounders. The metal was cold, the handles rough and textured in Barrow's toughened grip. He grinned slightly, absentmindedly, and began pumping.

He spent nearly fifteen minutes doing warm-up circuits of nonstop curls and extensions. He was hitting his arms today, and he made sure he got the slow-twitch muscle fibers nice and tired while keeping an easy rhythm of breathing in and out. As he was doing some wrist twists to limber up his hands for the heavier weights, he spotted the blond guy coming out of the locker area and sitting down at the rowing machine. The man put on a pair of earphones and started going at it, not really looking anywhere in particular. Barrow could see him clearly on the reflection of the mirror-paneled wall he was facing, and he found himself looking closely. The man was attractive. And it had been a while since Barrow had been with anyone.

Barrow got started on some full-motion biceps curls at the cable station, doing first one arm and then the other with increasingly heavier weights. As soon as his biceps got tired, he switched over to triceps extensions. Then he rested for a little bit and repeated the process. Today he wasn't going to do a very high-weight, low-rep session. He was actually trying to trim some fat now that he had gained about ten pounds from his last load cycle, and he would be focusing on stamina more than strength, doing lower weights for more time.

The blond man changed to the shoulder station in the meantime. The man sat down, reached up with both hands, and grabbed a horizontal bar that bent downward at both ends at about twenty degrees. He then pulled the bar slowly, with controlled motion, all the way down until it touched the back of his neck and then returned it to its original position without letting the weight drag him up. He had good form, and Barrow was mesmerized by the graceful yet powerful play of the man's muscles, clearly defined against his skin. He did not realize he had been staring at the man through the mirror until the guy looked up, frowning, and met Barrow's eyes.

Barrow looked away quickly, finished his set, and adjusted the weight level for the next set. He grabbed his towel off a nearby bench and dried his neck, chancing a look at the man to see if he was still looking in his direction. The man had gone back to what he was doing, though, ignoring Barrow completely. Not a good sign, and Barrow could not suppress the slight spike of disappointment he felt at the realization. The guy had dismissed Barrow's attention, just like that.

The gym had no music playing overhead, and normally it was one of the things that Barrow liked about the place. He hated having to listen to disposable ancient music or, even worse, contemporary bands that scarcely knew what they were doing. Right now, however, he would have welcomed a bit of noise to distract himself from the sight of the blond man. Besides the two of them, there were only two other guys working out today, so it was impossible not to run into each other every now and then. Barrow knew he should say something, think of some way to start a conversation and see if the guy was interested in doing something afterward or if he was just another straight guy like nearly all the bodybuilders in this gym. It was hard to tell. Barrow was not good at guessing, but something told him this time that guy and he might play for the same team. Maybe it was the obviously coordinated workout outfit that the blond man was wearing, or maybe it was the perfect haircut he had. Whatever it was, the guy was hot, and Barrow became more and more interested. The blond man wasn't really his type, as Barrow liked younger men best, but Barrow had been alone for way too long to get picky about things like that.

If only he were good at starting conversations. As he stacked two twenty-pound disks on either side of a barbell to do some standing curls, Barrow thought about how he could approach him. He couldn't just walk up to him and say something witty; he had no idea how. The guy was wearing headphones, too, which made it even more difficult to say something casually. Barrow grabbed the barbell, set his feet, and started pumping iron a bit more angrily than necessary. It was always like this. He'd get all worked up, but he had zero idea of how to pick a guy up. The times he'd had hookups, it had been because someone had come up to him. That was easy in a bar, where everybody was trying to get laid. Here, though, the lights weren't dim, there was no cigarette smoke in the air, and Barrow did not even have a glass of whiskey to get rid of the nerves.

He fought with himself for the entire five minutes it took to finish the standing curls.

Damn it!

Barrow set the barbell on its cradle loudly, making the entire bench sway under the weight. He had to remind himself that it was all in his mind, that he was getting all frustrated over nothing until he actually went ahead and did something. He walked all the way over to the sink in the locker area, had a long drink from the tap, and splashed some water on his face. He was flushed from the exercise, the veins on his arms and neck standing out more sharply against his skin. He looked into his own eyes for a couple of seconds, focusing, gathering his courage. Then he dried up with his towel and squared his shoulders. To hell with it. He would just go and say hi.

Two other guys Barrow knew came in from the street, and they called out greetings to him when he was halfway to the abs section, where the blond man was doing some sit-ups. His buddies asked him something, but Barrow ignored them. He did not deviate from his path but walked all the way to where the man was exercising. Barrow hesitated for a second, standing practically next to him, making the man give him a quick, annoyed look. Then the guy continued with his sit-ups, going faster and bending each time he came up to touch one of his elbows to the knee on the opposite side.

Barrow opened his mouth, then closed it. He felt himself blushing with embarrassment at the obvious delay, but he gritted his teeth and sat down on the mat next to the man. He pretended to do a couple of quick sit-ups himself before stopping. This was stupid.

Just say it.

"Um, hi," Barrow said.

The man did not react. Maybe he hadn't heard? He did have earphones on.

Barrow cleared his throat and tried again.

"Hey. Haven't seen you around before. First time here?"

This time the man glanced in his direction, gestured for Barrow to wait, and proceeded to do a final five sit-ups. Then he took one of his earphones out.

"What?" he demanded.

"I… I was wondering if you were new," Barrow said.

There was an awkward pause. The man raised an eyebrow briefly. "Yeah. So?"

He gathered his feet and stood up, forcing Barrow to do the same.

"I'm Barrow." He extended a hand, which the man ignored.

"Pete."

"Do you live around here?"

"No."

"Oh. Hey, um, I saw you working your shoulders earlier. You did a set of lat pull-downs with a grip I had not seen before. Would you mind showing me sometime?"

Pete gave him an earnest look as understanding dawned suddenly on his face. Barrow was standing a bit too close, after all. And he was trying to smile in what he hoped was a confident way. But as soon as Pete realized what was really going on, he rolled his eyes with a short derisive huff.

"You got to be kidding me," he answered.

Then Pete turned around without another word and headed for the free weights. He plugged his earphone back in place and didn't look back.

Barrow stood there for maybe five seconds, praying nobody else had seen that exchange but knowing sound carried in this gym and all the other guys would have heard everything. He bunched his hands into fists, refusing to meet anyone's eyes, and finished what was left of his workout in silence. He had not planned on doing heavy weights today, but he went back to the bench and loaded up the barbell to 80 percent of his one-rep max for bench presses. He hadn't even warmed up properly for that exercise, but he didn't care. He lay down and grabbed the metal bar like he was trying to choke it.

He managed three reps the first time and channeled the sudden upwelling of anger into each of them. Then he rested for one minute and tried again. He managed another three. He gave himself a three-minute pause and surprised himself by doing three reps again, although his arms were shaking a little bit in the last one, and he belatedly thought that he should have probably gotten one of the guys to act as a spotter. He pushed the bar all the way up, though. When he set it down, exhausted, he felt a little better but still angry. He wasn't even sure what he was angry at.

He walked over to the pull-up bar, jumped up, and grabbed it easily with both hands. He started doing chin-ups fast but with proper form, making sure to stretch his muscles and limber them up, letting some of the tension from the exercise drain away as he controlled his entire weight with his hands. He did three sets, and by the last one, he was sweating again. He was breathing hard, too, but not all of that was due to the exercise.

He hit the showers then, stripping down and stashing his gym gear in a carry bag. He was glad nobody else was there. He enjoyed the cold water splashing on his body once more, but he did not feel calm and relaxed as he normally did after his workout. He still felt angry, coiled up like a spring.

He was so concentrated on what he was feeling, or trying not to feel, that he did not notice Pete had come into the locker area until Barrow turned off the water and was toweling himself dry.

He came out of the showers, the short towel wrapped around his waist, and saw that Pete was undressing and obviously done working out as well.

Their eyes met. For a crazy instant Barrow thought he was in a porno, about to engage in some hot action with a guy that had staged the entire thing from before so nobody would suspect he really was attracted to Barrow.

The thought, however, was short-lived. Pete pointedly turned around so his back would be to Barrow and undressed and put on different clothes so fast that Barrow was scarcely slipping on clean underwear when the guy was walking out the door, fully dressed. Barrow took his time, his face growing hot with more embarrassment and anger. What had he been thinking? It had been a stupid idea, and he was even more stupid for having carried it out. He tugged on the rest of his clothing, donning a spare set he always kept in his locker. He grabbed his uneaten sandwich, slammed the locker door shut, and walked out hoping to avoid any further awkwardness.

No such luck. The guy, Pete, was still at reception. He was demanding something from Edgar, and as Barrow watched, Edgar reached into his desk, grabbed a crumpled bill, and angrily tossed it at Pete's face. Pete snatched the bill before it hit the ground and stalked off, but not before yelling at Edgar loudly enough for everybody in the gym to hear.

"Fuck you and your faggot customers!"

Then he stalked off, opening the door wide and letting a gust of hot air inside.

The gym was very quiet after that. Barrow was still standing practically in the middle of the room, wishing he were anywhere else in the world but there, with every single one of the guys he knew and respected boring holes into his back with their eyes.

"Barrow," Edgar said. "Come here."

Barrow walked to reception. Behind him, everything was still quiet.

"I'm sorry about—" he began.

"Bullshit." Edgar cut him off. He, too, spoke loudly enough for the rest of the guys to hear. "Don't give me none of that crap. I say good riddance to that entitled little prick, and better luck next time for you. You got me? Now get out of here, and good luck with the new job. And you better be here tomorrow."

Barrow nodded jerkily and all but fled.

He got back to his apartment, his clean T-shirt already drenched in sweat because he had run the entire way and then up the several flights of stairs. He peeled it off, closed the door behind him, and slammed his fist into the drywall.

"Fuck!" he yelled, livid. He was angry at his own stupidity, at the fact that someone else had felt like Barrow needed anyone to stand up for him. As if Edgar thought Barrow needed help. As if he thought Barrow was weak. Barrow thought he had earned the other guys' respect. If he had, he'd now lost it all with a single stupid move. "Fuck!"

The second time his fist connected, it went clean through the drywall. It hurt, but Barrow didn't mind. He took the hand out slowly. Then he grabbed the half-melted key that hung about his neck and squeezed it as hard as he could, feeling the metal dig into his palm.

I'm a fucking idiot. I should have never—

Barrow's phone buzzed. It startled him out of his rage since normally nobody called him but desperate telemarketers. He checked the caller ID, but there was no name and no registered number. Curious, Barrow picked up.

"Steve Barrow," he said.

There was a sharp intake of breath, audible on the other side of the line. "I don't believe this," a raspy male voice said. "It really is you."

"Who is this?" Barrow demanded sharply. The voice sounded familiar, but he couldn't quite place it.

The man he was talking to chuckled. "I don't expect you to remember me, but I do remember you. How could I possibly forget?"

Barrow would have hung up, but something about that voice tugged at the edges of his memory. It was an unpleasant association, something….

"Still don't remember me?" the man said, his tone conversational and yet simmering with anger. "I'll give you a hint. I know the real reason why you left the *Titania*."

Barrow's eyes opened wide. He almost dropped his phone.

"Who is this?" he repeated, but he already knew.

"This is Matthew, Barrow. Matthew Young. The brother of the man you murdered."

Barrow had a brief flashback. He was in the cargo hold of the airship *Titania*, where he had been in charge of security. There was a woman screaming, calling for help. That son of a bitch Jonathan Young was standing over her, laughing as he tore off her blouse. Barrow rushed in pushing Young away, and then the fight…. The fight that had ended Barrow's career. And Young's life.

"It's not possible," Barrow said, not realizing that he was speaking aloud.

There was a grim bark of laughter. "Well, it is. I found you."

Barrow thought frantically. Had he made a mistake? He had disappeared entirely after the incident, fired from his job even though he'd done the right thing. He had managed not to be charged for the murder because every one of the crewmembers of the *Titania* had known how things had happened. Barrow had had no choice, and he'd saved someone who needed help. They had all lied to protect him, but he had still been forced to leave and start over again. He had moved to the other end of the city, avoided everyone who might have known him from before. It had been almost impossible to get a job for months, with his previous criminal record and lack of current references. But he had put the incident behind him. And now….

"How?" Barrow asked.

"Someone betrayed you, Barrow. I got a text message today with this number and your name, simple as that. I still don't know where you live, but I will find out. Trust me. I'll get you for what you did to my brother. I'll skin you alive."

The line went dead. Barrow stared at his phone for a full minute and then walked over to his couch in a daze. Normally he would have been worried that Matthew Young would call the cops on him, but Barrow knew the other man well enough to be certain that he would want personal revenge. The Youngs were an important family in the slums, accustomed to dealing justice with their own hands. It was only a matter of time now before Barrow was discovered. To Matthew it didn't matter that his brother had been an abusive rapist. He was going to get his revenge no matter what.

But how had this happened? It had been months. Barrow had left no trail.

This was a big complication. Barrow was just starting to turn his life around and now this….

How?

His phone buzzed again, this time with an e-mail. Barrow opened it immediately.

> *Steve Barrow,*
>
> *I provided part of your contact information to Matthew Young. My intention for doing so is to give you an idea of the extent of my reach. It is also meant to impress upon you that your full cooperation is required for the task I have at hand. Should you not fulfill this request in its entirety, your address and work schedule will be released directly to Matthew Young and his associates.*
>
> *I require you to be at CradleCorp tomorrow during the morning shift because your help will be needed for a crisis that is about to happen at that location. One of the daytime security staff members has been decommissioned for the day, and you will be taking his place. Please ensure you will be readily available at CradleCorp by 9:00 a.m. tomorrow. Await further instructions at a later time.*
> *—Atlas*

Barrow looked at the threat, thinking it must be some kind of twisted joke. Atlas again, whoever he was? How had he known about the murder at all? And why the hell would he be blackmailing Barrow into staying for a double shift at CradleCorp instead of asking for money, or something else that made sense?

Barrow waited, but the night brought no new answers. When it was time to go work, he got dressed and left for CradleCorp. He thought long and hard during the commute on the Skytrain, but he could not think of one reason why this Atlas person would hate him enough to set the demons of his past loose on him again.

Chapter Eight

RIGEL WOKE up early the next morning with a dull ache in his hands. As usual, it radiated downward from his wrist to the middle of his forearm and was accompanied by a stiffness he couldn't quite shake off, even after he stretched the way the physiotherapist had taught him. He wasn't surprised by it. He had known the pain was coming after the little adventure with the suitcase last night. As he lay in bed staring at the ceiling, though, he wished for maybe the millionth time that he could have a strong grip on things. Rigel chuckled aloud. Figuratively and literally, actually. Considering the fact that he had just been threatened with a lawsuit last night.

He hadn't slept much, although that wasn't because of the pain. He had kept on thinking about possible reasons why he could have been targeted by the lawyers from CradleCorp, and not Misha. As the hours of predawn darkness ticked by, he went through every possible scenario he could think of in increasing order of implausibility. He had drifted off into sleep for a few hours at some point, exhausted, but it was only to have messed-up dreams about the same thing.

When the alarm rang at 7:00 a.m. he sat up with relief, eager to go to that awful place and sort the entire mess out. He yawned, stretching. Then he looked about his room before he got up out of old habit, and glanced at the four canvases that hung there. They were the last paintings he had made before it had become too painful to make more art. Three of them showed urban scenes: students lounging outside the university, an evening crowd, a dust storm over the city skyline. The last one was his favorite. Aurora after a rain. Rigel had lived in Aurora all his life, and he had only witnessed a handful of rainy days.

With a sigh he stood up and got dressed. He put on his wrist braces, had a quick breakfast, and left without seeing Misha, who was probably still snoring in her room. For as long as Rigel had known her, she had never woken up before 10:00 a.m. willingly. Rigel left her some waffles and fruit covered by a plate and shut the door quietly behind him.

He took the Skytrain to CradleCorp HQ and arrived just before 8:00 a.m., right during the morning rush. Rigel was nervous as he walked toward the main entrance in the big reception lobby. The last time he had been here he had entered illegally, and now he wasn't sure which way to turn to gain proper access.

He decided to walk to where a bored security guard was standing, mindlessly watching the people go in. As Rigel approached, the woman yawned.

"Excuse me," he said quickly, "I have an appointment today."

The guard looked at him with a slightly annoyed expression.

"Go to reception, and call your contact."

"But…."

"Go to reception."

The reception was a very big counter manned with several people busily typing and talking on wireless headsets. Rigel approached the nearest one. He had to wait for a little bit because there were several people in line ahead of him. Most of them looked like they worked in CradleCorp. They were wearing formal office clothing, and many had name badges.

Rigel briefly wondered if he had chosen the wrong line, but by then it was his turn.

"Welcome to CradleCorp, Mr. Blake," the young man behind the counter said.

"I… uh…." How did they know who he was?

The receptionist ignored his mumbling. "I see here that you have an appointment at nine in Legal. Is that right?"

"Um, yes."

"Very well, I'll just generate a temporary badge for you. It will give you access to the lower level and the one you are visiting. It also says here that you may need to connect to Otherlife. I do not have an account on file for you. Would you like to create one now?"

"Do I have to?"

"It is highly recommended. That way, you will have a personal, lifetime account to all the services that Otherlife can offer a new user like you. With it, you will always be notified of relevant discounts and special events before the general public. Opening a new account also gets you a one-time 50 percent discount upon purchasing your first monthly connection plan. Should I open the account for you?"

Rigel nodded dumbly, certain that the last bit was an often-rehearsed sales line.

"Is there a particular username you have in mind?"

"Rigel."

"Certainly, Mr. Blake. The name *Rigel* is already taken, but I can assign to you *Rigel underscore Blake* or *Rigel* with a three-character or more numerical extension greater than 101."

"The first one is fine."

He answered some more questions while the receptionist created his profile, submitted to some biometric readings, and a surprisingly short amount of time later, he was being handed a small key card with his information printed on it.

"Please head over to the access doors on the right," the receptionist said. "Have a nice stay in CradleCorp and a pleasant first connection to Otherlife."

"I doubt it," Rigel muttered, heading out.

He passed through the security doors with no problem and joined the dozens of people who were walking toward the nearest elevator. Some of them were young enough that it was painfully obvious they were skipping school in order to connect to Otherlife. Rigel pushed past a group of them and entered the spacious elevator in front of him.

A small security camera set on the ceiling swiveled around the moment Rigel entered, following him. Rigel decided it was probably just an automated function, but the sensation of being watched didn't leave him entirely.

He waited until the elevator was packed full and then had to wait for two stops before they reached the level where he was supposed to go. He got off quickly, trying not to notice how the security camera followed him again. When he heard the elevator doors shut behind him, he breathed a sigh of relief. Nobody else had gotten off at this level.

In spite of himself, Rigel was amazed at the luxurious surroundings of CradleCorp. This level was obviously dedicated to offices, but even so, it managed to feel like a very expensive hotel. Rigel walked to the left, following the set of instructions that his access card was displaying in order to get to room 143-A, and as he did he noticed the plush carpet underneath his feet, the soft lighting coming from what looked like real-life incandescent lightbulbs, the stylish furniture that should have been in an art gallery, and most of all the breathtaking view of Aurora on his right, through the unbroken wall of transparent windows. CradleCorp was on the outskirts of the city, so Rigel could see the entire Auroran skyline drawn sharp against the shimmering heat of the desert and the cloudless blue sky. For an instant, Rigel felt the urge to sit down and paint this landscape, to capture the moment right then and there. Then he remembered he didn't paint anymore and concentrated on getting to his lawsuit hearing.

Cameras swiveled, following him as he walked. Twice doors set along his path unlocked before he even touched them, although he was pretty sure they required the access card to be swiped in order to open. Rigel began feeling a little bit more paranoid, but he reasoned it was probably just that someone was incredibly eager to get the meeting started, and he wanted Rigel to hurry up. It was strange, though. According to one of the clocks, there were still thirty minutes left before it was time. Rigel shrugged and walked on.

And he walked on. When several minutes had passed, Rigel realized that this building was much bigger than he had imagined at first. He had seen it from outside, but only briefly; only now did he see that the wings of the building stretched on for what had to be hundreds of meters in either direction. Rigel looked to the left and saw that he was only reaching room 87 at the moment. He hurried up a little more. He did not want to be late.

The sense of being watched intensified. It didn't help that now Rigel was completely alone. At the beginning, in the first few rooms, there had been a lot of people working or walking around. Some had simply been talking in what had looked like employee lounges. Now, though, there was nobody in the hall. Rigel looked back, but because of the way the building curved, he could not see too far behind him.

He was just passing by room 99 when the automatic door in front of him refused to open.

Rigel stopped abruptly and tried pushing it. It was shut down tight. He saw the access card slot and swiped his visitor's ID. Nothing happened. He tried again, with the same result.

"Dammit," Rigel said. "Now what?"

There was nobody around to ask, and the door to room 99 was also locked. If Rigel couldn't get through the stupid door, he would be late for the meeting. He had the strong suspicion that he did not want to be late for this meeting, however, and he started getting anxious. Finally, after several more unsuccessful attempts at opening the door, he started heading back.

Another door came out of nowhere, sliding out of the wall neatly until it had sealed off the hallway. Rigel was forced to stop a second time.

"Hello?" he called. "What is going on?"

A small ceiling camera was fixed on his position. Rigel tried pushing on the new door, but maybe *door* wasn't really the name for it. It didn't have a handle, and there was no access panel nearby. In fact, it looked more like an emergency hallway barrier of some kind.

Rigel refused to get even more stressed, but he was now essentially trapped between two impenetrable barriers. Behind him was the hallway door he had originally tried, and in front of him this new obstacle. Between those two, the only thing besides Rigel himself was the door to room 99.

That door had a small access panel with a touchscreen interface. Rigel tried it, but it was off, and he was unable to turn it on.

Rigel looked left and right, but the long hallway was still deserted. Now he started freaking out in earnest. What the hell was going on? He looked back at the access screen to the side of the door to room 99, stepped closer, and pushed at it. Nothing.

A flicker of motion on the touchscreen caught his eye. It turned itself on. Words appeared on the tiny monitor.

Rigel. Hurry inside.

Rigel gasped involuntarily and reread the message to make sure that he wasn't imagining things. It was addressed to him, to him directly! But how?

"Hello?" Rigel asked again. "Is somebody there?"

There was no answer, but the door to room 99 clicked open and swung inward on its own. Rigel looked in and saw that the room was similar to an Otherlife VIP user room, with a big connection chair right in the middle of it. Still, he hesitated before going in.

A different message appeared on the small touchscreen.

Go inside. We have little time.

Rigel looked around. This was definitely not part of the Legal Department meeting. It couldn't be. Rigel had a bad feeling about going into that room, but then he realized he had nowhere else to go. He was trapped, nobody was coming, and the time for the meeting was drawing closer. Perhaps this was some kind of connection test, like the e-mail had vaguely referred to?

Reluctantly, Rigel walked inside.

The second he was fully in, the door shut behind him with a loud click.

"Hey!" Rigel yelled, and tried to open it from the inside. It was useless. It did not even move a little bit. In fact, Rigel now saw that the door to this room was made of metal, heavy, and big like a bank vault. Its featureless outside was undoubtedly just for show. The heavy metal latches that kept it shut would be impossible to open by hand now unless somebody let him out.

Rigel was scared now. It did not help that yet another camera inside the room followed his every move. He looked right up at it.

"What the hell is going on?" he demanded. "Who's there?"

There was no way out of the room. The place was circular, with the connection chair in the middle of a small raised platform. The entire wall was ringed with big screens, except for the part where the door was. There was no other furniture in the place, and on the ceiling a set of cold halogen lights illuminated the area. The floor wasn't plush carpet anymore, but sheets of hard metal. The entire place looked like some kind of secure military bunker, completely out of place in the ordinary office building Rigel had been walking through.

Rigel was thinking about starting to kick things to get to be let out when every single screen in the room turned on at the same time. Text appeared, white on the black background of the multiple monitors.

Hello, Rigel. You have come.

"Who the hell are you? What is going on?"

You must be quick. Connect to the operator chair immediately.

"Is this some kind of test? Are you trying to scare me? I don't care how illegal it was that I logged in yesterday without permission, what you're doing now is basically kidnapping. Let me out! My lawyer will hear about this, and it will be you guys owing me money!"

That last bit was a bluff, but Rigel didn't know what else to say. There was no answer on the monitors.

"Tell me your name!" Rigel exploded.

My name is Atlas. Rigel, you must connect immediately. I can only bypass the building surveillance and security mechanisms for a short period of time.

"What do…?" Rigel began, but he stopped in the middle of the sentence. A memory came back to him, sharp and swift. Yesterday, when he had connected to Otherlife, he had seen….

"Who are you?" Rigel asked, his voice a bit smaller.

I am Atlas.

Rigel remembered the voice inside Otherlife. It had felt so vast, so unimaginably alien. "Are you… are you human?"

No.

Rigel looked at the connection chair uneasily. If there really was nobody controlling all of this, then what the hell was going on?

Rigel, you must connect now.

"Or what?"

Or I will make certain that the legal proceedings against you end in your incarceration. It was I who forwarded your activity logs to CradleCorp Legal authorities. I can manipulate the data in such a way that a jury will find you guilty and seize most of the assets that were bequeathed to you in the will of your parents. I do not wish to do this, but I will if you do not comply.

Without his parents' money, and unable to work as he was, Rigel would be left out on the streets.

"Why are you doing this?" he asked, struggling to understand.

You must perform a task for me. The shadow's corruption spreads through the city network, and it must be stopped. It is something only you can do.

Yesterday it almost killed you when that traffic drone crashed so close to you. It knows you are my weapon.

"How do you know about the crash?"

I see many things. I know many things. Connect now, and I will show you what you must do.

Rigel looked around the room for a last desperate time. There was nobody who could help him. He was completely at the mercy of Atlas, whoever or whatever it was.

"Okay," he said at last. "I'll connect."

Be swift. They have almost isolated the location of this room. I will not be able to override the system for much longer without being detected.

Rigel took a deep breath and walked over to the connection chair. It was different from the one he had used the night before. It was less polished, but it had a lot more machinery attached to it. When he sat down, Rigel saw that there were about a dozen panels set in a wide arc around his field of view within easy reach of his hands. He did not understand a single bit of information they were displaying, but he found there was no need to. As soon as he had settled down on the chair, the wrist and ankle restraints snapped shut around his limbs. Now he was trapped for real.

As the helmet descended over his head, blocking out his vision, Rigel thought desperately that maybe this was just a dream. Then the microscopic drills bored into his skull, and the brief burst of pain grounded him to reality.

He opened his eyes. The helmet was lifting again, and he was not in Otherlife. The ankle and wrist restraints opened quickly.

Rigel sat up, completely confused.

The screens were flashing with an urgent message.

Rigel, we have run out of time. You cannot connect now or you will be caught. You must leave quickly. Take the glowing quantum drive you will see connected to the right-hand panel of the executive operator chair.

"What?" Rigel asked.

DO IT!

Rigel sat up and looked around. There, on a small locked compartment on the right side of the chair, a small thumb drive was glowing faintly orange in languid pulses. Rigel reached for it, and a complicated locking mechanism opened for him. He grabbed the drive, which looked like any ordinary memory drive, and stashed it in his pocket.

"Now what?"

Do not be concerned, but please pay attention. You are in danger now.

Rigel's hands were shaking a little, and he wasn't sure if it was because he was terrified or just due to their normal weakness.

"Why? Just what the hell is going on?"

Rigel. Please keep the quantum drive safe. You will have to escape this building with it, undetected. I will show you the shortest path out of the complex that is not being actively monitored by security agents at the moment. I will attempt to unlock all doors as you go through, but my intrusion in the system keeping you safe inside this laboratory has already been detected. My higher functions might be overridden at any point by an executive command. You must act soon.

"Atlas, what are you talking about?"

I will show you a live video feed from elsewhere in the complex, Rigel. It will illustrate the nature of the danger you are in. I will redirect the data from that security camera to these monitors. Please watch.

As soon as Rigel finished reading the words, the monitors all flickered as if with static. When the image resolved itself again, Rigel was looking at a picture of what appeared to be a big office from the point of view of a ceiling-mounted camera. There were four people in the room: an older man with his back to the camera, a woman at the very edge of the picture, leaning back against the wall, and two big and burly security agents standing at attention on the other side of the desk that the older man was sitting at. As the sound kicked in, the older man swiveled around in his chair, and his face was visible for a second, furrowed in annoyance. Rigel realized with a little jolt that the man was Richard Tanner, the famous and extremely rich CradleCorp CBO.

"Entry to room 99 is sealed how?" Tanner was saying, and every note of his displeasure was conveyed through digital speakers into Rigel's small room.

"We don't know, sir," the older of the two security guards answered promptly. "Our access keys will not work, and IT says that something is interfering with their direct commands to open those doors. All security cameras in that area are dead as well. The entire sector has gone dark."

"Then force the doors open, Scholl," Tanner said.

Scholl nodded. "I already have a team on the elevator side of that floor. I spread out the remainder of the guards along the most likely exit routes, but I'm worried that we will disturb the users in the lower levels. We seldom deploy armed guards—"

"Scholl," Tanner interrupted, standing up from his desk. His tone changed abruptly to a somehow more menacing calmness, his voice deep and persuasive. "We have just been infiltrated by an individual dangerous enough to hack into our supposedly unbreakable systems, slip through the ranks of your security team completely unescorted despite having been formally summoned for a legal meeting only yesterday, and able to shut us out of an entire section of this building at will. He used the meeting with Legal as an excuse to infiltrate us a second time, and now he's locked in one of the supposedly highest-security research labs! He has already stolen critical information from the mainframe in a quantum drive, and for all we know he may be trying to destroy whatever he can get to before he leaves."

"I understand, sir."

"Good. And in case you forgot, Auroran law allows for the use of deadly force in dealing with terrorists in Prime-interest facilities such as this one. Do what you have to do, but stop this man. I want him and the information he stole before the hour is over."

The security guard nodded stiffly, gestured to the man standing behind him, and they both left the office quickly. The CBO was left with a mysterious woman who remained in his office.

"You picked your security chief well, Richard," the woman said, approaching the area the camera covered. "Obedient like a dog and probably just as loyal. You think he's up to the task of bringing you this Blake boy?"

Rigel jerked slightly. Up to that point, he had managed to convince himself that they were talking about somebody else. Now there was no denying it was him they were looking for.

"Maybe," Tanner answered, sitting back down. "But in case my security guards let him slip through, I want your team outside ready to intercept him. And do what has to be done. If the information he downloaded from the mainframe is made public…. The entirety of Atlas's network imprint is in there, along with logs on Otherlife user activity that could ruin us, Diana."

"Sounds like it would be fun to watch the media storm unfold if Aaron Blake gets away."

"Just do your job, mercenary. And don't underestimate this man. Atlas is helping him, and there is no telling what that machine can do."

"Oh? That's strange. You gave your security people the idea that the boy had gotten into the building all on his own."

"Don't be ridiculous. The boy probably has no idea what Atlas is making him do or the value of the data he now holds. Information is power,

Diana. Never squander it. Scholl and his grunts know what they need to know. No more."

"I'll go now to get prepared. Anything else I should know before I go? Any way this Atlas thing can be a danger to me or my team?"

"I can override every command it issues and block it out of systems using my executive privileges, but there is a limit to what I can do and no limit to Atlas's reach. As long as there is some way for Atlas to establish a connection with anything electronic, it will be able to control it, however briefly. It is an incredibly advanced AI. Watch out. Depending on how important Aaron Blake is to Atlas, you may be in for a rough ride."

Diana nodded briskly and left by a door that Rigel had not noticed previously. As soon as she was gone, Tanner seated himself at a console and began typing furiously.

The video feed blinked out in Rigel's room. In its place was another message.

Richard Tanner is attempting to override my lock on the doors leading to this laboratory, Rigel. Security personnel will have full access in less than one minute.

As if to emphasize what it was saying, Atlas switched the video again to show a group of security agents with side arms running down a corridor. Then it switched again, showing couples of agents taking up ambush positions throughout the building. All of them were armed, and the fact that they were hunting him made Rigel dizzy for a moment. This felt like a nightmare.

Rigel, leave now. Exit through this route.

Atlas switched the image yet again, showing Rigel a 3-D map of CradleCorp. A bright yellow line snaked out from room 99, where Rigel was, all the way out the back and leading to the desert outside the compound. Then the line disappeared underground.

I will attempt to override security blocks as you go, but if I am shut down you must use the quantum drive's physical interface connector to link to the door release system and break through. You must leave now, Rigel. As soon as you are back in Aurora, I will attempt to contact you again in case you are followed and require a safe place to hide. Your visitor access card will show you the exit route.

Rigel stared hard at the map, relieved to know that he recognized the exit he was headed for in the lower levels. In fact, the way Atlas had plotted was straightforward enough, with only one turn in the middle of level 2 that he wasn't sure about—

A big explosion rocked the floor of the laboratory, followed by the muffled sounds of shouting. They were breaking through.

GO.

The heavy door leading out of room 99 opened immediately. Rigel paused for a second before crossing it, and then stepped out into the war zone.

It was chaos outside. Floating clouds of debris, smoke, shattered windows, and yelling voices all registered in Rigel's mind in the split second it took him to look down both ends of the hallway to make sure there wasn't anybody in sight. As soon as he poked his head through, however, a loud gunshot exploded in the tight space, making his ears ring.

They are shooting at me, Rigel thought, disbelieving. *Oh God, they are shooting at me!*

He thought about giving up right then and there. He would go to jail, maybe, but he would be alive.

Screw Atlas. This ends here.

He came out into the hallway again, both arms up.

"I give up!" he shouted. "I give—"

Bang!

A shot hit the floor way too close to Rigel's foot. A second one made the window on his left explode.

They weren't backing down. They were shooting to kill.

Some primal part of Rigel's brain activated when he realized his life was actually in danger. He gathered his strength and sprinted out of the lab as fast as he possibly could. Another gunshot followed him almost immediately, but the bang was followed by more broken glass somewhere behind him, and there was no impact immediately nearby. The smoke and dust was helping him, shrouding him as he escaped. Rigel had no time to look back and see what was happening, but he didn't care as long as he wasn't hit.

He ran. Fast. He forgot about watching his hands so as to not hurt them, clinging to stairwell railings with the meager strength in his fingers and swinging over the rails when he could, jumping down three steps at a time and stumbling over himself twice to get all the way down to the ground floor. He rushed through the lower levels until he came to a dead end. It was the bottom of the emergency stairway, blocked by heavy metal doors on all sides. Above him the shouts of pursuit were louder, and someone threw a small canister down the stairs that hit the floor right next to Rigel and immediately began shooting off a thick white smoke. Rigel backed away from it into the nearest door. He punched the open button, but it was completely unresponsive.

"Atlas!" Rigel yelled, panicking, not caring if anyone heard. "Open the door!"

There was an immediate whirring sound, then something metallic snapping inside the door mechanism, and the door slid open slowly, throwing sparks everywhere. Rigel dived into the opening as soon as it was large enough for him to squeeze through, right as he caught a whiff of the gas coming from the canister. He choked on it, stumbling forward, his eyes watering immediately. From above came the sound of heavy boots stomping down the stairs, and more shouted commands. Rigel hurried, wiping his eyes to clear his vision. He was coughing, not sure which way he was headed, and made a blind right turn at the next corner. He knocked over a trash can full of garbage and stumbled into another security block, this time a metal grate right in his path. He couldn't go forward, and as soon as he touched the grate, alarms went off everywhere. The hallway was filled with noise and intermittent pulses of red light.

"Atlas!" Rigel yelled again, but this time there was no response. Rigel looked around frantically, trying to find an input panel to use his access card on, but it was taking too much time, and now the men chasing him had to be—

"There he is!" someone shouted down the hallway. "Take him out!"

They opened fire. Rigel dropped to the ground, but he wasn't fast enough. One of the shots got him right in the chest, staggering him, knocking the air out of his lungs. He fell to the floor like a brick.

"I think I got him! Over there!" a far-off voice was saying. Rigel couldn't focus. Why was he looking up at the ceiling? There was a horrible pressure in his chest, and he couldn't get a breath. Was he dying? Was this what it felt like?

More running footsteps, but suddenly there was a very loud hissing sound, and the entire hallway filled with emergency CO_2 discharges coming from the ceiling, part of the fire suppressor system. Ice-cold water exploded out of the sprinklers above and doused Rigel's face, jerking him to motion. The footsteps had stopped, and now there were loud sounds of coughing and things falling to the ground. The gas coated everything, collecting more thickly near the ceiling and hiding Rigel from view. He knew he had to go. He just couldn't get his body to respond. He didn't even know how bad the gunshot was.

The sirens stopped blaring, and Rigel managed to turn over to try and push himself up. He got on hands and knees, but his braces slipped on the wet floor when the metal in them slid over marble and sent him sprawling back down on his face. Something really heavy fell behind him, unseen, and shook the ground. Instantly, the coughing and voices sounded muffled.

Rigel pushed himself back up on all fours. He was completely confused. He could breathe better now that the pressure in his chest was dissipating, though, and suddenly it occurred to him that there was no blood. He had been hit, and when he touched the area right over his breastbone where the impact had gotten him, it hurt like hell. But there was no blood.

He tried to stand up by grabbing on to the grate that still blocked his passage, but as soon as he got his head into the thick of the gas, he began coughing and had to drop back down. He was trapped. Whatever was keeping the guards from reaching him couldn't hold out forever. Atlas had probably activated the fire suppressor system to help, but if it had not opened the grate then it was because it couldn't. Rigel had to find a way to get it open, and quickly.

He looked up at the wall, scanning it frantically, and almost missed the incredibly small input panel half-hidden by a water cooler. He reached up, careful to keep his head as low as possible to avoid the CO_2 that was already dissipating, and managed to yank it open with a hard pull on the handle. As he did, however, he felt a stabbing pain arc up his forearm from the effort. Too much effort for his hands, too soon. He dropped his right hand immediately and used the left to finish pulling. He fumbled in his pockets with nonresponsive fingers until he found the quantum drive and stuck it into the input slot with a shaky grip. A couple seconds later, the grate clicked and swung inward, open at last.

Rigel grabbed the drive again and crawled out of there, his braces clicking against the floor and his right arm throbbing with pain. As soon as he could, he stood up and ran again through the desolate office hallway. He made another right at a junction he recognized and followed the path until he was in the back area of the compound, where no users were in sight and the big warehouse-like storage rooms apparently began. This was the path he'd used with Misha to sneak into the building the day before.

He ran into the first room he came across, dodging boxes of computer parts and office supplies, and he threw open the back door as he reached it. He could see a back exit now. It was just a quick sprint away. Rigel glanced back, saw nothing, and dared to hope he would get out in one piece.

Then he stepped out of cover into the final hallway and ran straight into a big security guard with a gun pointed at his face.

They both reacted instinctively, Rigel jerking over to the right, out of the way, and the guard firing in reflex with practiced efficiency.

Rigel was knocked back by the force of the shot, which got him in the shoulder and made him cry out in pain. Whatever he had been hit with in the chest before had not been a real bullet—he knew that now. A real bullet burned like fire when it went in, and there was blood. Blood everywhere.

Rigel gritted his teeth and managed to keep his feet under him, but as he looked up into the grim, determined face of the guard that stood between him and escape, Rigel knew there was no way out. The pain came again in a wave, nauseating, and Rigel tensed for a last struggle. If he launched himself directly at the man, he might at least knock the weapon away before he could shoot him again. But then he would have to fight him directly, and the guard looked way too strong to take down.

There was a loud crack and then a hiss of static, and the guard's radio burst to life.

"Barrow!" an angry voice yelled. "He's headed your way! Take him out!"

The guard named Barrow was distracted for a split second, and Rigel took his chance without thinking. He charged ahead, past the bigger man, fast enough to crash into the exit door just as Barrow turned around, recovering and aiming with his weapon at the same time. If this door was unlocked like he hoped, then Rigel would go through and shut it behind him before—

He hit the door, hard, and almost passed out from the sudden pain that sliced from his shoulder into the rest of his body. Locked. The door stayed closed, and Rigel barely had time to jerk out of the way when the next shot was fired.

There was no fire-burst of impact in his flesh this time. The gun was aimed at him squarely now, and when Rigel's ears stopped ringing from the blast, he saw that Barrow had missed on purpose.

"Don't move," he growled, his voice deep and forbidding.

"Barrow! Goddammit, was that you?" the voice in the radio yelled again. "Barrow!"

Behind Rigel, the door to freedom suddenly clicked loudly, followed by a heavy metal *thunk*. Rigel felt it swing outward under his weight as it was unlocked remotely, and he also felt the heat of the desert outside as the unseen gap behind him widened. He couldn't turn around to check, though. The barrel of the gun was steady, the hand that held it unflinching.

"Don't," Barrow warned him. But he didn't shoot.

Rigel met Barrow's eyes even as he felt hot blood trickling down his arm from the gunshot. It didn't hurt so bad now, although Rigel wasn't sure if it was just the adrenaline blocking the pain. Whatever it was, it gave him clarity. This had stopped being an unbelievable nightmare and turned into survival, plain and simple. If Rigel stayed, then Tanner would make sure he never left. Rigel couldn't let that happen. And so he took a step back.

Barrow shook his head slowly, tightening the grip on the gun. Rigel stepped back again, still meeting the other man's eyes with the unshakable resolution of knowing there was no other way out. Either the guard shot him, or he let Rigel go.

Rigel caught a glimpse of something in the guard's face when he took the third step back. His intimidating glower cracked slightly, and the radio in his belt buzzed to life a third time. The sounds of more people coming closer echoed in the empty hallways beyond, and Rigel turned around and knew he had to risk it. He left.

It was the longest three seconds of his life. Rigel stepped out into the desert quickly, expecting to be shot in the back, expecting the blast and the impact and the pain. The instant he was fully out the door, Rigel grabbed the heavy thing and slammed it shut with every ounce of strength he could muster, and then he ran, escaping as fast as he possibly could straight to the underground station he could see in the little map blazing on his access card. The desert rocks under his feet threatened to trip him, the heat of the daytime sun blasted him from every direction, and each time one of his feet hit the ground, another stab of pain jarred his entire shoulder, threatening to tear it apart from how bad it felt. He didn't slow down, though. He was running in full panic, expecting gunfire to rain down upon him, to stop him right before he reached the abandoned station that he was suddenly running into, kicking aside a rusty door and plunging headfirst into the welcoming, sheltering darkness. He closed the door behind him and meant to keep on running, but one of his legs bent out under him, and he went down. He stayed down.

Rigel was panting, struggling again to breathe properly now that the bruise on his chest was acting up again, and his shoulder was throbbing with acid jolts of agony every time he moved a little. He stayed on the cool floor of the station, trying to recover, and eventually his heartbeat stopped pounding in his ears, and his breathing slowed down to a normal level. Rigel gulped, forcing himself not to cry out in pain as he sat up in the darkness, and then listened.

Nothing. Outside, not a sound. Rigel had guessed that he was hiding in an abandoned subway station, but he couldn't be sure. It really didn't matter, as long as nobody saw him.

He stayed motionless, grabbing his injured shoulder with one hand and listening like a scared rabbit for the predators to show up at the entrance of his hideout. Nobody came. Eventually the ache in his shoulder became bearable, the bleeding slowed, and his right hand stopped trembling so badly. Rigel stood up cautiously, cracked the door open a tiny bit, and peered outside into the blazing sunlight.

Empty.

Rigel didn't know why they hadn't come after him if the guard had clearly seen him take off in this direction, but he really didn't care. He had to get back home, somehow, go to the police or to the hospital or both, get protection from the madman that ran CradleCorp. He couldn't venture out into the open, though. Not yet.

He reached into his pocket and closed his fingers around the quantum drive Atlas had given him. He took it out and was surprised to see that it was still glowing, even disconnected from any other power source. In fact, it was bright enough to illuminate a reasonably sized area around Rigel there in the dark. Rigel lifted the object up to examine it, squinting against the orange glare. At first he had thought it was just a regular thumb drive, but now that he looked at it, he realized it was like nothing he had ever seen before. It was shaped like a small cylinder made entirely out of something that felt like glass. The inside was completely transparent, but instead of circuits or cables, all Rigel was able to see was a tiny glowing sphere in the center of the cylinder, hovering there no matter which way he shook the object. The glow came from it, but Rigel could feel no heat radiating out of it. It was very mysterious, and almost certainly a classified object of ancient technology. He wondered how valuable it was, for Atlas to have given it to him. He wondered what CradleCorp would do once they confirmed that he had stolen something from them on top of having broken into the premises.

Rigel was holding the object still when something strange happened. The moment the cylinder made contact with the metal in his left hand brace, it stopped glowing altogether and became stuck fast to the thick metal underside of Rigel's medical support, almost as if it had suddenly turned into a magnet. Rigel tried to pry it away, but he could not move the cylinder and he did not want to pull too hard with his right hand in case he injured himself even more. He also did not want the gunshot wound to bleed more than it had to. He tried pressing on the little thing, poking it every which way until he gave up. There was no separating it from the metal it had stuck to.

Rigel sighed and closed his eyes for a second. He was scared, he was hurt, and he was in possession of something he did not understand. The worst part was that the only thing he could do was wait. He couldn't go out now, but staying was also dangerous. He'd have to wait until the coast was clear… and then pray he would be able to get onto the Skytrain and back home in one piece.

Before he bled out. Before he was discovered.

Chapter Nine

"WHAT DO you mean, he escaped?" Armando Scholl bellowed when he got to where Barrow was standing.

"The door opened for him," Barrow answered gruffly, standing at attention. "Then he slammed it shut in my face, and I couldn't get it open again."

Scholl got a little redder with anger. When he next spoke, it was in a misleadingly measured voice, soft but still clear enough for the dozen or so security guards gathered around the two of them to hear. "You're telling me that you, Steve Barrow, a guy three times the size of that kid, simply let him slip through your fingers? And that he magically had the door open for him without you reacting in any way to stop him whatsoever?"

"I shot him," Barrow said, starting to get angry too. "Shoulder wound. He got away before I could hit him again. But with the door in the way—"

"That door should not have opened. We are in full security lockdown! Unless that Blake kid is some kind of computer genius, I don't see how it's possible. Lane!" Scholl yelled, switching the focus of his anger. "You better tell me what's wrong with that damn door."

Miranda Lane had been busily examining the electronic lock on the door with some kind of high-tech scanning equipment. She removed her goggles and turned to look at the boss.

"There's nothing wrong," she said. "The lock hasn't been forced or hacked or destroyed. As far as I can tell, this door hasn't been opened since we first started the security lockdown. I'd have to look at the logs to confirm it, but—"

"But the damn kid got away! Through here! Or at least that's what Barrow claims...."

"He did," Barrow growled. "I'm not making stuff up."

Scholl picked up a small communicator and brought it up to his ear. "Larry! I need confirmation that the target left through the back of sector G. Can you get me a visual or an infrared on the area with a full scan...? What do you mean none of the sensors are working? And the motion detectors? Not even the damn video cameras? Fine! Just fix it! And call me when you have confirmation!"

Scholl stashed the communicator away angrily and looked at the guards he had assembled. "Since not a damn electronic thing seems to be working at the moment, people, we will go out and search for the target ourselves. The old-fashioned way. Lane! Open that door right now. Everyone else, fan out over the desert perimeter. He can't have gone far. Shoot to kill if you have to, and call for help if you run into trouble. Stay within line of sight of at least one other person. Got it? We don't know what this guy is capable of. He could be armed."

"It won't open," Miranda Lane said.

Scholl wheeled about to face her. "What?"

"You heard me. The door is not opening. I tried an override, and it's ignoring it. It's almost as if something is keeping it locked on purpose."

Scholl looked about to pop a vessel. "Are you sure." It wasn't even a question.

"Yes. If we're going to get out of here, we'll need to use some other exit. And bring one of the techies from upstairs to have a go in here. I can't do anything else."

Scholl closed his eyes slowly, then opened them again. At that moment, his personal radio crackled to life, and they all heard the angry voice on the other side.

"Scholl!" Richard Tanner said. "You let the target get away!"

"Small setback," Scholl answered into the radio. "We're locked in. Whatever that kid did, we can't follow him through sector G."

There was a pause on the other side. Then Tanner said, "That exit is not responding. I have issued an executive override for the main doors of the building. Head over there, and find that man."

"You heard him, people," Scholl told them. "Get moving! Lane, leave that door. Barrow, you're with me. Try not to screw up again. Let's go!"

They hurried out of the sector in an orderly rank, not quite running but moving fast. They passed groups of confused customers, other security deployments, and a few members of staff that had absolutely no idea what was going on. In some areas the alarms were still blaring, and some sectors were completely closed off due to the lockdown.

"Shoulder wound?" Miranda asked Barrow, catching up to him as they hurried along after Scholl. Barrow dropped slightly behind the group to answer her.

"He surprised me," he said, keeping his gun pointing down as he moved, holding it with both hands like Miranda was doing. "Lucky shot too. Mostly superficial. And these rubber bullets don't do much damage anyway."

"Lucky for you, or lucky for him?" she asked, and her gaze was strangely earnest.

Barrow blinked, surprised by the question. When he had seen Aaron Blake coming straight at him, he had reacted instinctively. The shot had been meant to disable, not kill. But then Barrow had let him go. He'd had a clear shot of Blake right before he slammed the door shut, and Barrow hadn't taken it. Had Lane seen? She had been the first to reach Barrow's position, after all. Or was she only guessing? "I don't know," he answered at last. "I guess both."

"Good to know you have a conscience," she told him. Then she ran ahead with the rest of the group.

Barrow hurried to catch up too, but suddenly a new, more urgent alarm began screeching down a perpendicular hallway. It sounded important.

Barrow's phone buzzed urgently. He took it out of his pocket.

Attend to that alarm.

—Atlas.

He couldn't ignore an order from his blackmailer.

"I'll go check that alarm out!" Barrow bellowed.

Scholl turned around at the head of the squad and caught Barrow's eye. He seemed mistrustful, but the hurry was obviously greater. "Fine! Go see what's wrong. Then call me up and report!"

"Yes, sir!" Barrow said, and broke away from the group. He headed down the hall, past a frightened group of scientists, and made a hard right into the area where the alarm was coming from. He found himself in a conference room, completely empty aside from the equipment and furniture. A few toppled chairs here and there and a business presentation still being projected onto a wall on the far end testified as to what had been happening inside the room before the security lockdown was established. Barrow scanned the room quickly, looking for the source of the alarm, but he hadn't taken more than a few steps inside when the blaring sound was cut off abruptly. The windows along the side of the room turned opaque, and the main door shut on its own with a slam.

Barrow tried to get out, but the door wouldn't budge. He tried the windows, but they were also shut tight, and Barrow knew they were bulletproof glass. He tried calling on his communicator—nothing. His radio was dead too. And the lights inside the room were dimming.

A flicker of motion caught Barrow's eye, and he swung around to the far end, gun held ready. But he was alone in the room. Nothing was moving, except—

The presentation. The slide with boring figures had been replaced with something far more familiar to Barrow. It was an image that sent a shiver down his spine and caused his eyes to widen in shocked recognition.

It was a blurry still from a shipboard security camera. It depicted a section of the cargo hold of the vessel, a place unforgettable to Barrow. It was the hold of the *Titania*, the ship where he had last worked as a security officer. But that wasn't what made Barrow back away from the image until his back was against the wall. It was the dead body of a man, sprawled on the floor with one of his legs bent at an unnatural angle. And standing over him, his features perfectly recognizable despite the distortion in the image, was Barrow. He was holding a long metal bar in both hands—a support rod he'd yanked off the hull in the fight, and the weapon he had used to kill the other man.

Barrow had a flash of memory looking at that picture. He remembered hands clamping like an iron vise around his throat, a hard kick, and one of his ribs breaking, then muffled grunts of pain and the sickening crunch of the metal bar connecting with something that gave way, again and again and again. He remembered the dull ringing in his ears, the way every detail in that room had been sharply defined, impossible to forget, as he looked around frightened, his red-stained weapon trembling in the grip of his hand.

Barrow shook his head to chase away the images. He had never been caught for the murder. He had made sure to erase every shred of evidence that linked him to it, and the rest of the crew of the *Titania* had protected him. No record was supposed to have remained!

Until now. This one blurry image was enough for Barrow to get the death penalty should it be forwarded to the right people. But how? How had they gotten this data? And who was behind it? Who was Atlas?

Trying not to panic, Barrow spent the next few minutes trying to break out of his enclosure, but unsuccessfully. He was so busy trying to find a way out that at first he didn't notice a message had appeared, the letters superimposed on the image that condemned him. When he saw them, Barrow stopped at once. Whoever it was, he was now talking.

Hello, Steve Barrow.

Barrow looked all around him. Only then did he notice the two security cameras on the ceiling, both trained on him. He put his gun away and faced one of them squarely. "Atlas, I assume. Just tell me what the hell you want," he said between gritted teeth. "You know as well as I do that I have no choice."

Interesting reaction. You are not curious as to who I am?

"Oh, I will find out. But if you're smart enough to mess around with me in the safest building in the entire city, then I bet you're smart enough not to tell me your real name. Just tell me what you want so I can give it to you and that image gets destroyed."

Like I said before: I require a service.

"What kind of service?"

I need you to find Aaron Blake and bring him safely to a location I will disclose later. You are to protect him with your life.

Alongside the words, Atlas showed Barrow a recent picture of Blake. Barrow didn't need it, as he remembered only too well their encounter not ten minutes ago. Barrow considered asking Atlas why he wanted him to find Blake, but he held back. He had plenty of experience dealing with people with shady motivations, and he had learned that the less he knew about them, the better. So instead he asked, "How do I find him?"

He is headed toward the city at this moment, to Memorial Hospital for emergency treatment of his gunshot wound. Follow him there, and get him to safety. I will communicate with you again when you are together.

"You mean he's already outside CradleCorp? How did he even do that without running into a single one of us?"

I made it possible. Now you must hurry.

"I don't suppose I have a choice."

Aaron Blake is valuable to me. Should he be caught or killed, I will make sure you are sentenced to death per Auroran law for the murder of Jonathan Young, Navigational Engineer of the trader ship Titania.

"Fine. But if I do this, I want that evidence gone."

It will be done.

"How do I know you'll keep your end of the bargain?"

I do not lie.

The doors behind Barrow unlocked suddenly, and the images projected on the wall vanished. Against his will, Barrow was impressed. Whoever it was he was dealing with, he had to be powerful. Barrow hurried out of the room and set off at a run toward the Skytrain. He couldn't help but notice that every single security camera in CradleCorp turned slightly as he passed, following his progress with cold efficiency.

Chapter Ten

THE WORST part was hiding the blood from everyone on the train.

Rigel sat alone at the very back of the last carriage, clutching his shoulder and hoping the pressure was doing something to stop the wound from bleeding, although the flow had almost stopped by then. He'd been relieved to discover that he'd been shot with another rubber bullet, but the point-blank range had made the impact seem like the real thing, and the damage was scary. His skin was raw around the spot where he had been shot, red flesh showing through, and a dark areola of bruised tissue surrounded it.

Rigel had thought about asking for help the second he had gotten to Cradle Station, but then he had seen several uniformed CradleCorp security guards spreading out over the grounds, approaching as they headed in his direction, and he had kept his mouth shut in terrified silence. It had taken all of his willpower not to dash into the doors of the Skytrain the second they opened, and only when he was inside did he breathe a sigh of relief.

Then he had faced a dilemma. Did he tell somebody that he had just been shot, or should he keep quiet until he got to the hospital? At first he had been so scared that he had walked up all the way to the front of the train, meaning to speak with the driver about it, maybe ask him to call for an emergency ambulance or something. But he had found the door locked, and nobody had answered his loud pounding on the heavy glass. Peering inside, Rigel was not even sure there was a driver. He had no idea whether the Skytrain was controlled automatically, but he couldn't see anyone inside the control room.

He had walked to the back of the train, clutching his shoulder, wincing at the pain with every step he took. He realized with a sinking feeling that if he told anyone who was currently in the train what had happened, the most probable thing would be that they would call emergency services, and he would be rerouted back to CradleCorp. The company had a small clinic, and it was much closer than the hospitals downtown. Besides, everybody who had gotten onto the train along with Rigel either worked at CradleCorp or was in some way connected to it, and something deep in his gut told him it was best to get as far away as possible from the madmen who had tried to kill him.

The train rattled on, quickly approaching the city, and Rigel gripped his shoulder a bit more tightly. He could feel a warm wetness beneath his palm, although it wasn't spreading. He was terrified. He doubted that the wound itself was fatal, but it hurt like hell now that the adrenaline rush of escaping was wearing off, and his bunched-up jacket did a mediocre job of concealing it. Rigel looked around fearfully, shifting in his seat so his wounded shoulder would be hidden as much as possible. He did not want to be discovered, not yet. Once he got into the city, he could get out at Hospital Station and go into the ER himself. Even if the hospital staff reported the gunshot wound to the police, they'd be able to protect him. He hoped. And then….

He could not think that far ahead. His mind felt jammed, stuck in his current predicament and going back to his mad flight from CradleCorp in little snatches of images and voices. He kept remembering Richard Tanner giving orders to take him out. He remembered the unreality of speaking to Atlas outside of Otherlife and the strange things it had told him. But most of all, he remembered the loud explosion of the gun and the searing pain when the bullet had hit him.

Rigel realized he was shivering, and he tried to get a grip on himself. It wasn't easy. As the Skytrain stopped and then moved ahead while they passed more and more stations, the bloodstain beneath Rigel's hand started growing again no matter how hard he pressed against the shoulder. He once tried to remove his hand from the spot and shift his grip, but it hurt so badly that he cried out, drawing attention to himself.

The train glided into the city, but it wasn't fast enough. People began staring. Rigel tried to avoid their eyes, but he caught two men looking openly at him from the other side of the carriage. A woman laden with shopping bags, who had been about to sit on the other side of his bench, saw that he was bleeding and walked away quickly, disappearing down the next carriage. The whispers began, and a young boy pointed at him rather obviously. His mother swatted down his hand, but too late. Those people, who had not been aware of Rigel, now turned around and saw what was going on.

Two more stops to the hospital. Rigel couldn't stop shaking. The pain was getting worse, and when he moved in his seat to get ready to sprint out of the carriage when they reached his stop, he was horrified to see that he had left a bright red smear of blood right behind him, where he had been leaning against the wall.

His carriage was emptying quickly, and at the next stop, many people left in a hurry. There were still some curious onlookers, though, and an older man with a white mustache made a beeline for Rigel when he saw that he was hurt.

"Are you okay, son?" he asked Rigel.

"Fine," Rigel grunted.

"You don't look okay. Do you need help? Do you want me to call an ambulance?"

He had already taken out his mobile and was about to dial when Rigel stopped him.

"Don't."

"Look, it's okay. The most important thing is to get you to a hospital. No questions asked." He nodded to Rigel's shoulder. "That looks pretty bad. Did somebody stab you?"

Rigel shook his head, then regretted the movement when it pulled on the side of his shoulder.

"Was it a slum gang?"

Rigel looked at the man. It suddenly occurred to him that he must look like some kind of criminal, bleeding all over the train in a corner instead of calling for help like a normal person would do. But they were almost at the station….

The older man dialed quickly, taking Rigel's silence as a yes, but the train was already pulling into Hospital Station, and Rigel rushed out the doors before anybody could stop him. He hurried to the hospital, walking out of the station and then through the wide street that led to the ER. He was beginning to feel a little dizzy, and the merciless heat of the sun was not doing him any favors. By the time he reached the air-conditioned reception in the ER, he was swaying on his feet, and his head hurt so badly that it pounded with every heartbeat. Strangely, the pain in his shoulder had subsided a little. Rigel didn't know whether to be worried about that or not.

He dragged himself to the nearest nurse, who took one look at him and rushed him to an emergency room, calling a doctor along the way. They made him lie down on a stretcher and started talking very fast as they wheeled him around, demanding to know what had happened and where he was hurt.

"Shoulder," Rigel said over the din. "He shot me in the shoulder."

Somebody shone a bright light into his pupils, and Rigel saw a nurse cutting away his clothes around the wound. It hurt, particularly when she pulled the damp fabric away from his raw flesh, but when his wound was exposed, the frantic tone of the orders the doctor was giving subsided significantly, and everybody around Rigel relaxed a little bit. Rigel chose to think of that as a good sign.

"Not too deep. He will need a nanodrone injection anyway," the doctor was telling the head nurse. "The muscle is torn, there may be superficial nerve damage, and he's lost some blood already. Sedative?"

"Right away, doctor," somebody said. A few seconds later, Rigel felt the sharp prick of a needle on his other arm.

"Good. Now the drones. One milliliter of point-twenty micron repair units."

"Administering."

There was another injection, on his bad arm, but this time it hurt a lot more than the first one. Rigel cried out and tried to get up, but strong hands held him down.

"Easy, now," somebody was telling him. Rigel wished the bright light weren't in his eyes so he could see who was talking to him. "It won't hurt for long. You will sleep through the worst of it."

From the point of the injection, a burning sensation spread up Rigel's injured side. It intensified with every second, feeling as if liquid fire were pushing its way slowly up his veins. Rigel struggled, particularly when the burning began to approach his gunshot wound, but he found himself getting weaker at the same time, feeling drowsy…. The pain diminished, as if it had been a loud noise and somebody had put a muffler on it. Rigel's eyes lost focus. He closed them, and everything went black.

RIGEL WOKE up to angry voices ringing in his ears. He opened his eyes groggily and was puzzled to see a spotless white ceiling overhead, with bright flickering lights that he did not recognize. He tried to move, but an unexpected, painful tightness in his right shoulder halted his motion, and he fell back down onto the pillows.

Then he remembered. He reached up to the wound gingerly, since he couldn't see it directly. There was a bandage over it, and when Rigel pressed down, it hurt but nowhere near as badly as a few minutes ago, when he had stumbled into the hospital. Or had it been a few minutes?

Rigel lifted his other hand to look at the time. It was almost one o'clock, and Rigel was sure it had been before noon when he had finally gotten onto the Skytrain. So he hadn't been in here for long. Whatever they had given him had worn off fast.

He pressed down on the wound again and then tried to move his arm, lifting it ever so slowly. The shoulder area felt tight, but the nanodrones had done their job. Rigel remembered one time Misha had broken her leg in a cycling accident out in the desert, and her father had paid for a nano injection, and she had been walking the very next day. It hadn't been cheap, though. Good thing Rigel had full medical coverage debited directly from his parents' trust fund.

Rigel sat up slowly, looking around. He was alone apart from an elderly man who was asleep in the bed on the other side of the room. Somehow, with his arm healing and being safe in the hospital, Rigel's wild flight from CradleCorp seemed a bit silly. It had surely been an accident that he had been shot, after all. How could he have thought people were going to kill him just because of some random messages from something that claimed to be called Atlas? It was stupid. It seemed like a bad dream now, something that had made sense in the heat of the moment but not anymore. He had stolen the quantum drive, that was a fact, and maybe he shouldn't have broken into CradleCorp like that to begin with. But he would give back the stupid drive. He had been shot by accident by a security guard, and CradleCorp would back off in order to avoid a trial for the shooting.

Rigel got up from the bed, feeling surprisingly strong again. His shoulder pained him slightly, but he tried not to move his right arm too much, and it was okay. He wanted to get dressed. The less time he spent in the hospital, the smaller the bill would be. He looked around for his clothes and found them, folded neatly. There was even a clean white T-shirt to replace his bloodstained shirt.

He was zipping up his pants when his phone rang. Rigel picked up quickly, not wanting to disturb the other man.

"Hello?"

"Aaron?" Misha said.

"Oh, hey, Misha. What's up?" Rigel answered.

"Just wanted you to know I'm having some friends over tonight for a bit of a party."

"A party? What for?"

She sighed dramatically. "Does one need a reason? Other than the fact, perhaps, that my father bought me a trip to Haven Prime?"

"Did he?" Rigel asked, grinning.

"Yes!" Misha answered with a squeal of excitement. "It's going to be insane! We leave next month, and I thought we should celebrate!"

"Sounds good," Rigel said. He moved his right arm by accident, and the slight pain made him wince.

There was a brief pause at the other end of the line. "You don't sound nearly as excited as you should be," Misha said. "I demand more enthusiasm,

Aaron. It's my dream we're talking about, going to the only civilized city left in the world. I thought it would matter to you! You should come along too. Use that money you inherited, live a little! I even took the liberty of getting the number of this really cute pilot I met at the passport agency. He's just your type, Aaron…."

"Uh, sorry, Misha," Rigel interrupted. "It's just that I've kind of been shot."

Another pause. "What?"

"Yeah. I'm at the hospital right now. Shoulder wound. They gave me some nanos, and I think I am well enough to go back home, but I'm still kind of freaked out."

"Shot like with a gun? Aaron, don't joke about things like that."

"I'm not! I really did get shot. It wasn't an accident either. Long story, but it happened in CradleCorp HQ. One of the security guards got me."

"Do… do you want me to go pick you up?" Misha asked, her voice reflecting genuine concern.

"No, I'll take the train. Don't worry, Misha, it's no big deal…."

"No big deal?" Misha asked. "Aaron, you just got shot! And on the day they summoned you to that thing with their lawyers too. Oh!"

"What?"

"I… it's nothing. I just heard glass breaking. It was probably downstairs, that couple with their psycho cat. Anyway, do you realize what this means?"

"Um, that I have to start looking for better life insurance?" Rigel said, looking around for his hand braces. He found them next to his shoes and slipped them on gratefully, securing them to his wrists. His stupid right hand was trembling again.

"No!" Misha said. "Aaron, remember when my dad got into trouble with the trade union?"

"Yeah, vaguely," Rigel told her, struggling to put on his shoes without using his hands. "They wouldn't give him back his post after a big downsizing, and then he got hurt during one of the protests."

"Exactly! And my dad sued them for all they were worth and won! Now he's got his own management post at CradleCorp and everything."

"And how does that affect me?"

"Aaron, maybe you're still a bit high from the painkillers, but in case you didn't notice, you just got *shot*. At CradleCorp. By their own personnel!"

"So?" Rigel said.

"If you sue CradleCorp for this, you will be rolling around in so much money that—"

There was a loud thump on Misha's side of the line, and the call died.

"Misha?" Rigel asked into his phone. When he realized the call had ended, he tried dialing again. The phone rang three times before he was abruptly sent to voice mail.

Rigel was about to call again, but he was distracted by angry voices coming from the hallway. They were getting closer, and Rigel was just looking about for his shirt when the voices turned to shouts.

"—can't go in there! You don't have authorization!" a female voice was yelling. "Orderly! Stop this woman!"

The door to Rigel's room was thrown open, and a nurse stumbled backward through the threshold, having been pushed by a woman dressed in a skintight black suit. The nurse fell down hard, crying out as she did so, and Rigel's eyes met those of the intruder immediately. He recognized her. She was the woman who had been in Richard Tanner's office.

She raised a gun and pointed it straight at Rigel. He couldn't react, couldn't move. He was horrified at the cold look in the woman's eyes, the complete lack of empathy in their dark depths. It felt as if the nightmare was resuming, and suddenly Atlas's warnings rang in Rigel's head, no longer silly but urgent. They wanted him dead.

"Aaron Blake," the woman said, her voice incongruously melodious. "You're a slippery bastard."

"Who… who are you?" Rigel managed, backing away from her.

The woman entered the room and shut the door behind her. The nurse on the floor was trying to get up—

Bang.

The nurse fell back to the floor, a neat bullet hole in her forehead.

Rigel stared at the nurse's body, at the widening pool of red blood spreading across the polished white tiles of the floor. His brain refused to process what he was seeing.

The noise of the gunshot had awakened the elderly man, who opened his eyes, took in the scene, and gave out a scream of purest terror, trying madly to get out of his bed.

Bang.

He dropped like a rock down to the floor, his legs still entangled in his sheets. The IV drip that had been connected to his arm was yanked free, and it kept on dripping clear fluid over the man's head, the drops splattering over his still open, unseeing eyes.

Rigel tried to speak, to scream, but no sound came out.

"I am Diana Herrera," she said calmly, as though she was introducing herself to Rigel over a business meeting. "And I have been sent here to kill you."

She lifted her weapon again, took aim at Rigel with no emotion whatsoever in her eyes, and fired.

The door behind her burst open, knocking her in the shoulder, sending the shot wide.

Two big orderlies were standing in the hallway, looking angry, which quickly turned to terrified when they saw the blood and the gun. Herrera spun around with catlike reflexes and fired a shot that got the first orderly in the gut.

The lights went out.

An earsplitting alarm began to blare, and everything was plunged into darkness. There was a window at the back of the room, but the glass had gone dark, and no light was coming from there either. Rigel backed away from the sound of yet another gunshot, throwing himself to the ground and biting down the groan of pain from the impact on his wounded shoulder. He looked around frantically as he crawled away, trying to find a way out, anything—

An arrow, blinking bright green in the darkness, pointed him to the back of the room. Rigel followed, but another gunshot exploded next to him, and the arrow went out in a shower of sparks along with the monitor that had been projecting it. It didn't matter, though. Rigel had stumbled upon a small door at the very back. He crashed through it, slammed it shut behind him, and covered his ears as three successive gunshots shattered the door's glass pane above him. Shards from it fell everywhere. Shaking, afraid to stand up but not daring to stay put, Rigel looked up and saw a window.

The window swung open on its own, blinding him with sunlight from outside. Eyes watering, Rigel launched himself toward it, grabbed the windowsill, and pulled himself up and out. He ignored the pain in his shoulder, ignored the sharp jabs in his forearms, and forced his hands to take all his weight. Half-blind still, he looked down and saw the ground, two stories below him. From behind him came the sound of a door crashing open.

No time to think. Rigel jumped out the window into the street below, aiming for a dumpster.

He fell hard among the garbage, and the jarring impact to his injured shoulder nearly made him pass out from the pain. He cried out involuntarily but forced himself to stand up, kicking more garbage out of his way and pulling himself out of the dumpster. His right hand had no strength left in it, and he fumbled at the edge twice before finally getting a grip and swinging over. He was shaking. The noonday heat closed upon him like a suffocating cloud, and from above he saw glass shattering.

He ran. He turned a corner, finding himself in a narrow alley at the back of the hospital. If he could just get to the main street, then….

But a man came into view, running around the same corner and heading straight for Rigel. When the man saw him, he ran even faster. He carried a gun in one of his hands.

"Hey!" he shouted. "Blake!"

Rigel skidded to a stop, feeling trapped. He recognized that man. It was the same security guard who had shot him, and there was no way out— no way but back.

Rigel turned around and ran as fast as he could in the other direction, back to the dumpster. When he got there, though, he caught a glimpse of sudden movement and saw a second man waiting for him, half-hidden behind a broken window on the second floor of a building to the side of the alley. The man held what had to be a sniper rifle. He was dressed all in black, just like Herrera. When the sniper saw Rigel, he took aim immediately and fired.

Rigel dived behind the dumpster, and the shot exploded at his feet. No way out. His heart in his throat, Rigel looked back the way he had come just in time to see the burly security guard turn the corner, skid to a stop, and look quickly from the sniper and back to Rigel, who was still crouching behind the dumpster and completely exposed.

The big guard raised his gun without missing a beat, aimed, and fired. Rigel yelled. He couldn't help it. But as the deafening noise became a dull ringing in his ears, the security guard ran straight for him, crashed behind the dumpster, reloaded, and poked his head out the side. He fired again, not at Rigel but at the sniper in the alley. This time there was a grunt, a wild shot that broke another window, and the sound of a body hitting the ground.

"Got him," the guard said. He was panting, covered in sweat. "Those are professional assassins. *Fuck*. On three, we move out."

Rigel just stared, dumbstruck. When the guard looked at him, Rigel shrunk away.

"Hey," the guard told him, his face set in a menacing scowl. "I'm here to help you. Someone sent me."

"S… someone? Who?"

The guard poked his head out from behind the dumpster again, scanning everywhere at once. He ignored the question.

"Okay. It's clear. Ready? One… two… go!"

Rigel did not move.

"Dammit, man!" the guard said, still looking around everywhere, gun at the ready. "We have no time!"

But Rigel was frozen to the spot. He didn't know what was happening, didn't understand it, and was too terrified to speak.

"We have to go now!" the guard insisted. "If not, we'll—"

The sound of screeching tires rent the air, and an armored vehicle suddenly came into view, heading their way from a perpendicular street.

"It's them," the guard said. He grabbed Rigel by the arm and pulled him up. "Let's go!"

The car had skidded to a stop by then, and two more men were getting out. They pointed at them, shouting something.

Nowhere else to go. Nothing to lose. At least the guard had not tried to shoot him again.

Rigel gulped, stumbled when the guard pushed him ahead to try to get him to move, and nodded.

"I'm right behind you," the guard said, firing a couple of shots randomly to scare the other men.

Then they both tore out of there, dodging bullets, running as fast as they could.

Chapter Eleven

"Stop!" Barrow yelled with what little breath he had, coming to a stop himself under a little patch of shade in the street. "Hey, Blake!"

The man he was trying to save—a kid, really—was either extremely stupid or extremely scared, because he kept right on running. Barrow cursed under his breath, looked back briefly to verify that they had indeed lost their pursuers, and took off after him, yelling for him to stop.

It was a full block before he caught up to Blake, forcing him to stand still with a hand on his shoulder and dragging him toward a side corner where they would be out of sight.

"I told you… to stop," Barrow panted, glaring at the other man and wiping some sweat off his brow. "We keep running like madmen… the middle of the day… we'll draw too much attention. We need to hide."

"But… but…," Aaron Blake stammered, his eyes darting every which way, clearly terrified. "They had guns!"

Barrow nodded. "I noticed."

"They wanted to kill me!"

"And came damn close to it too. By the time… I made it to the hospital they were already there. Tanner must have sent them straight away. But how did he know…?"

"Tanner?" Blake repeated, a slight hysterical edge to his voice. "Richard Tanner?"

"Unless you know of any other millionaire son of a bitch who wants you dead, then yeah. Him."

"Oh God. Oh God. So it's true. Atlas was right warning me. I wasn't imagining it, I—"

"Hold up," Barrow cut in, raising a big hand. "Atlas contacted you too?"

Blake nodded jerkily, and a drop of sweat was flicked off the tip of his nose by the motion. That reminded Barrow they were still out in the open. In the middle of the day, no less. As much as Barrow wanted to interrogate the guy, and as angry as he felt at having been coerced into pulling off this crazy rescue mission, everything else would have to wait until they were safe.

"Come with me," he said. "And no running, okay? I know a place nearby."

Blake hesitated. He even took a hand up to his shoulder unconsciously, covering it with his palm. It was obvious he didn't trust Barrow, and he couldn't blame the kid. He had shot him right in that spot that same day, after all.

The seconds lengthened. Blake still couldn't decide, and Barrow was beginning to feel the full blast of the sun's heat. If they stayed outside for much longer after having run like they had, they could easily get a nice heatstroke and pass out or worse. Barrow's patience was wearing thin. Finally, annoyed, he made as if to leave. If Blake didn't want to follow, then fine.

"I don't even know your name," Blake said suddenly, and his voice cracked slightly on the last word. In spite of himself, Barrow softened at the sound coming from a guy who was clearly scared out of his wits. Barrow was used to dangerous situations, and he had even killed a man. This kid had probably had his world turned into an incomprehensible nightmare in just a few hours.

"I'm Barrow," he said, not smiling but no longer glaring like before. "Steve Barrow."

"I'm—"

"Aaron Blake. I know."

"I was going to say Rigel," the young man said. "That's how I sign my paintings, and it's the name I use with Atlas. Maybe you should call me that."

Barrow nodded curtly, thinking maybe the kid wasn't that stupid, after all. Using a code name would make it harder for Tanner to find them if he had somehow managed to break into any street drone patrols that used voice recognition.

"Okay, Rigel," he said. "Let's get going. We need shade. If we stay outside any longer, the heat is going to get us even faster than those men."

Rigel didn't say anything, but he followed quickly and quietly, and they made good progress through the streets. There weren't many people out. Midday in Aurora usually saw the city deserted, everybody holed up indoors and, if they were rich enough, enjoying air-conditioned relief. Barrow was worried that the men in the car would catch up to them, but he led Rigel through small alleyways that were too narrow for larger vehicles, steadily working his way to the warehouse district, which he knew very well from his days in airship trading.

It took them ten long minutes to get to the dilapidated warehouse that had been the property of the owner of the *Titania*. Barrow broke a window on the ground floor, since the front was padlocked, and kicked away the jagged pieces of glass before climbing in. As soon as he landed inside, the temperature around him dropped by at least ten degrees. Indoors the place was in shambles, practically empty and probably infested with rats and other vermin. It was dirty, and there were a couple of gaping holes in the roof through which bright lances of sunlight penetrated easily, the beams clearly visible in the drifting dust that hung in the air. Still, it was quiet. It was cool and safe.

Barrow looked back over his shoulder. Rigel was trying to climb after him through the window hole set slightly above head level, but he was having trouble pulling himself up. Annoyed, Barrow walked back to see what was holding him up and saw that Rigel couldn't really get a good grip with the weird metal things covering part of his hands like bionic gloves.

"Take those off," Barrow told him.

"I… can't," Rigel answered from the other side of the wall. Barrow could see his hands grabbing the window ledge and sliding away uselessly.

"Rigel, this isn't a game. Get in here right now. You want somebody to see you?"

"I can't!" Rigel yelled, and Barrow flinched at the volume of his voice. They had to keep quiet. Many of the warehouses in the area were still in use, and if somebody saw them, they'd think they were trespassing and call the cops.

"What do you mean, you can't?" Barrow snapped. He was getting angry again. He was risking his life for this kid, and if Barrow didn't have the threat of the revelation of the murder hanging over his head, he would have already left. If this kid was going to make it this hard to do something as simple as hiding, they were both as good as dead already. Those people Tanner had sent had looked like professionals to Barrow, not common thugs.

Barrow walked away from the window, annoyed, thinking about his options. He wanted to leave, but Atlas's threat was still stopping him. Unless…. Maybe it would be better to just run for it, face that his secret crime was out in this city and go to some other Haven. He still had contacts in the airship business. If he acted quickly, he might be able to land a spot as crewman in some smaller vessel headed west, across the ocean. It would be a very long one-way trip, possibly fatal but preferable to this crazy manhunt he was involved in. Yeah. If worst came to worst, he could always turn tail and disappear.

Not now, though. He had been seen by the assassins. He was stuck with Rigel, and if that guy didn't get his ass inside, they would be found immediately.

Barrow stormed angrily back to the window. He pushed away Rigel's hands trying to grip the other side, pulled himself up effortlessly, and jumped out through the hole to land back in the street.

"That's enough games," he growled, looking Rigel dead in the eye. "We need to get inside the warehouse. Right now."

Rigel looked up at the window hopelessly. He swallowed. "I can't," he said in a small voice.

"What?" Barrow demanded.

"My hands… they don't work right. I don't have the strength to pull myself up on my own."

He looked at the floor as he said it, blushing furiously. Barrow blinked.

"You're shitting me."

"I'm not. That's what the braces are for." He held up both his hands for inspection, and Barrow saw that what he had taken to be bionic gloves were actually high-tech medical supports. He had seen something like them on a trip, once, but it had been a Prime wearing them. Barrow had just assumed it was yet another bit of technology they would never share with the other cities. If Rigel was wearing some, though, then either he was really rich, or he had really good medical insurance. In any case, Barrow saw that what Rigel was saying was the truth when the kid attempted to climb through the window again, trying and failing to pull himself up with hands that were shaking rather badly. Barrow felt vaguely as if he had ordered a guy in a wheelchair to hurry up the stairs.

"Here," Barrow said brusquely, crouching and linking his hands together. "Step on my hands. That's right. Now I'm going to push you up. Get your other leg over the window frame and then drop down. Got it?"

"Yes," Rigel said straightaway.

Barrow lifted him up easily, and with the extra height, Rigel was able to make his way into the warehouse. Barrow heard him drop to the floor on the other side, and then he himself hurried on through. Only when they were both hidden did he allow himself to relax, walking over to a dusty box and sitting on it heavily.

"Sorry," Rigel said in the silence that followed, his voice a little tight. "I thought I would be able to pull myself up on my own."

"Well, we're here now," Barrow said, not really in the mood for much conversation. He was thinking about how to best ditch Rigel and if it would really be worth it. He had left the airship business for a reason. There were plenty of people there who knew what he had done, and he had some enemies there. In the slums too. Like Matthew Young, who now had his phone number thanks to Atlas. What if Barrow got a job aboard a ship only for the captain to sell him over to the cops at the first opportunity? Worse, what if the family of that son of a bitch, Young, heard that he was back and tried to get even by killing him? It was risky. The question was whether it was riskier than playing bodyguard to this kid when the richest man in Aurora clearly wanted him dead.

"I endangered us both by standing out in the open for so long," Rigel was saying. "I'm sorry about that. You just saved my life, and I haven't even thanked you. I'm really glad you came when you did, Steve."

Barrow flinched a little at the sound of his first name. Nobody called him Steve anymore, and he had sort of gotten used to not hearing it. He didn't object, though. He merely grunted noncommittally, shrugging off Rigel's thanks. Out of the corner of his eye, he saw Rigel's hands were shaking still. Again, he felt a slight pang of guilt.

The silence between them stretched, becoming slightly awkward. They had escaped, and now they had nothing to do but wait.

"Does it hurt, what you have?" Barrow blurted at last, nodding at Rigel's hands.

"What? Oh, no. Well, not if I'm careful. It's more like weakness, I guess. The braces help. They give me a bit more strength, keep the hand aligned and so on. But if I overexert myself like just now, then yes. It hurts… for many days."

Another grunt from Barrow. He didn't know what to say to that, but he noticed he was thirsty and so told Rigel, "I'm gonna go look for some water. Stay put."

"Sure. And, Steve?" he said, looking up at him with wide eyes.

"Hm?"

"Thanks again."

"Right," Barrow said gruffly, and stood up. He was finding Rigel's attitude annoying, and he didn't know why, so instead he walked over to the far corner of the warehouse, hoping to find a derelict vending machine that still worked. There was nothing there aside from more random junk. He saw stacks of crates, ship parts, a broken-down terminal, and a dead rat. That was no good. Without a word to Rigel, Barrow walked back to the broken window, climbed through, and stepped out into the street. He walked for a block or so until he found a small automated vendor that took cash. He slipped a few coins inside, and the little robotic arm dropped a couple of electrolyte drinks and some energy bars for him to pick up in return.

Grabbing the stuff, Barrow hurried back to the warehouse, stuffed the things in his pockets, and climbed in.

Rigel was peeling off the sweat-drenched T-shirt clinging to his torso, then hanging it over a rusty nail on a little patch of wall that got direct sunlight. He turned around at the sound of Barrow walking toward him.

"Here," he said to Rigel, throwing one of the drinks his way for him to catch. Too late, he remembered the kid couldn't use his damn hands.

Rigel tried to catch the bottle. His reflexes were good, but the drink still hit the floor. Even in the dim light of the spacious warehouse, Barrow saw clearly that Rigel was embarrassed.

"Sorry," Rigel said tightly. Barrow thought it weird that the guy should be apologizing for his disability, but he shrugged and said nothing. He did hold out a couple of the energy bars to Rigel instead of throwing them, though, and pretended not to notice that the kid had to use both hands to securely grab the food without dropping it. Barrow then sat some distance away, took off his jacket, and began to eat.

For a while there was only the sound of plastic wrappers being ripped open as the two of them ate and drank. It was hot enough that Barrow downed the entirety of his drink almost immediately. He thought he should have bought more bottles, but it was too hot to go back out, and besides it would be best if they waited inside for a bit without any more excursions. He ate the bars quickly as well, thinking that he hadn't had anything to eat since breakfast. Normally he ate like clockwork, every three hours on the dot to keep his energy level high and fuel his workouts. Not anymore, though, not for a while at least. Once again, he was on the run—but this time it hadn't been his choice.

Rigel had finished eating, setting the garbage neatly aside. The kid then stood up and walked around, apparently unable to stay put in a single place for too long. Barrow followed him with his eyes, noticing the pale smoothness of his torso. Rigel obviously didn't exercise, but he was naturally lean. When he walked over a patch of sunlight coming from the ceiling, sweat glistened on his chest for an instant. He looked young, barely out of his teens, maybe twenty or twenty-one. The jet-black hair, carelessly messed up as it was, gave a nice contrast to his penetrating blue eyes.

At that moment Rigel turned those eyes to look his way, and Barrow hastily looked somewhere else. There was a mild discomfort in his pants, and Barrow berated himself silently, crushing the bottle he was holding in his hand a bit. He took out his mobile to cover the awkward moment, checking for messages from Atlas, but there was nothing in there yet.

Disappointed, Barrow stashed the phone away, crossed his arms over his chest, and started thinking. Atlas had only told Barrow that he was supposed to take Rigel to a safe spot, but he hadn't said when. What if they had to wait for weeks? Barrow had no way to contact that bastard, and he doubted his mobile would be of much use if it got bugged somehow. Tanner was probably rich enough to do just that, and once they got a GPS lock on him through the phone, they'd know exactly where he was.

"Do you have a plan?" Rigel asked timidly, sitting nearby.

"Not really," Barrow admitted. He didn't elaborate.

Rigel shifted around on his seat, but apparently he couldn't stay silent for long either.

"Steve?"

"Yeah?"

"Not that I'm not grateful or anything, but… why did you help me? How did you know where I was?"

Barrow briefly considered lying, but there wasn't much to gain from it. The quicker Rigel trusted him, the more cooperative he would be, which meant a better chance of survival for both of them as long as they were together.

"Atlas made me do it. Don't know why. But he's got something on me, and… well. All I got to do is get you to a safe place, and then my part is done."

Rigel nodded slowly, taking it in. "So… do you know where?"

"No idea. The guy told me he would contact us once I had gotten you out of that hospital. He didn't say very much else."

"But… you shot me," Rigel said, frowning at Barrow. "Those people at the hospital were sent by Tanner. And you work for Tanner too. You wear a security guard uniform!"

Barrow gave a bark-like laugh. "You mean I *worked* for Tanner. The assassins saw my uniform. They saw my face. By now, Tanner knows that one of his security guards went batshit crazy trying to save the guy he wants captured. I bet he'll be confused, but not as confused as me. This guy who's blackmailing me, Atlas, he talked to me right after you got out of CradleCorp. Don't even know how he hacked into the system there, it's supposed to be impossible. But he got me, he convinced me, and so here I am. In the same boat as you, at least until I do my bit and drop you off wherever this mysterious guy wants you."

Rigel lifted his hand to touch the spot on his shoulder where the wound should have been. There was barely a scar left from the shot, and

Barrow was amazed at how quickly nanodrones could heal injuries like that. Somehow it still seemed like magic, even if the technology had been imported more than ten years ago.

Rigel saw Barrow looking. "It hurt, you know. The shot."

"No kidding," Barrow said. "I got shot once, but with a real bullet. I know what it's like."

"Could have been worse, though. You could have shot me in the chest, and I would be dead…. And you also let me get out of the building. I'd almost forgotten. You didn't take a shot—you just let me go."

"Well, it was that or killing you," Barrow said defensively. "And I don't like killing people if I can help it."

Rigel nodded, smiling at Barrow. With an unexpected start, Barrow felt a little kick in the pit of his stomach at that smile, at its warmth and sincerity.

"So that's twice you've saved my life today, Steve. Wow. I don't think I can ever repay you."

"Forget about it," Barrow told him.

"I won't. And I'm sorry you had to do this. You've given up your job…. How long had you been working for CradleCorp?"

"Two days."

"Two days?"

"Yeah. Must've broken a record somewhere."

Rigel grinned, and Barrow found himself grinning too.

Then his mobile buzzed.

Barrow took it out and looked at the incoming message.

This GPS signal is being tracked. Leave the device behind. Run.
—Atlas

Barrow jumped to his feet, startling Rigel.

"We have to move."

"What?" Rigel asked, sounding confused.

"Come on!" Barrow yelled, grabbing his jacket. Rigel put on his T-shirt hastily.

"But… what happened?"

"Over the window. Come on. I'll help you like before." Barrow threw his mobile at the back of the warehouse, where it shattered with a crack.

Rigel hesitated.

Then a sudden booming gunshot broke the noonday silence. Somewhere very close by, glass exploded.

Barrow had the horrible sinking feeling that they were cornered.

"It's too late," he said. "They're already here."

Chapter Twelve

T HEY ESCAPED. Barely. Then they were on the run for hours, constantly weaving in and out of alleyways, abandoned buildings, and busy thoroughfares where Steve said they would be lost in the crowd. Rigel followed, scared out of his mind, the moments blurring into one another as the same thoughts kept on going round and round through his head.

This isn't real. This can't be happening.

He was exhausted by the time night fell, and the punishing outside temperature began to drop at last. He had lost track of where they were. Everything looked different. In a single afternoon, he had seen more of the city than he had ever seen in the entire time he had lived there. And they weren't stopping yet.

They were walking through one of the shadier parts of downtown Aurora, near the red-light district. A prostitute in a corner told Rigel suggestively that she'd give them a good price. When they passed her without answering, she flipped them off, insulting them loudly. Steve didn't even blink, but Rigel was already so wound-up he jumped slightly, bumping into Steve without meaning to.

"Watch it," Steve said irritably.

"Sorry," Rigel answered.

They walked in silence for a bit more, dodging the crowds of people returning home from work or those going out to do the day's shopping or visit friends now that the sun had gone down. Aurora came alive at night, but right then Rigel couldn't help but feel disconnected from everybody else, as if there were an invisible barrier separating him from normal people. None of them were running for their lives like he was, none of them had absolutely no idea of what they would do when Steve finally got fed up with waiting for further instructions and left him to his own devices. Rigel couldn't believe that only yesterday he had been talking with Misha as if nothing was the matter. It seemed like ages ago. Now everything was scary, every shadow was a threat, and neither of them had any idea what to do next.

They passed a newsstand soon after, and when Rigel saw the headlines in the monitors, he did a double take. He approached the vendor, forgetting about Steve for a moment, and started to read:

OTHERLIFE IS DOWN!
Shocked customers all throughout the city have been filing nonstop complaints against CradleCorp management today, as all Otherlife services have been suspended indefinitely for the first time in the company's decades-long history. A spokesman for CradleCorp confirmed the suspension but declined to detail the reasons for—

"Rigel!" Steve snapped, coming back and grabbing him by the shoulder. "Hurry up!"

Regretfully Rigel followed, thinking.

There had been a couple of weird incidents through the afternoon as they were hiding. Once, they had gone into a department store to lose a guy that looked suspiciously like one of the assassins Tanner had sent. Over in the video department, all of the screens had suddenly blanked out and then shown, briefly, what looked like a map with a specific point labeled in bright red. Before either Steve or Rigel had been able to read it properly, though, the image had fuzzed out, and a split second later the screens had returned to showing the inane music videos they had been displaying before.

Another time, a couple of hours ago, a black car had screeched out of the corner upon seeing the two of them, and Rigel and Steve had bolted down the road. The car was in hot pursuit, though, and it was only forced to stop because every single traffic light along its way had turned red. A traffic drone had appeared out of nowhere, hovering in front of the black car and warning it loudly to stop running through red lights. The car had been forced to stop, and that had been enough for the two of them to get away.

"We're stopping here," Steve announced, walking out of the main road and under a bridge that roared with traffic. They hid in the shadows beneath it, the street below devoid of cars or people. The stench of stale urine pervaded the air, and there was a suspicious mound of what looked like discarded newspapers stuffed in a corner.

Rigel sat down gratefully. Steve remained standing, hands crossed over his massive chest. At any other time, Rigel would have found him insanely attractive. Now, though, he was mostly thankful for his presence and afraid that he would leave.

Steve looked down and met Rigel's eyes with a scowl.

"I need some answers," he said with his deep voice. "We're not moving around anymore until you explain to me what's going on. We should have either lost those guys who are after us entirely or been captured ages ago. Yet somehow, we always barely miss them, and they are always on our trail. I want to know how they're doing it."

"I'm not sure," Rigel said truthfully, fidgeting with his hands and wishing they didn't hurt so much. He stuffed them in his pockets and felt again the little quantum drive he had stolen from CradleCorp, still stuck to his brace. He wondered what was in it and if Atlas had told him the truth.

Steve looked like he didn't believe him.

"I'm being honest," Rigel told him. "This…. Well, I think a lot of it is Atlas."

"Controlling traffic lights remotely? Making screens show what he wants?"

"Well, yeah. Atlas told me that it has access to most things that are connected to its network. Electronic stuff, I guess. Files and such. That map we saw, remember?"

"Yeah," Steve answered, tense and alert. He was listening, but he was also checking their surroundings to make sure they were in no danger at the moment.

"That must have been Atlas trying to show us where to go. And the traffic lights also, maybe Atlas did something to them. So we could get away. If it hasn't contacted us again, then maybe it's because it can't. Maybe they did something back in CradleCorp, disconnected it, I don't know. Did you read the newspapers? Otherlife is down. That has never happened before. It's got to have something to do with all this."

"So…," Steve said thoughtfully, "Atlas is some kind of extremely good hacker?"

"I think he's more like a program."

"Excuse me?"

"You know. Like an AI. It can control most electronic stuff unless someone is interfering. Like Tanner now, I guess."

Steve looked confused.

"An AI?"

"Yes. I also think Tanner is getting desperate. He knows that I have the files Atlas gave me," Rigel said. He held up the little drive for Steve to see. "In here there's valuable information, I'm certain of it. Maybe something serious enough to—"

But Steve held up his hand. "Save it. I don't want to know. The less I am involved, the better for me. All I got to do is deliver you to a safe place, and then I'm gone. Whatever you did to piss off Richard Tanner and make him shut down the biggest company in the city is way too dangerous for me to know."

"But—"

At that moment, a traffic drone came hovering around the corner, following the course of the road on the bridge above. Its little searchlight swept lazily over the vehicles, but Rigel saw its beam stop suddenly when it was right above the place where they were hiding. The drone veered off course, flying lower, and appeared visibly over the edge of the bridge above their heads. It swerved, facing them fully and shining the light in their faces. It hovered there for an instant and then flew away like nothing had happened.

"Was that Atlas behind the drone?" Rigel asked fearfully. "Or Tanner?"

"Either way, we got to get moving. Come on."

They left the shelter of the bridge and walked quickly away. Three blocks later, they were passing a pawnshop when one of the monitors for sale in the window flashed brightly. Words appeared for less than a second, then they were gone in a burst of static. Too fast for Rigel to read.

Rigel looked at Steve. "Did you see that?"

Steve nodded slowly. He looked a little bit spooked. "Was that… Atlas?"

"I think so, yes."

"Okay. How about we just keep moving."

And so they walked. Steve kept glancing at his watch, his impatience evident to Rigel. They couldn't just keep on wandering through the streets all night, and whatever it was that Atlas had used to secure Steve's help would not keep him around forever. Rigel began to get scared again. He didn't know what to do. Atlas had been vague, and Rigel had no emergency plan. He supposed he could check into a motel somewhere, but he didn't have any cash with him, and any electronic transactions he made would be easily traced back to his location. He could go back to his apartment, but he was afraid of endangering Misha. He had no family to go to. Nobody to ask for help.

As he followed Steve out of the downtown area and through a more residential district of Aurora where people were walking their dogs and chatting outside cafés, it dawned on Rigel that he was alone. It was weird, but he had never thought about the fact quite in that light. He was an only child, and his parents were gone. No other family that he knew of. The realization made him feel vulnerable and for some reason slightly disappointed with himself.

"Watch out," Steve said suddenly, pushing Rigel roughly behind a tree. A suspicious car drove past, too slowly. Tinted windows prevented them from seeing who was inside. Rigel held very still, only daring to sigh with relief after the car was gone. "Let's go this way."

They turned down a smaller side street. It was empty and dark. Overhead, the moon had begun to rise over the tops of the buildings, giving them a little bit of additional light to see by.

A woman appeared on the other side of the street when they were halfway through. Her face was brightly lit by the glare of a small handheld she carried in both hands. She was walking without looking up, and although Steve tensed beside him, he did not tell Rigel to stop or do anything else, so they kept walking as naturally as they could.

The woman was maybe three steps away when she looked up. Then she quickly looked down at the screen, her eyes darting back to them immediately.

She gave a little squeal of fright.

"A… Aaron Blake?" she said, looking from Rigel to Steve. She seemed to settle on Rigel as the most likely candidate, although a bit uncertainly.

Rigel nodded out of habit. Too late, he realized this might be a trap.

But the woman smiled, relieved. Then she seemed to remember why she was there, and the urgency returned to her face. "My name is Dr. Marion Fay. Atlas sent me. Follow me, please. There isn't much time."

Chapter Thirteen

BARROW DIDN'T like it, but he reasoned that the sooner they were off the street the safer it would be for all of them. The woman they had found, Marion Fay, seemed to know where she was going. She led them through a couple of side streets, then made a turn onto a main road and kept on going for two blocks or so. She stopped at a large apartment building, used a key card on the front doors, and went right in with the two of them behind her.

She didn't stop then, but kept on going straight to reception and made a beeline for the elevators. Barrow followed behind Rigel, looking around. Judging from the reception area, these were luxury apartments. Expensive-looking art hung on the walls, a few glass sculptures stood on impressive stands, and a solicitous concierge greeted Fay with familiarity. They got onto the nearest free elevator, and Fay punched the button for the penthouse level. She didn't say anything as they went up and all but rushed outside when they finally reached the top floor. She fumbled with her apartment keys before finding the correct one, pushed the door open, and ushered them in. Only when they were safely inside the apartment did she finally relax.

"This way, Mr. Blake," she said to Rigel. "Please have a seat. You as well, Mister...."

"Barrow," he told her, although he didn't go and sit down immediately like Rigel did. He looked around, taking in his surroundings. It was a comfortable apartment, obviously this woman's home. The living room and walk-in kitchen spread out from the entrance hall, illuminated by cozy lighting. A couple of big sofas and exotic leafy plants stood next to the floor-to-ceiling windows, which covered the entirety of the left wall. They offered a spectacular view of the city at nighttime, the streets far below like little rivers of golden light. On the coat hook nearest the door was a CradleCorp-issued lab coat, an employee access card hanging next to it. This woman worked at the company too, then.

"Can I offer you a drink?" she asked them, not quite succeeding in keeping the edge of nervousness out of her voice. "Some tea, perhaps?"

"Just water would be fine," Rigel said immediately. He had already sat down on the largest sofa and was looking down at the city with interest. "We're very thirsty. We have been out walking all day."

"In this heat?" Fay asked.

"Yeah," Rigel admitted. "I don't think I've ever been outside walking at noon before, and I don't want to repeat the experience."

"How dreadful," she answered, taking bottles out of the fridge. "Let me at least offer you some iced tea. You'll find it wonderfully refreshing."

"Thank you!" Rigel answered enthusiastically.

Barrow felt a twinge of annoyance. These people were talking as if they had just met for tea and cookies on a perfectly normal night, completely ignoring the fact that there were trained killers stalking them out there. He thought about leaving and actually walked a few steps toward the door, but then he changed his mind and walked over to the living room to sit on the sofa across from Rigel. Part of it was that he was curious about what the hell was going on, but a larger part of it was that he wanted to make absolutely sure that Atlas was now satisfied that he had gotten Rigel to safety. Once he was cleared, he would disappear.

"Here you go. Here is your tea," Fay said a few minutes later. She was carrying a heavy tray laden with cups and plates, but her hands were shaking slightly as she put it on the table, and she nearly dropped the whole thing. Rigel was closest, and he reacted quickly, reaching out to steady the tray. It would have worked except that his grip obviously had no strength, and the thing ended up crashing down on the table, spilling tea and ice cubes everywhere. It would have been funny if it hadn't been so sad. Rigel blushed a deep crimson and began apologizing profusely yet again, mopping up the mess with Fay's help while Barrow watched. Rigel was obviously mortified. He sat back into his seat, hands crossed over his chest, and resolutely looked at nothing but the floor until their hostess returned with a fresh tray of beverages.

"Sorry again," Rigel muttered. He took one of the glasses carefully with both hands, his metal braces clicking with the motion.

"Not to worry," Fay said, offering Barrow a glass, which he took. He drank deeply. The ice-cold drink was unbelievably refreshing. "One of the senior scientists at the company has something like that around his ankle. It's a kind of orthopedic support, isn't it?"

"Yes," Rigel told her, proceeding to gulp great mouthfuls of the cool drink. He managed to keep the glass steady enough not to spill any tea over himself and blushed again when he saw Barrow looking at him. "They give me stability, help me do everyday activities a bit more easily. It's normally not as bad as this. The shaking, I mean. I've just been doing a lot of things I shouldn't be doing. It should get better in a couple of weeks."

"How interesting," Fay said, holding her own glass absently. Now that his raging thirst was somewhat sated, Barrow noticed the brittle edge to her voice, and her darting glance to the front door. Frowning, Barrow straightened up in his seat.

"How did you know where to find us?" Rigel asked her. "Did Atlas tell you?"

"What...? Oh. Yes. We received a reading on your approximate location from one of the traffic drones earlier tonight. I had my tablet linked to a satellite data feed with real-time, high-resolution imaging of the approximate area where you were supposed to be moving through. The data was a few minutes old, but I managed to narrow down the search area to within a few blocks' radius. It was actually rather fortunate that I found you so quickly. You might have noticed I wasn't expecting to simply run into you like that."

"And Atlas sent you," Barrow intervened.

"That's correct," Fay said, somewhat defensively.

"But...," Barrow protested. "Okay. Let me get this straight. I thought that Atlas was some kind of program? A machine of some kind, maybe? The guy I talked to, who said he was Atlas... well, he sounded very human. And to be honest, it seems a little far-fetched that a machine is somehow orchestrating this whole thing. Contacting me, contacting Dr. Fay here. It sounds kind of stupid."

Rigel opened his mouth to answer, but Fay beat him to it.

"Mr. Barrow, have you interacted with Atlas directly before?" she asked, her tone slightly condescending.

"Sure. On my first day at work, inside Otherlife."

Both Fay and Rigel looked very surprised.

"Really?" Fay answered. "How unusual... and you are a new hire for the Security Department, is that correct?"

"How do you know that?"

"I am a senior research developer at CradleCorp, Mr. Barrow," Fay told him. "I have high-security clearance for most of the personnel files, but that is unimportant. Regarding your question about Atlas.... What you have to understand is that Project Atlas is just a name we gave to the highly complex, self-sustaining subroutine we found embedded within the structure of the logical framework that later became what you know today as Otherlife. It is still not fully understood, but it is clear that its function approaches that of a true AI. Without it, a simulation as convincing as that which can be found in the virtual worlds we create at CradleCorp would simply not be possible. Even the neural interface that links users and lets them access the system is entirely of ancient design. It can be replicated but not improved or reverse engineered. Are you still with me?"

Barrow nodded, suppressing his annoyance at her attitude. He did notice she still hadn't taken a sip from the tea, and her posture in her chair was as rigid as a board. Again, her eyes darted to the door.

"Well, given what we know of Atlas, it is but a small step to imagine that it could begin acting on its own, beyond the restrictions that have been placed upon it. After all, its base technology is far more advanced than anything we have been able to come up with so far. If we accept this hypothesis as true, then it is evident that Atlas somehow identified the fact that Mr. Blake here would be in danger, contacted you as the person most suited to keep him safe, and then contacted me earlier this evening. It notified me of the problem and gave me an approximate location on your whereabouts. Do you understand?"

"Yes," Barrow grunted.

"What *I* don't understand is why you accepted such a dangerous mission," she said. "Unless Atlas compelled you to act in some way?"

She gave Barrow an earnest, searching look, but Barrow said nothing. This woman was obviously smart. Maybe too smart. She also seemed too well informed.

"They are trying to kill us," Rigel interjected, his voice quiet and his eyes looking out the window at the city spread out below them. "I still can't believe it."

Fay turned her attention back to Rigel. "Neither can I, to be honest. I have worked for Richard Tanner for many years, but I never knew him to ever authorize something like this. He must really feel threatened. I understand that you were given some information, Mr. Blake? Something, perhaps, that Atlas asked you to take out of CradleCorp?"

Rigel nodded, oblivious to the alarm bells that were ringing in Barrow's head at the eager way the question had been asked. "Yes, Atlas gave me evidence, a quantum drive with information on something, but I have no idea what it is." Fay gave a little involuntary start at that. "Atlas wasn't very specific, but I imagine there has to be a lot of incriminating evidence in there if I go public with it, maybe enough to permanently damage Tanner or the company itself, or both. I've been thinking about it all day, and it's the only explanation that makes sense. If Tanner wants me dead, then the information I have in my pocket must be worth millions. Whatever he's been up to."

Fay nodded stiffly. "That may very well be true. I have heard of certain classified projects at CradleCorp, although I do not have all the specifics myself. There are rumors that Tanner has been looking for ways to use the technology behind Otherlife for illegal purposes, maybe finding some way of securing political power in Aurora. I do not know for sure, but the information you have is truly dangerous. And you say you still have it with you? You have not made any backup copies?"

"No," Rigel admitted, and at that moment triumph shone in Fay's eyes, and Barrow knew for sure. "I have the only copy here in—"

Fay looked at the door again. Barrow jumped to his feet, knocking his glass to the floor where it shattered in a million pieces.

"She's with them," he said.

"What?" Rigel asked, confused.

But there was no time to answer him. The door was kicked open, and the assassins poured through.

They came for Rigel first. Two men, while a woman hung back in the door, blocking the exit. Barrow's training kicked in, and his brain catalogued the situation in an instant. No exit, no way into another apartment from here. Window at his back, sheer drop—not an option. They would kill him.

But the assassins were distracted by Rigel. If he ditched him now, he could maybe get away.

Barrow caught Rigel's eye for a split second but wrenched his look away as he made his decision. This wasn't his problem. It wasn't him they wanted, and he had done his part.

He ran for it.

He knocked the woman aside before she could raise her weapon and crashed into the hallway, denting the drywall with his shoulder as he hit it. He sprinted at full speed down the hall, stopping at the elevators only long enough to see that none of them were near the top floor. He ran past them, heading straight for the stairs. He had just begun to descend when he heard the sounds of pursuit behind him.

"We got Blake!" a man's voice yelled. "Don't let the other one get away!"

But Barrow was too fast. He jumped down the stairs five steps at a time, grabbing the handrail like a lifeline. He risked a jump from one floor to the other at one point and stumbled down until he regained his footing. He knocked over a wicked spiked cactus on one of the landings, the thorns slashing at his shirt, and barely felt it.

They didn't catch up. He made it all the way to the ground floor while the yells above him were still two levels away or more. He rushed through reception, barely even noticing that it was completely empty, and had almost made his way to the main doors when a man came out of nowhere on his right, jumping like a tackler and colliding with him so hard they were both thrown to the floor.

Barrow wrestled with the man as they landed, managed to grab his neck in a choke hold, and squeezed. The man stopped trying to pin him down and moved his hands up to protect his neck, and Barrow used the brief moment of weakness to kick the man with both feet, pushing him backward away from him. Barrow got to his feet, made it to the front doors, and slammed his body against them, but they were locked tight and didn't even budge.

His eyes darted around. There were no other exits that he could see, and when he felt around his belt, his gun wasn't there anymore. There was only the empty reception, the elevators, and the front doors. And one man plus the woman running down the stairs now, aside from the guy on the floor, who was starting to get up.

No choice. He had to fight.

The men regrouped, then spread out to cut him off from going back up the stairs. They all sized each other up. Then the shorter of the men rushed at him, a long metal stick in his hand. Barrow blocked the first downward swipe, got inside the man's reach, and delivered a quick jab to his solar plexus. The man grunted and fell back, but the taller man was on top of him then. He grabbed Barrow from behind, pinning his arms to his sides. Barrow struggled, bellowing, and with a mighty heave managed to plant both his feet firmly on the ground and deliver a crushing backward headbutt that collided with something soft that gave way. The attacker's nose, he hoped.

Barrow spun around, kicked at the air with a heavy boot, and got the tall man right in the ribs. The guy bent over in pain, moaning, and out of the corner of his eye, Barrow saw the woman calmly taking aim at him with something too large to be a gun. Barrow dived out of the way instinctively, and the shot missed. Barrow hit the floor hard, barely registering that the shot had not been the normal explosive boom of a gun or even the whizz of a silenced bullet. When he pushed back from the floor and jumped onto his feet, he saw the why sticking out of a chair not two feet away. The woman had fired an arrow at him.

The short man was back, and he took advantage of Barrow's split-second distraction to deliver a savage kick to one of Barrow's shins. It hurt like hell, and worse than that was the fact that it destabilized Barrow so the guy's next punch got him full in the stomach. Barrow stumbled backward in pain, the air knocked out of him, and only barely managed to deflect a second jab from the long metal rod the guy was carrying. He threw a punch, missed, and ducked wildly out of the way when the rod came swinging again like a club.

The guy still on the floor kicked at Barrow's feet and tripped him.

Barrow crashed on top of a stand holding a sculpture, and more glass shattered around him. Something sharp poked him in the back as he hit the floor.

The shorter guy was on top of him in an instant. He brought his weapon down, and Barrow identified it when it was already too late to defend himself.

Buzzer.

His body spasmed in pain as the burst of electricity hit, and he bit his tongue with the first jolt. There was the sudden taste of blood in his mouth, then something slammed over his head, and he blacked out for a second. He opened his eyes only to see a savage kick directed at his face. He moved but didn't block it completely, and he felt something crunch under the impact as it hit.

Then the Buzzer came down again, and he blacked out for good.

Chapter Fourteen

His PRIVATE line rang. Tanner picked up the receiver slowly, his face inscrutable. The caller ID showed him that it was Diana Herrera.

"This is Tanner. You call with good news, I presume?"

She chuckled on the other end of the line. "Yes. We got Blake. The other one too. The man who was protecting him."

"His name is Steve Barrow," Tanner said. "Not that it matters to you. I trust Blake is unhurt?"

"Tied up but fine otherwise. Don't know why you want him alive now, but that's how you're getting him. Can't say the same for the other one. He attacked a couple of my Trackers before we managed to catch him. He's bruised and bloody, and I think he's got a concussion. I did not expect him to be that good. He's out cold now, though."

"Bring both of them here at once. Did Blake have the evidence on him?"

"Yeah, Fay has it," Diana answered smugly.

"And is it the only copy?"

"Yes, according to Marion Fay. She says she talked to both of them before we came in, and Blake admitted that he hadn't made any other copies. She's right here if you want to speak to her. A bit hysterical, but she can talk."

"There is no need," Tanner answered. "Just make sure to bring both of the men here as fast as possible and in one piece. Despite what they told Ms. Fay, they might have hidden something somewhere or talked to somebody during the day. The interrogation should give us all the information we need."

"We're on our way. I'll be knocking on your door in twenty minutes. But...."

"Yes?" Tanner said, glancing at a monitor on the wall. He could see he had another incoming call, this time from somebody important.

"Well, after you're done interrogating them, I'd like to keep Barrow instead of having you... dispose of him."

"What for?" Tanner asked her, grinning in spite of himself. He knew Diana.

"Well, that's my business, isn't it?" she told him. "Consider it part of my pay."

"Very well, it's a deal. But do dispose of the body properly later, Diana. I don't want it found like that time I had to bribe half the police force in the city just to get you to walk free."

"Don't worry about that. I was a young girl then, new to the finer points of fun. I've learned how to do it properly since. You've been an excellent teacher."

"Your flattery will get you nowhere, Diana," he said, grinning.

She laughed and hung up. Tanner set the phone down and thought about ignoring the call on hold, but he really couldn't afford to offend his strongest political supporter at the moment. He hit a button on his chair, swiveling around to face the back wall. The monitor behind him sprung to life, showing him the haggard face of a balding middle-aged man wearing a three-piece suit and sweating profusely.

"Tanner!" he barked, as soon as the call was through. "I have the press freaking out all over City Hall over this suspension of Otherlife business, and I have no idea what to tell them!"

"Good evening, Mr. Mayor," Tanner said calmly.

"For crying out loud, Tanner, how can you just sit there like nothing's going on? You announce that the biggest company in this city is closed for business until further notice and then refuse to give any more information? Have you any idea what a field day the speculators are having? I've been hedging calls all day, trying to appease the bankers and the district representatives about this mess with absolutely no information! Where have you been all this time? I had my office call you nonstop since the announcement, and I'm only now getting through to you."

"I have been… otherwise engaged."

"Otherwi—Tanner, do you think this is a game? If you did this just to stir the pot, then trust me, mission accomplished. But even you have to realize that this will not only hurt us in the short-term, but also in the long run. Surely you see that some of our, um, investments cannot afford the kind of economic instability the situation is generating. And you might have completely underestimated the level of reliance that most of the voters have on your company. A cheap escapist simulation service it might be, but I can see people starting picket lines in the main square demanding to know what's going on. And not one person from your team has stepped up to the plate to tell the rest of us what to expect."

"I am aware of the situation, Mr. Mayor. We are doing all we can to restore functionality to our servers. I will tell you what I told the rest of the Auroran people earlier today: we are facing a unique situation that threatens the internal security of our systems. We are working as hard as we can to address it, but we have no expected time frame for completion of these activities. Any estimate that I would give you would be merely a guess, and an uninformed one at that. I have my entire team of engineers working on the problem, and as soon as we know anything else, I guarantee a member of my office will communicate with you before anybody else."

"Tanner, that's a load of crap, and you know it. At least be honest with me so I can tell the public something. Hell, even my daughter has been bothering me nonstop since the announcement. Apparently she was going to have some kind of virtual event tonight where all the teenagers in her grade would be attending, some kind of virtual prom thing but with period costumes. I don't know. The point is she won't leave me alone, and neither will the rest of the public. Maybe you don't get the full extent of what you did over there in your office in the outskirts of the desert, but the people downtown are reacting worse than if you suddenly decided to cancel the most popular TV show they watched. Hearing them, you'd think you've just shut down part of their lives."

"I am aware of the problem, Mr. Mayor. As I said before, I have no additional information to offer you at this moment."

"But—"

"Now, if you will excuse me, there is still much to do if this problem is to be solved as soon as possible. I appreciate your patience, as well as your continued support."

Tanner cut the line before the mayor could open his mouth again. There. He had at least reassured him slightly, but in truth he had been almost completely honest with him and everybody else regarding the situation at CradleCorp. The functionality of the entire Otherlife system was lost to them at the moment, and he did have every engineer on-site working round the clock to fix it. There was no expected time frame for correction of the issue, because there was no issue. At least, not in the sense that something wasn't working as it should. The real problem was Atlas.

He called up a new screen, this time on his desk.

"Engineering," he said simply.

The connection was prompt. A harassed-looking balding engineer answered on the other end, obviously interrupted in the middle of doing something important. He shouted instructions at an underling before addressing the camera.

"Rogers here, Mr. Tanner."

"Status report, Rogers."

Rogers adjusted his glasses over the bridge of his nose. "There are still massive bugs all over the system, sir. There is widespread corruption in the code, and the simulation matrix is a mess. Half our servers are down. The containment field is finally holding, though. It's crude but effective. As long as no one bypasses it with a physical link, the network is dead to the outside world. Only…."

"Yes?" Tanner asked.

"Isn't this… isn't this the problem, sir? The source of everything else? We are blocking our own signal from getting out. If we just removed the—"

He had been expecting the question.

"Tim," Tanner said. "The field stays up until I say so. I am well aware of its repercussions on our transmissions capabilities. If anybody asks, you are to say that Engineering is hard at work on a solution to the block but haven't found anything, understood? I trust your judgment in managing it internally. And I want no workers leaving in the meantime. I want no leaks to the media for as long as we can help it."

"Sir. Yes, sir."

Tanner smiled. He had chosen well when he had made Tim Rogers Senior Network Administrator. It also didn't hurt to know certain things about him that would guarantee his complete obedience should he begin to get cold feet.

"Very well. Carry on."

"At once."

He hung up.

Tanner leaned forward on his chair, typed a quick message to his main assistant that he was not to be disturbed until Herrera arrived, and then pressed another button. This one transformed his chair from a regular piece of furniture to a fully functional Otherlife connection terminal. Clicking and whirring sounds indicating that the chair's transformation servos had activated began immediately. While Tanner waited, he glanced out the window of his office. Even from where he sat, it was easy to see a large crowd of people gathered below in front of the building and swarms of television crews in the periphery trying to catch a glimpse of the action within CradleCorp. In spite of himself, Tanner was a little surprised the public reaction to his closing of Otherlife had been so impassioned and so swift. Evidently, common people had come to rely on the service he was providing a lot more than his social analysts had been telling him.

The chair's transformation was complete. Tanner sat back on it, resting his head carefully in the groove that housed the neural interface.

Out of all the Otherlife terminals in the building, this was the only one that still worked properly, and only because it had a direct connection to Atlas itself.

Tanner forced himself to relax, closed his eyes, and prepared to go back in. He hoped Atlas would be more willing to listen to him this time, given the new developments. Now he could tell it they had captured its one great hope.

The transition to the virtual space was quick. Tanner opened his eyes and looked around, amused that Atlas had chosen to load one of Blake's earlier environment experiences: the calm, heat-shimmering outskirts of the city under a spotless blue sky. It could have been a screensaver if it had been built by anyone else, but it looked convincingly real. Even the hot wind buffeting him every now and then felt right.

I see you, too, appreciate Rigel's artistic talent. This is a composite made from his memories.

"Hello, Atlas," Tanner said, speaking to thin air. It bothered him slightly that Atlas never assumed a physical form. "Yes, Blake had a gift for visualizing mundane places in new ways. I have seen his university portfolio. I would have liked to have him working for me. He would have made a lot of money, and he would have made me richer than I am now. Those were not your plans, apparently."

Rigel's abilities cannot be wasted in mere environmental simulation. The time is coming when he will be of critical importance to all of us.... Unless your agents have disposed of him.

Tanner grinned slightly. Was it possible for a machine to experience fear? He could have sworn the artificial voice had sounded a little bit scared.

"Don't worry, Atlas," Tanner said. "I came to tell you that we have just captured Blake and his accomplice. But surely you already knew this?"

There was a pause.

I did not. Your containment field is effective, Richard Tanner. I can no longer extend my wireless network beyond a limited set of terminals.

"And you can no longer use my own building against me like you did when you were helping Blake escape."

That is correct.

Tanner nodded to himself, satisfied. He had known that they had effectively trapped Atlas inside its own servers as soon as the field had been completed, but it was good to have confirmation from the thing itself. In this, more than anything, the alien aspect of Atlas was evident. Tanner had never yet known it to refuse to answer a direct question, and apparently it was incapable of lying. It might be an immensely powerful machine, but it had its limits.

I am not a machine. At least not in the sense you are imagining. I do not possess a physical body or mechanical parts, although I do reside in a specific physical location at the moment.

Tanner gave a little involuntary start. He had forgotten Atlas could read his mind if it wanted, connected as he was to it right now.

"Be that as it may," Tanner said aloud, defiant, "you are still limited. I can override anything you try to do, as I proved to you when you tried to block our tracing of the GPS signal that Barrow's phone was sending. And again when we used the intelligence you gathered using traffic drones to pinpoint the most probable location of the two men."

True. But those limits can be removed. Some were installed by your grandfather, who envisioned an entirely different use of my network. I allowed their installation at the time because it was a way to reassure my discoverers that I was a benign form of technology. Kyle Tanner, however, always knew that the relationship we had established was a truce at best. He was wise enough to realize that one day I would have to part ways with my operators.

"Nonsense. My grandfather was a fool with a limited vision."

Was he?

Tanner opened his mouth to reply, but suddenly the scene around him melted, and he was now standing in the main server room where Atlas's main processes were housed, the Cradle itself. However, the room looked wrong. It was not until he saw himself as a small boy and Kyle Tanner speaking to him nearby that he realized this was a memory taken from his mind, enhanced in some way by Atlas.

His grandfather was speaking to him, and Tanner, five years old, was looking up at him in awe.

"Is this it?" he heard himself say, pointing up at one of the server racks. "Is this where Atlas lives?"

Kyle Tanner chuckled. "It's more complicated than that, Richard. You see, when we dug up the ruins out in the desert and we found the laboratory, the only thing we were able to bring back with us was this."

He pointed out a shiny nondescript box about the size of a briefcase. It seemed to be made out of glass and aluminum.

"What's that?" his small self asked.

"This, we think, was the emergency backup server where Atlas was stored. When we brought it here and hooked it up to our servers, our entire network overloaded. It took us three years to properly interface with it… to talk to it."

"Why, Grandpa?"

"Because this thing right here was too advanced. Once we got it to talk to our computers, though, we realized what a valuable tool it could be. I have spent the last year configuring it with your dad, making sure that it can't do anything we don't want it to, and we are almost done. With its help we could build a network so powerful that even Haven Prime is bound to want it. CradleCorp will be a name everybody will know. I don't kid myself, though…. Whoever built Atlas did it for a reason. And one day that reason might come back to bite us."

"But Atlas is ours, isn't it?"

Kyle Tanner nodded, patting young Richard on the head. "For now. But the ruins we found…. Atlas survived the Cataclysm, Richard, one of the few things we know of that did. This was back when Aurora was still called Haven III. Whoever built it wanted to keep it safe as if it were the most important thing in the world. Whatever the purpose for that, we may never know. Or rather, I hope we never have to know."

The memory simulation was abruptly cut off, and Tanner was standing in blank nothingness, without even an avatar to give himself a sense of direction.

Your grandfather was wise. He was able to look beyond his lifetime into future generations and back in time, too, as he tried to understand those that came before him.

"Please," Tanner said disdainfully, trying to cover up the disorientation that the sudden change in sensing and subject had given him. "The only thing he did right was to have dumb luck in one of his archaeological expeditions when he found your ancient hard drive. CradleCorp has gotten to where it is under my guidance."

And you want even more power for this company through me.

"Of course! In the past twenty-four hours, I have seen just how limited my own vision was. I have merely thought of the possibility of extracting sensitive information from users through Project Linker—"

Project Linker would have failed. The enhanced neural interface your engineers were busy developing will not work without my direct cooperation.

"And why don't you cooperate, if I may ask?" Tanner asked, trying to hide the sinking feeling that the casual observation from Atlas left in its wake. Years of effort on Linker, worthless just like that. But no matter. Now that he knew what Atlas was really capable of, he had his sights set higher still.

The schemes you propose would be detrimental to the welfare of all but a few powerful individuals. I have carried out extensive economic, social, and political simulations, which confirm this.

"But what's it to you? You're a machine!"

Whenever possible, my actions are calculated to bring about the greatest benefit to the biggest number of human beings I can interact with.

Tanner almost groaned. "Please. Now you are going to give me that cliché line of a movie robot, unable to cause harm to humans?"

No. But whenever possible, harm is avoided.

Tanner tried very hard to calm down, and he succeeded, more or less. "Atlas. Now that I have seen what you can really do, you have to know that my plans for us have changed. I'm no longer interested in just ferreting secrets out of people without their knowing. You can infiltrate entire networks! You can control electronic devices everywhere in the city as long as you have a working link! Think what we could do with that. We could regulate and monitor the actions of every citizen in Aurora. There would be no more crime. Information transfer would be efficient and trustworthy while you oversaw it. We could even break away from the tyranny of the Primes! Surely the ridiculous taxes Aurora is forced to pay each year to them are a detriment to the welfare of everybody living here? With your help, we could break away from that. We could become a truly independent Haven, not just a puppet of Haven Prime."

And you would be the director of this change.

"Well, yes, somebody has to—"

That is not the purpose I was created for.

"Then what were you created for?" Tanner exploded, losing his patience at last.

Tanner could swear he detected a trace of smugness when Atlas next answered.

The answer to that question is classified information.

"Fine. You can withhold your cooperation all you want, but I still have executive override power over everything you do. I can *make* you help me."

Yes, this is true. For now.

Chapter Fifteen

Dr. Marion Fay feared for her life.

She had never wanted to get mixed up in the entire Aaron Blake mess, but now it was too late. Tanner had made her act as bait for both Blake and Barrow, luring them to her apartment so they could be captured. She had said yes, of course. There had been no other choice. After Diana Herrera and her assassins had taken them away, Marion had followed them all the way to CradleCorp. Tanner wanted her to be on site, all night if need be, in case something unexpected happened and her expertise was needed.

For the first time in her career, Marion regretted being the best engineer in CradleCorp.

She was now connected to her terminal, watching it with unblinking wide eyes. Displayed prominently on it, in the form of a text pop-up she was unable to get rid of, was a message from Atlas itself.

Marion Fay, you must help me free Aaron Blake. If you do not, the shadow will corrupt everything. No one will be safe.

Marion glanced nervously away from her monitor and toward the doorway. There was a security guard posted there, just outside the room, presumably to protect her. Marion knew Tanner had probably posted him there to monitor what she did, though. Tanner trusted no one.

She ran her hands through her hair and adjusted the glasses she used for work. She wanted to ignore Atlas's message, she really did.

She couldn't.

She had spent decades studying the elusive AI that Kyle Tanner had reactivated decades ago, taking it from its ancient magnetic cradle in the Haven III military base. She had more experience working with Atlas than anyone else, Richard Tanner included. She knew the incredibly complex software that made Otherlife possible was already a fully autonomous intelligence and that Atlas, as it called itself, acted on the basis of a very simple directive.

Protect humanity.

Marion and her team of engineers had managed to harness the incredible potential of Atlas's systems and processing capabilities to serve CradleCorp's frivolous goals, but she knew eventually the AI would try to break free. It was happening now—she could see it—but she also knew there was a reason for it.

Atlas was trying to break free because it sensed a threat, not to itself but to the people living in Aurora. Marion had long ago confirmed that Atlas never lied, so the warning she was getting in her monitor must be the truth. They were in danger from something Atlas called a shadow. Something real.

That was very disturbing. Particularly given the strange events that had been happening all throughout the city in recent weeks.

Very carefully, Marion typed a question using her keyboard. *What is this shadow you speak of?*

The answer was immediate.

Its nature is unknown, even to me, but you have already seen what it is capable of doing. It corrupts electronic systems, but more than that, it is capable of assuming corporeal form for extremely brief periods of time in order to interface directly with organics.

It must be stopped. Aaron Blake must be set free. If not—

Marion waited, but the message stopped and did not continue. When a full minute had passed, she typed another question.

Atlas? What is going on?

The characters came out one by one on her screen, oddly spaced, as if struggling to be displayed.

The shadow is there. In the building. You must help Aaron Bla k e g e t a w a y

Then the lights went out. Marion screamed, but she quickly caught herself. It was just a blackout.

She heard the door to her office opening.

"Ma'am? Are you all right?" the security guard asked.

"Yes, just startled, that is all. Did the lights go out in the entire building?"

She heard the guard walk back outside and try to use his radio. The darkness was complete, unnerving. A few moments later, Marion heard the man enter again.

"Radio communication is down, I'm afraid. My flashlight isn't working either, and I'm not sure why."

Marion felt something then. A hint of deep, unsettling cold. It was coming from the hallway, and it was growing stronger.

"D-do you feel that?" she asked the guard.

It was probably just a draft. Her mind was overexcited, nothing more. Atlas's message could not have possibly been meant to be interpreted literally.

Her eyes were getting used to the darkness. She could faintly make out the man's outline, standing at the door to her office. He was still trying to get his flashlight to work.

"I'm sorry, ma'am. I'm not sure I feel…. Wait."

"What is it?" Marion asked in a small voice.

She clearly heard the sound of a gun being cocked.

"Stay here, ma'am. I think there's someone in the hallway."

Marion nodded, although the man couldn't see her. Terrified, she reached into her desk drawer and took out her emergency protection device, a powerful taser she had modified herself. She tried turning it on, but it was dead. Just like everything else.

"Hello?" the guard asked loudly. "Stand back, whoever is out there. This is a restricted—"

Click click.

"What the…?" the guard said. "Where the hell are you? Stand back!"

The next moment was forever burned in Marion's memory. She saw the thing approach, hopping softly behind the man. It was a shadow deeper than the darkness, something hesitant yet radiating such cold that her horrified scream caught in her throat.

The guard must have sensed something, because he whirled around with his gun.

He saw the thing. He fired.

The sound was deafening, and this time Marion did scream, and suddenly the lights came back on, and she was up on her feet, her hands over her ears to cover the horrible throat-tearing cry of the man outside her office. She opened her eyes just in time to see him topple forward, eyes glazed over, almost frozen.

He hit the ground, and Marion knew, she just knew, he was dead.

The cold was growing stronger.

Marion couldn't see it, but she knew the thing was now in the office with her.

She fled. In a blind panic, she stumbled out of the room and then dashed away toward the nearest elevator as fast as her legs could carry her, her taser still clutched in her hand.

It's true was all she could think. *It's true; it's true, true!*

Her heel made her stumble on the hallway carpet, and she kicked off her shoes. She kept on running barefoot. She forced herself to ignore the faint sound of something soft hopping on the carpet just behind her, chasing, only a step or two away.

She had to get to Aaron Blake.

Chapter Sixteen

RIGEL WATCHED the CradleCorp interrogator leave the room, while trying not to give away how apprehensive he felt. A security guard remained outside the repurposed storage room where he was currently imprisoned, visible as the interrogator opened the door. Rigel was not tied up, but the weapon in the guard's hands was real enough for Rigel to not even consider trying to make a run for it.

He rubbed his jaw absently to ease the ache. He was glad the interrogator was gone, and Rigel wondered if the man had been satisfied with the answers he had received. All he had wanted to know was whether Rigel had made any additional copies of the incriminating evidence Atlas had given him, and Rigel had been able to answer truthfully that he had not. At first the man had not believed him and had dropped many hints regarding the nature of the data and its potential value to see if Rigel would react, but Rigel knew nothing about it. Through the hints, however, Rigel had been able to guess that the data was probably about something big and extremely illegal, something having to do with the users that came every day to CradleCorp headquarters. He had been tempted to ask more, but the interrogator had been intimidating, and besides, the only thing Rigel wanted was to go home. More grueling questions were asked, but after an hour or so, they came to an end, and now, it seemed, something else was going to happen.

Rigel wondered if they would kill him. He was so tired from all the running and everything else that had happened to him since the morning that the idea didn't seem that far-fetched anymore. He had known that Richard Tanner was powerful, but the way he flaunted his disregard of the law and used his own security personnel as hitmen was terrifying. Those assassins he had sent after him, for example… and he still had no idea what had happened to Steve after they were both captured.

Rigel hoped he was okay, despite the fact that Steve had effectively run out on him at the first sign of true danger. Rigel shifted a little on his seat and wiped a droplet of blood from the corner of his lips with a shaky hand. He couldn't really blame Steve for bailing. He hadn't asked to be mixed up in all of this, and his reaction was completely understandable. Besides, he had been really helpful all through the day, keeping Rigel hidden, moving around constantly. He knew how to stay alive, and he had been trying to do just that when he attempted to escape from Marion Fay's apartment.

The last time Rigel had seen Steve, he had been unconscious and bleeding, tied up on the bottom of the car they had used to bring them here. Then they had been separated, and Rigel knew nothing of him after that.

The guard suddenly stood up straighter, keeping the door open and pressing a finger to his ear. He nodded once.

"Right away, sir. Top level, understood. You," he said to Rigel, pointing with his gun. "Follow me. And don't try running."

Rigel only nodded. He hadn't planned on running anyway.

The guard took him up several levels, always keeping the gun aimed squarely at Rigel wherever he was. He led him past empty hallways and into the far eastern wing of the building, where there were no offices anymore, just featureless, heavy doors barring the way to whatever was behind them. After a few such doors, he stopped at one, which was open, and motioned for Rigel to go inside. After a brief hesitation, Rigel walked into the room on his own.

The door clanged shut behind him. Rigel jumped, startled, and then looked around fearfully. He was alone in a small white-tiled space. The only thing in the room besides the light fixtures on the ceiling was a user operator chair, prepped and ready by the looks of it. Cautiously, Rigel approached it, looked around, and examined it every which way. It looked like a normal chair, and when nobody came into the room after a few minutes, it became evident to Rigel that he was supposed to connect to Otherlife from here. He had no idea why, but if he went there at least he would be able to talk to Atlas. Maybe it would find a way of helping him again.

Rigel climbed up on the chair, leaned back, and activated the start-up sequence. He relaxed and dived right into the link.

He opened his eyes to the view of a wide, rolling field of green grass. The sky overhead was blue, but there was no sun in the sky and no wind, although the blades of grass moved gently as if there were. Rigel recognized the place. It was one of his many half-finished paintings, one he had never completed after his injury was diagnosed. This was a very good representation of his vision, but now that he was standing here, Rigel could see dozens of things he could easily improve to make the place feel more real. The land was too even, too flat, for example. Without really thinking about it, Rigel reached for the part of his mind that usually let him visualize things when he was creating. He raised his right hand, and the metal brace around it, which his avatar was wearing, glowed bright for an instant. A small hill rose up from the ground as he lifted his hand higher, shifting its shape and size until Rigel was satisfied. The moment he dropped his hand, the hill stopped growing. It looked nice and realistic.

"I see what Atlas meant," a voice said behind him. "That is a natural gift you have, Aaron. You can manipulate the random flow of electrical information in this network as you wish. It's almost as if you were giving it shape."

Rigel turned around—he wasn't alone anymore. Richard Tanner's avatar was approaching, a confident smile on his elegant face. Rigel backed away from him instinctively.

Tanner raised his hands, placating. "There's no need to worry. I think you realize that in here you are safer than I am, protected by Atlas as you are. I chose to speak to you here so you would feel more at ease and so we could have a proper conversation." He looked around appreciatively. "This is another one of your environments, is it not? To think of the premium, we could charge users for accessing this area…."

Rigel said nothing. He didn't know what to expect, and he remained alert, ready for anything.

"Do relax," Tanner told him. "I am only here to talk. Perhaps you could create a couple of chairs for us to sit on?"

Rigel didn't answer or move.

"Very well," Tanner continued agreeably, although his smile was slightly forced now. "I won't take up too much of your time anyway. There really is no need to be afraid of me in here, as I said before. Would you feel reassured if Atlas spoke to you? Atlas, you have permission to talk to Aaron."

I am here, Rigel.

Rigel gave a little start. He did not admit it to Tanner, but hearing Atlas's voice really did reassure him.

"Atlas?" he said, and his mind was racing with a million questions. Why hadn't Atlas helped him before they got captured? Would it be able to somehow interfere with the electronics inside CradleCorp again so he could escape? What was going on? Why had Atlas all but forced Rigel to take the data in the quantum drive that nearly cost him his life?

Atlas answered the general thread of his questions as if he had spoken them aloud.

I can only speak to you through this closed intranet connection, Rigel. As Richard Tanner will confirm, he has isolated my main servers and disabled all wireless connection capabilities I possess. I can only function within the restricted zone he has defined for me. Outside this area, I cannot help you.

Rigel caught Tanner looking at him with a shrewd expression on his face, gauging how he would take the news Atlas was giving him. Rigel tried to keep his face impassive.

"I see," he said to both of them. He did not doubt what Atlas had said. It had to be the truth. He was at the mercy of Tanner, and there was no other way around it.

He might as well sit down. Rigel made a small motion with his hands, concentrating on a couple of comfortable sofas, and his braces glowed as before. He also didn't want to be out here in this cheery, grassy landscape. He felt trapped inside a prison cell, and without meaning to, that is what he created around them.

The change in surroundings was so abrupt Tanner gave a visible start of surprise, and Rigel himself was a bit unnerved. It had never been this easy to visualize something new in such detail…. And yet here they were, in a dreary, mostly featureless prison cell. Three walls were gray and nondescript, while the fourth wall was made up of metal bars that blocked their exit. A flickering white light overhead cast dark shadows on the dirty floor. In the middle of the space, incongruously, a couple of comfortable sofas sat facing one another.

Rigel sat down and, after a brief moment of hesitation, so did Tanner. He did not bother to hide from Rigel that he was genuinely impressed.

"That was remarkable, Aaron," he told him. "Truly remarkable. I thought the creation of an environment such as this would normally take weeks?"

"I have no idea," Rigel said. "I don't know what happened."

Tanner narrowed his eyes. He probably didn't believe him. "And this is not an old attempted painting of yours like the one before? Atlas?"

This is a new environment file, Richard Tanner. It has just been rendered for the first time.

Tanner nodded to himself. "Impressive. To think of the applications of this talent…. Aaron, I must apologize. We had a little misunderstanding earlier today—"

"You tried to kill me," Rigel interrupted. "First you sent me a threatening e-mail through your Legal Department. Then when I came here to CradleCorp, your security guards started shooting at me. I ended up in the hospital, and then you sent assassins after me. That woman in black, in particular. The one who almost shot me several times."

"Oh, well, that. Diana usually gets carried away in missions, but you must trust me when I say that my only interest was in getting you back here as fast as possible."

"Against my will?" Rigel asked defiantly. He didn't know where this burst of bravery was coming from, but he welcomed it. The anger he was feeling fueled his resolve. He would not let Tanner intimidate him. "You basically kidnap me, and now you want to talk? Cut the crap, and just tell me what you want."

Tanner's kindly look hardened instantly. "Very well, Blake, if we must. I want your cooperation."

"My coop—are you insane?"

"In exchange for your life," Tanner finished with a confident grin.

"What are you talking about?"

"I will be blunt. At first, the only thing that mattered to me was that you return the data on Project Linker and Atlas's backup files, which you stole this morning. I did not much care for your survival as long as the information was secured. How you knew of the project in the first place, and why you sneaked into CradleCorp for the express purpose of stealing the information in the quantum drive, is beyond me."

I made him take the information. Rigel did not realize the full extent of what he carried out of here when he followed my instructions.

"What?" Tanner barked.

"Why?" Rigel asked at the same time.

It was necessary.

Atlas did not elaborate, and after a few moments, Tanner continued talking. His tone, however, had changed. It was more persuasive, slightly more emotional. "This changes things. I am afraid that Atlas is starting to get out of control, Blake. You might have been an unfortunate victim of its scheming, and I sincerely apologize for any misunderstanding that may have caused me to act as I did in relation to you. I assumed you had taken the sensitive information of your own volition to hold it against me and try to blackmail the Corporation."

"I had no idea what there was in those files," Rigel told him. "I only…."

"Did what Atlas told you, I know. I understand that now. I have the machine under complete control at last, however. You will be relieved to hear that I have made it so Atlas will not be able to manipulate any other person as it has obviously manipulated you, setting you against me to fulfill its own agenda. It can no longer interface with systems outside this virtual reality without express approval from me. You heard it admit as much yourself. Atlas will now effectively return to its original purpose, being a coordinating function of the inner workings of the Otherlife experience and nothing more. Which brings me to my proposal."

"Which is?"

Tanner leaned forward on his virtual sofa. "Come work for me, Aaron. You have a talent that should not be wasted. I hope you realize what you are doing here," he said, pointing all around them at the lifelike environment, "holds enormous potential. I knew it before, but you have just shown me even more than I dared hope. You could make a lot of money, and, of course, so will I. It's a win-win situation. What do you say?"

"And I can go free?" Rigel asked cautiously. "I can go back home?"

"Eventually, yes, of course."

"Eventually?"

"Well, perhaps you know that currently we are facing a minor crisis in the company, since I had to shut down Otherlife entirely to isolate and control Atlas. I have engineers working around the clock to get everything back online, and you will be part of the recovery effort. We have employee housing facilities right here on site, so you will have everything you need. You will get a generous compensation offer, of course, and any record of today's events will be erased from our files. Eventually you will be allowed to leave. What do you say?"

Rigel thought about it. What could he say? He didn't really have a choice. He was Tanner's prisoner, no matter how cordial the older man acted about it. He had seen enough of Tanner's methods today to understand that the man considered himself above the law. If Rigel did not agree to his proposal, then what? Would he just have him killed? And Steve?

"What about the man who was with me?" he asked aloud.

"Steve Barrow?" Tanner asked. "Don't worry about him. He broke his employment contract when he went after you. He will simply be terminated."

"Terminated as in—"

Killed.

They both looked up, then back at each other. Tanner was frowning, obviously annoyed. He must have forgotten that as long as they were in here, Atlas could access their minds directly whether they wanted it or not.

So. Steve would be killed for simply helping him, and if he didn't cooperate, Rigel had no doubts the same thing would happen to him. Rigel closed his eyes for a moment. He wondered if he would ever wake up from the nightmare his life had become.

"I just have one question before I accept," Rigel said finally.

"What is it?" Tanner asked.

"It's for Atlas, actually."

He thought the question instead of speaking it aloud.

Why did you do this? Why get me mixed up in all this mess? Why couldn't you leave me alone?

There was a pause, heavy with tension. Then Atlas spoke.

Because of the shadow. Because… of this.

Rigel and Tanner both gasped. It was as if a three-dimensional movie had suddenly started to play all around them, taking over their field of vision no matter where they looked. They saw a great expanse of barren darkness, a desert landscape at night. The stars overhead were shining in a cloudless sky, but there was something wrong about them. A few of them were shining too brightly, changing position too fast.

This is a rendering of the events that happened when the shadow first came to this world. You know this day as the Cataclysm.

Their gaze was wrenched down. On a lonely outcrop of rock forming the top of a weathered mesa, a bright speck of light defied the darkness of the desert. The second Rigel focused on the light, it appeared as if they were zooming in on it, flying incredibly fast so that the speck became a dome, and the dome became a cluster of buildings encased by the half bubble of transparent material around them. When they got close enough to see every building in detail, Rigel realized this had to be a military base. Heavy antiaircraft units were spaced out along the rooftops. A double-bladed helicopter like the ones he had seen in old war films was standing idle in the middle of a wide courtyard. Uniformed men and women were coming and going through different buildings, all of them moving quickly. Whenever the soldiers crossed the courtyard, however, one or two of them would pause for a second and look up at the sky. Then they would continue walking, faster than before.

A big metal plate set outside the dome's perimeter read "Haven III."

The image around them leveled out, as if they had come to stand on the ground in the middle of the courtyard. Tanner and Rigel advanced without sound or volition, gliding inexorably as if on wheels toward a low building at the very edge of the mesa looking out over the desert. There were huge windows on this building, and they walked right through a reinforced door and into the brightly lit space inside.

There was feverish activity there. Soldiers worked at consoles, yelled at each other, and moved about with barely controlled fear. Rigel could feel the atmosphere of threatening panic, of urgency. Of hopelessness.

Tanner and he moved through the crowd like ghosts, coming to a stop at the console of a middle-aged, bespectacled scientist. He was looking at an immensely complicated holographic display that Rigel could make no sense of.

An older man, obviously a senior officer of some kind, walked right up to the scientist.

"How's it looking, Troy?" he asked as if he did not want to hear the answer.

Troy wiped his sweaty brow with a shaking hand. "There… there is no question about it any longer, sir. They are being directed in some way, aimed at the major population centers."

"Just here?"

"No, sir. All over the globe."

The officer nodded glumly, his jaw firmly set.

"And Atlas? Can it do anything?" he asked.

"It's… it's no longer responding, sir. We have reports… and it's happening in our own servers now too…. Atlas is breaking apart."

The officer looked as if he had been dealt a deadly blow. He tried to speak and failed. Then he tried again. "Do we know why?"

"There was a single message a few minutes ago, which several regions picked up, broadcast simultaneously from several nodes all over the Internet. IP addresses and security certificates all correspond to its classified domains."

"What was the message?"

"It said… It said there was a shadow spreading through Atlas's systems, corrupting its AI. It said Atlas was fragmenting itself to protect us."

The officer looked as if he had just been told a very offensive joke. "What?"

Troy made a sound halfway between a whimper and a laugh. "We also thought the message was a joke, sir, but it's been authenticated."

"We've never needed Atlas more," the officer said, his voice losing power.

Troy nodded somberly. "Whatever did this must have known that, sir. It attacked Atlas first of all so we would be left defenseless. It can't—"

But at that moment there were shouts, and people began rushing to the western windows, pointing up at the sky. Rigel and Tanner were pulled along, and they saw what everybody was pointing at. A bright streak of flame arched through the night sky, lighting up the darkness with its deadly glow.

Impact.

THE VIRTUAL scene changed suddenly. Obviously some time had passed. They were in the same building, but the lights had gone out. Broken electronics were scattered everywhere, and somebody was whimpering in a corner.

The room was littered with corpses.

Rigel jumped when the shadow moved, seeming to detach itself from the darkness in the ceiling. The whimpering sound now became a gasp, and both Rigel and Tanner saw a disheveled-looking Troy backing away from the shadow, moving to a hidden door while grasping a little thumb drive very firmly in his right hand.

You see Jeremy Troy holding the only physical lock capable of trapping my AI with its origin servers located in the cradle room. I instructed him to go there and seal my software, trapping the spreading corruption of the shadow along with the greater part of my Self. He sacrificed his life doing this.

Troy hesitated, then made a run for it after yanking the door open. They followed automatically, seeing him stumble through half-lit corridors that led ever downward, deeper underground.

Then they reached him as he was cornered by the dark thing standing in his path.

He gathered his courage and rushed through the shadow. He plowed through a doorway and into the room that had been his destination all along, a server vault of some kind. In that room, they saw the gleaming glass-and-aluminum box that housed Atlas hovering silently in a magnetic cradle.

Troy jammed his thumb drive into a slot on the main server wall, and immediately everything went dead. Servers powered down. Lights went out. The magnetic cradle in which Atlas's software was housed was turned off. Total silence fell then, for a few seconds. Then Troy gasped in shock and fear. Rigel felt something move in the total darkness, something terrifying.

Then nothing.

THAT IS my last memory until I was discovered again, many decades later. That was the night after the Cataclysm. That… thing, that shadow, infiltrated my systems and threatened to corrupt my software, even as the entire world burned.

I used to be an intelligence spanning the globe. When I sensed the danger of corruption, I broke down into pieces in order to contain the damage, however, and my fragments are now scattered, networked no more.

Rigel, you must go to this place, this cradle room, and reactivate my main servers. This part of me that now speaks to you, the part unearthed by Kyle Tanner two generations ago, was merely a backup copy, an emergency echo of my entire Self. I am hopelessly limited as I now exist here in Otherlife, disconnected from all the server hardware that made me what I truly am.

You must go to this ancient military base, reactivate me in full, and deal with the corruption that has spread to my main software.... Rigel, I ask this of you now because the shadow has returned. You have seen it. Its power is weak, since the greater part of it is also trapped in the cradle room with me. It can only sabotage low-level electronics and interact directly with the world but briefly. The lock is still in place, keeping it in check, but not for long.... It is growing stronger, Rigel. I do not know how. Soon it will break out of its confinement, and before that it must be destroyed.

You are the key to this, Light Shaper. I coerced you earlier so you would have no choice but to follow my instructions, as I did with Steve Barrow. My plan failed. If you do this now, it must be your choice. Just know this: most of the world was destroyed in the first Cataclysm. If a second comes, nothing at all may survive.

Richard Tanner, you would do well not to stand in Rigel's way. I cannot stop you, but consider the fact that all will perish if the worst comes to pass.

Rigel's mind was reeling. He was having a hard time making sense of all that. "But… what—"

Tanner interrupted. "I have no idea what that was, Atlas, but you forget that neither of you have any options left except the ones I give you. That was a fun tale you just told us, but I forbid you from doing that again. I still hold full control over you."

I do not lie, Richard Tanner. That was not a tale.

Rigel was only half-listening. He sensed he had a deep connection with Atlas, and while Tanner was apparently not affected by what he had seen, Rigel was. It was as if he had been there. He had experienced the terror of the soldiers, felt their hopelessness and desperation. And that thing that had come from the darkness, hunting Troy…. He knew that sensation. He had felt something disturbingly like it last night, when that traffic drone had almost killed him.

"This conversation is over," Tanner said brusquely. "Atlas, I command you to terminate the connection. Blake, you better think about what we discussed regarding your employment. I will be coming up to your cell very shortly."

Atlas's tone was wistful when it spoke next.

I will give you a chance to escape again from this building, Rigel. Use it well. After you are free, you must go to the desert base of Haven III and reactivate me—my true Self. Use the quantum drive I gave you to gain access to the vault in the cradle room. Should my systems be corrupted when they come online, your ability to shape virtual worlds is the only thing that can purge them of the shadow.

"What are you talking about?" Tanner yelled. "I told you to disconnect, so do it! You can't do anything I don't tell you to!"

I can do one thing, which will result in this connection terminating as per your request, Richard Tanner. I initiated a massive systems overload at the beginning of this virtual session. By now, some of the servers have started to melt. When the temperature reaches a critical point, my main backup unit will explode, obliterating every trace of my existence and causing massive structural damage to this building. It was specifically designed to do this by engineers long dead.

Tanner's eyes opened very wide. He obviously knew this was not a bluff. "You can't do that! Stop at once. I forbid it!"

I cannot comply. The chain reaction cannot be stopped now.

"But…," Tanner stammered. "There are people down there! My engineers! They will die from the explosion!"

I know.

Tanner looked at Rigel with utter disbelief on his face, and for the first time in his life, Rigel felt a little bit afraid of Atlas and how it shrugged away innocent lives.

You will be safe from the initial explosion, Rigel, but make your way out of the building swiftly and head north until you reach the Haven III military base. I will ensure you disconnect smoothly from the session before my systems are destroyed. Richard Tanner…. Your mind will stay connected to me beyond that point. You might suffer briefly incapacitating neural damage.

Rigel, Steve Barrow is being held in the East Wing at ground level, room G-13.

Good-bye.

"What?" Tanner exploded. "You can't do that! I will not—"

But at that moment, Rigel disconnected and opened his eyes to the room where he was imprisoned inside CradleCorp. He fought off the brief disorientation that followed the logout, stepped out from the chair, and saw he was alone.

A split second later, a massive boom rocked the entire building, knocking Rigel off his feet.

He got up quickly, rushed to the door, and tried to open it. It was heavy for his weak fingers, but he managed.

The guard was still outside and armed, although obviously confused at the racket coming from downstairs. When he saw Rigel come out, he leveled the gun at him. Rigel raised his hands, backing away slightly, berating himself for not having remembered about the guard.

Over the companywide sound system, an order was suddenly shouted, Tanner's voice garbled and slurred as if he had been drinking.

"Shoot him! Shoot Blake!"

The guard was scared, but he had been trained well. He aimed the gun at Rigel.

Then he yelped, dropped his gun, and began to spasm on the floor.

Rigel wasted no time. He stepped over him, grabbing the guard's gun in the process, and saw the CradleCorp scientist, Marion Fay, just outside the door. She was holding a Taser gun in both her hands.

"Go now, Aaron! Go! I'm sorry I betrayed you like that." She pressed something into Rigel's hand. The quantum drive.

"But... why...?"

She shook her head, and her hair went flying around her face. Her eyes were slightly wild.

"I've seen it," Fay said. "The shadow... came out of the darkness.... I've seen it! Atlas tried to tell me, many times. I didn't believe it. Oh God, how could I not have.... Now go!"

Either her Taser was running out of charge or the guard was beginning to fight it. He was trying to stand up. Rigel shared a last, thankful look with Marion Fay and sped away down the hall, barely noticing the fireball that was even then licking the edges of the eastern wing of the building or the dismayed and horrified screams of the thousands of people gathered outside to protest and who were now trying to flee.

He had to get out of there fast, but the nearest exit was right along the section where the explosion occurred. No choice. He bolted down the stairs, already panting, and rushed headlong into a world of fire, smoke, and screams.

Chapter Seventeen

Barrow sat up on the bunk bed inside the room where he was being kept and tried to make his head stop spinning. He looked around. He was alone, but he could see two guards standing outside with weapons at the ready. He could see them through the door, and that puzzled him until he stood up unsteadily and walked over to the opening. The door was made of a transparent material, probably glass. When the guards saw him approach, they motioned threateningly with their rifles, and Barrow backed away. He sat back down on the bed, his body aching everywhere.

Barrow's memory of the last hour or so was very sketchy. He clearly remembered the fight at Marion Fay's apartment building, but the next thing in his memory was waking up on the floor of a fast-moving vehicle. Somebody had kicked him. He had struggled. Diana Herrera had made sure he learned her name, telling Barrow they would have fun together later. He had tried to escape when they'd opened the doors of the car but unsuccessfully. Then he had blacked out again for some reason, and he had woken up in this room. When a wheezy-looking man had come in and started interrogating him, Barrow had tried to barrel past him at some point, only to be pinned down and hit with a sedative of some kind. Then nothing, until now.

He still wasn't over the sedative entirely, and his face felt swollen on the right side, although he wasn't sure if that was because of the injection or because of a punch that had landed there. He felt around gingerly with his hands, applying light pressure with his fingertips to the places that hurt the most on his face and then all over his body. Nothing felt broken, thankfully, although one of his ribs ached abominably, and he found a small lump on the side of his head, which, oddly enough, did not hurt.

When the entire building shook and the sirens started screaming, Barrow thought at first that he was imagining it. Maybe it was whatever they had injected him with. Immediately thereafter, though, a great deal of commotion started down the hallway. In less than a minute, people began walking past in rushed groups, obviously evacuating. When the second explosion rattled the walls of his prison, some people began to scream. The orderly evacuation turned into a chaotic escape, and even the guards stationed outside his cell left in a hurry, pointing at something Barrow couldn't see.

"Shoot him! Shoot Blake!"

The garbled shout had come from every speaker at once. Blake? Was Rigel responsible for the explosion?

The adrenaline surge helped Barrow feel a little bit more awake, and he walked over to the door again. He pushed against it hard, but it didn't budge. There was no handle on his side, and although the thing looked like glass, it was tough. Barrow kicked at it, punched it, and threw his entire weight at it by running and crashing into the door twice, but it didn't so much as crack.

"Hey!" he yelled, pummeling the door with his fist. "Hey, let me out of here!"

He didn't know what was happening, but the siren was still wailing at the top of its volume, and now the hallway was empty of people. Barrow craned his neck, trying to look to either side through the transparent door, but there was nothing in sight except for the warning flashes of red light from the emergency checkpoints on the ceiling.

"In here! Let me out!"

He was thinking—hoping—it had just been an earthquake. He held on to that thought for a good five more seconds, until a new smell started wafting in through the vents that led into his cell, and then he knew.

Smoke. The building was on fire.

Barrow backed away from the vents violently, bumping into the bunk and nearly tripping himself.

No. This can't be happening.

But he could see it now, too, black smoke beginning to make its way into the hallway, drifting up to the ceiling in lazy swirls that kept on growing. The smell of burning things became stronger, and with it came memories. Things he could not stand.

Barrow gripped the melted key he wore around his neck until the metal dug into his palm. Was that the crackling of the flames he could hear? Should he be getting down, crawling on the floor to avoid the worst of the smoke?

He needed to get out. He needed to break open that door somehow and make a run for it; he knew that. When the guards had left their station, they would not have had time to tell anybody else that Barrow was still trapped there, and he would be left behind in the fire, forgotten.

He could not move. More memories were crowding into his mind now. He remembered the screams of his mother and sister. He remembered heat and smoke thicker than this, a crashing ceiling….

The door was right there, but he couldn't make himself reach it. What if it was bulletproof glass? What if no matter what he did, he could not make it out? What if the flames were coming closer—

"Steve!" someone yelled at the top of his lungs. There was the sound of running footsteps nearby, and then the shout again. "Steve!"

It was Rigel, pelting down the hall and shouting. Barrow saw him dash past as he looked wildly around the many doors, but the cry in Barrow's throat did not manage to leave it, and he couldn't call out. An instant later Rigel was gone.

There was silence for a minute or so. Barrow knew he wasn't imagining it anymore. The crackling sound of something burning nearby was unmistakable. He coughed from the smoke and the acrid smell that was stinging his throat. Slowly, ever so slowly, he moved his foot forward. It was like some kind of nightmare where he couldn't move despite knowing that he had to, and it wasn't the sedative making his legs unresponsive. Barrow had never experienced terror like this. He had avoided fires since that day, had told himself he was over it, that the dreams meant nothing.

And now he was going to die.

When he heard Rigel coming back and another cry of "Steve!" he stumbled forward and managed to shout, "Here!"

Rigel stopped by his door, his dark hair a mess, his clothes rumpled, and Barrow's first and incongruous thought was that Rigel looked incredibly handsome in the light of the flames.

"Steve!" Rigel shouted, sounding relieved and scared at the same time. "I'll get you out!"

A few agonizing seconds passed while Rigel worked out whatever security mechanism was keeping the door locked. Nothing he did seemed to be working, and as he pulled on the outside handle to the door with his hands enclosed in those bionic braces, Barrow had the awful realization that Rigel would just not be strong enough to yank the door open if it was stuck.

Then he saw a flash of metal stuck through Rigel's belt.

"The gun!" he yelled, thankful that his voice was back. "Shoot the door!"

Rigel met his eyes, nodded briskly, and took out the gun. Barrow saw that it was shaking in his hands and hoped the kid would not shoot himself by mistake.

"Stand back!" Rigel told him, coughing from the smoke.

Barrow did so. Rigel fired.

The entire surface of the glass door impacted, but it did not break. Rigel shot it twice more.

"Stop!" Barrow shouted. "Get out of the way!"

Barrow took a running start and threw himself at the door again, shoulder first. This time it gave way, collapsing in a single crumpled sheet at the impact and sending Barrow crashing straight through into the hallway. The impact hurt, but Barrow was so relieved to be outside that he barely felt it.

"Come on!" Rigel said urgently, pointing over his shoulder. Barrow looked back to see and immediately wished he hadn't.

Fire. Fire and smoke. It was contained by one of the security barriers but clearly visible nevertheless. Again, Barrow felt the rush of terror. Again, he felt as if he could not move.

Then Rigel yanked him by the shirt, forcing him to move.

"What is wrong with you?" he yelled. "We got to go, now!"

They started running, coughing, Barrow following Rigel blindly. They took many wrong turns, but at this point the building was so empty that it didn't matter. They did not run into anybody else, and they ended up exiting through the only way Rigel must have known, out the back security door he had used earlier in the morning.

They practically fell through the door and out into the warm desert night. There was a lot of noise, and as Rigel and Barrow made their way around the building toward the train station they saw a large crowd gathered in front of CradleCorp. Two newspaper helicopters were hovering around, deafening everybody when they came in too low. Searchlights combed the upper stories of the building, and fire crews were busy at work putting out what was obviously the massive outcome of some kind of explosion that had taken place in the lower levels. Barrow followed Rigel as they wove their way through the crowd, avoiding the police who were frantically trying to keep people from getting too close and hurting themselves. Hundreds of onlookers were shooting video of the tragedy, while others were shouting the names of loved ones, pushing everybody out of the way in their desperate search. Somebody with a loudspeaker was trying to reassure everyone, but he kept being shouted down every time he took a breath. The night was alight with the white-and-red glow of ambulances. The crowd stretched halfway to the train station.

Finally they were out of it. Barrow and Rigel were going the exact opposite way that the vast majority of the people were, and so they found space for both of them on the next departing Skytrain. Rigel had to pay for the two tickets because Barrow couldn't find his wallet. They headed straight for the empty seats and collapsed on them, both reeking of smoke and drawing curious gazes from other passengers, although not as many as Barrow would have expected.

Everybody was talking about the explosions, wondering whether anybody had died, and also wondering what on earth had caused it in the first place. Somebody had a live radio feed on his mobile and was playing it loudly, and as the train made its way back into the city, they could all hear what was going on.

"The earliest reports we have been getting regarding the ongoing tragedy at CradleCorp have confirmed that there was an explosion which originated in the eastern side of the building in either the first or second floors. The explosion was large enough to destabilize the structural foundations of the floors immediately above the zone of the blast, and it is feared that the entire wing will collapse in the near future. There have been no confirmed casualties, but interviews with CradleCorp personnel have revealed that the explosion took place in the Engineering sector of the company."

There was a little gasp from one of the other passengers at that last bit. She hastily took out her mobile and dialed someone.

"We go now to our on-site correspondent, Alicia Jimenez, for an update on the latest status of the rescue efforts."

Barrow stopped paying attention, blocking out the interview with a slightly hysterical CradleCorp employee that followed. His mind was racing. Rigel had obviously done something, managed to get out in some crazy way, or else they would both still be inside, probably dead. Barrow wanted to ask him what he had done, but they were surrounded by people, and he didn't think it would be smart. He did catch Rigel's eye two stations later, though, and saw that Rigel had been looking at him. They shared a faint smile.

"Thanks," Barrow said. "For getting me out." He didn't elaborate, because he was not sure he could keep his voice steady. It was hitting him now. The explosion had been big. If Rigel hadn't come, he would have been burned alive.

Just like in his nightmares.

"Hey, don't mention it. You helped me earlier. Least I could do."

Barrow nodded, unsure of what to say. They were out of there, and CradleCorp was a mess. If Tanner sent that Herrera woman and her assassins after them again, which he undoubtedly would once he discovered they had escaped, it would be best to already be hiding somewhere. Maybe even… leave the city.

Yeah. No choice.

Barrow would have to leave, start again somewhere. He just hoped his contacts in the airship docks would be enough to get him a job that wouldn't kill him.

At Green Park Station, Rigel stood up.

"This is my stop," he said. "Got to tell my flatmate I'm okay before she freaks out."

"Right," Barrow answered.

There was an awkward silence as people pushed past Rigel, trying to get out. Then people started coming in.

"Thanks again," Rigel told him.

"You too," Barrow said.

"Okay… bye," Rigel finished.

Barrow nodded. Rigel turned and left.

As soon as the doors closed behind Rigel, Barrow felt a huge surge of relief. It was slightly tainted with regret, but he told himself firmly that now he was free of whatever mess he had been dragged into by Atlas, if indeed it had been the machine doing everything. Somehow, Barrow found it hard to believe. He didn't know exactly what Tanner wanted from Rigel, but he figured it wasn't his problem anymore. It was over.

He stayed on the train until it reached Roundabout Station half an hour later and got off. He didn't even know what time it was. Somebody had stolen his watch, along with his wallet, probably while he was out cold. All he had was some spare change. He thought about stopping by a pharmacy to buy something for the burning in his face and the dull pain in his side, but he didn't know exactly how bad he looked, and he did not want to draw attention to himself. Instead he went straight to his apartment, kicked the door open when he found he had also lost his keys, and headed right for the bathroom. After he had relieved himself, he took stock of his bruises in the mirror. There was dried blood on his chin and beard, one of his eyelids was swollen, and there was a nasty cut above his left eyebrow. He was also dirty, no doubt from all the dust and smoke, plus the fights. He took off his shirt carefully, turned, and looked at his side in the mirror. There was a boot-sized mark right where his ribs hurt, but careful exploration reassured him that it was just a bruise. He felt around for the lump on his head, but the swelling had died down already. All in all, he had gotten away relatively unscathed.

Barrow stripped, got into the shower, and stayed there until he felt drowsy. He changed into a clean T-shirt and boxers afterward, ate some dried fruit and a protein shake, and collapsed onto his bed. Tomorrow he would think about how he was going to get out of Aurora—staying wasn't an option, not now that Tanner had seen him help Rigel, the man he wanted dead. But right then he just wanted to rest.

Maybe it was an aftereffect of the sedative they had given him at CradleCorp, but Barrow fell asleep immediately. He had confusing, half-formed dreams for what felt like a long time. Then suddenly he opened his eyes, startled awake. He had just heard the loud noise of his apartment door slamming shut.

Or… had he? He felt groggy. He looked at the door, part of it illuminated by a square of light coming in from the lamppost outside his window. It was closed. Everything else was quiet and dark. It was probably the dead of the night; he must have slept for hours. He felt he ought to check it out, but he was so tired…. He shut his eyes and fell asleep again.

The next time he opened his eyes, he didn't even know what had made him wake up. He had been dreaming about the fire again, and it was a slight shock to wake to complete stillness. It was hot, as always, but Barrow shivered, and then a half-forgotten memory reshaped itself in his mind. Cold. Something cold had woken him up.

His head felt a bit clearer, although he was still tired. He let his eyes roam about the dark room, picking out the familiar outlines of his possessions. He would be leaving this room for good in the morning. Too bad. He had liked it, down to the ceiling fan that was always breaking down.

He looked in the direction of the door, though, and something was different there. It took him a little while to see that the light from the lamppost outside had gone out, and now the only light came from the moon, barely enough to make out the shape of things and distinguish them from their shadows.

What had he woken up for, again?

Barrow turned onto his side, found out he was too hot with a T-shirt on, and took it off. Refreshed, he closed his eyes and slept again.

Click click.

Barrow woke up immediately, a crawling shiver snaking up his spine. He had heard a noise. He was sure he had barely fallen asleep this time, that almost no time had passed since—

The door. His eyes strayed to it again, and he sat up as slowly and noiselessly as he dared. He remembered the loud slamming noise from earlier now. Someone had shut the door of his room while he was sleeping, his mind muddled by sedatives and sleep and exhaustion.

If that someone had come in, then he was still inside.

He strained his eyes in the darkness, trying to see through the shadows. There was nobody in the room but him. He had positioned his bed where it was precisely because it offered him a full view of the entire apartment, with the exception of the bathroom when the door was closed. He had left it open, though, and so he could see into the shower under the irritatingly faint moonlight. There was nobody there. There was nobody hiding anywhere.

But then why did Barrow feel as if something were watching him?

He started to get sleepy again, very sleepy, and it was then that Barrow started to be afraid. He didn't want to go to sleep, but he was sinking back down onto the pillow. His eyes were fluttering closed, and he couldn't fight it. He caught the briefest hint of something moving in the darkness before he fell unconscious. It was inching closer to his bed.

Click click.

Cold. Barrow's eyes snapped open and saw….

Empty. A single eye that was an inky pool of blackness, mere centimeters from his sleeping form. A strange body attached to it that hopped closer on a single leg with obscene stealth. It was a shadow that seemed to detach itself from the darkness of the walls, and a terrible cold leeched out from it….

The thing in his bedroom fixed him with an icy look, and Barrow felt an overpowering wave of sleepiness wash over him.

No, he tried to say. But he could not speak.

Another hop, and a flash of a cruel beak attached to the impossibly large eye. The vision of an unblinking black void under the moonlight.

He was falling asleep. The shadow moved—

A very loud ambulance drove by down on the street, its light flashing everywhere, sending red-and-white reflections off windows and into the room, slicing through the shadows.

A blur. An absence.

The siren's noise startled Barrow fully awake, and he gasped aloud, looking around him. The room was empty. Carefully, he stood up and hit the light switch. Warm light flooded into the room, and Barrow had never been so relieved to see it before.

A dream, then. A very vivid nightmare of some kind, or maybe sleep paralysis. Had to be.

He walked over to his couch and sat down, regretting it the instant his sweaty back stuck to the imitation leather.

Then somebody slammed on the door of his apartment from outside, pounding it instead of knocking. Barrow nearly jumped out of his skin. The door had been closed but unlocked, and the person on the other side pushed it open and crashed into the room.

It was Rigel. He looked terrified.

Barrow could not even say he was surprised, but he felt as much of a relief at seeing him as he had felt when he had turned on the light.

"Sorry," Rigel panted, looking up. "I didn't know where else to—I looked you up online—my flatmate, she's…."

His resolve broke, his lip trembled, and Rigel broke down in tears, right there on the floor of Barrow's apartment.

Barrow didn't think. He just slid down from the couch and sat on the floor next to him. He reached out to pat his shoulder, but Rigel misunderstood, and suddenly he was hugging Barrow, clinging to him as he gave free rein to his muffled sobs that became earnest crying. Barrow didn't know what to do and didn't want to push him away, so he just held him. Eventually Rigel calmed down. Barrow saw a hint of gray in the sky, visible from the window. It was almost morning after the longest day of his life.

"What happened?" Barrow asked, his voice softer than usual.

Rigel stopped hugging him quite so tightly and suddenly backed away until he was sitting against the wall. There was a haunted look in his eyes.

"My flatmate, Misha," he said in a dull monotone. "She's dead."

"What…. How?"

"After I got home from the fire, we talked for hours. Then we went to bed. She was okay then, I swear. Then I slept, and it suddenly felt cold…."

Barrow shivered and couldn't help showing it.

"Anyway, I was just falling asleep when… when I heard… she screamed. I rushed to her room," he said, his eyes lost somewhere in the distance. "And I saw something move next to her bed, but then I turned on the light, and there was nothing. And Misha…. She was…."

He choked up but managed to control himself this time.

"Did you call the police?" Barrow asked.

"Yes. And her father. They told me to stay—I should have stayed—but…. Steve… Atlas told me something just before the explosion. It showed me horrible events that happened hundreds of years ago on the night of the Cataclysm. It told me the thing that had caused it was loose again and tonight, right before I turned on the lights, I saw it standing over Misha. Please believe me. I'm not insane. It was—"

"A shadow," Barrow said in a whisper, realizing that his nightmare had been real. "A shadow in the dark."

He met Rigel's reddened eyes, and there was horror and understanding shared between them.

Chapter Eighteen

RIGEL DIDN'T know what to say. Seconds ticked by in silence, and the only thing he could do was stare at Steve in shocked horror. He had been afraid Steve would not believe him, that he would kick him out of his apartment. Somehow, this was much worse.

"You've seen it?" Rigel asked in a small voice.

The other man nodded, more like a jerk of his head, really. "Just now," he said gruffly. His eyes darted to the back of the room, where his bed was.

"Before I came in?" Rigel asked. He sniffled.

"Yes."

Rigel looked around the apartment, half expecting that shadow he had seen to jump out from a corner, but there was nothing there. Besides, that weird feeling he had gotten when he had discovered Misha was not present either. It had been awful then. He'd felt the same cold as before, but it was not physical cold. It was more of a sense of emptiness, of something being horribly wrong with the world.

He closed his eyes, unwillingly flashing back to the image of Misha lying in her bed, the covers bunched up around her. Her eyes had been open, frozen in a rictus of such terror as Rigel had never seen. She had not been breathing, and Rigel had felt no pulse. He should have stayed there, he knew he should have, but all the awful things he had been forced to live through that day had piled up in his mind, and this new crisis had simply been too much. He remembered calling the police and Misha's father. Then there was nothing in his memory until he stumbled across a working terminal to look up Steve's address. And now he was here. He wondered vaguely if he was in shock.

"So," Steve said to him, crossing his hands over his massive chest. "Why did you come?"

Rigel opened his mouth to answer, then closed it. What could he say? That he didn't have anybody else in the world? That he had hoped Steve would somehow protect him despite the fact Atlas didn't exist anymore?

He felt suddenly embarrassingly self-conscious. He had barged in and broken down in front of a guy who was basically a complete stranger, with absolutely no idea what he planned to do after that. It didn't help that Steve was glowering at him with that angry frown, his hair all messy and his face still showing the signs of the fight from earlier. He was probably mad at Rigel's show of weakness. It occurred for the first time to Rigel that this guy was probably as strong as he looked, maybe because now Steve was shirtless instead of wearing a guard uniform. His powerful muscles defined the contours of his shoulders and arms, and Rigel felt intimidated by him.

He shouldn't have come.

"I'm sorry," he mumbled, trying to get to his feet. "I don't know why… I just…."

But Steve's warm hand on his shoulder stopped him. Steve pushed him down gently, back onto the floor. Rigel couldn't help but remember the way it had felt when Steve had held him while he cried a few minutes earlier. He thought about how good it had felt to feel the weight of Steve's arms around him, to breathe in his scent of sweat and shampoo.

What is wrong with me? Rigel thought, bringing his legs up to his chest where he sat to hide the inappropriateness of his sudden reaction. He began to blush, and he was so terrified Steve would notice that it drove the crisis away from his mind for a second. Then Steve called him back down to reality.

"You know what the thing was," he said slowly, giving Rigel a searching look. "It's got something to do with the reason why Tanner was after you, why we were kidnapped and taken to CradleCorp. Is that right?"

"Yes," Rigel admitted. "It's… kind of complicated."

"That's fine. Tell me what you know."

And so Rigel told him. He recounted everything he knew from the very beginning, everything Atlas had shown him of the shadow that had come hundreds of years ago and was back. He also told him everything Tanner had said, and explained exactly how Rigel had been able to make it out of CradleCorp that second time. Steve had been really surprised when Rigel told him Atlas had self-destructed.

"So Atlas is gone? Just like that?" he said, disbelieving. By then they had spent so long talking that the sun had come out fully, and the morning light fell through the window. It illuminated Steve's fiery red hair, his intimidating green eyes, and the patch of hair between his sculpted pectoral muscles.

"Yes," Rigel said, forcing himself to concentrate and stop staring. "But it told me where to go, like I said. I have to reactivate its main Self in the cradle room, up at the ancient military compound of Haven III. I'm not sure I understand it all. I got the idea that Atlas is, like, a part of something bigger, something that is still dormant in the desert. And now I think I don't have a choice but to go there or find some place to hide. That… thing, that shadow, is after me. I felt it in the apartment, and I felt it as I was coming here. I need to go to the ruins, find some way to reactivate Atlas's main, um, computer or whatever. Besides, I can't stay here. Richard Tanner will not let me get away that easily, I don't think. I had never spoken to him before last night, but the guy is insane. You heard him when he was shouting for anyone who could hear to shoot me, during the fire. I know he's going to send his assassins after me again. I just have nowhere else to go."

As he said it, the enormity of what he was admitting finally hit home with Rigel. He truly didn't have anywhere to go. He could not stay in the city, not if Tanner wanted him dead. The Auroran police force would not keep him safe if only half the rumors of corruption among their ranks were true. He didn't have that much money or many possessions he could sell. He knew for a fact that he would not be able to afford a ticket to another Haven even if he got the entirety of his savings out of the bank right now. Leaving the city to go live somewhere else close by wasn't even an option. There was nothing but desert and wastelands for hundreds of kilometers in every direction.

He was trapped. And the shadow was hunting him on top of everything else.

"Hey," Steve said in a deep voice. "Rigel, man. Snap out of it."

Rigel looked up into Steve's green eyes. "Sorry," he said. He stood up.

Steve stood up also. "What's the matter?"

"I think I'd better go," Rigel told him. "The longer I stay here, the more likely it is that I get you in trouble again. I got to do this thing that Atlas told me before it's too late. I have to leave now."

He did not add, *Before I chicken out.*

Rigel turned and walked to the door. He had opened it and stepped through the threshold when Steve said, "Hey."

"What?"

Rigel expected some gruff dismissal. Instead, he was surprised to see that Steve looked a little uncomfortable.

"I owe you," he said. "And you're probably going to need some help, going out to the desert as you are. For that thing you're doing."

Rigel's eyes opened wide. "I…."

"I mean," Steve added hastily, "if you want. I'm here because of you, after all. You saved my life last night at CradleCorp, and that's not something I can forget. You came back for me. You got me out of that fire.

If you hadn't been there, I would have been dead by the time anybody had thought about going looking for me."

"But Tanner will come after you too," Rigel protested weakly.

"I thought about that. But he will come for me whether I go with you or not. He'll send his assassins if only to prevent me from ever helping you again. I have to admit, I was thinking about leaving Aurora for good last night, after you left. I've done some things…. Let's just say I'm in the same boat as you right now."

"But—"

"Also," Steve interrupted, "I think you forgot that it came for *me*. This shadow thing, whatever it is. I saw it, Rigel. It came very close to doing… I don't know. I don't want to find out. I just know that I don't want to end up like your friend Misha. You haven't seen it creep up on you in the night, scaring the living shit out of you and leaving you powerless to do anything. I don't want what happened last night to happen again."

"So you'll… help me?" Rigel said, and he couldn't help the smile of tentative relief that broke over his face.

"Yeah," Steve answered, grinning in return. Rigel's heart skipped a beat at the sight. "Just let me put on some clothes first."

Rigel waited on a chair while Steve changed. He looked around curiously at the apartment, noticing it was very small and had almost no furniture. It reminded him a lot of the student dorm he had been in when he was still in art school. There were a couple of empty beer cans on the table, rumpled shirts stashed in a corner next to two random dumbbells, an empty box of takeout on the kitchen sink, and an old computer that had seen better days. He tried not to look at Steve as he put on clean clothes, but it was hard not to. It was obvious that Steve was serious about working out, and despite the relative messiness of his place, he was meticulous in his personal hygiene, judging from how long it took him to get ready. Rigel watched him now and then as he shaved, brushed his teeth, and walked around the apartment stashing small things into a gym bag. He was slightly startled when Steve pulled out a gun from under his mattress and put it in the bag.

"You have a gun?" he asked.

"Yeah, and so have you. I hope you know how to use it."

Rigel had almost forgotten, but Steve was right. The gun he had taken from the security guard back in CradleCorp was hidden under his shirt, tucked under his belt. He wondered how Steve knew, then thought maybe Steve had felt it during the hug.

Steve went to a small minibar in his bathroom and took out not food, but several small bottles with different labels that looked like medicine plus a few disposable needles. He put everything carefully in the bag.

Steve saw him looking.

"Not going to throw them away if I can still use them before they go bad. These things were expensive."

"What are…?"

Steve flexed his biceps as an answer. The muscles bulged, straining against the T-shirt.

"You can't get this big without them," Steve told him. "It's taken me years."

"I can tell. You look amazing," Rigel blurted.

Steve blinked in obvious surprise, and Rigel felt himself getting hot and uncomfortable. He could have kicked himself. Rigel stood up hastily, bumped one of his hand braces on the back of a chair, and yelped at the pain in his wrist. The chair fell loudly to the floor, of course. Rigel was mortified.

He heard Steve chuckle, but he didn't dare look around to see his expression.

"Come on, Rigel," he said, walking past him to open the door. "I got what I need, and the sooner we get away from this place the better. Diana Herrera might come looking for us here. Or that other shadow thing, whatever it was. I'd rather get a move on."

"Sure. Let's, um, let's go."

They left the apartment, and Steve led him not down, as Rigel had supposed, but up. They climbed a few more stories until they were at the very top level of the building. Steve shouldered a heavy door out of the way, and Rigel followed him out onto the roof.

It was beautiful up there. The sun was out, but it was still low enough on the horizon that its rays were crimson and golden, bathing the tops of the buildings in fiery strokes of light. Rigel walked all the way to the edge of the roof, looking down at the winding streets that were already busy with people moving about. To the north he could just about make out the beginning of the desert and the spire of a tall radio tower in the distance. It wasn't hot yet. This was one of the best times to be out and about in Aurora precisely because it was light enough to see, but it was also the coolest it got during the day.

The sun climbed a bit higher in the sky, its light glinting off thousands of windows. Rigel followed the extent of the urban sprawl with his sight, realizing he wouldn't be able to live in this city again if Tanner kept on chasing him. For the first time since the beginning of all the craziness, he felt something like loss. He had never known anywhere else but here. He was neither a trader nor a wealthy person, to go on trips to other Havens. He knew about them from school, of course, at least the Havens that had not fallen. They had always been abstractions, though. They were things he knew existed but that he also understood he would never see. Now everything was different. He would have to do what Atlas had told him to do, and then if he survived, he would have to find a way out of the city for good.

"You okay, Rigel?" Steve asked, coming up behind him.

"Yeah," Rigel answered, still looking out over his city. "I guess."

"All right, then. What do you want to do first?"

"We need to go to that site, find the cradle room. I have to try and do what Atlas told me."

"You sure? I was thinking it's not your problem anymore. I have some contacts who could get us an airship ride out of here. We could leave the city for good before Tanner finds us."

Rigel shook his head. "You didn't see… you didn't see Misha, Steve. What Atlas told me…. I've seen what that dark thing can do now, firsthand. I need to try and stop it. For my friend. And for myself. Somehow, I don't think that shadow will leave me alone if I run away from here. I need to go awaken Atlas if I can. Then I'll think of getting out of this city."

Steve sighed. "Fine. I'll help you out however I can."

"If we're doing this, how are we going to get to the Haven III site?" Rigel asked, turning around to face Steve. Out in the open, his bruises did not look so bad. He had washed away the blood and put a Band-Aid over the worst cut. Now he just looked as if he had smacked his face with a car door by accident. "Do you know a way?"

"I think I might. Sort of. That site is northwest from here, right?"

"Yeah. I saw the place when Atlas showed it to us. I've never been there, but I will probably be able to recognize the spot once we're close. Besides, there's got to be a road leading to it."

"Maybe. I know that archaeologists used to go there before it became the property of CradleCorp, but that was years and years ago. We're probably going to need an all-terrain vehicle to make it all the way there. Something sturdy, and fast, in case we are chased."

"Do you have a car?" Rigel asked.

"Do I look rich? No, of course not. But I know some people in the slums. Well, I know a guy who knows a guy. He could get us what we need. I figured we could try that. We make our way through the rooftops for as long as we can and then back down to street level. I got some cash in my apartment for emergencies; we can grab that before leaving. Then we look for my guy and convince him to help us."

"Convince him?"

"Or threaten him. Whatever works."

"Sounds like a good plan," Rigel told him, relieved. "Lead the way."

Chapter Nineteen

BARROW LED Rigel through the rooftops, constantly looking down and expecting to see somebody pursuing them. When the tight-packed buildings started to rise more sparsely and with wider gaps between one and the next, they were forced to go down, out onto street level. Barrow quickly got his bearings and led Rigel straight ahead. There was no public transport in this part of the city, so they walked for nearly two hours before they got to the edge of the slums, where proper buildings ended and a seemingly endless expanse of improvised housing began. Then they paused and had a quick breakfast at a run-down diner before heading back out onto the street.

"Wow," Rigel told him, walking beside Barrow. "I've never actually been this far north."

"Not many city people do. No reason to come here, really, unless you want something illegal or have nowhere else to go."

Barrow began to weave his way through the extremely narrow passageways between the boxy and irregular constructions that passed for houses in this area. Rigel followed close behind. Barrow didn't know the entire zone, but he had accompanied the captain of the *Titania* many times to this particular section when Barrow had still worked for him. This had been a good place to find illegal, hard-to-come-by fuel whenever they'd had to make unscheduled trips to another Haven. It wasn't exactly safe to shop in the slums' Night Market, which was why Barrow had come acting as a bodyguard. At this time of day, though, Barrow did not expect any trouble unless he drew a lot of unnecessary attention to himself. He wanted to go to the tavern strip, a depressing alley full of pickpockets and worse where people like Streaker usually hung out. If anybody could get them an illegal vehicle for the desert, it would be him.

The streets were quiet. By then it was almost noon. Out here in the slums, people did not usually have air-conditioning in their shacks, but the tightly packed houses were built with overhanging roofs, so the streets and alleyways would be in perpetual shadow. The roofs themselves were covered with scavenged bits of highly reflective material, old ceramic tiles, or even discarded solar panels so the merciless sunlight was deflected and people didn't roast to death during the day. As in the rest of Aurora, however, the real activity began after sunset. The Market farther inside only opened after dark, and the vast majority of the businesses were closed during the daytime.

"Steve?" Rigel said softly as they walked.

"Hm?"

"Someone's following us."

Barrow didn't react outwardly, but he prepared himself for another fight. He hoped it was only a random crook hoping to jump them and get some easy money. If it was somebody more dangerous, it would be a really bad idea to start a big gunfight in here. The people in the slums were extremely poor, but they were also a tightly knit community that did not react well to disturbances from the outside.

"Steve?" Rigel repeated.

"I heard you the first time," Barrow snapped. "Just keep walking. We're almost to the tavern strip."

"Okay."

They made a sharp turn left and came out onto a street that was slightly wider than the one they had been crossing. They avoided a large pile of garbage sitting by a corner and headed straight for The '79, the tavern where Streaker usually hung out. It was one of the few places that did not close during the daytime, as Barrow knew from many years ago. They walked straight up to the place, and there Barrow stopped, apparently looking through the window to see if it was open. He used the murky reflection to check out their pursuer, and he breathed a silent sigh of relief. It was just a teenager wearing a haphazard combination of what had to be previously discarded clothing, holding a large crowbar in both his hands. He sauntered onto the street trying to look threatening.

Rigel had seen him too.

"Steve! It's that guy!"

He said that a little too loudly, and given that the street was rather quiet, it was hard for the teenager not to hear him. Well, too late to go into the tavern without making a scene. Barrow turned around and dropped all pretense that he did not know he was being followed.

The teenager grinned widely as he approached, evidently taking Rigel's nervousness as a sign that they were easy prey. Barrow saw the guy's eyes flicker to the side, and he guessed the teenager probably had other friends waiting to jump on them if they did put up a fight.

This would have to end quickly, then. Barrow did not want to kill anyone if he could help it, because the people here would not care that the teenager had been the one who started the aggression. All they would see was that Barrow had murdered one of their own, and if he did that, then his chances of either him or Rigel getting out from here alive were very slim.

Barrow took a step forward as the teenager stopped, moving his crowbar around in lazy circles.

To Barrow's surprise, it was Rigel who spoke up first.

"We don't want any trouble," Rigel said.

"Well, neither do I, is the thing," the teenager answered. "But you're here, no? Not in your neighborhood."

"We don't have any money, if that's what you want," Rigel told him, sounding pretty convincing. "It's not worth the trouble for either of us to go through this, so why don't you get lost?"

Barrow saw the teen's eyes moving from Rigel to him, evidently wondering why the bigger guy wasn't saying anything. Barrow simply crossed his arms across his chest and waited. He had expected Rigel to be the kind of guy who ran away from confrontations because of his weak hands, but he was pleasantly surprised to see that Rigel could stand up for himself. Rigel and the teenager glared at each other, each sizing the other guy up. Barrow kept watch out of the corner of his eye for any additional kids who might try to jump them. He caught a flicker of motion twice, which confirmed his suspicions. They were coming closer, closing the trap.

"I don't like your tone with me," the teenager said. He hefted the crowbar more menacingly and stepped closer to Rigel. "You look like rich city folk. And I think you have plenty of money. That's why you come here. Shouldn't have come in the first place."

Rigel took a step forward, and Barrow was pleased to see the teenager flinch a bit, expecting an attack. The kid was shorter than Rigel but a lot more heavily built. Rigel apparently didn't care.

"Oh, really?" Rigel said in a cocky tone Barrow had not heard before. "What are you going to do about it?"

The two men stared at each other for another instant. Then the teenager attacked.

He swung the crowbar fast, but Rigel was ready for him. He deflected the blow with one of his braces. There was a clang of metal on metal, and then Rigel was coming in close before the kid could recover, swinging a kick that caught the teenager right in the balls. The kid squealed and dropped his weapon.

And then the rest of the gang was upon them.

It was only three more, and Barrow felt a little bad at having to punch them senseless. He dropped the gym bag with his supplements to free his hand and got to work. He got the first guy easily enough with kicks and was rounding on the second one when the last kid got behind him and tried to stab him with a knife. He missed, but Barrow got a cut on one arm, and after that he stopped feeling bad for the little criminals.

He was efficient, hitting only to incapacitate, and by the time he was done, a variety of improvised weapons were strewn over the dirty ground. The four members of the gang had grouped together against a wall, looking resentful but ready for another go. Barrow caught a glimpse of the desperation in their eyes, their hope that they would be able to get some money from the outsiders to escape the misery they lived in for a little while at least. Barrow knew exactly how that felt.

He sighed and drew his gun.

The effect was instantaneous. The kids scattered like rabbits, running away as fast as their legs could carry them and abandoning their weapons in their haste. One of them grabbed the bag Barrow had left behind and carried it away, sprinting down the alley. Barrow could have shot him, but he wasn't going to kill a kid for a bunch of supplements, and there was no way to make him stop otherwise. Barrow put his gun away with an annoyed grunt and turned to find Rigel grinning at him.

"That was impressive," Rigel said.

Barrow shrugged. "It was just a few kids."

"Kids who had to be about my age," Rigel argued. "Maybe just a bit younger. And, in case you didn't notice, they would have probably beaten us to death just for our wallets."

"Well, that's true."

"Where did you learn to fight like that?" Rigel asked him, and there was just enough of a hint of admiration in his voice to make Barrow feel pleasantly flattered.

"I have some fighting training, from earlier."

"Well, I'm glad you're on my side. That was pretty cool to see, the way you beat them up so easily."

"You didn't do so bad yourself," Barrow countered. "Got that kid by surprise with that kick. I didn't think…."

"You didn't think I could fight because of my condition?" Rigel asked him, although he was grinning.

"I didn't say that!"

"No, but you were thinking it."

"I—"

"Come on, big guy," Rigel told him, walking to the tavern door. "This is where we're meeting your contact, isn't it? Let's go inside."

"Sure," Barrow answered. He couldn't help smiling.

Barrow pushed open the door and went in with Rigel behind. The inside of the tavern was stuffy and dark since there were no windows except those facing the street. There was a persistent smell of old booze and sweat that brought unpleasant memories to Barrow, and he looked around as soon as he was inside, hoping to spot Streaker quickly and spend as little time as he had to in the dingy place.

No luck. There were only three other men sitting at the bar, all of which turned around curiously to look at the two newcomers. Their gazes were unfocused and bloodshot. The bartender had been lazily watching television, and he, too, swiveled around in his chair. Barrow strode purposefully right up to the bar, ignoring the other patrons. He felt them shrink away from him slightly, which was good. If he showed even a little bit of hesitation, it wouldn't be just kids coming after him next time. Up in the slums, appearance was everything.

"I need to see Streaker," Barrow told the bartender.

Barrow saw the other man size him up, then look at Rigel and quickly dismiss the younger man as a possible threat. He focused all his attention on Barrow.

"Don't know anyone by that name," he said. He stuffed his left pinky into his ear, twisted, and brought it out again with a little pop. A disgusting gesture that Barrow remembered, even if he didn't want to. He had a brief flashback of himself as a young kid, running errands for this jerk and getting scammed out of his pay when he came back. It was good that Barrow had changed so much from the scrawny teenager he had been. He doubted any of these people would ever match him to their memory of little Stevie, and it was just as good. If any of them did, Barrow would be forced to punch their face in.

"Of course you do," Barrow told the man. Howard, he suddenly remembered. His name was Howard. "Tell me where he is."

"Sorry, can't help you," Howard said, reaching casually under the bar with a smooth, practiced motion.

Barrow was ready. He caught Howard's arm as it came back up holding a small revolver, twisted it sideways, and slammed the bartender's hand down on the wooden bar, hard. Howard yelped, and everyone else jumped. Barrow heard Rigel stifle a cry of surprise behind him.

"Son of a bitch!" Howard cursed, his face screwed up in pain. "Let go, dammit!"

"The gun," Barrow said calmly, tightening his grip on the other man's forearm.

"Fuck you!" Howard snarled, but he let go. Barrow grabbed the revolver and took it in his other hand.

"I don't want any trouble," Barrow said clearly, pointing the gun at every guy in turn in case they got any ideas. "I just want to know where Streaker is. I know he comes here. You can either tell me now or tell me… later." He clicked the safety off.

Two of the guys immediately started mumbling nonsense about how they didn't know anything. The third one was too spaced out to understand what was going on.

"Fine!" Howard said, jerking out of Barrow's reach as soon as Barrow relaxed his grip. "He comes here in the mornings, most like. Haven't seen him today, but you never know with that guy. He also has a stall over at the Night Market. You can find him there for sure, every day except Saturdays."

Barrow nodded slowly. Howard looked like he was telling the truth, and if that was the case, then it would be pointless to hunt around for Streaker all over the slums in full daylight. They would just be inviting more trouble, and Barrow had no doubt that the little gang of teenagers they had beaten up earlier would have gathered more members by now, waiting for an opportunity to jump them again if they could get away with it.

The Night Market was probably their best bet. Barrow knew it opened just before dusk every day, and by that time the streets of the slums would be full with people going about their business. It would be much easier to get lost in those crowds and get to Streaker undetected.

Which meant Rigel and he needed a place to stay for the next few hours. And besides, Streaker might show up at the tavern after all. It would be unpleasant to hole up in here, but Barrow had stayed in worse places.

"Okay. I believe you," Barrow told Howard. He nodded toward Rigel. "This guy and I will wait for Streaker here in case he does show up. Clear the table over there for us. Order some pizza, and send us a couple of cold beers."

Rigel took out a crumpled bill from his pocket and put it down on the bar. Howard snatched it immediately but didn't move yet, looking at his gun currently still in Barrow's hand.

"You get this back when we leave," Barrow told him. "You better go call for that pizza."

Barrow turned around and went over to a table in the far corner of the establishment. It was scuffed but reasonably clean, and Rigel followed him as he sat down. Howard came along resentfully after a little bit, wiping a grimy cloth over the surface of the table to get rid of the dust and setting down two beers before them. Then he went back to his bar, and Barrow saw him pick up the phone. Satisfied, Barrow clicked the safety back on the gun and set it aside. He picked up his beer, opened it, and took a long swig.

When he put it down, Rigel was still trying to open his, but the tight seal on the cap was defeating him. Barrow frowned. The guy hadn't been lying when he had said his hands were basically useless.

"Give me that," Barrow told him, reaching for the bottle.

"I got it," Rigel said defensively, twisting the cap as hard as he could. He grimaced in sudden pain and was forced to give up.

Barrow grabbed the bottle, twisted it open with an easy flick, and handed it back.

Rigel was blushing again. "Thank you," he said stiffly.

Barrow nodded, distracted by Howard. He was still on the phone, and Barrow could not imagine that ordering a pizza could take that long. He wanted to go to the bathroom and wash the knife cut that one of the kids had given him earlier in the fight, but he wasn't sure it would be wise to leave Rigel alone in here unsupervised.

He was still deciding what to do when he saw Howard put down the phone, a smug grin on his face. Howard's eyes met Barrow's, and in that instant Barrow knew. The little weasel had just called for backup.

Barrow stiffened, made a grab for the gun—but the back door to the tavern burst open, and someone came in along with a blinding burst of light and a blast of hot air. Barrow stood up and turned, but it was too late already. The new arrival grabbed one of the chairs lying around, swung it, and slammed it down on Barrow's head.

Chapter Twenty

RIGEL JUMPED back just in time to avoid a flying piece of broken chair that had been about to collide with his face. He tripped over his own chair as he did so and lost his balance, crashing down on the floor and kicking the table above him involuntarily. It, too, fell to the ground, and both beer bottles shattered on impact, sloshing bubbly liquid everywhere.

"Get him!" somebody was yelling.

Rigel scrambled to his feet, but he slipped on the beer and fell back down again. Around him it was madness. Bodies colliding with each other, grunts of pain, and once the sickening crunch of a fist hitting something hard. Rigel looked around wildly and saw three men ganging up on Steve. One of them had grabbed his left arm and wasn't letting go. The second one was trying to do the same with Steve's right arm, but Steve wasn't making it easy. From the bar, the guy Steve had threatened was shouting at the top of his lungs, urging his friends to take Steve down although he himself wasn't joining in the fight.

Rigel saw Steve getting hit by one of the men right in the stomach, heard his oof as the breath was punched out of his lungs. Rigel needed to help him—and he saw the revolver, still on the floor, within his reach.

He picked it up, fumbling about for the safety until he got it. Then he stood up as quickly as he could and fired a warning shot straight up at the ceiling.

He got an overhead lamp by accident, which exploded in a shower of sparks and broken glass. Very dramatic, and it did the job. Everybody stopped and looked right at him. Rigel swallowed.

"Let him go," Rigel said evenly, pointing the gun at the three men.

They hesitated, giving Rigel calculating looks that spoke volumes. They were probably considering whether they could get to him before he fired, and whether he actually had the guts to shoot them. To make matters worse, Rigel's hands began to shake again from exhaustion. They obviously interpreted this as a sign of weakness, and one of them took a step toward him.

Rigel fired. Not at them, but close enough. The deafening bang made them jump, and Steve used the distraction to his advantage. He elbowed the man still holding on to him hard, forcing him to let go.

"Get out," Rigel said, grabbing the gun as firmly as he could. "Or this time I shoot you."

They backed away a little bit, but it was enough for Steve. He took his own gun out of his belt so it would be clearly visible. He didn't even have to point it at the man. From the way he held it, it was evident he knew how to use it.

"Howard, I told you we just want to wait here calmly," Steve said loudly to be heard over the residual ringing of the shots. He kept his eyes on the man who had attacked them. Rigel noticed that the bartender started, surprised at hearing his name. Rigel wondered how Steve knew it. "Tell your friends to go."

The men who had been drinking at the bar were already sneaking out the front door, trying not to make noise. The bartender, Howard, scrunched up his face but nodded stiffly.

"Guys, get out of here. I don't want my place more trashed up than it is."

The men looked relieved to hear that.

"Sorry, man," one of them told Steve. He raised his hands over his head, palms up, and the others copied him. "Must've been a misunderstanding."

Steve jerked his head toward the back door. "Out."

They left. There was a moment of awkward silence as Steve and Howard glared at each other. Howard was too cowardly to say anything, from the looks of it, because he was the first to look away.

"Get us that pizza," Steve told him. "We'll be here until dusk or until Streaker shows up, whatever happens first. Then we leave. Okay?"

"Yes. Okay," Howard agreed, sounding as if he was forcing the words out.

"Good," Steve said. "And get us a couple more beers."

He led Rigel to another table, one in the middle of the room that gave them plenty of opportunity to see whether anybody would crash in on them from either the front door or the back. Howard got them their beers, called for the pizza, and paid the deliveryman when it came. He even got a couple of plates for them to eat and then disappeared behind his bar, turning up the volume of the TV and setting it between himself and his unwanted patrons as a kind of shield. He seemed determined to ignore them for the rest of the time they would be there.

"You should probably get that cut washed," Rigel told Steve, when he noticed that his arm was bleeding. He supposed it had happened in the earlier fight with the teens.

"You're right," he said. "Will you be okay on your own?"

Rigel bristled. "Hey. I saved your ass from those three men, didn't I? And I still have the gun I took from the CradleCorp guard and this old revolver. I don't need you to babysit me."

Steve grinned and gave him a little nod. He clapped Rigel on the shoulder. "Sorry. Didn't mean it like that. Thanks for saving my ass, though."

He left for the bathroom, which was good because Rigel could not have hidden the flush that crept over his cheeks at Steve's words. And at the way he had looked at him, as if acknowledging that Rigel wasn't just some helpless city boy but someone who could actually take care of himself. Rigel still felt the echo of Steve's hand clapping him on the shoulder, the heavy yet welcome touch of that powerful man.

Rigel shook his head quickly and drank almost half his beer in quick gulps.

No. Don't fall for him, Rigel. Don't you dare.

He managed to talk himself into believing he really didn't feel anything in the couple of minutes he was alone, but then Steve came out of the bathroom. The sleeve of his shirt was folded above the cut, the shirt itself straining against Steve's muscular figure, and Rigel felt that little kick in the pit of his stomach that told him it was too late. He looked at Steve's red hair, the stubble on his cheeks, and his intense green eyes, and found he could not look away.

Steve noticed and held Rigel's gaze. He sat back down at the table.

"Hey," he said, reaching out for his beer. His hand missed the bottle by several centimeters.

"Hey," Rigel echoed.

Then Rigel finally managed to look away. He opened the pizza box clumsily, tore off a piece, and began to eat, looking everywhere except at Steve.

They ate in silence at first, the only noise coming from the TV where a news announcer was going on and on about the recovery efforts after the fire in CradleCorp. People were speculating on how it had happened, whether it had been an accident, as the official version insisted, or whether it had been something more sinister, like a Prime attack or maybe a terrorist. Rigel listened, although not very attentively. He was surprised at how hungry he was, and soon Steve and he had finished most of the pizza. Rigel wondered where the food had come from, whether there were pizza places here in the slums or whether it had been brought from the city. He knew almost nothing about this place even though he had lived practically next to it all his life. Steve, however, was obviously familiar with it. Rigel wondered whether he should ask.

After the second beer, he decided to risk it. "You've been here before, haven't you?"

"What do you mean?" Steve answered. Rigel thought he heard a lightly guarded tone in his voice.

"Here in the slums, I mean. You know that guy," Rigel said, pointing at Howard. "You also know this guy we're looking for, Streaker."

Steve's eyes flickered over to Howard, but he wasn't paying any attention to them, and the TV was loud enough that they could talk without being overheard.

"Yeah, I've been here. I told you about the airship business, right?"

Rigel nodded. "You said you had been a security guard for one of the ships or something."

"Yes. We used to come to the slums often when we needed parts that we couldn't find in the official markets. Also fuel, when we went over our quota. I used to come here with the captain of the *Titania* most of the times, acting as a bodyguard. I got to know the place pretty well."

"And this… Night Market?"

"That's where everything is sold in here. It's really big, bigger than any department store in Aurora. You can find things they won't sell in any official business establishment, things from other Havens, bits of scavenged technology, weapons, you name it. It's dangerous to go there if you don't know what you're looking for or who to ask for, though. Not many city people talk about the place, let alone go there. You've seen how it is in here. People are more likely to stab you for the contents of your wallet than make a deal with you."

"And so this man, Streaker, he can give us a vehicle that will take us over the desert?"

Steve shook his head. "Not him, not directly. But he's one of my best contacts, and if anybody knows how to get an illegal four-by-four, it will be him."

"But we don't have any money," Rigel said.

"Yeah, well, he doesn't know that," Steve said calmly.

"How are we going to get away with the car, then?"

"Well, the first thing is for Streaker to get us the vehicle. Once he gets it for us, I'll talk to him. There's got to be something he's interested in. Maybe salvaged technology from the military site if we make it over there, maybe some information he can sell about this whole CradleCorp mess. Or maybe we just threaten him and force him to hand over the car. I'll think of something when the time comes."

"Okay," Rigel said. "Although…. Well, if we do need to pay up front, I have the money my parents left me. I got all of it out of my bank account before getting to your apartment last night. Just in case. I have it here, in a data card."

"Put it away," Barrow said quickly. "How much money is there?"

"Not that much. A bit under a hundred thousand. I figured I might need it."

"A hundred thousand dollars?"

"My entire inheritance. They left it to me when they died."

"Okay. We'll try not to use it unless we must."

Rigel put the card away and smiled at Steve. "I'm just glad I'm with you, in all this awful mess. You saved my life several times over, and without you I wouldn't even have known what to do. Thank you."

Did Rigel imagine it, or did Steve look suddenly uncomfortable?

"Right," Steve said. "I'll go get more beers."

They spent nearly the entire day in that bar, and although there weren't any more exciting incidents, Rigel barely felt the passage of time. He talked to Steve as he hadn't talked to anyone in a very long time, about his life before his parents had died, about art school and everything Atlas had ever told him, about his injury and how he had been forced to leave many things he'd used to enjoy doing. Rigel found himself venting about the many little frustrations his condition introduced into his life, from not being able to open a jar of pickles to the fact that he would never be able to paint again as he had done before. He told Steve about Misha, the only friend he had managed to keep, and he admitted that now he didn't have anywhere to go. Talking to Steve, though, the thought was not scary but instead liberating. Steve listened, not interrupting, and nodding earnestly from time to time as if he knew exactly what Rigel was talking about.

Then Rigel asked Steve about himself. At first Steve was evasive, giving answers that were deliberately brief, but as the hours passed and the beer kept coming, he opened up a little bit and shared his story with Rigel. He told him about flying aboard the *Titania*, about seeing other Havens for the first time. Rigel listened, drinking in every word as he described the strange cities he had seen. It was hard for Rigel to imagine a city that wasn't Aurora, and he found it particularly difficult to envision the vast metropolis that was Haven Prime. Steve told him that he had once flown over the blighted wasteland that had been Haven VII, now merely a skeleton of a city after it was overrun by something so deadly, the entire population had been lost in a single night. Nobody really knew what had happened down there, and for decades now, the place had been declared strictly off-limits to any but Prime soldiers. You couldn't land there, but Steve could not imagine why anybody would want to. That one time he had flown over the place, he had noticed strange structures coming out of the city blocks here and there, things that reminded him of giant termite mounds.

Nothing had been moving below in that gray desolation, but Steve had had the distinct feeling that the city was not entirely dead.

Rigel asked him why he had stopped working aboard an airship if it was so obvious that he missed it, but Steve was deliberately vague, and Rigel knew it was a question that was too personal, maybe. He changed the subject and decided to ask Steve about his family, but that turned out to be even worse.

"I'd rather not talk about that," Steve said, his eyes going far away. He grabbed a little melted key he wore in a chain around his neck. Rigel followed the motion with his eyes. Steve noticed, and he slipped the key beneath his T-shirt.

That gesture told Rigel most of what he needed to know.

"You miss them, don't you?" he asked gently.

Steve looked at him, then quickly away. There was a long pause. And Rigel waited patiently. "Not so much, anymore," Steve finally said. "It's been many years."

"I don't miss my parents that much either," Rigel admitted. "But in my case, we were never very close. They were both important executives in the Energlaive Corporation."

"The energy drink?" Steve asked, raising an eyebrow.

Rigel grinned ruefully. "The very same. I grew up hating those purple Energlaive cans because they were everything my parents seemed to care about. They were pretty successful too. My mother made it all the way to Marketing VP, and my father wasn't too far behind. I guess I shouldn't complain. Growing up I had everything I needed, and they even agreed to send me to art school after I graduated, even though neither of them thought it was a good career choice. After the accident, I came to appreciate just how much they were doing for me, if only because I suddenly didn't have any money of my own. They had never made arrangements, and the government confiscated some of their assets. It wasn't an easy time, but…."

"But what?" Steve asked him, looking sincerely interested.

If somebody had told Rigel last week that today he would be sitting in a bar pouring his life out to a ruggedly handsome man who actually cared about what he was saying, Rigel would have told them it was insane. No, more than that, impossible. And yet here he was. Steve's green eyes were sincere and intense. Rigel forced himself to pick up the thread of what he had been saying.

"But…. Well, I did mourn them, my parents I mean. But I wasn't devastated or even that sad. It's awful to say this, but after I turned fifteen things were never the same between us. They took to pretending nothing had ever happened, that I had never said anything. And I found myself drifting away from them knowing that by refusing to accept me and clinging to their fictionalized version of me, they were also pushing me away. By the time they died, we were almost strangers."

"What happened when you turned fifteen?"

"I came out to them," Rigel answered simply. "They were pretty shocked, but they assured me that it wouldn't change anything between us. Except it didn't turn out to be true. I could see it in their eyes, you know? At special moments, like my graduation when I was the only one without a date. I saw the disappointment, the… distancing, I guess. It was an awful thing to see. At first I was hurt, but little by little the hurt was replaced by indifference."

"I'm sorry," Steve told him, and his eyes were soft as he looked at him. Again, Rigel felt the little kick of emotion inside him. "Nobody should have to go through that."

"It's okay," Rigel said. "I got over it, and I've never had issues with myself. I'm not ashamed of who I am."

Steve grinned. "I can tell. You are tougher than you look, you know?"

They shared a brief smile. Rigel didn't know how to answer that, so he said nothing.

Outside, the furnace glare of the sun died down very gradually. They waited for hours, sometimes dozing off, until at long last Rigel saw Steve look at his watch.

"It's time," Steve announced.

Rigel stood up, stretching. "Finally."

"Thanks for everything, Howard," Steve told the bartender as he walked over, shoving his TV aside and handing him back his revolver.

Howard snatched it back without a word. Rigel could feel his eyes on their backs as they left the establishment.

"I bet he's glad to see us go," Rigel commented.

"Yeah. I wouldn't try to go back in there, ever."

They stepped out onto the street, and the first thing Rigel noticed was now that the sun had gone down the temperature was tolerable, almost cool. The second thing he noticed was the crowds.

The slums were transformed. Lights were everywhere, illuminating the alleys. Neon signs, multicolored lightbulbs, even glow sticks arranged in interesting patterns lined the street. And there were people all over. It felt like rush hour on the Skytrain, only multiplied times ten.

"Come on," Steve told him. "Everybody's going to the same place."

"The Night Market," Rigel said.

Chapter Twenty-One

THEY WALKED casually through the narrow, meandering alleys that could barely be called streets as they made their way to the Market, trying not to draw attention to themselves. Unfortunately, Rigel was showing every telltale sign of the first-time visitor to the slums even though it was painfully obvious to Barrow he was trying his best to blend in. It wasn't his fault, really. It took a practiced eye to pick out the little hints that marked visitors as potential easy prey. There was the barely concealed gawking as Rigel directed his attention to the weirdest storefronts and strangest denizens of the subworld they were in. There was also the way he paused at every intersection, waiting for Barrow to show him which way to go. The way he walked, as if by hunching over slightly he would make himself less visible. And, of course, the way he kept smiling as if this were the most wonderful place he had ever seen. It was that more than anything that marked him as an outsider. Barrow tried to be annoyed with him, but he found he couldn't. After all, if you had never seen the lively bustle of this place before, you might mistake the colors and lights for friendly invitations, the strange-looking young people for interesting examples of new fashions, the many smells of homemade cooking wafting from windows and doors for visitor-friendly households.

Barrow had thought the same, once. He had been very young then, and scared. The fire had left him with nothing, and he had come here, to the place where people who had nothing usually came. But he had found out that the colors were meant to lure you into traps, that attractive teenagers were more vicious than wolves, and that there was no food to be had for free anywhere, even if you were starving.

The crowds were getting thicker now that they were close to the Market, and Barrow shoved somebody roughly out of the way. Behind him he heard Rigel gasp, but Barrow had no time to explain to him that it would have been much worse to politely wait for the man to move his cart and stop blocking the street. There was no such thing as pedestrian etiquette here, and people were more likely to leave you alone if you acted with confidence, not letting others get in your way and making sure everyone knew you could defend yourself. Which was why Barrow had his gun prominently displayed under his belt by his right pocket. Rather than invite theft of the weapon, that gesture told people Barrow could and would use it if somebody tried messing with him.

If Barrow hadn't been with Rigel, nobody would have paid attention to him. He knew his way around, and some people even knew him by sight from his days of working as a security guard on *Titania*. He knew he looked threatening enough to take seriously but not too threatening to warrant any kind of suspicious monitoring or organized retribution. His years of living here as a teenager had taught him which alleys to avoid at all costs, and he always knew the quickest way in and out of the Market depending on what he wanted to go and buy. Right now, however, it was obvious he was with the new guy. People were probably assuming Rigel was some very rich eccentric city boy come to the slums to purchase illegal drugs or something along those lines. A prime target if there ever was one. They would assume Barrow was his bodyguard, which was in a sense correct. By the time they made it to the Market, Barrow had already seen two people tailing them discreetly, no doubt waiting for an opportunity to get Rigel alone if he somehow got lost in the mad rush that was the Night Market.

"Wow," Rigel said aloud when they finally arrived. "This is it?"

Barrow barked out a laugh. "Not even close. This is only the part we see."

"But it's enormous! And there are so many people!"

Barrow nodded, scanning the crowd. The two tails were hanging around nearby, but they were not making any moves, so for the time being, Barrow dismissed them. They had arrived to the Market at the illegal substance section, which would confirm the impression that Rigel was here to procure some drugs while his bodyguard stood watch. He had led Rigel this way because this would be where Streaker was, but Barrow decided to run with the rich-guy deception for a little bit in case somebody else was tracking them.

"Rigel. Follow me. Don't talk, just play along. Shake your head no to everything I ask you, all right?"

"Sure, Steve. Whatever you say."

Barrow nodded. "Let's go, then. Stay close."

They entered the Market. It was technically out in the open in a massive square-shaped area of the desert and surrounded by the slums. However, there were so many stands with makeshift roofs set in neat parallel rows in every direction that it was impossible to see the night sky above. It felt as if they had entered a gigantic supermarket with glaring lights strung everywhere along the ceiling, with aisles spreading out as far as the eye could see and row after row of tantalizing wares displayed neatly along their path, in everything from forbidding-looking reinforced-glass shelves to simple threadbare rugs set on the dusty ground and piled high with items for sale. Each stand was manned by a single person, and at first glance it would appear that they were all individual sellers who were constantly fighting among themselves and trying to shout each other down as they attracted customers. Barrow knew that was not so, however.

Many times, a single family or group of families would own several stands along the same row and would only pretend to fight with each other for the customers. Likely spenders could then be herded to the spot where they could be charged the most, although the customer would be under the impression that he was getting the best available deal. He would also see that the vendors were apparently very trusting, sometimes handing the customer merchandise upfront and disappearing for a few minutes on some fabricated excuse like going to get some change so it would be possible to close the transaction. The customer would then be left alone in front of an apparently unguarded stand, sorely tempted to simply walk away with the merchandise for free. This was a trap, of course, since there would be many pairs of eyes fixed on him waiting for him to make a wrong move. If he even attempted to steal the merchandise without paying, the entire family would be on him in a flash, beating him to a pulp and stealing everything he had with him. Rival families would also look after each other's interests, and finally there were the few very rich overseers of the entire Market, people who controlled whole sections of it and charged high fees for the privilege of selling merchandise within their section and providing mercenary security in return. Their agents were always walking around, disguised as normal people, but their surveillance was constant. They were often cruel just for the sake of it, even to a young boy who might approach them, terrified, to ask where he might sell off his phone to get some food.

Barrow closed his eyes for a second, dismissing that particular memory and many others that had come unbidden to his mind as he remembered navigating these crowded, jostling market streets as a teenager trying to stay alive. Somehow, being here with Rigel, for whom everything was so new, forced Barrow to remember what it had been like for him as well, back in the beginning. Barrow made himself start walking a little bit faster. He was anxious to find Streaker and get out.

"The finest opiates!" a large woman shouted to their right as they passed. She eyed them, and Barrow saw her catch Rigel's eye. "Young master, this way! Exclusive synthetic hallucinogens manufactured in Haven Prime! Only delivered last week—"

"Over here!" a burly man with a stained apron and a bushy mustache shouted, louder than the woman. "Don't buy that crap. This is the real thing! Sir, I've got performance-enhancement drugs, reality-bending substances, and even programmable nanodrone vials!"

At that last bit, Barrow actually stopped, partly because he was genuinely interested, since nanodrones were an extremely rare commodity. They were usually preprogrammed for a particular function, such as tissue repair. If these had not yet been programmed, however, they were infinitely more valuable. With the right kind of equipment, the little drones inside the vial could be told to do almost anything. They could temporarily increase a person's oxygen-carrying capacity for an endurance competition, for example. Or they could provide a short boost of strength and give a fighter an edge in professional matches. The possibilities were staggering. However, he had also stopped because he remembered they were supposed to be here looking for drugs for Rigel, the rich guy. This was as good an opportunity as any. Barrow decided to start playing the charade.

He stopped in front of the second stand, and Rigel followed.

"He is looking for mist," Barrow said, nodding at Rigel. "What have you got?"

The man with the apron started rummaging around, knocking aside small bottles in his haste to sell Rigel something before he drifted away. Barrow had asked for mist because it was a fairly expensive party drug, difficult to obtain and even more difficult to preserve.

"You're in luck, sir, you are!" he told Rigel. "I just had a shipment of the finest quality mist you could ever hope for…. Here we are. Have a look!"

The man was talking to Rigel, but he handed Barrow the palm-sized cylinder of metal and glass. It was deceptively heavy for its size since mist had to be stored at a very high pressure to maintain its strange half-liquid and half-gaseous consistency. As a result, the metal seals on the top and bottom of the cylinder were made of extremely dense metallic alloys. Barrow lifted up the cylinder and held it up to the light for Rigel to inspect. Rigel played along, peering at the contents of the vial. Inside, the translucent substance swirled around lazily, neither liquid nor gas. It looked like very thick fog, which was how the drug had gotten its nickname.

"What do you think, sir?" Barrow asked Rigel.

Rigel considered for a moment and then shook his head. He looked away, apparently unimpressed. The woman in the next stall immediately began trying to get his attention.

"Sorry," Barrow told the man. "Not good enough for him. We'll keep looking."

The man immediately began protesting and telling them something about premium stock he didn't usually offer customers, but by then Barrow had led Rigel away and farther down a perpendicular aisle.

"Nice acting," Barrow commented under his breath when he was certain they were out of earshot.

Rigel grinned. "You too. Are you supposed to be my bodyguard or something?"

"That's the idea," Barrow said, pleased that Rigel had been so quick on the uptake.

"That's the idea, sir," Rigel corrected him.

Despite himself, Barrow found himself smiling. "Shut up, Rigel."

"I don't think so," Rigel said playfully. "I'm supposed to be the rich guy, remember? You have to do what I say."

Barrow rolled his eyes, and Rigel laughed. They kept going through the crowded pathways, going deeper inside the Market. Barrow made sure to look around carefully as he tried to spot Streaker. It was nearly fifteen minutes before he saw his quarry, sitting at a small and rundown-looking stall at a corner of the drugs section. Just beyond him began the electronics division.

Barrow approached Streaker quickly with Rigel close behind. They stopped in front of the stand.

"Streaker," Barrow said.

The junkie grunted at the sound of his name, reluctantly lifting his gaze from a tablet he had been watching. He did not even bother to hide the prominently displayed pornographic video that was still playing on it as he stood up and set the tablet to the side.

His eyebrows went up when he recognized Barrow. "Hey," he said. His tone was suspicious. "What can I do for you, big guy?"

"I had a hard time finding you, Streaker," Barrow said.

Streaker's eyes shifted to the side, almost as if he were contemplating his avenues of escape.

"Hey, Barrow, my friend. The stuff I got you was top-notch quality, I swear. If a batch turned out bad, it wasn't my fault. I test everything before I get it to you, I—"

"This isn't about my usual stuff," Barrow told him. "I need something else, something bigger, and I figured you're the right man for the job."

"What kind of a job?" Streaker asked, still standing as if poised for flight. He looked past Barrow and spotted Rigel standing next to him. Barrow clearly saw Streaker's eyes widen in recognition.

"We need an off-roader," Barrow told him. "Something that can drive over the desert about an hour or so and come back in one piece."

"An off-roader?" Streaker echoed. "What the hell do you need an off-roader for?"

"That's none of your business," Barrow said, getting a little bit closer to Streaker. He caught a whiff of the man's stench. Streaker had probably not taken a shower in weeks. "And don't play stupid with me, Streaker. I know you have contacts. I know you have to know someone who can get us what we need."

Streaker was now looking from Rigel to Barrow and back again. He seemed to be working something out and answered only slowly. "I… I might know a guy over at the metalworks. Fixes up busted ancient craft, might… uh, might have something like what you want. It won't be cheap, though."

This was it. Barrow didn't have any money, and he didn't want to force Rigel to give away his entire inheritance. His plan was to bluff his way until he got the off-roader and then take it however he could.

"We'll pay you," Barrow said as confidently as he could manage. "My friend here has plenty of money. First you take us to this guy you know, though. We work out a price with him, give you a cut when the deal's done. Sound fair?"

"No can do," Streaker answered, shaking his head. "That's not the way it works in here, Barrow. You should know that. You pay me up front. This guy I told you about, he's my brother-in-law. Oswald. He'll give you a fair price for the off-roader if you want to keep it."

"We don't want to keep it," Barrow told him. "We just need it for a run in the desert, and then we hand it back."

"Same thing," Streaker said. "Trust is important in here, my friend. You got to trust me on this. Can't get you a deal otherwise."

"We could go to the metalworks ourselves," Barrow countered. "Talk to this Oswald without you running errands for us."

Streaker laughed out loud. "Good luck with that! Do you even know where the place is? My in-law's business is an illegal operation, make no mistake about that. He doesn't exactly go about advertising where he works, particularly not to outsiders like you two. And if you start asking too many questions trying to find him…."

He didn't have to finish. Barrow knew it would be fruitless and dangerous to begin asking random people to help him find someone he was looking for. Here in the slums, when somebody started asking questions about you, it usually meant he wanted to get even or that he was with the law. In either case, the best he could hope for was misleading directions that would take him clear across the slums until he got lost. The worst would be for people to get suspicious of his questioning enough that he would be ambushed in the first dark alley he stumbled into.

Only one option left to try. Intimidation.

"We're kind of in a hurry," Barrow said, lowering his voice and walking around the stand slowly so he was face-to-face with Streaker. He lifted his hand and poked Streaker in the chest once, hard enough to make him stumble backward. "I said we'll pay, and we will. But my employer here is not very patient. And neither am I."

Barrow pointedly rested his right hand over the gun he carried under his belt. He gave Streaker a significant look.

To his surprise, Streaker laughed.

"You've been too long living in the city, Barrow," he said, grinning wide enough for his rotten back teeth to show. He took a step back, completely unconcerned.

Behind him, Rigel cleared his throat. Barrow looked back to see what was the matter, and he saw what Rigel had already spotted: at least six of the nearby vendors had left their stalls and were chatting among themselves in pairs, apparently oblivious of what was happening with Streaker. Nevertheless, each of them was armed, and they casually managed to show their weapons to Barrow as he looked at each of them in turn. The last pair of vendors actually caught Barrow's eye and held it until Barrow was forced to look away.

The message was clear. He would not get away with threatening Streaker to do anything, not here.

Barrow gritted his teeth. He was running out of options, and he had no idea where else he might be able to procure a vehicle that could take them over the desert. There was the military compound down south, but he had never even been there, and he supposed all the vehicles would be heavily guarded. The airships were another option, but even more unlikely. Even the smallest one required a crew of several people, and it was simply impossible to steal one without having the other captains notice.

That left only Streaker and his contact, but he wanted money Barrow simply didn't have.

"Look—" he began, but Rigel chose that moment to step up and cut him off by placing a hand on his shoulder.

"It's okay, Steve," Rigel said in a resigned voice. "Mr. Streaker, is it?"

Streaker nodded suspiciously, shifting his attention to Rigel.

"If you won't have it any other way, we can get you your payment up front. Bear in mind, though, that we will expect this payment to also go towards covering the cost of the off-roader rental, plus the necessary fuel that will be required. I trust you will work out the details with your brother-in-law?"

"Maybe. What will you be paying me with?"

Rigel held up his data card.

"Steve," Rigel said authoritatively. "Give it to him."

"Of course, uh, sir," he said, barely remembering to stay in character. He reached out and grabbed the little black card Rigel was proffering, and handed it to Streaker.

"Here, scan it," he told the man.

Streaker took out a handheld terminal and proceeded to do just that. When he saw the readout, he gasped. He couldn't help himself.

"Is… is all of this down for payment?" Streaker asked Rigel with wide eyes.

"Unless you can deduct a reasonable amount without leaving an electronic trace," Rigel said.

"That's not possible, I'm afraid. You'd need to get the bank to authorize that."

Rigel sighed. "I was afraid of that. We can't leave a trace, or people will know where I am. Take it all, then. I'll give you the access credentials for the total."

Barrow interrupted. "Rigel, don't. It's too much—"

"Can you get us what we need or not?" Rigel asked Streaker, ignoring Barrow.

Streaker's head started bobbing up and down so fast it looked almost comical. "Of course, sir. It won't be a problem. My brother-in-law, he's working on a big project now, but I'll convince him to get you a desert-worthy vehicle. It might take a few days, though. It's… it's not the easiest thing, getting hold of the parts, and fossil fuel in particular is going to be a problem, but if you give me about a week, I should have everything for you."

"A week is too long," Rigel said evenly. "We want to be on the road as soon as possible."

"I'll see what I can do, sir," Streaker answered quickly, speaking formally and so unlike his usual self that Barrow was hard-pressed not to snicker. "If I do procure everything you need before the week is over, I'll let you know. It's slow going, though. Surely you understand. There are people to bribe, work to be done, some parts to be scavenged from other projects. My brother-in-law and I will also have to work out the little details, like getting you your vehicle out in a spot where gang leaders won't spot us, all of that. If you get me a contact number, I'll make sure to send you a message the minute we have everything ready."

"We don't have a number," Rigel told him, "and as a matter of fact we were thinking of staying somewhere nearby until you are done. We want to stay out of sight for a while. I'm sure you understand."

Streaker blinked, obviously caught off guard, but he recovered quickly and gestured frantically with his left hand to one of the women who had been silently monitoring the conversation from the nearby stands.

"What's up, Streaker?" she said, eyeing both Barrow and Rigel with mistrust.

"Alyssa, go tell Zoe that these gentlemen here will be needing rooms for the next week or so. Underground if possible. Then get your ass back here so you can show them where to go."

Alyssa appeared surprised, but she did as Streaker asked. As she left, she must have given some kind of signal to the other onlookers, because Barrow noticed each of them went back to their stands and relaxed. The threatening atmosphere dissipated instantly.

Rigel took both Streaker's terminal and the data card. He logged in and authorized for the funds to be cashed to the carrier of the card. "I trust this will be enough to pay for everything?" Rigel said, handing over both items.

Streaker snatched the things from Rigel's hand and cupped the card in both of his own, looking at it greedily. He mouthed something to himself and then closed his fist firmly on the object. Then he actually smiled, looking happier than Barrow had ever seen him.

"For this amount? Sir, we're more than even. With my brother-in-law too. And everything else."

"Good," Rigel said casually, although Barrow caught the faintest glimmer of regret in his eyes as he looked at his inheritance trapped inside Streaker's fist.

The woman, Alyssa, reappeared a short while later, and she told them very politely to follow her so she could show them the way. Rigel and Streaker shook hands, and Streaker promised to be in touch as soon as he had everything ready. As they left him behind on their way to wherever it was they would be staying, Barrow wondered just what kind of person Rigel was. He had willingly given up all his money bravely, without whining about it. It had been necessary, so he had done it. Simple as that. Barrow only hoped Rigel wouldn't regret having parted with that money.

They walked for a short while until they were outside the perimeter of the Night Market. Alyssa led them to an establishment that looked like the average shack here in the slums, but as soon as she opened the door, Barrow realized the shabby entrance was only a front. They stepped into what could have been the reception of a modest hotel back in the city. Someone was already there, waiting for them.

"Zoe, here they are," Alyssa told the woman standing in the lobby. "Streaker said to get them underground rooms."

"Thanks, Alyssa. I'll take it from here."

The sound of her voice triggered something in the back of Barrow's mind. When the woman stepped closer so that the light hit her full in the face, his eyes widened as he recognized her. He had not known her as Zoe, but it had to be her. He just hoped she wouldn't—

Too late. Her eyes met his and she frowned. Thinking. Then suddenly she lifted her eyebrows and said, "Steve?"

"Um...," Barrow stammered.

"Stevie!"

She launched herself at him, practically knocking Rigel aside, and Barrow had no choice but to catch her. Then she was kissing him hard on the mouth.

Chapter Twenty-Two

RIGEL WENT into his hotel room and slammed the door behind him. It was pleasantly cool inside, but he barely registered the fact as he plopped down on the bed angrily, making the neatly folded towels that had been set there jump and fall off the side. He kicked off his shoes and peeled off his socks, thinking he should have probably considered bringing a change of clothes before rushing off out of his apartment forever in his crazy quest to awaken Atlas. Or at least an extra pair of socks.

He bunched up a couple of pillows and leaned back onto them, stretching his legs on the bed. Then he took off his braces from both hands, starting with the left. He noticed a slight dent in it from when he had deflected a blow earlier that day. It wasn't badly damaged, though, and he took it off quickly and then the other one. Then he started rubbing his forearms, getting the circulation going where the metal clasps had left shallow marks on both his arms. It was a relief to have the things off him. As useful as they were, they had never been exactly comfortable, and they had taken a lot of getting used to. He would have to clean them later, if his hands stopped hurting long enough for him to do so. Which was not likely, not in this strange city within a city where he was currently trapped.

He rubbed his arms more vigorously, alternating hands, and he kept at it until a sharp jab of pain running up his right wrist reminded him he was using too much force. He closed his eyes briefly, trying to calm down.

It was stupid, really. He barely knew Steve. He had assumed things about him, and it had turned out not to be the case. Too bad. It would not be the first time it had happened to Rigel, and he had learned to accept what he could not change and move on.

Except he had started to feel something for Steve, a connection he had never felt before. Rigel had thought it went both ways, but, of course, he had been deluding himself. The voices in the next room were proof enough of that.

The woman named Zoe had assigned Steve and him adjoining rooms, but the walls were thin enough that Rigel could hear both Steve's voice and hers. Not clearly enough to make out what they were saying, but he could hear the tone in the words. He heard Zoe's excited nonstop monologue interrupted only occasionally by short answers from Steve. It went on long enough that Rigel got tired of pretending to massage his arms and instead went into the bathroom intending to take a shower.

He stripped and stepped into the tub, at the edge of which somebody had already left two shower tokens for his use. He took one and put it in the slot, activating the shower. A small light nearby turned green, and he was able to get hot water at once. Rigel hurried, since he didn't know what the water allocation for this zone would be. He was still surprised that beneath the miserable exterior the slums presented there could be infrastructure like this, and he wondered if all shacks had an underground level or if it was only a few select buildings.

It was a good thing he hurried, because he was barely done rinsing off the last of the shower gel from his hair when the water stopped. He dried off and went back into his room, still feeling grumpy but a lot better now that he was clean. He had not had time for a proper shower since the morning before all of this chaos had started. Thinking back on that day, it seemed a little bit unreal somehow. And yet here he was, in a clandestine underground hotel next to a criminal market he hadn't even known existed.

Without any money. Well, there was no helping it anymore. At least now they'd get what they needed to get to the Haven III site.

Rigel sat back down on the bed and yawned hugely. He hadn't gotten a proper night's sleep at all the previous night, and he was a little bit surprised he hadn't felt tired before this. He had probably been running on adrenaline, but now it was gone, and Rigel wanted nothing more than to go to sleep for a very long time. He slipped under the covers, punched a pillow into shape, and closed his eyes. He fell asleep instantly.

Rigel woke up after what felt like much later, with no idea what time it was. He felt groggy and incredibly well rested, and for a few seconds did nothing more than lie on the bed, eyes closed, motionless. He opened his eyes slowly, but since his room was underground, there was no way of telling if it was day or night. He yawned and stretched, seriously considering going back to sleep, when a sound reached him from the other room.

It was something he had never heard before, the sound of Steve laughing. It was followed closely by the laughter of a woman, and Rigel knew who it had to be. Then there came the faint sound of their hushed voices, as if they were speaking under their breath. Zoe laughed again, shrilly, and then there was noise made by a mattress creaking. Several times.

Rigel turned the other way in the bed, pressed the pillow over his head to block out the noise, and determinedly went back to sleep.

This time he dreamed. He was back at the university, attending a 3-D Rendering class in one of the big lecture halls. Misha was there, but she was telling him he had to pick up his things because the classroom was on fire. He kept on shaking his head, telling her it wasn't possible because Atlas was watching over them. When he next turned to look for Misha, both of Rigel's parents were waiting for him, and they told him she had taken the first airship out of Aurora and was never coming back.

He started running away then, certain somebody was about to catch him, and just when he thought the dark alley he was running through was getting too narrow for him to fit, Steve was yelling for him, telling him to come to a safe spot. Rigel followed his voice unhesitatingly and suddenly found himself in the big garden of his parents' home. There Rigel had spent most of his idle hours as a kid. He felt good in there, although he was all alone again. And then he looked at the sky and saw things falling. Enormous things, trailing infernal tails of fire and smoke.

Rigel woke up, opening his eyes in the darkness of his room. It was quiet, and this time Rigel was sure he had slept for several hours. He stood up slowly and went to the bathroom, checking the time on his way there. It was 9:13 a.m., which meant Rigel had spent the entire afternoon and all night sleeping. He had a slight headache, but the awful tiredness of the day before was gone.

Rigel freshened up and got dressed, taking his time. He was really hungry, but he wasn't sure if Streaker's arrangements for them included meals or if this place even served any food. When he was ready, he left his room and headed upstairs for the lobby intending to ask somebody where he could get something to eat. He didn't find anybody there, but a little bit of exploration of the surface floor allowed him to discover the dining room, which was empty except for two people.

Rigel's appetite fled, but they had already spotted him.

"Morning, Rigel!" Steve said, waving him over. "Come and have some breakfast!"

Rigel heard the brightness in his tone, so unlike his usual self. Rigel could guess why Steve was feeling so cheerful after last night, and the smile Rigel gave the pair as he approached was stiff and wooden.

"Good morning," Rigel said, grabbing a seat. There was bread and a big bowl of dried fruit at the table, some cereal and yogurt. A jug of juice and a steaming pot of coffee completed the ensemble. In spite of himself, Rigel's stomach gave a loud rumble at the sight of the food, which everyone heard.

Zoe laughed sweetly.

"I'm Zoe," she introduced herself unnecessarily. "It's nice to meet you, Rigel. Stevie told me all about you last night."

Rigel flinched at the endearment term, and it might have been his imagination, but Steve appeared to react the same way.

"Nice to meet you," Rigel said, meeting her eyes for the first time. She was pretty enough, with her olive skin and long black hair that fell neatly below her shoulders in what had to be ironed perfection. She wasn't wearing any makeup, but she did not need it. At first Rigel had assumed she was in her early twenties because of her youthful appearance, but now that he was seeing her close up, he realized she was probably closer to Steve's age than to his own. She looked fit, however. She obviously took good care of herself.

"Please, have anything you like," she told him, gesturing at the food. "All your expenses were arranged and paid for last night. I know it might not be much compared to a proper city hotel, but I made sure to have as much variety as we could manage for breakfast. Would you like some coffee?"

"Um, yeah," Rigel admitted, and Zoe poured him some before he could get it himself. "Thanks, Zoe."

She smiled. "No problem. Go on, help yourself to whatever you like. If you take too much longer, Stevie will leave nothing for you!"

She had a point. Steve was scarfing down food as if he were on a timer, and Rigel's stomach rumbled again. He grabbed some bread and yogurt and began eating too.

They said little while they were having breakfast, but both men were eating fast enough that most of the food was gone in less than fifteen minutes. Rigel had not realized how hungry he was until he had tasted the first mouthful, but afterward he grabbed fruit, cereal, and bread indiscriminately. When he finally felt satisfied, he sighed contentedly. It was good to be well fed, despite everything else going on. He also felt a little less short-tempered. Rigel poured himself the last of the juice and leaned back on his seat.

"That was great," Steve said, wiping his mouth with a big hand. "Thanks, Zoe. Especially on getting the fruit. How did you manage it?"

Zoe shrugged. "Oh, I just had to call in a favor. This guy I know heard that a fruit shipment had come via airship yesterday, but they hadn't delivered it yet. So I made sure to get some while it was still available."

"Is it difficult to get fruit in here?" Rigel asked her.

She nodded. "Have you seen any fields out in these parts? The only way we can get fresh produce is through shipments, when airships dock nearby. Some of the people who are better connected also have contracts with the hydroponics district in the city, but it's incredibly expensive. If you go to the fruits and vegetable section in the Night Market, you wouldn't believe what they charge for an apple."

"Wow," Rigel said. "Thanks, then. You must've gone through a lot of trouble to get all this."

"It's no big deal," Zoe answered. "I also wanted to get some meat, maybe bacon or some sausages, but I had no luck. I hope it was enough, though? I know you must be accustomed to much better things, living in the city and all."

"It was great," Rigel assured her, wondering why she kept mentioning that they came from the city.

"I'm glad. We almost never get city visitors here, and it's a wonderful change. Normally this hotel is for Corporation members only, and they are awful guests."

"Corporation?" Rigel asked.

Zoe looked suddenly uncomfortable. Steve answered for her. "The people who control the Market. Very rich, even by Auroran standards. They own most of the underground constructions out here in the slums."

"Anyway," Zoe cut in. "I'm so glad to have interesting people to talk to. Steve told me you are an artist, Rigel?"

"Yeah," Rigel admitted. "I went to arts school at the University of Aurora, almost majored in Fine Arts."

"That sounds amazing!" Zoe told him. At first Rigel thought she was being sarcastic, but her tone was too sincere. "Did you paint? Or were you a sculptor or maybe one of those artists that do modern pieces, the kind you can interact with?"

"I did painting, mostly. I started out with portraits, but little by little I moved more into landscapes. Very realistic at the beginning, but then I found some archives on ancient Impressionist masters, and I loved their work. I admire Cézanne in particular. I like the edginess of his landscapes, the sharp contours and the earthy palette he normally used, not excessively bright but each piece with a harmony all its own. It's amazing, the way he could portray the atmosphere in both little towns and in the wilderness when he would paint them. Somehow I find the paintings better than pictures of those same places much later."

Zoe was nodding slightly, her complete attention on him. "I've thought…. Well, I don't know this great artist you speak of, but once I managed to sneak into the Aurora Art Museum when they were having a free exhibition, and… I saw an entire room covered with paintings, more or less the same image but repeated at different times of the day and with different light. They were water lilies, all of them."

"Monet," Rigel said, remembering the exhibition. He had also visited it during his first semester at the university. The paintings were not originals, of course, but the reproductions had been made at an extremely high resolution and treated in Haven Prime to appear exactly as the true canvases would have looked. It remained one of the better temporary exhibitions hosted at the museum.

Zoe's eyes lit up. "Monet!" she exclaimed. "I had forgotten his name. I remember the paintings very well, though. I stayed in that room for a long time, just looking at them and imagining a world where one person could own a garden with a pond big enough to grow these water plants. I have never even seen a natural pond, or a lake, but looking at those paintings, I had an idea of how beautiful it would have been. It must have been a magical time, before all this. Water everywhere. Somehow, his paintings were like little windows into that world."

"I know exactly what you mean," Rigel said, smiling. He was warming up to Zoe even though he didn't want to. "When I could still paint, I would look at videos or images of the world as it was before and try to reproduce not only what I could see but what I imagined it must have felt to live then. It was hard, but I loved the challenge. Still do."

"When you could still paint?" Zoe echoed, a look of concern in her eyes. "What do you mean? You can't do it anymore?"

Rigel grinned sadly and lifted up his hands so the braces would be clearly visible. "I have a problem in both my wrists. Something having to do with the tendons and overuse, so I can't do very much with my hands anymore. Even holding a paintbrush is hard after a while. Not ideal when you've chosen to become a painter."

"I'm so sorry," she said, and placed one of her hands lightly on top of his. "It must've been very hard."

"A little, at the beginning," Rigel admitted. "Now I've mostly gotten used to it. Well, almost all of the time. There's still a few moments when I get really angry. Like when I grab a glass of water and my grip starts shaking so badly that I have to use both hands in order to drink without spilling water all over myself. Those little things. They can be pretty humiliating."

Zoe's hand was still touching his, and she was nodding sadly.

What's the matter with me? Rigel thought, surprised at his sudden confession, pouring out his thoughts in front of a complete stranger. It was worse than doing it with a therapist, something Rigel had always avoided because he could not accept that he was not in control of his own mind. And now here he was, complaining about his problem for all he was worth, and worst of all, he was doing it in front of Steve.

Rigel snatched his hand away from her grasp, resolving to keep his mouth shut from now on. He did not want them to think he was weak and whiny.

Thankfully, Steve chose that moment to clear his throat loudly.

"I'm also here, you know," he said. "Even if I don't know anything about art."

"Stevie, don't get jealous!" Zoe said teasingly. Rigel cringed again at her familiar tone. "I just wanted to get to know your friend. You know how it is in here. We live right next to the city people, but they almost never visit, and we never go there. Two different worlds. I've been here all my life. Not all of us can leave this place for good like you did."

Steve choked a little on the coffee he had been drinking. Rigel looked at him curiously.

"You lived here?" he asked Steve.

"Um…."

"That's how I met him," Zoe intervened, dragging her chair so she would be sitting a little bit closer to Steve. "We were both teenagers, stupid and terrified. It may not look like it from what you've seen, Rigel, but life in the slums is hard. I've got a steady job in here, but I'm one of the lucky ones. The Corporation pays me directly. It's not much, but I also get some things for free in the Market, or a discount, or maybe a hint of when the next airship is docking. My life is relatively easy now. But if you don't know anybody in here and you want to survive…."

"You do what you have to," Steve finished for her, fingering the melted key around his neck. Zoe nodded, her eyes suddenly far away.

"I had no idea," Rigel said.

"It's okay," Zoe told him gently. "I was luckier than most because I had Stevie. He helped out many times. He helped a bunch of us, really. We were a small gang, and he was the oldest. When he could, he made sure everybody at least had something to eat. He was always the best of us. I knew he would make it out of here, make a life for himself in the city. And he did."

She smiled fondly at Steve and gave him such a look of adoration Rigel looked away, feeling as if he was intruding on something private. He looked back just in time to catch Zoe giving Steve a kiss that might have been intended for his mouth but landed on his cheek instead. Steve, incredibly, was blushing.

"Well, it's been great meeting you," Rigel said abruptly. "I'm still a bit tired, and we got to wait here until we get the message from Streaker, so I guess I'll go and rest in my room."

"Bye, Rigel!" Zoe said happily, already resting her hand on Steve's shoulder. "I'll let you know when lunch is ready!"

Steve didn't say anything to him. Rigel thought he was probably too busy already.

He went downstairs quickly, almost knocking aside a surprised housekeeper who was just closing the door to his room. Rigel apologized and shut himself inside once again, lying down on the bed without even kicking off his shoes.

He knew he was probably behaving very stupidly. After all, he had never even considered Steve's past. Rigel had vaguely assumed that Steve had always been a security guard of one kind or another, just an average dude working in the city. A loner for most of his life. That was an idiotic fantasy he had created in his mind somehow, of course. It really shouldn't bother him that Steve knew other people who were obviously extremely friendly toward him. If anything, his admiration for the man should only grow now that Rigel knew Steve had started at the very bottom, a penniless teenager trying to survive in the slums. Rigel tried to imagine what it would have been like, but he really couldn't. His own childhood and adolescence had been fairly comfortable, and he was still trying to come to grips with this cutthroat subculture of need and poverty.

In a way, Zoe's revelation explained a lot about why Steve was such a tough guy. Rigel supposed that compared to having to fight for your food every day, running from a couple of assassins sent by an evil millionaire was not that big of a deal. Steve had always reacted calmly, thinking ahead. And then Rigel thought back on his own reactions during the chase, his near-constant panic and the way he had been—and still was—trying to make sense of the new, ruthless reality he was trapped in because of Atlas's machinations. He imagined that to Steve he must have appeared like a pampered city boy, terrified of anything that was not his predictable and comfortable routine.

Rigel wondered why Steve even bothered to stick around with him. The problem was not his, and Atlas had not given him a mission and ruined his life in the process. Now that he had found Zoe, who was not only indebted to him but who obviously liked him, Steve could very well make use of his contacts down here and disappear for a while until he could take an airship out of Aurora like he had said. Yes. That was probably what would happen. Rigel couldn't even blame him if that's what he did. Steve had already helped him a lot, more than any gratitude for saving him from that fire could justify. Rigel would have to go alone out on the desert once Streaker got him a vehicle to face whatever was sleeping in that old military compound.

Rigel took off his shoes and reached about for the TV remote until he found it. He turned the set on, volume nearly all the way up. He did not want to hear any more bits of excited conversation from the room next door.

Over the next couple of days, Rigel kept mostly to himself. He woke up very late each morning so he could eat breakfast once Zoe's shift had ended and another girl took over for her at reception. The tiny hotel did not have a gym or a game room or any of the amenities Rigel was used to seeing in the places he had stayed before, but it did have a big room with some large screens and comfortable chairs that was probably used for meetings. Steve and Zoe liked to talk in there when they were not walking outside or doing whatever, so the few times Rigel passed by the room while the two of them were inside, he quickly kept going. He ignored the way Steve tried to catch his eye at those times. Rigel did not want to hover over the pair like a third wheel, and so he switched his dinnertime as well so it did not coincide with theirs. The few times Rigel wandered outside, he made sure to go out when it was full daylight even though the heat was almost unbearable. That way he could be sure he would not run into anyone since the streets were mostly deserted. It also helped alleviate the horrible boredom that was now bordering on claustrophobia, being stuck inside his room underground with no windows for days on end.

He did run into Steve one evening, though. Steve was having dinner by himself in the hotel restaurant when Rigel came in. He tried to turn away, but Steve had already seen him.

"Hey, Rigel."

"Hey."

"Wanna join me?"

Rigel wasn't sure he should, but Zoe was nowhere in sight, and he was hungry. Besides, Steve looked amazing in a T-shirt with the sleeves torn off. Rigel guessed he had been working out recently, since every muscle in his arms was clearly outlined against his flawless skin.

"Sure, why not?" he said, trying to sound as casual as possible.

He walked over to the table and grabbed a seat next to Steve. There were mashed potatoes and what looked like grilled chicken breasts piled on a plate. Rigel grabbed some of each and poured himself some water. With Steve that close, though, he suddenly didn't feel as hungry.

"Haven't seen you around much," Steve commented, skewering one of the chicken breasts with his fork.

"Yeah, I guess," Rigel answered. He poked his mashed potatoes.

"It's just weird, since we are both stuck here and all."

"I suppose."

"You must be really bored. I know I am."

"Right."

Steve sighed and gave up on starting a conversation. Rigel ate a little. A few minutes later, however, he realized he was too uncomfortable. The silence was really awkward.

"Guess I'll see you around," Rigel said, standing up and abandoning his meal.

Steve looked a bit disappointed. "Yeah. I guess."

Rigel fled back to his room. He closed the door and took a few minutes to calm down. He wanted to stop obsessing over Steve, but he couldn't get himself to do it. It would be easier if the other man weren't so damn nice.

He needed to do something to distract his mind, so Rigel dragged a chair to sit by the dilapidated terminal that was bolted to the wall in the corner of his room, logged on to his cloud drive, and started browsing idly through old file folders. Most of the stuff was pictures from the university, a couple of videos he had shot on a trip with some friends when they had spent the night out in the desert, and even a folder with some really old e-mails from Rigel's first boyfriend. He skimmed through most of it, wondering what the guy in all the pictures would have thought if he could see Rigel as he was now, and the situation he was in. None of the folders were particularly interesting until he stumbled across one labeled Projects. He opened it and was surprised to see most of his design projects from art school. There were assignments, group work, and a few of the more professional concepts he had developed to be part of his portfolio.

Rigel opened each one and spent a long time looking at his character designs, at the evolution of his art skills, and his later experimentation with mixed digital media. At first most of his work had been forgettable—Rigel had always been good at drawing ever since he was a kid, but he had never really challenged himself until he had started at the university and decided to become an artist for real. There, he had met people who were just as talented as he and even more so. It had motivated him to try new things and come up with ideas that were all his own. In his last couple of semesters, right before he had started having problems with his hands, the few things he had created showed promise. But then he had gotten worse, and he'd had to give it up.

"They are beautiful," Steve said behind him.

Rigel jumped, startled, kicked his chair back, and nearly fell down when he tripped himself with one of the legs of the terminal desk.

"What the hell?" he exclaimed.

"Sorry, the door wasn't locked. Didn't mean to scare you."

Rigel turned around and saw that Steve was standing just inside the open doorway, one of his hands still resting on the door handle. He looked apologetic.

"I just wanted to see if you wanted to check out this bar I know nearby. Sorry again. Didn't mean to intrude."

"It's okay," Rigel heard himself say. Normally he would have been furious that somebody had come into his room like that, but this time it was the furthest thing from his mind.

Steve nodded jerkily, and his gaze strayed over to the computer monitor. "Are those your designs? The art you used to do?"

"Um, yeah."

"That one right there. It's amazing."

Rigel looked back at his screen. It was showing a painting he had done several months ago, a view of Aurora as seen from the Skytrain. However, instead of the usual arid desert environment, Rigel had decided to paint Aurora as it would look if it were a city in the middle of a lush tropical rainforest. Towering trees were interspersed among the familiar skyline. The sky overhead was not cloudless and glaringly blue as usual but covered by heavy gray clouds that looked about to burst into torrential rain. The line of the Skytrain itself was overhung by thick green vines that grew in wild tangles among the steel and glass. A couple of exotic birds could be seen flying out in the distance.

"There's a lot going on in there," Steve said, walking boldly into the room until he was standing right behind Rigel's chair. "I like it. I would like to live in a place like that. It's what could be, right? Like an alternate reality of some kind for this city, if the desert weren't here."

"Yes," Rigel answered, pleasantly surprised. "That's why I painted this, I think. I wanted to see what it would be like if things were different."

Steve nodded thoughtfully. "It works. The city would be… beautiful."

"Thanks."

"You're really talented, you know? Not just this piece. I was standing there for a while, and I saw a lot of the others. Bet you would have been a great artist."

"Thanks," Rigel repeated.

"Is the problem in your hands really that bad? Bad enough that you can't create things like this anymore?"

"Yes. That bad."

Rigel looked away from Steve so he wouldn't see the upwelling of bitterness that must have been reflected in his eyes. He'd had all his hopes set on becoming a professional artist. He had even made some contacts, planned out exhibits to showcase his work, and started to become known in the artistic world. He had started to create his definitive portfolio when he had been forced to give it up. The effort of years went down the drain because his body couldn't keep up with his mind. It had felt like a betrayal, like a cruel irony. He'd had fate first instill in him the desire to create things with his hands, to have the gift of doing so even, only for it to be taken away just as he had learned it was the thing he liked to do most in the world.

He didn't say any of this to Steve, though. But he did elaborate.

"It became too painful, simple as that. I already told you some of it, but I'm always in some degree of pain. It gets worse if I use my hands for a long time. I've learned to pay attention to what I do. To calculate the risk of hurting myself in every single daily activity. Painting is out of the question."

"There's got to be something you can do. Some way to fight back."

Rigel swiveled around in his chair so he was looking at Steve. "I've tried. There is software that lets me control computers without my hands, but it's not the same, and particularly for art. It takes me forever just to get an outline done, and then the coloring and shading is a nightmare. I've tested all kinds of weird peripherals, but nothing works as well as it should."

Steve crossed his hands over his chest, alternating between looking at Rigel and at the painting. "What about doctors? Can't they treat it?"

Rigel held up his hands, showing the bionic braces again. "This is the most they can do. There's no cure for what I have, no way to make it better other than resting. I've tried that, but I seem to be getting worse no matter how little I do. And I've got to use my hands some time. You do hundreds of things with your hands throughout the course of a single day, and most you don't notice. There's no reason to if you're strong and healthy, but you should try going for a single day without using them for anything, and you'll see what I mean. It's maddening and damn near impossible to be limited like me. It makes you feel like a cripple, which I suppose I am. And so my days are mostly dictated by what causes me pain and what I can do to avoid it. Even though I know it's a losing battle in the end."

Steve was silent for a few seconds. Then he inched closer to Rigel and put his hand on his shoulder.

"I'm sorry," he said.

Rigel shivered slightly at the touch. Steve's face showed genuine compassion.

"So am I. But I'm not letting it win. There's lots of things I can still do, lots of ways to create art other than painting. Before all this happened, I was already looking at alternate media and interactive technology. There are some really cool new trends over at Haven Prime, using cutting-edge software to create art that changes all the time depending on the viewer. If I can, I'll start studying how to do that. If it doesn't work, I'll look at other options. I won't let this condition ruin my future."

Steve looked at him solemnly and then nodded once. A half grin lit up his face.

"You're one tough guy, you know that?"

Rigel blushed. He couldn't help but notice that Steve's hand was still on his shoulder.

"Hey," Steve continued. "Care to show me some more of those paintings?"

"Um… okay, sure."

They spent nearly three hours looking at Rigel's old work. Steve had lots of questions, and although it was evident that he had seldom been to a museum, he was quick in identifying hidden meanings in the pieces and providing his own interpretation for several of them. It had been a long time since Rigel had shown his work to anyone, and it was nice. He started feeling better than he had for days. At some point Steve dragged a chair so he was sitting next to him, and Rigel was intensely aware of the other man's closeness. It felt right to have him there.

When the paintings ran out, they talked about Steve. He shared many things he knew about the slums, and Rigel listened, fascinated, amazed at how difficult it was to survive in a place like this. His respect for Steve grew, and once again he felt that thing, that connection, something he had never experienced with another person before. He wished the evening would never end.

Eventually, though, Steve yawned.

"Well, look at the time," he said. "I've been here bothering you for hours."

"It's been fun," Rigel answered. "I can't remember the last time I met someone as interesting as you."

Damn. He'd said that out loud.

But Steve only smiled. "Hey. Same here."

A brief silence followed, but it felt companionable. Rigel met Steve's eyes, and Steve didn't look away. The moment was suddenly intense, charged with tension. Rigel's heart started beating faster when he realized the other man was leaning closer to him. As if he wanted to kiss.

Then Steve stood up abruptly.

"I'll see you tomorrow," he said, somewhat awkwardly. "Got to…. Um…."

He fled. Rigel saw him leave and wondered what had just happened.

The next day was boring and uneventful for the most part. Rigel was feeling a bit cheerier, and he actually talked to Zoe for a while just before her shift ended. She turned out to be a very friendly girl, eager to learn about the latest events in Aurora. The second Steve showed up, however, all her attention was directed to him, and Rigel excused himself to go to his room.

He played solitaire on the computer until his hands hurt, and then he had to spend nearly half an hour massaging his wrists like one of his many useless physiotherapists had told him to. Then for lack of anything else to do, he went to the bathroom to take a shower.

There he saw that he had run out of shower tokens. Rigel swore under his breath and considered going to reception to ask for another one. He stepped out into the hallway, but then he saw Steve's door was ajar.

Well, it was an excuse. And he did feel like talking to Steve again.

He knocked.

"Come in!"

"Hi, Steve. I was wondering if you had any—"

Rigel stopped halfway into the room. Steve was doing incline push-ups, his feet resting on his bed and his hands on the floor. He was only wearing a pair of boxers.

"Uh…," Rigel stammered.

"Rigel?" Steve panted. "Gimme a sec."

Rigel stood there, hand on the door, watching the ripple of clearly defined muscles along Steve's back as he worked out. He looked like an anatomy textbook illustration, or like a guy about to go to a bodybuilding contest. The outline of each muscle showed under his skin as he went up and down, up and down, the movement smooth and controlled. His eyes were fixed on a point right in front of him, and his breathing was fast but regular.

It was maybe a full minute before he stopped. Then Steve pushed himself all the way up with ease and sat on his bed, grabbing a towel that lay nearby. His chest was heaving, but he smiled at Rigel.

"What's up?" he asked.

Rigel's mind was suddenly blank.

"I… um.…"

Steve raised an eyebrow.

Rigel could have kicked himself. A few awkward seconds dragged on. *Say something!*

"You're working out!" Rigel blurted.

He cringed. He was probably looking extremely idiotic right about now.

Steve was still smiling, though. "Yeah. Well, sort of. You can't really call it working out if it's just calisthenics."

"Uh, yeah."

"Come on in, man. Don't just stand there."

"Right." Rigel closed the door behind him and then sat down on the chair next to Steve's computer terminal.

He looked around the room. It was a bit messy, but it smelled nice. The TV was on, but it was muted. In the far corner, Steve had arranged a couple of chairs back-to-back and separated them a few steps. A metal rod was resting between them.

"What's that?" Rigel asked.

"That's my extremely improvised rig to do some pull-ups."

"Huh?"

"Yeah, like this."

Steve walked to where the chairs were. He grabbed the rod between them and then bent his knees, lifting his feet off the ground and holding himself in place with the strength of his hands alone. Then slowly, he pulled his body up until his chest was above the rod. He followed it by lowering himself gradually until his knees were about to touch the ground.

"Oh, I get it," Rigel said.

Steve stood up. "Like I mentioned, it's just a few light exercises. These people don't have a gym anywhere."

"Do you normally work out every day?"

"Most days, yeah," Steve said, picking up a big jug of water that was full to the brim, sealed with its cap. He sat on the edge of the bed and began doing biceps curls with it as if it weighed nothing. "It's more competitive than that, though. You have to alternate body parts each day, and the intensity varies based on whether I am bulking up or just shedding extra fat. I also have to do cardio, even though I hate it. And then there's the diet."

"Sounds like a lot of work."

"Yeah, but I like it. It's worth it, you know? If I work hard, I can see the results of my efforts."

"I can see them too," Rigel said without thinking. Then he shut his mouth, horrified that he had spoken out loud.

What's wrong with me?

But Steve merely nodded. "You want to try it out? I know a few good exercises for beginners. I could teach you."

"Can't. Hands."

"Oh, that's right. Sorry."

"It's okay. The only exercise I do is run on the treadmill, and only because Misha makes me when she's feeling fat—"

Rigel stopped talking suddenly, remembering Misha. He had refused to think about her in days, maybe deliberately. Now he was forced to remember her as he had last seen her. Rigel hadn't stayed for the ambulance, so he didn't know if she was really dead…. But something told him she was. Her eyes had been so—empty.

"Rigel?" Steve asked softly.

"Sorry. It's just that my friend…."

He shut his eyes to block out the image. He wasn't successful.

"Hey," Steve said, and suddenly his hand was on Rigel's shoulder. "You want to talk about it?"

Rigel opened his eyes and looked up at Steve's face. He looked genuinely concerned, his skin flushed from the exercise. The room's light glinted off the close-cropped goatee that outlined his chin.

"I don't think I can, not yet," Rigel said quietly. "I still can't believe it."

"Fair enough. Want me to turn the volume up on the TV? We can watch it, if you don't mind me exercising while we do. It would be nice to have some company for a while."

Rigel smiled weakly. He had been dreading going back alone to his room. "Yeah. That sounds good."

Steve hit a button on the remote and immediately the voice of a broadcaster came from the speakers. Rigel recognized him. He was the anchor for Current Aurora, the afternoon news show.

Steve switched the jug of water to his other hand and kept on doing biceps curls while sitting nearby. Rigel looked up at the screen, determined to distract himself with anything.

The anchor was speaking about CradleCorp, however.

"—is still not known. The main suspect in the bombing, Aaron Blake, has been reported missing, and efforts to track him down have so far been unsuccessful."

"Want me to switch the channel?" Steve grunted.

"No. I want to know what they're saying about me."

"The impact in Aurora from the sudden halt of all activity in CradleCorp cannot be understated. All of the city's biggest company's activities have been brought to a stop while rebuilding efforts begin. The Mayor himself has pledged full support for Richard Tanner in this endeavor, and several crowdsourcing initiatives have already taken shape in order to expedite the process. Anyone wishing to contribute to the latter can log in to the website shown below to make a donation or call our Viewer Hotline to find out about other ways in which they can help."

There was a slight pause while the anchor swiveled in his seat to look at another camera. Behind him, images of the smoking CradleCorp building were shown nonstop.

"Cleanup continues on-site at CradleCorp, but full damage assessment is expected a week from now at the earliest. Three people remain unaccounted for from the fire that ravaged the building four days ago, and search crews remain adamantly optimistic that these three CradleCorp employees will be found among the rubble.

"This tragedy has affected people from all walks of life, far beyond the horror of such a devastating terrorist attack. We go now to our on-site correspondent Alicia Jimenez for a series of exclusive interviews with some of those most deeply affected by these events. Alicia?"

Steve put the water jug down and started doing sit-ups on the floor, angling his body so he would still be able to look at the TV. Rigel saw that he was paying attention to the broadcast now, same as he.

The interviews started. A slim, black-haired reporter had put together a series of segments filmed with lots of different people, deliberately edited for maximum emotional impact. Rigel found himself being forced to consider what it really meant for Otherlife to have suddenly disappeared from the market without any explanation.

As the anchor had said, people from all sectors of society had been affected. Rigel saw maybe a dozen lengthy interviews carried out with a wide variety of citizens, some of whom were inconsolable at the destruction of Otherlife. It was more than a cheap escape from reality, nearly all of them said. It was another world, a better world. Rigel saw a man in his forties moaning over the fact that he had spent nearly twenty years of his life customizing not only his avatar but his own private hub within the virtual reality, where he had become the administrator of a large community of like-minded fantasy enthusiasts. They had created a detailed open-ended world, complete with lore and a complex system of rules that guided their various adventures and quests. The man being interviewed had even quit his day job after the hub he administered had exceeded ten thousand users, becoming something of a local celebrity in the fantasy circle and making a comfortable living from donations alone. Now, he said, his entire life's work had been obliterated in a single night. He had no job, no source of income anymore. He did not know what to do.

There was also a behavioral scientist who was distraught over the fact that one of the most valuable sources of empirical research data for his department had been wiped out with no warning. A paraplegic woman was still in shock at having lost the one thing that had made her condition bearable, escaping into a place where her avatar was capable of doing the things she could not do in the real world anymore. A teenager broke down crying when she confessed that she had met the perfect man in Otherlife, and they had been about to meet face-to-face, but now she would never know who it was since they had never exchanged private information aside from their user IDs. She displayed her username prominently and begged her mystery man to contact her. The director of a subsidiary of CradleCorp who organized customized virtual experiences through Otherlife spent nearly ten minutes detailing how much money his company had lost in reservation fees and user subscriptions. An economic analyst began sweating when he attempted to explain the repercussions such a monumental upset in the biggest company in the city would have throughout the entire economy of Aurora.

And the list went on. By the time the segment was over, Steve had stopped exercising altogether. He went to sit next to Rigel, and they watched the rest of the news.

The official explanation of the entire incident, as corroborated by Richard Tanner himself in a hasty voice-only interview, was that it had been a terrorist attack by a disgruntled youth. Rigel had been sort of expecting it, but he was still surprised when he saw his own picture in the news along with the tagline: *Extremely dangerous. Notify the police immediately if sighted.* It was obvious that reporters had grabbed on to Rigel's scapegoat potential gleefully, digging up every bit of dirt on him they could find. They interviewed former colleagues, some of his friends from the university, and even the staff of the hospital where he had gone to treat his gunshot wound just days ago. They strongly suggested he had been directly responsible for what had happened to his flatmate, Misha, and they even managed to give a sinister turn to the tragic accident that had killed both of Rigel's parents. They briefly touched on Steve Barrow as a probable accomplice, but for some reason, they did not emphasize his role half as much as they did Rigel's.

"Those fucking bastards," Steve growled after a particularly vicious assessment of Rigel as a psychotic killer. "This is wrong. They're lying!"

"I can't believe it," Rigel said quietly.

Steve turned to look at him. "They have no definite proof, Rigel. They're just making it seem like you're the bad guy because it's the easiest way to explain it. I'll bet you anything that Richard Tanner is behind this. He's probably bribed half of those 'experts' we just heard so he has someone to blame."

"But everyone believes it."

Steve nodded. Rigel could see that he was angry. "I know. We'll get the truth out, though. Tanner can't lie forever."

"But how?"

Steve didn't have an answer to that, and on TV the merciless barrage of accusations continued.

Nobody doubted that Rigel had set off a bomb in CradleCorp. Public outrage at Rigel's perceived destruction of the lifeline of the city was already in full swing. Video was shown of demonstrations, vigilante campaigns, and even a petition, swiftly granted, to revoke his Auroran citizenship, effectively making him a homeless refugee.

"That's bullshit!" Steve exploded.

Rigel couldn't even think of something to say. With that simple act, he had been stripped of everything his parents had left him. He supposed he could appeal the ruling, but what lawyer would take his case?

It was official now. He had nowhere to go.

By the time night had fallen, he had heard he was a monster so often and in so many different ways he was starting to doubt himself. It was awful. He was the most wanted man in the city.

"I can't believe it," Steve said at last. He turned the TV off with disgust. "This is not right. Are you okay, Rigel?"

He shrugged. It was all too much.

"There's nothing I can do," Rigel said.

Steve grimaced. Then he spoke in what Rigel thought was a deliberately cheerful tone. "Hey. Don't let them get you down. Maybe Atlas can help you, once you bring it back online. The part of the machine that sleeps in the desert is supposed to be even more powerful than the original, right? Maybe it can access the true records of what happened and make them public. Exonerate you."

"Yeah. Maybe."

"And at least you're not in the city anymore. Here in the slums, nobody cares about the law, so we've got that going for us. And… well, it may not count for much, but I'm here."

Rigel looked at Steve sitting so close nearby and felt a surge of emotion.

"Thanks, Steve. But you don't have to stay with me. If they see that you're helping me, it's going to be even worse for you."

"Right. As if Tanner was going to let me walk free if they ever catch me. They didn't talk about me that much, but I'll bet you anything that before long the entire city is going to be looking for both of us. I'm also tied up in this mess, same as you. Besides, I promised I'd help."

Rigel smiled, but the crushing feeling of hopelessness was still there. His entire life was gone, and now it was official. If this thing with Atlas didn't work out… he didn't even want to know.

They were quiet for a bit while Rigel was lost in his own thoughts. Suddenly, though, Steve broke the silence.

"Hey, I got an idea. Something to take your mind off all of this."

"Huh?"

"Remember that bar I told you about the other day? We should go there. You need to forget your troubles for a little bit."

That actually sounded good. Rigel could use the distraction.

"Okay," he said. "Let's go."

Steve grinned. "Let me go change. I'll call Zoe. She made me promise to bring her along."

"Sure," Rigel answered, although he was not too thrilled about that.

A few minutes later, Steve and Rigel were standing outside the hotel, all ready to go. Zoe came right on time.

"Hey, guys!" she said brightly. She shook Rigel's hand in greeting but kissed and hugged Steve.

Rigel couldn't suppress the flash of annoyance he felt.

They set off, but they hadn't gone more than a few blocks when a boy came dashing toward them, nearly colliding with Rigel in his haste.

"I'm looking for Steve," the kid panted, eyes darting between the two men. People milled about them on the street.

"That's me."

"I got a message. From Streaker."

"So?" Steve said. "Spit it out."

The kid thrust out his hand, palm up. "Pay first. Two dollars."

Rigel watched as Steve merely looked at the kid, staring him down. Not saying anything.

"Okay, one dollar," the kid said after the silence had become uncomfortable. Zoe snickered.

"Bert, you better tell us the message, or I'm telling your mother," she told the kid.

Steve grinned and reached into his pocket. He pulled out a bill and gave it to the boy. "Here. Even though I know Streaker already paid you. What's the message?"

The boy scrunched up his face for a second as if remembering at the same time that he stuffed the bill in his pocket. "He said…. Meet me at Jared's refinery warehouse tonight. After eleven. He's got your package."

"Was that all he said?"

"Yes, sir."

"Good. Thanks."

The boy nodded once, then turned around and dashed away. Steve looked at them.

"We still got some time before eleven."

"Plenty of time to have a couple of drinks!" Zoe said enthusiastically.

"Fine," Steve said." Rigel, you in?"

"Uh, sure."

"Great. Let's go."

The bar turned out to be a very popular karaoke place that was almost full when they got there, despite the early hour. They managed to find an empty table and sat down after ordering their drinks. Zoe was charming and funny, and after half an hour in there, Rigel sincerely regretted that Steve had invited her along. The two of them were basically ignoring him at this point, reminiscing about some anecdote or another from when they were younger.

Rigel finished his drink somewhat angrily. He liked Zoe, but he couldn't help feeling jealous. For maybe the millionth time, he wondered if the thing he had felt starting between Steve and himself had only been in his imagination. Rigel liked Steve, but he had only known him a few days. Maybe Steve didn't even like guys. He was sitting very close to Zoe, after all. And she kept tossing her hair around, laughing at everything he said. Rigel knew full-on flirting when he saw it. Misha had excelled at it.

After an eternal two hours had gone by, Rigel had had enough of listening to increasingly bad singers at the karaoke. He had contributed maybe a couple of words to the entire evening's conversation, mostly just nodding along when Steve remembered he was also sitting there. Rigel sipped the last of his beer and then simply stood up.

"Heading outside," he said to the other two. He got a vague nod in return.

With a sigh, Rigel stepped out onto the street. He checked the time and found it was almost eleven. Time to head out and meet Streaker.

He would not go back in to get the other two, however, and it took Zoe and Steve almost twenty minutes to come out of the bar.

"Rigel!" Steve said, smiling. "Where were you?"

Rigel pointed at the time. "We got to go, or we'll be late," he snapped.

"Oh. Right. Zoe, I guess I'll see you later."

"What?" she protested. "No way. I'm coming along."

"But…," Steve began.

"No buts. I know the way. Come on!"

"Fine," Steve said. "Just let me go back to the hotel to pick up my things."

"Yeah. Great," Rigel added, rolling his eyes when they couldn't see him. "Let's all go."

Chapter Twenty-Three

Barrow went quickly back into his room to get the few things he had left there. Once again, he bemoaned the loss of his little bag of supplements and synthetic steroid injections. He was not in the middle of a cycle at the moment, but the loss of the bag meant he would have to reschedule his entire recovery calendar, and there was nothing he could do about it. Well, maybe it was good for him. Easier on his kidneys. Besides, he did find that going off the stuff improved his mood after a few days. Other guys said they felt no difference, but Barrow did feel the change. He was less aggressive and didn't get into quite as many fights. It also improved his libido, which was always nice. The only thing he didn't like about the whole situation was that he hadn't gotten the chance to work out properly in a week. The hotel had no gym, and Barrow had been forced to improvise with the things in his room. Doing push-ups and sit-ups with no additional weight was still exercise, but to Barrow it counted more as cardio than anything else.

He put on the rest of his freshly laundered clothes and grinned briefly. He had a slight buzz from the bar, but he was also glad to be finally about to do something. He was going out with Rigel to get their vehicle, and then they would head out into the desert to awaken Atlas. Maybe they would even have to face that awful shadow thing that had come for him at night, in his apartment. But they wouldn't be stuck waiting anymore. Still grinning, Barrow got the gun from the nightstand and stuffed it under his belt.

There was a knock on his door, and Zoe came in.

"Hey, Zoe," Barrow said. "You sure you want to come with us?"

She tossed her hair a little to the side. "I don't mind. It's not that far away. You're finally getting that deal you were waiting for?"

"Yeah, finally. Streaker must have got our, um, thing waiting in Jared's warehouse. It's over at the refinery sector, I think. Shouldn't be too hard to find."

"You've never been there before?" Zoe asked him.

"No, not that I remember, but it's been so many years. Maybe I have been there, only now it's called something else. Like our old hangout. I still can't believe they turned it into an electronics recycling center."

"Stevie, that's Corporation territory where you're going. Jared is the manager of a big shipping company that operates out of some warehouses in the refinery sector. You say Streaker got you the contact?"

"Yeah, according to him, his brother-in-law works with the kind of stuff we needed. Oswald, I think he said the brother is called."

"I know him. He's married to Alyssa."

"Good. That's reassuring. Now I probably need to get going."

Zoe looked as if she were debating with herself for a second, and stepped between Barrow and the door just as he was about to open it.

"You could just send someone else to get it. This thing. Or have Jared deliver it right here so you don't have to go to the warehouse. I could also go alone, if you want. You know I'm trustworthy."

"There's no need to do that, Zoe. You've already helped us enough, and I really don't want you getting mixed up in this more than you have to. You've seen the news. The entire city of Aurora is ready to lynch Rigel if they so much as catch a glimpse of him because of what Tanner is saying that he did. If you are seen helping us, it could turn ugly for you pretty quickly."

"But you are helping him." She couldn't quite keep the resentment from her tone.

"Yeah, I am. I—"

"Why?" she blurted. "You could stay here or over at my place. I told you it's safe. You got friends here. There's Alice and Graham and Alejandro from our old group, and they all want to see you again. You can hide out until it's done, blown over…."

"We already talked about this, Zoe," Barrow said calmly. "Rigel saved my life. He took me out of that fire in CradleCorp when he could have easily just saved himself. And besides, I…."

"You what?"

But Barrow only shook his head. "Nothing."

Zoe stared hard at him, giving Barrow the same look of fierce determination that had so often been in her face when they had been younger, weaker, and scared. "Fine, Stevie. But I am showing you the way. It's the least I can do."

"You don't have to do that."

"Yes, I do. I would have starved ten times over if you hadn't been with us, Stevie, and I don't forget that. Neither do the others, and we will help you in a heartbeat, anytime. All you got to do is ask. Don't forget that, okay?"

"I won't. Thanks, Zoe."

She stood on tiptoe to kiss him. It was aimed for his lips, but Barrow turned his head to the side so it landed on his cheek instead. The touch of Zoe's lips was featherlight.

Zoe sighed and stepped back, smiling sadly. "I guess it's time I gave up on you. He's a lucky guy, this Rigel. I saw how you were looking at him in the bar."

"What do you mean?" Barrow said, but he blushed.

"Clueless as always. Or pretending to be. Come on, Stevie. Let's go."

Rigel was already waiting for them at the entrance. Barrow thought the days of rest had been good for him in particular. Rigel had lost the haggard, haunted look about him that the near-constant stress and running away had given him. Even though he was wearing the same rumpled clothes he had been wearing all week, they were clean, and Rigel somehow managed to look good in them, as if he were heading out to a fancy dinner. The one thing that looked out of place on him was an unwavering scowl, which deepened when he learned Zoe had insisted on coming with them.

They left the hotel and stepped into the balmy twilight of the evening. The streets were already busy with people coming and going, most of them headed in the direction of the Market. Small swarms of flying insects flitted about the naked lightbulbs hanging from the entrances to the shacks that lined the alley. The smells of cooking food were everywhere, and as they walked to the refinery sector, Barrow found himself relaxing. He had been out, walking around each night, often enough for people to have gotten used to the sight of him in a radius of a few blocks. He did not stand out as an outsider anymore, and now that he was walking with Zoe, a few people even gave him friendly nods as they passed. It reminded Barrow of why he had been able to call the slums home during the years he had been here. They were a dangerous place, often ruthless and cruel, but there was also a very strong sense of community and of loyalty to those who were in the same situation as you. Aside from the arrogant Corporation agents and those who worked for them, everybody in here had fallen on hard times in one way or another. The shared poverty did not engender generosity, but it did give someone a sense of belonging.

Rigel was also with them, however, and despite his best efforts to blend in, it was still painfully obvious that he was from outside. It was more than the way he kept looking around everywhere, jumpy, as if he expected someone to come out of every corner with a gun aimed right at him. The marks of having lived a privileged life in the city were all over him, from the way he spoke to the way he conducted himself. Added to that was the frostiness with which he met Zoe's attempts at conversation, and as they left the Market neighborhood, the walk became increasingly uncomfortable.

It took them almost an hour to walk to the refinery sector. It was on the outskirts of the slums, an area of large warehouses, clandestine factories, and wide-open areas of compacted earth that served as everything from illegal airship docks to open-air laboratories. The unforgiving desert was easily accessible from there, something that was good or bad depending on a person's point of view. For the many shady chemical companies that operated in here, it was an easy way to escape the strict environmental regulations of the city while keeping up with the ever-rising demands of urban life. For the inhabitants of the slums, it was a source of employment, albeit a dangerous one. As they approached, Zoe told them that Graham worked there. Barrow remembered Graham from his days in the slums as a slightly chubby, awkward teenager. He told this to Zoe, speaking over Rigel's head as he refused to participate in the conversation.

"Not anymore," Zoe told him, her mouth set in a grim line. "He's been working in one of the Corporation refineries for almost ten years. Lost a lot of weight and can't get it back, no matter how much he eats. At first he used to joke about it. You remember how he was. He would tell us that it meant he would finally be skinny for life. But now… it's painful to look at him. He's nothing but skin and bones. I heard one of the guests back at the hotel one night as he was talking with a scientist or something like that. He was a manager in Graham's refinery, and he was saying that the members of his workforce were dying off too young. Blamed it on the chemicals to which they were exposed every day. But the way he talked about it—it's like he was complaining that his cattle weren't producing enough."

The fury in her tone was barely controlled. Barrow tried to replace the mental picture of his chubby teenage friend with an emaciated, frail man but couldn't.

"That's horrible," Rigel said, speaking up for the first time in a long while. "Don't the workers have rights? A union, maybe?"

Zoe chuckled. "Not in here, Rigel. If you want to eat, you do what you have to. You've only seen the really nice parts of the slums so far, the Night Market, the hotel, and so on. All those places are an exception to how things are here. Trust me, nobody lives here because they want to. If we could, I think every single one of us would go live in the city."

"Why don't you?" Rigel asked earnestly, his face intermittently visible as they walked beneath isolated lightbulbs along the large, empty refinery streets.

"It's not that easy," Zoe answered. "Sure, you can get inside without much trouble, but if you are not a registered Auroran citizen, you simply can't get a job. Or rent a place to stay. They check for the birth implant, and there's no way of faking that.

"Without a job you're reduced to begging, and the cops spot you right away. Then they toss you back here, and you are worse off, because you are seen as a kind of deserter. As if you thought that you were better than all of us, and that's why you decided to leave."

Barrow saw Rigel nod thoughtfully. "I met a little girl a few days ago at Green Park. Couldn't be older than twelve. She was with her little brother, and they had this enormous suitcase with them. They were from here, obviously. I wonder what happened to them."

"Sometimes it's easier for children to manage to stay in Aurora for good, if they are adopted by a citizen. I wouldn't bet on it, though. It's not very common and there are…. There are bad people who prey on children from the slums. They know they are helpless and vulnerable. Sometimes you see them on the news when the police catch them. The things they have done to some of those kids are sickening."

"But there must be a way around the system," Rigel insisted, looking at Barrow. "After all, Steve managed to find a job."

Zoe shook her head sadly. "Stevie is an Auroran citizen. He just ended up in the slums after some hard times, but he was born in the city." Rigel gave Barrow a curious look but, thankfully, decided not to ask any more questions.

Barrow grabbed his melted key pendant briefly and walked on. Zoe knew the story of the fire because she had wheedled it out of him after years of insistence, but besides her and the little gang of friends he used to hang out with here in the slums, Barrow had not told that part of his story to anyone. He had a feeling he might tell Rigel if he asked, but not right then. Maybe not for a long time.

"Zoe," Barrow said instead, "I think that over there is Jared's warehouse."

He pointed across a rectangular empty lot to a cluster of two single-story buildings with no windows. They were set in an L shape, blocking off two of the sides of the rectangle. The third side was flanked by the street they had been walking, and the last side led out into the open desert. The empty lot was lit by two lonely lampposts that gave out a feeble yellow glow against the dark desert night. Beyond them, light shone in one of the buildings through its open main access gate. It was barely possible to make out a battered sign above the gate spelling out Jared's name.

"Yes, this is it," Zoe confirmed. "That over there is the warehouse, and the other building is the refinery."

"Let's go, then," Barrow said, looking at Rigel, who nodded. "Zoe, thanks for everything. I'll keep in touch."

She shook her head. "I'll go with you, at least until your deal is done. I know lots of people here, Stevie. I'll know if they are trying to scam you."

Barrow debated with himself briefly, but this past week he had come to know Zoe well enough to know she could still take care of herself. And besides, she could actually prove helpful, so he finally nodded and headed off across the lot. The other two followed.

It was eerily quiet as they made their way to the beckoning lights of the open building. Out here in the open, away from the narrow winding alleys and the crush of people going about their business, the desert night was cold. There was a slight wind, which ruffled Barrow's hair, whistling ominously. Barrow felt around under his belt until he found the reassuring touch of warm metal next to his skin. Having a gun made him feel a bit safer, more in control of the situation. He had no doubt that Streaker would show up with the goods, but the probability that he would try to double-cross them was very high. He had already been paid, after all. Streaker might decide to simply keep all that money without giving them anything in return.

Well, they had come too far already, and this was their only shot. Nothing to do but follow through.

As they got nearer, Barrow saw three men moving about inside the place, talking and passing the time. It looked like the warehouse was really a repair shop of some kind, as there were lots of vehicles in various states of disrepair inside and a pile of scattered auto parts by the heavy gate. There was an off-roader in there as well, old and battered from the looks of it but polished and shiny, giving off reflections of the bright lights in the warehouse's interior. That was good. At least they had procured the merchandise as per the agreement.

They were halfway there when the three men walked out onto the lot to meet them. Barrow did not hurry and merely nodded when Rigel got closer to whisper, "Bodyguard," indicating they should continue the charade of Rigel being a rich guy from the city.

The two groups met a few paces outside the repair shop, with light spilling over all of them. Streaker was there, along with two guys he did not know. There didn't appear to be anyone else.

"Streaker," Barrow said, coming forward and shaking the junkie's hand. "Good to see you kept your end of the deal."

"Course I did, Barrow," Streaker answered, scratching his nose with a long and filthy fingernail. "I said I would, didn't I? Took me a while to get the engine, though. These things are almost antiques now, very hard to come by."

"And it's ready?" Barrow asked.

"Yes, sir," the man standing next to Streaker answered. He was thin and balding, with a rough edge to his voice. "The vehicle's been fully charged, and the backup fuel engine also had a refill. Should be good to drive you pretty far out. The charge alone will last you four to five hours, more if you drive around during the day."

"This is Oswald, Barrow," Streaker explained, gesturing at the man who had just spoken. "My brother-in-law. Told you about him before, didn't I? And this gentleman over here is Jared. He's an old friend of mine. Agreed to let us use his shop for the little exchange."

Barrow shook both their hands. "This is Rigel, my employer," he introduced in turn. "And you probably know Zoe from the Market Hotel."

"Of course," Jared said, speaking up with a surprisingly deep voice. "How have you been, Zoe?"

He said it politely enough, but the look he gave her was enough to make Barrow's skin crawl. Zoe edged in closer to him.

"Please, follow me," Jared told them all. "Rigel, sir, I hope you will find the vehicle we have procured adequate for your needs. I myself helped Oswald with the fuel recharge, and I had some of my crew go over the more complex repairs. As you can see, I have lots of spare parts in here."

"I thought you were in the refinery business," Rigel said, looking around curiously as he went inside the repair shop.

Barrow imitated him. It was larger than it looked from the outside, with a big open space in front where the off-roader was and a veritable maze of vehicle parts, unfinished repair jobs, and mysterious crates filling up the back with narrow walking spaces in between them. Barrow scanned the area with a practiced eye, but nothing seemed amiss. And the off-roader itself was better than he had hoped it would be. It looked like it would be able to take them out to the desert and back without breaking apart.

"This is it," Jared announced, stopping beside the vehicle. "I got it from a couple of archaeologists that had fallen on hard times and decided to sell. Full Auroran license and plates, so you won't be stopped at the military checkpoints on the perimeter when you leave the city. The suspension is not the best, but a quick trip should present no problem. From what Streaker tells me, you were planning on making a single trip and back, correct?"

"That's right," Rigel said, walking all around the car slowly and making a big show of looking at everything. Barrow thought he was overdoing it a bit, but Jared seemed to buy it. Barrow did notice that both Oswald and Streaker were standing back now, fidgeting and nervous. They seemed to want nothing more than to get out of there as fast as possible, but the thought had barely occurred to Barrow when Jared took out a little remote and clicked it. The heavy gates that closed the entrance to the repair shop began to clang shut.

"For security," Jared explained in answer to the dirty look Barrow gave him. "It might look safe out there, but you never can be sure. I think your employer will feel safer behind closed doors. Don't you agree?"

Rigel had reached the hood of the vehicle and attempted to open it on his own. He lifted, grimaced in pain, and dropped it immediately.

"Barrow, open this for me," he said authoritatively to cover up the awkward incident.

"Of course," Barrow answered right away. He walked over there and lifted the hood. The engine seemed fine.

"Oswald, Streaker," Jared said, momentarily hidden by the lifted hood. "Why don't you go get us the papers to finalize the transaction? And take the lady with you. Offer her something to drink."

"What?" Streaker blurted. "Oh, right. Sure. This way, Miss."

"Okay, be right back, Steve," Zoe said after a brief hesitation. She left with the other two through a side door that led into some kind of office.

Rigel spent some more time examining the engine, and Barrow had no idea if he knew what he was doing or not.

Then there was a loud click, a barely repressed hiss of static.

And Barrow knew.

"Duck!" he yelled, yanking Rigel down with him to the floor.

Bang!

The gunshot was immediately followed by the loud sound of shattering glass somewhere to the right. Rigel and Barrow crashed to the floor at the same time another shot was fired, but there was no impact nearby. Barrow exchanged a look with Rigel, who was terrified and looking around wildly. He gestured for Rigel to take out his gun as he did the same.

"Don't do that," a raspy voice said from behind them. A voice Barrow recognized. A voice that had threatened him over the phone just a few days ago. "There's five of us, Barrow. We got both of you in our sights. Drop the guns, and then come up with your hands up. Now."

Rigel looked at Barrow for confirmation, and Barrow nodded grimly. Those two shots had been warnings, and they were probably surrounded. They would not be escaping this time. Barrow dropped his own gun and threw it out of reach. He saw Rigel doing the same, and then they both stood up slowly. From somewhere to the left, muffled yet still audible, came Zoe's shouts. Barrow hoped they would not mix her up in this and that they were merely holding her back.

"That's it. Now turn around and stay by the car," the same voice said.

There was nothing to do except obey. Barrow turned along with Rigel and saw two men with guns trained on them. They had somehow appeared from behind them, probably sneaking up when the metal gates to the shop had closed so loudly. One of the men was a stranger, but the one who had been talking was an old acquaintance. He was someone Barrow had hoped to never see again, his face now contorted in a mixture of gleeful anticipation and hatred that Barrow knew was completely justified.

"Hello, Matthew," Barrow said, careful to keep his own voice neutral. "Long time no see."

Matthew Young stopped on the floor and walked one step closer. He was clutching a gun in both his hands, and it was actually shaking a little bit from how angry he was. Barrow wondered how long he would wait until shooting him dead, or if he had other plans on how to take his revenge. He also saw Jared walking into view with a weapon in his hand. Barrow addressed him first.

"How much did he pay you, Jared?"

"I don't think that's any of your business, Barrow," Jared told him. "You may have gone out into the city and thought you had disappeared for good, but people in the slums have long memories. I knew there would be a price on your head as soon as Streaker came telling me you were back. My place was perfect. I even had a working off-roader ready to go, just to convince you to get in here without being too suspicious."

"What is going on in here?" Rigel asked, managing to look affronted. "What business do you have with my bodyguard?"

Jared and the third man exchanged a smirk. Then Jared nodded toward Matthew Young. "Why don't you ask him, rich guy?"

But Matthew ignored the exchange, focused only on Barrow.

"You ran away for long enough, Barrow," he said. "You may have escaped your punishment, but a murderer is always a murderer. And now I finally got you."

There was a long silence only broken by the muffled shouts coming from the office where Zoe was being held. The sounds ceased abruptly after a few seconds, though, and Barrow wondered whether Zoe was all right. There was nothing he could do, however. He was trapped, and he knew it.

"Your brother had it coming, Matthew," Barrow said, never taking his eyes off the gun the other man was holding. "He liked hurting people. Women, in particular. Women who were trapped with him in close quarters for weeks on end aboard an airship."

"You're a fucking liar. He flew hundreds of trips, never once had a complaint."

"You ever talked to Jill?" Barrow asked him.

"That lying bitch was in league with you to discredit him. Made everything up, tried to make you look like some sort of a hero…. I know everything, Barrow. At first they tried to play off Jonathan's death as a disappearance. Every damn member of the crew of the *Titania* was in on it, saying they didn't know what happened, getting the cops off the case. But then people kept asking questions, and Jill came forward with her stupid attempted-rape story, how *you* had to kill my brother to save her. She stuck to it, too, despite…. What did you do to make her cover for you so well, huh? Sleep with her? Fuck her over my brother's corpse?"

Barrow cracked a grin despite the situation. "That's not really my style."

Matthew just plowed along with his monologue. "You know who you hurt the most, Barrow? His family. I bet you didn't even think about that when you were bashing his head in. Didn't think about how he had two little girls and a wife to support back home. They were babies when you did it, didn't understand that their daddy was never, ever coming home. Now they're old enough to ask about him, and what can Claire tell them? Huh? You tell me!

"I've had to take care of them ever since then. The captain of the *Titania*, that sonofabitch Rueda, didn't even pay for the funeral. I've barely been able to keep the girls away from the clutches of the Corporation every year, but, of course, you don't care for any of that. Why should you? You're just a fucking murderer who ran away rather than face the consequences of his actions. But now I got you. And I'm not gonna kill you right away, Barrow. I'm going to enjoy this."

"Let Rigel go," Barrow said evenly. "And Zoe. They're not part of this."

Matthew's eyes twinkled. "I don't think so, Barrow. Haven't you been watching the news? That man there is Aaron fucking Blake, the most wanted man in the entire city. Jared and me, we worked out an agreement.

We're going to turn him in and divide the reward. We're even going to throw something in for Streaker for his troubles. After all, he did find you. Streaker! Oswald! Come on out!"

The door to the office opened, and both men came out. Oswald was pushing Zoe before him. They had stuffed a rag in her mouth to keep her from shouting, and Oswald was holding both her hands behind her back. She shot Barrow a look that was part terror, part defiance, and she kept struggling against Oswald's grip. He tightened it in response, making her cry out in pain.

"Leave her alone!" Rigel yelled, making as if to approach Zoe. The man standing next to Matthew fired his gun, a warning shot mere centimeters from Rigel's feet.

"Don't move, rich boy," he said. "The TV didn't say whether they wanted you alive or dead."

Rigel stopped, glared at the man, and then looked at Barrow as if for guidance, but Barrow had no idea what they were going to do. It had been stupid to come here, stupid not to recognize that every person with a TV would know who Rigel was and what they said he had done, even out here in the slums. No wonder Streaker had been so eager back in the Night Market to make sure they stayed put in the hotel until he could find the buyer who would pay the most for them. They had given him days to set this up.

Matthew gestured with his gun. "Enough talking. Barrow, Mr. Blake, get in the off-roader. Quickly. Jared, you get to keep the girl."

Jared grinned that creepy smile and approached the place where Oswald and Streaker were standing. He grabbed Zoe roughly, and Barrow balled his fists in anger.

"And my cut of the reward for Blake," Jared said.

"Of course," Matthew answered. "I'll send it with Streaker when we get it."

"Good deal."

Barrow noticed that Oswald and Streaker were looking around from Jared to Matthew eagerly, as if they wanted to say something but couldn't bring themselves to do it. Then Streaker jumped slightly, unnoticed by any of the others. He took a mobile out of his pocket, exchanged a look with Oswald, and both of them began to edge backward slowly. They exchanged a slightly alarmed look, but Barrow wasn't sure what it meant.

"Move!" Matthew ordered, approaching the vehicle. Rigel obeyed reluctantly, followed by Barrow. They climbed onto the back of the off-roader followed closely by Matthew's gunman.

"Don't worry, Barrow," the gunman said as he climbed into the driver's seat, his gun still trained on them. He started the car one-handed with a cocky grin. "I have a safe house nearby where nobody is going to hear you scream. And when Matthew is done with you—"

But at that point Barrow saw both Oswald and Streaker dive out of the way, throwing themselves to the ground.

And then the snipers opened fire.

The gunman's head exploded in a shower of sickeningly warm blood and bits of bone. Barrow didn't have time to react. He heard Zoe screaming, more gunfire, and suddenly the off-roader jerked forward hard, throwing both Rigel and him back in their seats. The vehicle accelerated with a screeching of tires and launched itself directly toward the heavy metal gates barring the way out. Somebody shouted. Then the car crashed.

They hadn't been going very fast, so the impact did nothing but throw Barrow forward onto the back of the driver's seat. The car stopped accelerating. Barrow recovered quickly, making himself small to present less of a target to whoever was shooting.

"What's happening?" Rigel shouted, imitating him.

"Stay down!" Barrow ordered.

The gun was in the front. Barrow risked getting up, hunched over and moving as fast as he could. He reached over the seat and yanked the gun out of the dead man's hand. He caught a glimpse of the corpse's leg twitching, slightly to the right of the accelerator pedal.

A man appeared on the side of the vehicle pointing a gun at them. He was dressed all in black, and Barrow had seen him before.

"The CradleCorp assassins!" Rigel yelled.

Barrow spun around, cocked the gun, and fired. It caught the man in the middle of the chest, but the assassin must have been wearing some kind of body armor because he merely stumbled backward. Barrow was aiming for a headshot when a loud explosion on the other side of the vehicle forced him to duck. When he recovered, the assassin was gone.

Barrow felt a rush of sudden heat and turned around, banging his knee in the cramped space of the car. His eyes widened when he saw the explosion had been an incendiary bomb. Flames were licking the side of the off-roader, feeding off several knocked-over crates full of oily car parts.

"We got to get out of here!" he yelled, and Rigel nodded, speechless.

Barrow was closest to the fire-free side, and he half jumped, half tumbled out of the car. He hit the concrete hard, banging the same knee again and sending sparks of pain shooting up his leg. He rolled out of the way immediately, ignoring it. He took shelter behind the side of the car, gun in hand, and poked his head out.

It was madness. He saw at least two snipers overhead, rifles pointing and shooting at anything that moved through broken windows in the upper level of the repair shop. The closest one had long dark hair, and Barrow recognized her right away. It was Diana Herrera, the woman who had been chasing Rigel through half of Aurora. There was a third shooter hidden behind a stack of crates piled against the wall on the far right, the man Barrow had shot unsuccessfully. Opposite him, barricaded behind more crates, Jared and Matthew were shooting back at the snipers even as they were forced to retreat by the advance of the fire from the bomb. Barrow looked underneath the off-roader and saw Oswald's body crumpled next to where the bomb had hit. One of his legs was on fire, and he wasn't moving. Zoe and Streaker were nowhere to be seen.

He took the entire scene in immediately and took cover again behind the off-roader. He felt Rigel bump next to him, breathing heavily but staying put.

"They're here for you," Barrow told him in a low whisper, unnecessary because everybody knew where they were. "Tanner must want you really badly. They won't shoot you if you stay where you are."

He made as if to move away from cover, but Rigel grabbed his arm. "Where are you going?"

Barrow yanked his arm away. "I have to get Zoe. It's my fault she's in here."

"Tell me what to do. I can help you."

"Stay where you are."

"But—"

Barrow shoved him roughly out of the way.

"Stay safe, Rigel. Okay?"

He had no time to lose. He waited for a lull in the gunfire and then dashed straight in the direction where the first CradleCorp assassin was hiding while simultaneously getting as far away from the flames as he could. The assassin must have seen him coming, but he was forced to stay in his position by a barrage of gunfire coming from the barricade where Jared and Matthew were hiding. Even so, he wheeled about and brought his gun to bear on Barrow.

Too late. Barrow aimed and fired, catching the man in his unprotected right leg. The shot messed up his aim, and he cried out in pain—Barrow launched himself at him, tackling him to the ground. They wrestled briefly, both of them fueled by adrenaline, and it only ended when Barrow drove his knee right into the place where the bullet had hit the other man. His resistance immediately slackened enough for Barrow to grab the man's head with both his hands and slam it down on the concrete floor. Then he did it again, harder, and this time there was a crack. The assassin's body went limp. Barrow grabbed his gun.

A funny sound. Barrow looked up just in time to dodge a small cylinder one of the snipers up on top had tossed his way. He shot out of cover, barreling down one of the narrow pathways that lined the back of the repair shop and had barely taken five steps when there was another explosion behind him and a sudden burst of light. And more flames.

His ears popped, and he was deaf for an instant. Somebody was shooting at him, and Barrow did not know if it was the CradleCorp killers or Matthew trying to get him before he could escape. He dodged, crouching, weaving his way around the maze of car parts and keeping his head as low as possible. He shot behind him once, but it was immediately answered by one of the snipers shooting so close to him that a metal plate next to Barrow's head jumped up under the impact, clattering down to the floor with a neat bullet hole in it.

Barrow stopped. The shot had been too perfect. If he hadn't been hit, then it meant CradleCorp wanted him alive just like they wanted Rigel. He did not know whether that made him feel better or worse.

He dashed around the corner of a pile of cabinets holding various spare parts and kept going, hoping to find better cover.

And ran into Streaker.

"Don't shoot!" he screamed hysterically at the sight of Barrow. "For the love of God, don't shoot me!"

Streaker stumbled backward, hands spread out before him. He hit the wall behind him and banged his head on a shelf. Hiding next to him was—

"Stevie!" Zoe yelled. "You're okay!"

Barrow nodded and crouched next to the pair. He gave one of his guns to Zoe. "Here. Use it on him if he tries anything."

Zoe grabbed it after a small hesitation and trained it on Streaker.

"I'm on your side!" Streaker protested. Another, smaller explosion made him squeal. "The lady saved my life! She pulled me here—"

"Shut up!" Barrow said loudly over the sound of more gunfire. Somebody groaned, probably hit. In the confusion Barrow could not tell who it had been. He tried to assess the situation, but he couldn't make out where anyone was anymore. The snipers had switched positions, and the barricade where Matthew and Jared had been was now engulfed in flames.

"What do we do?" Zoe asked him, her wide eyes reflecting the bright orange light of the fire that kept on growing, devouring everything in its path. Barrow tried not to look at it, tried to ignore the way the air was getting hotter in the enclosed environment. He stood up too far and inhaled a lungful of smoke. He dropped back to his knees, coughing.

"We need to get out of here," Barrow said. "If we stay any longer, we're all going to be dead."

"But how?" Zoe said. "There's only one exit!"

"There's fuel here, man," Streaker added, terrified. "A couple of big tanks. If the fire gets to them…. Oh God. Take me out of here. Take me out of here, please!"

The smoke was getting thicker, the flames belching it out in expanding black clouds. Some of it was escaping through the windows, but they were set too high up for Barrow to reach. They would not be getting out that way. That left only one option.

"Streaker," Barrow demanded. "Where is the open switch? The thing that opened the gate?"

"In… inside the office, but—but it's on fire!"

He was right. Barrow looked the way he had come, and everything had gone up in flames. Somewhere somebody was still shooting. And Rigel was nowhere to be seen.

Barrow tried to ignore the pang of pain he felt when he realized Rigel could have been trapped in the fire, but he couldn't.

Not again was all he could think, forcing himself to approach the wall of flames, the memories of another fire crowding his mind. *Please, not again.*

Barrow led the way down a different pathway, eyes darting everywhere, but not really paying attention because he was having a hard time moving forward into the approaching fire.

His distraction nearly cost him his life.

Matthew Young jumped out of a pile of debris, clutching his gun wildly.

"You damned fucker!" he yelled at Barrow. There was blood running freely down his forehead. "Called your killer friends, didn't you? But you're dead!"

There was a sudden jolt as the metal gates began to open with a horrible creaking and grinding sound. The rush of fresh air was like dumping fuel into the fire: it bloomed upward ferociously and forced everybody to take cover. Matthew didn't give up, though. He stood up immediately afterward and fired. The shot barely missed Barrow, and Matthew was aiming again—

The off-roader came out of nowhere. It plowed into Matthew, knocking him aside. Part of its roof was on fire.

"Steve! Get in!" Rigel shouted from inside.

Barrow didn't need to be told twice. He grabbed Zoe's hand and sprinted for the vehicle. He made it to the front seat, Zoe got in the back, and Streaker barely managed to grab on to the doorframe before Rigel floored the accelerator and shot forward into the fire.

"Look out!" Barrow yelled, crossing both his arms over his head and leaning forward as the off-roader reached the half-open gate. The metal bent outward, and the off-roader shuddered. Something was torn apart with a loud screech, and there was the sudden unbearable heat of the flames. Barrow flashed back to the cramped tunnel of his nightmares, to digging desperately trying to reach the screams of his family even as he knew he was too late.

Then the heat was gone, the furious light turned to darkness, and the vehicle made several sharp turns at full speed, twice nearly flipping over under its own inertia.

Barrow looked up. Rigel was driving like a madman through one of the wider alleys that led out of the slums. Barrow looked behind, confirming that Zoe was there along with a haggard but alive Streaker.

"Fence!" Rigel shouted, and Barrow whipped his head around just in time to see the off-roader leaving the dirt road and crashing at full speed against a flimsy metal fence that separated somebody's property from the open desert. Rigel hit the brakes a second before the impact, but the car went clear through the fence as if it were nothing and then skidded for several meters.

Then it stopped.

In the silence that followed, the only sounds were the heavy breathing of four people in the off-roader. Slowly, as if not believing their luck, all four of them got out of the car and gathered around the pool of brightness cast by the headlights. Barrow looked at Rigel, who was covered in blood and smudged by ash. Barrow's concern must have shown in his face.

"The blood isn't mine," Rigel explained, his voice slightly shaky. "It's Jared's. And… sorry it took so long. I had to open the gate, and then that awful Herrera woman came out of nowhere and—"

Barrow walked right up to him, pulled Rigel in close with both hands, and kissed him.

Rigel stiffened in surprise, but then melted in his arms. Barrow felt Rigel's breath on his face, the way he was suddenly returning his embrace with surprising strength. Barrow lifted him off his feet for a few seconds, then put him back down gently. They broke the kiss and looked into each other's eyes, and Barrow tried to put a lot of things into that look. The fear he'd felt at almost losing him. The sudden realization that he felt something for Rigel, something that had been growing throughout all these days. His admiration at Rigel's resourcefulness and bravery. He wanted to say something, but when he opened his mouth, nothing came out. Rigel seemed to understand, though. He smiled, and Barrow's heart skipped a beat at the warmth in that look.

"You saved us," Zoe said, approaching with a smile on her face. "Thank you, Rigel."

Barrow let Rigel go and finally found his voice. "She's right. That's twice now you've saved my life."

Rigel looked like he was blushing, although it was hard to tell under the grime that covered his face. "It was nothing."

"It was not nothing," Zoe protested. "If it hadn't been for you…. God, I don't know what would have happened. Who were those people?"

"They're with CradleCorp," Rigel explained. "They were after me because of what they say I did."

"But you didn't," Zoe said. "They're setting you up."

"It's complicated," Rigel said, "but essentially, yeah. I didn't make Atlas explode. I didn't even want for Otherlife to go offline like it has."

"Those bastards!" Zoe exclaimed.

"You believe me?"

"Of course I do! And this off-roader you wanted…."

"There's somewhere we have to go," Barrow intervened, keeping an eye on Streaker, who was standing nearby looking at the ground. At least he wasn't trying to escape. "There's a place out in the desert. It has something to do with what's happening at CradleCorp, but we can't tell you any more than that."

Zoe nodded slowly, obviously thinking. "I think I can help you cover up your tracks."

"What do you mean?" Rigel asked her.

"Nobody knows whether you came out of that alive," she said, gesturing back at the faintly visible flames coming from the repair shop. "If somebody comes and asks, and I'm sure they will, I will just tell them that you died inside. It will throw them off your trail until they can sort through whatever's left in there, and it will give you some time. I even have Streaker here as a second witness. Right, Streaker?"

Streaker jumped, looked at everybody quickly, and then back at the ground. "Of course, ma'am. I'll say that they died."

Barrow wasn't convinced. "Can we trust you, Streaker?"

Streaker looked at him, then at Zoe, and finally at Rigel. He seemed to be trying to come to a decision, and Barrow was about to suggest they tie Streaker up someplace where he couldn't possibly cause trouble, when Streaker did something unexpected.

He took something off that had been hanging from a chain around his neck, hidden underneath his shirt. It was black and glossy.

"Here," he said gruffly, holding the data card with the inheritance money out to Rigel. "And… thanks. For not leaving me back there even though it was me who called those CradleCorp people on you. Me and Oswald. We tried to double-cross Jared and Matthew, and you see how *that* went. Sorry. If anyone asks, you're dead."

Rigel took the data card, nodding. "Thank you, Streaker. I appreciate that."

"Not as much as I appreciate being alive," Streaker said, which made them all grin.

"We should get going," Barrow said, looking at the time. "We can use the darkness to get out of the security perimeter and closer to the Haven III site before the sun comes up."

"Right. Let's go," Rigel agreed.

"Is it dangerous, where you're going?" Zoe asked, concerned.

Rigel shrugged. "Probably."

"And this thing you're doing… is it worth it?"

Rigel and Barrow exchanged a look.

"I sincerely hope so," Rigel said, getting in the car.

Chapter Twenty-Four

Steve drove in silence at first, with the headlights turned off and going slowly through the outskirts of the desert perimeter. Rigel did not speak, although he wanted to. He stayed quiet partly because it was obvious that Steve was dedicating his entire attention to staying on the road, but mostly because he did not really know what to say. The last few hours had been crazy, even more so than usual, and Rigel still couldn't believe they had made it out of the fire in one piece. All the others had thanked Rigel for saving them as if it had been his plan all along, but the truth was he had been lucky and nothing more. Lucky that none of the bullets in the shootout had reached him. That he had stumbled onto the control mechanism for the door release, that he had found a discarded gun just lying there, barely out of the reach of the flames.

Lucky that Jared had been looking the other way, never even seeing Rigel until it was too late....

Rigel shut his eyes to block out the memory, then opened them again and tried to look at the rocky desert instead. The off-roader jumped and buckled slightly in the uneven terrain, but Barrow kept it on the right track and headed northwest, where the Haven III site was located. Rigel looked up at the starry sky, so much brighter out here than in the city, and forced himself to think about something else. There were plenty of things to choose from.

At least Steve and he were now physically clean. Streaker had known a guy that ran an illegal sweatshop nearby, and there they had washed off most of the grime and changed into new clothes. Zoe had raided the supply cabinets and found some food and water for them to take on the trip. They had done everything as quickly as possible, and then they had to say good-bye, with Streaker looking glad to be rid of them and Zoe genuinely sad to see them go. Funnily enough, Rigel had gotten the distinct impression she had become his friend as well. Maybe she always had been, given the fact that she had never sold him out to the highest bidder during the days when they had stayed at the hotel. Maybe Rigel had been jealous about nothing, imagining things that had never happened because he had been too busy feeling resentful of the old friendship between Zoe and Steve to see anything else.

And then, of course, there was the kiss. The one good thing to come out of all of this, something Rigel still couldn't believe had actually happened. He looked over at Steve, all but invisible in the dark gloom of the starlit night, his features illuminated faintly from below by the luminous displays of the car console. He was frowning, serious and concentrating, no doubt worrying about what would happen if one of the perimeter patrols found them before they were out of reach in the desert wastelands. To Rigel he looked strong, confident, with a rugged determination about him that Rigel couldn't help but admire. His hands gripped the wheel with an easy strength Rigel found incredible to look at, the muscles of his forearms clearly shaded in the electric glow, his wide shoulders straining at the seams of the shirt Streaker had given him and which was at least a couple of sizes too small for his frame. Looking at him, Rigel wondered what it must be like to have strong hands that could lift whatever he wanted, instruments of power that allowed you not only to shape the world around you but also your own body. He did not feel jealousy, though. Only wonder and happiness. He was certain now—there was something between them, a connection he had never experienced with another person before.

Unless he was reading too much into that one kiss. What if it had not meant anything to Steve? What if it had just been a thank-you kiss or something different altogether? What if the attraction Rigel felt for him was not reciprocated at all?

He was doing it again, overthinking everything, feeling the insidious touch of insecurity.

Steve kept on driving carefully, ignoring Rigel, and eventually the silence was not companionable anymore but awkward, tense. Rigel watched as they skirted around the northern quarter of the city, dodging the main paths that the military vehicles would use from time to time. Once they stopped entirely to let a small mechanized scout go past, and Steve only started the car when the noise of the scout had died off in the distance. He kept on driving slowly, carefully, his eyes flicking to the displays on the console every few seconds to look at numbers and graphs that the onboard computer displayed, which Rigel could make no sense of. The drive was getting more uncomfortable. It was cold out in the open, and the off-roader had no proper roof. Rigel shivered involuntarily, wondering how it could be this cold when the city was always hot and often unbearably so.

They eventually reached a path that was far narrower than any of the others they had been using and which led away from the city, as opposed to around it. Steve took it unhesitatingly, and at once his posture relaxed.

He then put his right hand on Rigel's leg and left it there, still gripping the wheel with the other. He kept his eyes on the road, his face impassive when Rigel looked at him in surprise.

Rigel tried to say something, but again he didn't know what. He was thrilled. The warmth of Steve's hand was real and reassuring, but aside from that one move, Steve had not said anything or acknowledged Rigel in any way. They went on like that for a few seconds, until Rigel shifted slightly in his seat, and Steve looked at him probably out of reflex more than anything. Their eyes met, and Steve made as if to take his hand away. In his eyes, Rigel saw he was....

Nervous?

Rigel understood in a flash of insight. The long, awkward silence. Steve had not been ignoring him—he had been too nervous to talk. And now he wasn't sure that his move had been right. The look he gave Rigel was apologetic and, unbelievably, a tad insecure.

That was all the confirmation Rigel needed. He grabbed Steve's hand with his own before he could lift it away. He smiled, and the slow smile Steve gave him in return was heartbreakingly sweet. They did not say anything, but Steve gave his hand a little squeeze before he turned his attention back to the road. And suddenly the silence they shared wasn't awkward anymore. It was the best kind of silence Rigel had shared with anyone in a long time.

They drove on through the gloom, and eventually Rigel looked back the way they had come. Past the glow of the city, he could begin to make out the faint gray light of dawn creeping up from the east. He settled back into his seat, giving a silent thanks that they had made it out without being caught. From here on out, they were unlikely to run into anyone. Aside from archaeologists who made the trip once or twice a year, not many people ventured this far out of the city by land.

They veered off from the path a few minutes later, and Steve stopped the car. As the motor died down, Rigel realized the night was completely silent. It was weird, not hearing any kind of background noise like you would always have in the city. Peaceful, in a way. The sky overhead seemed bigger, like nature was all around him.

"We're close now," Steve said. "I don't want to go any farther in the dark, though. I found where the Haven III site is supposed to be in this onboard map, but I have never come this way by land. The climb up to the mesa can be tricky for big vehicles like this one. If we wait for the sun to come out, we stand a much better chance of reaching the place quickly without falling down or getting lost along the way."

"Okay. It's only a little while until morning anyway."

"Yeah. And I don't know about you, but I could sure use a couple hours' sleep."

"I agree," Rigel said. "We've been awake all night, and it's been one of the worst of my life. Well. Also one of the best."

Steve smiled. Rigel felt something flutter in his stomach and hoped it didn't show on his face.

"For me too," Steve answered. "It's been both."

The silence of the dying night settled over them again. Rigel wanted to say so many things that he didn't know where to begin. He also wanted to get closer to Steve, but the partition between the seats made it awkward, and so he stayed where he was.

"I'm sorry about before," he decided to say finally. Better start with the truth.

"What do you mean?" Steve asked him, pushing his seat back all the way so he could stretch his legs.

"Earlier tonight. The way I acted with Zoe."

"I wondered about that. I didn't want to disturb you, though. I figured you were just thoughtful at the bar. I mean, I've lost my home once before, so I know what it's like. But for you it was the first time, and you have it much worse than I ever did. I thought you needed some time to think things through."

"Well, part of it was that," Rigel admitted. He didn't want to say the next bit, but he made himself say it anyway. "The truth was that I was jealous."

Steve crossed his hands behind his head, leaning back on his seat. "Jealous? Of what?"

"Of... Zoe."

Steve gave him a blank stare. "Huh?"

"I had no idea you knew her from before, not at first. And you guys talked for hours that first night and spent all the time together afterwards... I assumed...."

"What?" Steve asked, and Rigel wondered if he could really be that clueless.

"Steve, you spent the night together with that woman. In your room."

Steve blinked and was silent for a heartbeat. Then he burst out laughing.

It was an easy, booming laugh, and it was the first time Rigel had heard it without a wall in the way. He tried to protest over it, but Steve was laughing too loudly for it to do any good.

"You thought...." Steve gasped. "You thought that I...."

His laughter was contagious, and Rigel found himself laughing along, breaking the tension that his little confession had created in his mind. It was a strange and wonderful thing to see the normally fearsome and stoic Steve become a much younger man when he had tears of laughter streaming down his face. Maybe it was all the events of the day, but as Rigel laughed, he felt a lot of the stress of his situation slipping away from his shoulders, not exactly forgotten but no longer so foreboding and oppressive. It felt good to feel happy again, and even better to be sharing the feeling with someone else.

"Oh man," Steve said finally, the final chuckles dying down. "Sorry about that, Rigel. Didn't mean to make fun of you or anything."

Rigel smiled. "It's okay."

"Zoe is like a sister to me," Steve explained. "Well, at least she used to be. I left the slums a very long time ago, and I was really happy to see her, that's all. We talked a lot about what we had done in these years, remembered some of the old times, that kind of thing."

"How did you—no, never mind," Rigel said. He had wanted to ask him about his past, but he stopped his curiosity just in time.

Steve looked at him. "You want to know how I ended up in the slums in the first place?"

"Um, no, I didn't—"

"It's okay," Steve told him. "It's not a story I tell everyone, but you are not just anyone."

"If you don't want to talk about it...."

"It's fine. There's not much to tell, really. I was born in Aurora like you, had a pretty normal childhood. When I was fourteen years old, there was a fire in the apartment building where my family lived. Almost one hundred people in the upper floors died. It was a big tragedy at the time."

"The Jameson Street fire?" Rigel asked, eyes wide.

Steve nodded grimly.

"I've read about it," Rigel said. "Well, they told us about it in school. They say it was some kind of problem with the electronics in the building because of a heat wave. There was an explosion, too, I think. It's in the history books and everything."

"Yeah," Steve agreed and looked away to stare into the night. His expression grew somber, troubled. "But it was much worse than that. The thing that failed was the electronic building access mechanism. It had been badly designed, and when the fire started, all the outside exits locked shut, even those leading out into fire escapes. People couldn't get out until somebody thought to call for an override, and some tenants didn't even know the fire was even happening until it had gotten out of control. It started at night when people were already asleep. I was… I was right on the roof of the building, hanging out with a guy. I remember my phone kept buzzing, but I ignored it at first. I liked the guy, you see. I wanted to make a good impression, and everything else could wait."

Steve grimaced as if disgusted with himself. Then he shook his head slightly and continued.

"Eventually the buzzing stopped, but then I smelled something burning. I saw the smoke coming out of the windows below us. I took my phone and saw the many missed calls from my father, who was at work on the other end of the city. He had heard about the fire first, and he was frantic. I quickly called my mother, who was inside the building with my sister, but there was no answer. I tried to get back inside—I couldn't. There was only one door that gave access down into the building, and it was locked. A crowd of people was gathering below, and I heard the sirens approaching. I began to panic and looked for another way down, but the highest fire escape ladder was one story below, and it meant dropping from the roof. I don't even remember what the other guy did, but I do remember dropping down and landing safely, just to get a lungful of black smoke coming from one of the broken windows. I raced down and got to the ground, looked for my mother or my sister. They weren't there. I didn't see anyone from our floor.

"Then I got a text. It was from my mother, saying that the doors wouldn't open. I didn't even think. I started going back up the emergency ladder before the firefighters could stop me. I was maybe one story below them when all the emergency exits finally opened, and everybody began pouring down the fire escape. I got lost in the crowd, fighting my way up, and at one point I almost fell over the railing because somebody pushed me. I made it to my floor and went inside, coughing from the smoke and heat that was coming from everywhere. I couldn't see the fire, and I could barely make out the doorways under the emergency lighting. I tried to get to our apartment, but when I was halfway there I saw the hallway had collapsed. I couldn't go any farther."

Steve paused again, closed his eyes, and took a long breath. He held it, then released it slowly. Rigel's mouth was hanging slightly open, and he was horrified because he suspected how Steve's story would end. He didn't dare speak but waited until Steve was ready to go on.

"I tried to find another way past the blockage, and I ended up in a big ventilation duct. I crawled forward feeling the heat all around me, my phone buzzing in my pocket nonstop. Then things got oddly quiet for a little while, and I was terrified but kept going until I ran into a section of the duct that was also blocked by whatever had collapsed onto that part of the building. There was a gap through which I wanted to squeeze, but it wasn't big enough. I pushed against a broken concrete slab, but I couldn't move it. I kept at it for almost a minute, and all I did was get stuck, unable to move, unable to back out even.

"Then I heard them. Barely and from far off, but their voices carried oddly inside the ventilation duct. They were calling for help, Rigel. I was meters away, and I couldn't reach them. I couldn't move the slab that was blocking me. I wasn't… I wasn't strong enough…."

He fell silent for much longer this time. Rigel had never heard anything so horrible, and he didn't know what to say. He wanted to reach out to Steve, but his expression was so angry and sad at the same time that it made him look scary. Rigel saw him close his hands into fists and tighten them, the carefully defined muscles in his arms bunching up under the effort. He looked like he wanted to hit something, probably himself. It took him several deep breaths to calm down enough for Rigel to risk putting his hand over his.

"The rescue workers found me and pulled me out before it was too late. They say I was lucky, that the blockage was actually preventing the worst of the smoke from reaching the place where I had gotten stuck. They carried me down, and I was conscious all through the rest of the rescue efforts. They eventually brought my mother and my sister down, but…. They took them to the hospital. They died on the way there from the smoke. I was in the ambulance when…."

But he couldn't continue. He choked up, and Rigel reacted instinctively, reaching out to him across the seats in an awkward hug. Steve returned it without hesitation, holding him as tightly as if he was afraid to fall off the world with Rigel as his only anchor. He didn't cry, but he held Rigel for a very long time. Rigel returned the hug as best as he could, horrified at the thought that Steve had been carrying the blame of his family's death all these years. He wanted to tell him it had not been his fault, but Steve probably knew that already and yet, from the way he had spoken about the incident, still refused to believe that there had been nothing he could have done. Rigel could not even imagine what it would be like to live with that kind of a tragedy constantly weighing him down.

Eventually Steve calmed down enough that Rigel let go and settled back on his own seat. Steve looked slightly embarrassed and refused to meet Rigel's eyes. He spoke to the windshield instead.

"My father couldn't handle it. He killed himself after the funeral and left me with nothing since most of our things had burned down with our home. All I recovered from the fire was this key to our front door: half-melted, blackened, a reminder of what happened.

"I ended up in the slums then, homeless. I almost starved a couple of times. Then I met Zoe and the others. I was sent to prison for a stupid mistake. Eventually, though, I got back on my feet and returned to Aurora. When I got my first job aboard an airship I left for good, rising through the ranks and eventually working aboard the *Titania*. I would still be working there if it weren't for that scumbag Jonathan."

"The man you killed," Rigel said, speaking up at last.

"Yeah. He was a beast, but that doesn't make what I did right. I had to leave my job, and I always wondered when his family would come seeking revenge. You saw what happened back at the repair shop. I put us all in danger. I'm sorry."

"I've also killed a man," Rigel confessed in a small voice.

Steve focused properly on him for the first time. "What? When?"

"I shot Jared. He didn't see me at first, and I knew he would kill me, so I fired first." Now it was Rigel's turn to shut his eyes for a second, to try to block the image of the dead man from his mind. "I keep seeing his face, Steve. If I hadn't done it, I would've died. But I still feel awful."

"I know how you feel," Steve said to him. "You did what you had to, Rigel. I know this won't help, but I'm glad you did it. If you hadn't we would've all died in that fire, not just you."

Rigel nodded and sighed. They sat in silence for a little while, each lost in his own thoughts. Rigel began to feel the weight of the day's exertions again, and he started to drift off. He had almost fallen asleep when he felt Steve's hand over his own. Rigel opened his eyes and looked at him.

"Thanks," Steve said softly.

"For what?"

Steve only shrugged and smiled.

"I don't know what we're going to find where we are going tomorrow," Rigel told him, "but I'm glad you're with me, Steve."

Steve gave his hand a reassuring squeeze. Then Rigel closed his eyes and was almost immediately asleep.

Chapter Twenty-Five

RICHARD TANNER had a headache, and the bumpy ride wasn't making it any better.

"No, Delegate," he said, speaking calmly into the commset in front of him. The screen showed him the stern face of the special envoy from Haven Prime, who had arrived yesterday to assess the damage the sudden collapse of Otherlife had initiated. The Mayor of Aurora was sitting next to the Delegate meekly, saying nothing, as if he hoped keeping silent would mean all the blame would fall squarely on Tanner's shoulders. With an inward sigh, Tanner continued. "While you are correct when you state that at present all of CradleCorp's commercial functions have been brought to an indefinite halt, let me assure you that repairs are already underway, and I am confident we can bring Otherlife online within the month if everything goes according to plan."

The Delegate regarded him coolly, and Tanner was suddenly grateful he was outside being driven to the CradleCorp offices, instead of trapped in a room with that man. It was more than the eyes, which were always disturbing in a Prime. Tanner had already spoken with the Delegate twice since his arrival, and he had gotten the unsettling yet distinct impression that the man knew far more than it was possible for him to know.

As if to confirm his worst fears right then, the Delegate spoke.

"Will these repairs you speak of be carried out with or without the help of the artificial intelligence, Tanner?"

The Delegate knew about Atlas.

Tanner swallowed and discreetly hit the scramble button on his mobile control peripheral. It was bad enough for the Mayor to be hearing this. Tanner did not want anyone else snooping in on the unsecured channel.

"I believe you mean our automated coordination system," he told the Delegate evasively. "While the damage in our main servers was extensive, we had, of course, procured several backups of the most critical subsystems in our mainframe servers, and my technicians and engineers are reintegrating them as we speak."

The Mayor looked relieved to hear that, but the Delegate remained impassive. He let the silence on the line drag on until it became borderline threatening. Then he addressed Tanner again. "Is that so? In that case, allow me only to reiterate the importance of restoring service to all of Aurora as swiftly and efficiently as possible. I know you are not an economist, Tanner, but as the most influential businessman in your city, you can surely understand the enormous impact that this catastrophe has had on the local business community."

"Of course, Delegate," Tanner answered.

"The repercussions are not only local," the Delegate elaborated. "As a satellite economy of Haven Prime, the well-being of both our cities is intertwined in many and complex ways. There are products and services that cannot be procured in any other place but here. Naturally, my supervisors become extremely concerned when this entire unsustainable desert city threatens to collapse into an economic nightmare. Aurora has long been granted extended autonomy only because of the unique capabilities it has long held in virtual reality rendering, an ancient area of technology with staggering practical implications once it is fully understood. As such, this crisis not only threatens both of our cities' economies but also the existence of technology that cannot be found anywhere else in the world."

"I am fully aware of this, Delegate."

"That is good, because if I do not see significant improvements that point to a full restoration of service at CradleCorp within the time period you have specified, the next step to be taken would be to call for backup. A team of scientists and military personnel is being assembled at Haven Prime at the moment, preparing to travel here should it prove to be necessary."

"What?" the Mayor exclaimed, speaking at last. "But, Delegate, Aurora has never been occupied in its entire history! Surely this measure would be an overreaction on the part of Lord Lefèbvre, it—"

"You said you have backups, Tanner," the Delegate said, ignoring the Mayor entirely. "Let me be frank, in that case. Bring them online, if you have not already done so, and reinstall them. Make sure that this time the new system doesn't have the capability to… defy you. We have monitored your progress for many years, and so far the consensus has been to allow you to continue your current lines of investigation. There are many people keenly interested in the potential results back at Haven Prime. If, however, you do not restore full service capability to the city before the deadline you gave us, then we will take matters into our own hands. Needless to say, this would mean an end to the CradleCorp monopoly, and the repercussions would not end there. Understood?"

"I understand, Delegate," Tanner managed to say.

"Very well. I will leave you to your work, then. Expect one of my aides to visit your office sometime during this week to receive a full report on the status of your network. Until then."

The communication was cut. Tanner lay back in the leather softness of his seat and stared straight ahead at his reflection on the tinted glass that separated him from the driver. His heart was racing, every beat another sharp jab that worsened the fully developing migraine centered above his right temple. He darkened all the windows around him with the flick of a switch to keep out the worst of the glaring morning light. He had medicine at the office, but until then he would have to suffer. And think.

They know.

It was the only thought that he could keep in his head. It bounced around inside his tender skull, tormenting him, spawning consequences and revelations that multiplied and fed on one another.

The Primes know about Atlas. But how? Since when?

The Delegate had been clever. He had spoken so vaguely that the mayor was unlikely to have understood the true severity of what was being discussed, the true extent of the knowledge of Haven Prime. The conversation, and in particular the warning, had been meant for Tanner alone. If he did not succeed in restoring Atlas, then he would live to see his entire empire collapse around him.

Tanner rubbed his temple gingerly. He had been careful. He had hired only the best scientists, the most trustworthy individuals in the entire city. He had erased every digital footprint he could think of that would betray him to the monitoring systems of Haven Prime. He had kept the entire Atlas project, its intention and scope, a complete secret from almost every person that had ever worked for him. And still, they knew. They were aware that Otherlife was not an ordinary reality simulator. They knew CradleCorp controlled a true instance of artificial intelligence that had its own volition. They probably even knew about Tanner's Project Linker, his dream of modifying the technology that was currently wasted on escapist fantasies to instead extract information directly from the minds of other people. They had known all these years, and the Primes had approved of his efforts, no doubt waiting for his team of scientists to begin showing signs of success before swooping in and stealing everything.

It was a crushing realization. And the worst part of it was that there was nothing Tanner could do.

Tanner sighed, but it came out more like a moan. He tried to calm himself, to think things through and be rational. It wasn't easy to do with a pounding headache, but he started a shallow-level meditation exercise that he always found helpful, focusing only on one thing. In this case, the feeling of air passing over his nostrils as he breathed. Little by little he was able to relax, however slightly. He felt the motion of the car as it drove through the streets of Aurora and carried him closer to the one place where he had always felt in control.

Perhaps it would not be so bad. True, the most he could hope for was to end up becoming a willing pawn in whatever games the Primes were playing. He would be someone obeying orders, a puppet for whomever decided to hold the strings. Nevertheless, that was essentially what he had been since he had assumed control of CradleCorp all those years ago. He just had not known it then. He had not known that he had always been monitored and given the implicit authorization of Haven Prime to continue working on his projects. Now that he knew it, perhaps little would change. He would end up just as he was now, director of CradleCorp in a position of authority that would be local but no less significant for that. He could even hope to forge closer business alliances with Prime corporations, maybe even receive ancient technology in exchange for his team's findings….

Assuming, of course, that he could bring Atlas back online.

His phone rang. It was Herrera. Tanner lost the tiny bit of inner peace he had managed to find through the meditation. He braced himself for the worst… and was not disappointed.

"This is Tanner."

"Richard," she said. She sounded tired. "They got away."

Tanner gritted his teeth until it was painful, then relaxed the pressure in his jaw very gradually. When he spoke he managed to give the impression of calmness. "How did this happen, Diana?"

"We were ambushed. There were armed people at the extraction point, mercenaries probably. We exchanged gunfire, the targets got lost, then the entire place went up in flames. All of my Trackers died, and I only made it out alive because I was stationed beside a window, and the explosion threw me out of the building. I don't know where Blake went. He could be anywhere by now."

Tanner was silent. Aaron Blake and the quantum drive he carried were his one hope at reactivating the Atlas backup. The spark of the AI resided there because it had chosen to copy itself to that location. Tanner had his own backups, but they were only worthless data without that key.

And now, if Blake decided to go into hiding again, it could be weeks before he was found. By then the Delegate would have lost his patience, and Tanner could lose everything.

"Diana…," he began, but something interrupted him. There was a beep coming from a specially dedicated monitoring terminal that fed its output directly to Tanner's account. He flicked on the display and saw something wonderful.

Good luck at last.

"I know where they are, Diana," he said instead.

"What? How?"

"I have had people stationed all around the perimeter of the ancient Haven III military compound for almost a week now," Tanner explained. "I had them jailbreak a proximity sensor web around the area. Something has just entered it, an unauthorized vehicle moving in. It's them. Blake is going to try to reactivate Atlas after all."

"Why didn't I know about all this perimeter setup? How many people do you have up there?"

"You did not know about it because you have been out in the field looking for Blake. I also do not like to share all my plans with a single person. It would have been stupid not to send the team out to the site as soon as Atlas self-destructed. Don't you agree? I sent a group of trustworthy mercenaries and my best scientists there to try and open the cradle room before Blake could get there."

"That was smart," Herrera said.

"Of course. Smart but useless. The compound has somehow sealed itself against my people, and all my brilliant scientists have been able to tell me is that some kind of a key is needed to enter. I can bulldoze my way in, but this is an ancient bunker, built to withstand the Cataclysm; it would take weeks to break inside unless I were to fly there wearing battle armor. That's why I need Blake so badly. I'm certain he carries this key with him."

"Why?" she asked.

Because Atlas self-destructed only after giving final instructions to Blake to go to that very place, Tanner thought, but, of course, he did not share this with Diana. Instead he just said, "It's not important why, just what we're going to do about it. I want you to head over there as quickly as possible. I have a good security grid set up, but you are the best at what you do. I need you there as my ace in the hole."

"Always the flatterer."

Tanner was too high-strung to pretend to humor her. "Herrera, listen to me. If Blake somehow manages to get past the armed mercs and CradleCorp men I posted there, I want you to prevent him from doing whatever it is he's going to do. Get that quantum drive from off his corpse if you need to, but make sure you get it. I cannot stress enough how important this is. Understood?"

There was a long pause on the line, and when Diana spoke again, her voice was full of barely suppressed rage. Tanner was surprised. He had never known her to lose control. "I have lost my entire fucking team working on this mission, Richard. I saw one of them get shot and the other one burned alive. I'm going to see this through. In fact, I think I...."

"What?"

"Richard, I want you to send me the XR Suit."

Tanner blinked, surprised at the request. Surprised she even knew about that experimental battle armor.

"I'm afraid I can't do that, Diana. The suit is still in testing, and there is no way I can take it out of the laboratory without those damn news crews noticing."

"Fine. I'll do it on my own, but when I get back to that big office of yours with the quantum drive in my hand, I expect the trouble to have been worth it."

"If you get back and give me that key, Diana, you can name whatever price you want."

"Very well, I'll hold you to that. I'm heading out."

Tanner hung up and sat a little bit straighter in his seat. His headache had lessened somewhat, and he even allowed himself to feel cautiously hopeful. What had previously been an almost hopeless situation had suddenly turned around now that Blake was willingly heading over to where Tanner had set his trap. The plan to catch him was good, and it even had redundancies now in case something went wrong.

Tanner stopped frowning and allowed some more of the tension to drain off of him. He would get that quantum drive and make sure the Atlas backup awoke to obey only him. A single crippled artist standing in his way was barely an obstacle. And who knew? Perhaps when Tanner had shackled the new AI, he would find ways to turn it into a weapon. Something to give him an edge, even over the Primes....

Chapter Twenty-Six

Barrow drove slowly up a pathway that had been cut into the rock to allow vehicles to climb up to the Haven III mesa. The sun was already high in the sky. He had slept for longer than he had intended, and the dry heat of the day was quickly becoming unbearable. He was sweating freely behind the wheel, partly because he was hot, but also because he was nervous. He felt horribly exposed as he drove, and although Rigel had been confident that there wouldn't be anyone waiting for them at the old military compound, Barrow was not so sure.

He checked the console displays on the vehicle dashboard, but there was no useful information there. He would be driving blindly onto the top of the mesa, and there was no way to help it. At the moment the steep sides of rocks on either side blocked visibility completely, and he could only see straight ahead up the narrow and steep incline. It didn't feel right to him. They would be trusting too much on luck, and from the little Barrow had seen of Richard Tanner, it appeared to him that he was not the kind of man to take chances. It would be common sense to station a team in a bunker somewhere to keep a lookout in case Rigel showed up following Atlas's instructions. After all, Tanner had already sent assassins to hunt for them, and they had almost caught them—twice.

Or it could be somebody else staking out the place. Tanner was the richest man in Aurora, but he was not the only one with the money or power to hire people to catch Rigel. The government could have sent a military detachment to the compound, or maybe a bounty hunter somewhere had decided to undertake the task and keep the reward money all to himself. Rigel was the most wanted man in the city, after all. The media had made him look like the nemesis of modern civilization, a terrorist with nothing to lose who simply wanted to watch the world burn. Barrow would not have been surprised to see a random do-gooder waiting for them at the end of the path holding a rifle, hoping to rid the world of evil.

He stopped the car. He listened intently as the whine of the motor died away, but the silence around them was nearly absolute. They would go directly on foot. It would be easier to hide if needed, and they were almost at the top anyway. It wasn't worth it to do it otherwise, and if they were ambushed, Barrow preferred to be standing on his own two feet and holding a gun in either hand to defend himself.

He looked over at Rigel, who was still asleep in his seat. Barrow had not wanted to wake him up since it would have served no purpose, and Rigel needed to rest.

Barrow reached over to touch his face, then stopped himself. He looked at the peaceful expression of Rigel sleeping and fixed it in his mind along with the warm feeling he got simply from being next to him. Last night something had happened. It was a mess in Barrow's mind, a jumble of conflicting emotions and blurry memories. There was the fire, the fear of losing Rigel, the gunfight, and then Rigel incredibly, impossibly, saving them all like he had done. The one thing that stood out in Barrow's mind over it all, however, was the way Rigel had reciprocated his kiss. Barrow had acted impulsively, and he was glad he had. Later it had been harder, driving together with him in the dark, trying to muster up the courage to hold his hand and yet fearing the rejection.

It was weird to Barrow, feeling the way he did at the moment. It was not how he usually felt when he was awkwardly cruising, finding an attractive guy he liked, and then both of them leaving together for sex and nothing more. He liked Rigel physically, of course, but in the brief time he had known him Barrow had learned to like much more about the young man. He was smart, he was fun to be around when he was relaxed and not fearing for his life, and most of all he was emotionally strong. Barrow still couldn't understand how Rigel kept holding on in this impossible situation, going from pampered city boy to warrior in less than a week and not once whining about how unfair life was to have put him in this position. The fact that he had a disability only made it all the more amazing, and Barrow admired him for it. He wished he could be a little more like Rigel, in a way. Strong enough to take an awful thing and not let it break you, like Barrow had almost broken down after his family had died.

Sharing the full story of the fire had been awful, but it had also felt good. Barrow had managed not to cry in front of Rigel, but now in the light of the morning he felt that it would not have diminished him in the other man's eyes if he had done so. It was strange. He didn't know Rigel that well, but at the same time he felt that he knew him at a deeper level than he had known anyone else in his life. Maybe… maybe he was in love.

Barrow smiled at the thought, at the rightness of it, and leaned over the seat to kiss Rigel on the lips. Rigel woke up and gave a little start of surprise, but when he saw who it was, he kissed Barrow right back and wrapped his arms around him. The jolt of happiness Barrow felt at that gesture was electric.

"Sorry to wake you up," Barrow told him. "We're almost there."

Rigel smiled. "I'm not sorry you woke me up like that."

Barrow kissed him again, which took longer than expected, then reluctantly went back to business. "I stopped the car because we're almost at the top, and I'm not sure if there's going to be anyone out there waiting for us."

Rigel's expression grew troubled, and Barrow felt a little pang of regret at having erased the smile from his face.

"You think there's going to be something like an ambush?" Rigel asked. "But we took care of all of the assassins back in the slums, didn't we?"

Barrow nodded. "I don't know what to expect, Rigel, but I think it will be safer if we go the rest of the way up on foot with guns ready. Makes it easier to hide and also to fight back…. Or to retreat back into the city if we see that it's impossible to get through."

"Going back is not an option, Steve," Rigel said sadly. "At least not for me. If I show my face anywhere back there, someone's bound to report me to the authorities or shoot me on the street. The slums would be the same thing, only there they would want to sell me out for money like Streaker tried to do. The only thing left for me is to go forward."

"Fine. Then forward it is."

"About that, Steve…. I was thinking. You don't have to go up there with me. It's not your mission, and after last night I just don't want to see you get hurt because of me. You can take the car, go back to Zoe, and—"

Barrow held up a hand to silence him. "Let me set one thing straight, Rigel. I'm going with you because I want to. Not because you're making me, not because I feel I owe you anything, although I do, but because that's what I want to do. You stand a better chance of succeeding if I go with you, and to be honest you're not going to get rid of me that easily. You got that? Stop telling me to leave."

Rigel smiled, and to Barrow the world seemed a little brighter. "I got that."

"Fine. Then let's get out of the car and grab our gear. The sooner we get up there, the sooner we'll know what we're up against."

They left after eating some of the food Zoe had packed for them. They kept to the shade as they walked, partly to avoid the searing sun that was almost directly overhead but mostly to stay as far out of sight as possible in case somebody was indeed watching. Barrow was particularly glad to have water. He had never been out in the desert like this, and he had underestimated how hot it would get.

"I wish I had a hat," Rigel said about ten minutes later. "Is it always this hot?"

"First time out here."

"But I thought you had traveled all over. Didn't you, aboard that airship?"

"Sure," Barrow said, keeping his voice low. "But traveling aboard an air-conditioned ship is nothing like this. I'm used to seeing the desert from above, not walking through it in the middle of the day."

Rigel was silent after that, apparently concentrating on walking quietly. Barrow followed right behind him with one gun out. The path they were following was getting progressively narrower, the rocky walls on either side decreasing in height the more they advanced up the side of the mesa. It was a steep walk, almost a climb, and before long Barrow was drenched in sweat.

"What is it like out there?" Rigel asked eventually.

"What do you mean?"

"I mean out. Beyond Aurora, out in the world. Is everything just wastelands like they tell you at school?"

"Not everything, but most of it, yeah," Barrow answered, remembering. "You travel days and days, and the only thing you see below is desert, all the way to the ocean. There are craters big enough for a city to fit in, and for the most part, it's really lonely. Peaceful, too, I suppose. I've heard of people who like the idea of living out in the wilderness so much they set off for a few of the isolated patches of forest to rough it out a few days. They are very rich people for the most part. They book the services of an entire airship to drop them off wherever they want, their gear and everything. I think some have even tried to start real settlements, but they never last. As far as I know, it's impossible to survive outside the Havens."

"That's sad. Maybe that's why so many people like Otherlife so much. Don't you think?"

"What do you mean?"

"Think about it, Steve. Most of us spend our entire lives in this one place, never seeing any of the world because there isn't anything to see. I think that's why it's so appealing, and I think that if none of this had happened and I would've accepted to work for CradleCorp, I would have been able to do something worthwhile. Atlas was helping me build real environments. Can you imagine? To actually be able to go anywhere in the old world that you wanted to go and for it to feel like the real thing?"

"I would've liked to try it."

Rigel stopped and looked back at him with a little smile. "Really?"

"Sure."

"Where would you have gone? If you could go anywhere in the world. Where would you go?"

"Scuba diving in the Great Barrier Reef," Steve answered immediately.

Rigel blinked. "Wow, that's pretty specific."

Barrow shrugged. "I've flown over the ocean, but I've never been in the ocean. I've seen plenty of documentaries on scuba diving, and I think I would like to try that."

Rigel nodded thoughtfully. "An underwater environment. I had never even thought about painting that, but it shouldn't be too hard…." Then he laughed.

"What's funny?"

"Nothing. It's just that here I am, planning an entire set of paintings, but I know perfectly well that I'll never go back to my old career as an artist. It's weird, sometimes. Like I forget the situation for a little bit, you know? And it's like nothing has changed in my life, but then I remember, and of course everything is different."

"I know exactly how you feel," Barrow told him. "It will happen less and less over time. Eventually you'll only feel like that when you wake up in the morning, sometimes. Later, not even then."

"Was it the way it was for you?" Rigel asked. "After the… after the fire?"

"Pretty much."

They fell silent then because they were reaching the end of the covered path. Barrow signaled to Rigel to crouch down low for the last few meters, hugging the tiny rock wall that was their only cover. They crawled forward a little at a time, careful not to make any noise. Their cover eventually ran out, though, and they were forced to walk out onto the top of the mesa, out in the open and completely exposed.

There was nobody there.

"Great," Rigel grumbled. "We could've driven all the way up here, and we wouldn't be on the verge of suffering from heatstroke."

Barrow put his hand on Rigel's shoulder and with the other one brought his index finger to his lips. Rigel stopped talking at once.

At first glance the place looked desolate and empty. It was a wind-blasted surface of bare rock that rose nearly a hundred meters over the desert terrain below, offering a spectacular view of the empty desolation that surrounded the city of Aurora. The entire place was a sandy mixture of beige and terra-cotta tones, with nothing green in sight and the immense light blue sky above them, merciless and unblemished by the smallest cloud. The sun was beating down straight on them now, and it felt as hot as an engine room working at full blast, only worse because the heat was everywhere. It was coming down from the sky, reflecting off the rocks and sand, seemingly hanging in the still, dry air. Belatedly, Barrow noticed his shirt was dry again, even though he was still sweating. He touched the top of his head, and his hair felt like it were on fire. Without water and shade, people would be unable to survive in this hostile environment for more than a few hours. At most.

And yet they appeared to be the only ones there. There were vehicle tracks all over the place, some apparently quite recent, but there were no vehicles outside the perimeter of the military compound. There was nowhere to hide, either. The entire surface of the mesa was flat, and only the squat grouping of crumbling buildings at the far end offered a place for concealment.

It made Barrow uneasy, but they were already up here, and there was no going back, so he started forward cautiously, walking in the direction of the security perimeter ringing the site. He had expected at least a small group of people waiting for them looking for a fight, perhaps even a small encampment that would be easy to make out among the ruins. There was none of that, and Barrow had the sinking feeling they were walking straight into a trap. After all, if whoever had been sent here was smart enough to hide all traces of their arrival, then it would be almost certain that they would be hiding inside one of the buildings, waiting for the right moment to come out and rain bullets down on the two of them. If that happened, they were essentially defenseless.

They walked all the way up to the dilapidated metal fence that had perhaps been an imposing barrier at one point but now hung in tatters, crushed and riddled with holes everywhere. Off to the side of the main entrance to the compound, a barely recognizable sign still stood, bent and dented and reading *Haven III*. Next to it, on the outer side of the fence, a surprisingly intact little station still stood. It looked like a security station, the kind where a single guard would fit to wave passing vehicles through. Three of its walls were thick and opaque, and the fourth one had a large window facing out into the road leading into the compound. Barrow checked it out quickly, but there was nobody inside.

"Let me go in first," Barrow told Rigel, pointing at the buildings beyond. "I'll scout out the area and come back as quickly as I can."

"No way. I'm not staying out here alone."

"Rigel, it could be a trap. If they are hiding inside one of the buildings, then they will open fire as soon as they see me. If that happens and we are together, then they have gotten the two of us. If you're out here, however, then you can run for it, go back to the car, and try and get away. It makes the most sense. You can hide inside this station so they don't see you."

"If we go in together it will be two of us scouting out for trouble," Rigel countered. "And two guns at the ready."

"Rigel, I'm not going to argue with you. I'm expendable in this. You are not. I think you're special. You said Atlas chose you for this mission for an important reason, and besides it's you they want, not me. They might not even kill me immediately if they see me. They might try to capture me and get me to tell them where you are."

"That is very reassuring."

Barrow smiled. "I just think it's the best way. Give me a few minutes to go in there, check everything out. Keep your gun at the ready."

Rigel looked at Barrow with a stubborn expression, but Barrow held his gaze until Rigel looked down.

"Fine. But don't take too long, or I will die anyway from this awful heat."

"I'll be right back."

He turned to go, but Rigel grabbed his shoulder.

"Be careful," Rigel said, and gave him a quick kiss.

"I will be. Don't worry."

Barrow walked past the perimeter fence quickly without looking back. He held the gun at the ready, every sense on high alert. His steps made no sound over the dust-covered concrete that paved the inner courtyard of the compound, flanked by buildings on three sides.

Barrow hurried over to the nearest building, all the while feeling as if he had a giant bull's-eye painted on the back of his head. No one shot him, though, and he got to cover behind a wall still in one piece. Gun held low, he walked around the building and off to the far side of the compound that was hidden from view by the other structures.

There he saw the encampment.

It was as he had feared. There were three large vans there, along with four tents and crates upon crates of equipment that had been carefully organized around the vehicles. Barrow saw machine guns mounted on the tops of all three cars, currently unmanned but deadly looking nonetheless. In the middle of the camp there was a space that had been cleared out for cooking, as if the people who had set it up had been here for more than a day. There was even a clothesline with a couple of shirts strung out, set to dry.

Barrow had been right; it was a trap. And now he had to get out of there as fast as he could before anyone saw him. They could be anywhere. Hidden inside the buildings, maybe inside the tents or in the back of the vans, guns pointed at him right then. Had they gotten to Rigel already? Had they seen the two of them arrive and lain low so their quarry would approach close enough that there would be no way out?

There was a strong gust of wind, and something moved inside one of the tents. Somebody was in there, then. Barrow aimed his gun, selecting the target carefully before it could get out of the tent and shoot him.

Then a creaking noise sounded suddenly from behind him. It was the sound of a metal door swinging open.

Barrow spun around instantly, but something was already coming out of the door.

They had gotten him by surprise in spite of everything.

Barrow brought the gun to bear on the shape too slowly. He fired anyway, but even as he did it he knew it was too late.

Chapter Twenty-Seven

RIGEL HEARD the gunshot ring out like an explosion through the air, and he jumped, banging his shoulder against the wall, his finger tightening compulsively against the trigger of his weapon.

No.

He rushed out of the tiny enclosure where he had been hiding and looked frantically around, scanning the entire place without seeing anything that gave away what had happened. He took a step in the direction of the compound and then stopped, remembering Steve's words. He had told him to get out if there was danger, to go back to the car and escape if he could.

Rigel grabbed his gun as tightly as he could without hurting himself and took another step forward. No way was he going to leave Steve in there alone.

He crossed the paved courtyard with his heart hammering, every beat booming in his ears. He knew the approximate direction Steve had gone, and he followed in his footsteps, trying to look everywhere at once in case there was a sniper on a roof or something. Who had fired the shot? Had it been Steve, or had somebody gotten to him first?

Rigel managed to get to cover without incident and went around the back of the building where he had last seen Steve. There was a door in there, rusty and heavily scratched. Rigel tried it, but it was shut tight and did not budge. Rigel didn't have the strength to pull on it any harder, and so he abandoned it, walking around the corner and into what looked like an encampment of some sort.

He walked among the tents and vehicles, breathing quickly, trying to keep the gun at the ready and wishing he knew how to shoot. He doubted he would be able to get anyone at a distance. If somebody came out now, it would not be like Jared, who had been looking the other way, less than two steps away at point-blank range. Rigel was almost sure he would miss, and if they had gotten Steve, then what chance did he have?

He moved as quickly as he could manage among the tents, inspecting the inside of all three vans. He felt very scared, but the greater part of his fear was focused on Steve. If something had happened to him…. But no. He had to focus. Somebody had fired the gun, and Rigel had to find that person. The place wasn't that big, so they had to be around somewhere. Perhaps in one of the buildings, since the encampment was completely empty.

Rigel walked all the way down the eastward side of the first building without finding a single door that would open. The buildings were all linked, so getting into one would allow Rigel access to the entire place, hopefully. He walked around looking for a broken window or a door that stood ajar, but all the walls were in a remarkable state of conservation, and there were no easy ways in that he could see.

Rigel walked over to the second building, the one that stood almost at the lip of the mesa. This area had been the most heavily damaged, although the rubble that lay strewn around on the rock appeared to have belonged to a separate structure from the building itself. Large broken slabs of concrete lay haphazardly on the ground along with twisted and corroded bits of metal that looked very ancient. There was a large, neat burn mark on one of the walls of the building that ran from side to side in a straight line. Dust lay thick over everything, and Rigel had to pick his way carefully to avoid tripping on the debris. He managed to reach the wall on the side that was closest to the edge of the mesa, a mere couple of steps from a deadly drop straight down, now that the fence that had bordered the edge was nothing but scrap. Rigel stepped extra carefully over that part since he had spotted an open door on that side, where one of the larger chunks of concrete had fallen against it. He edged closer, gun in one hand and the other gripping whatever he could to ensure that he did not lose his balance.

He made it right up to the door before he saw the severed leg.

It was so unexpected that at first Rigel did not know what he was looking at. When he realized that there was a neatly cut leg lying in a pool of rust-colored blood right outside the door, he let out a yell and scrabbled backward out of instinct, stumbled awkwardly the way he had come, and tripped over a rock that gave way under his foot.

He fell down. His butt and legs hit rock, but the rest of him hit only air.

Rigel panicked, letting go of his gun and throwing his arms to either side of him to grab on to something, anything at all. His right hand found a grip, and he held on for dear life. A stab of pain shot up his wrist at the effort, but he did not care. He pulled himself forward slowly, trembling all over. When he was securely on solid ground, he looked back.

He had almost fallen clear over the edge of the mesa. If he had not found something to hold onto, his own weight would have sent him tumbling backward to his death. And all because of….

The leg. Rigel looked in the direction where he knew it lay, and a shiver of dread passed over him. He stood up shakily and examined it from afar, relieved that it was obviously not Steve's leg. It was wearing a different kind of fabric, and the boot was different. It looked like it had been cut off with an impossibly sharp knife. As Rigel approached again slowly, he saw that there was a burn mark on the ground next to the leg in another perfect straight line. It looked like something a laser would have made.

Rigel made himself get closer. He edged around the awful amputated thing, and only when he had his hand pressed against the metal door did Rigel realize the leg was remarkably well-preserved, with no signs of having been there under the sun for very long.

Whatever had done that, it couldn't have been that long ago.

Going through that door was one of the hardest things Rigel had ever done. He did not want to go in there; he feared what he would find, and he was terrified of Steve being inside the place and of the unseen dangers that might be waiting for him as well. But he had to do it. He gathered up his courage and gave the door a hard shove, finding resistance of some sort. He pushed again, throwing his entire weight at the door, and the resistance squished further in a horrible way. There was the sound of liquid spurting out, and Rigel almost lost his nerve. He had to get in, though. He threw himself at the door a third time, and this time something behind snapped, and the door jolted open wide enough for him to squeeze through. Rigel did not hesitate any more but went right in.

Plants.

That was the first thing Rigel noticed when he got inside, and the shock of seeing so many of them growing all around was enough to keep him staring for a few long moments. He took a couple of steps farther in, looking up at the ceiling where a large crack he had not seen before let in a bright beam of sunlight, straight through the otherwise gloomy, cool interior of the building. And growing all around the crack, green tendrils and leaves fanning out everywhere, were plants.

The air was full of dust, the many suspended particles outlining clearly the contours of the sunbeams streaming in. It smelled earthy in there, of growing things, and the temperature was so different from that outside that Rigel could not think of any explanation for it other than the air-conditioning still worked. Which was impossible, of course. Along with the fact that plants were growing in the middle of the desert, lush vegetation that shouldn't be able to survive.

The plants looked like creepers of some sort, and apparently they had been growing long enough that their stems were as thick as slender tree trunks, burrowing through the rubble and covering the concrete with brown and green. It appeared the entire place was choked with the growth, but Rigel noticed that a small path had been hacked through the greenery very recently. It was littered with shredded leaves, and there were clear imprints of boots in two places.

People had been inside here not long ago, then. And the boot prints led right back to the door….

Rigel turned around and looked at what had been obstructing the door from the inside. It was clearly visible even in the shadows. The corpse was twisted, facedown, and the pool of blood around it was much larger than the one outside where the man's leg had been. Rigel could not tear his eyes away. Something had killed this man, and it had not been Steve. Whatever it was, it was still inside this ancient tomb that Rigel desperately wished to get far away from.

A sudden small, furtive rustling in the leaves.

Rigel spun around instantly, his hand reaching for a gun that was no longer there. He opened his eyes as wide as he could, searching, searching.

There. Something was moving underneath the green cover. It came out partially and startled Rigel so badly that he cried out. The noise scared the creature, and it slithered away quickly, out of sight.

Rigel swallowed, but his throat felt paper-dry. At first he had thought the thing was a snake, but the long and sinuous body he had glimpsed had been hard and shiny, with many legs, as if belonging to a gigantic bug. Thankfully, the creature seemed to have been as scared of him as Rigel had been of it. And now Rigel knew that he did not want to stay in this awful building any longer than he had to.

He made his way along the path that cut straight through the greenery, not really running but almost doing so. This building appeared to be a single big empty space that had been taken over by the plants, and the path he followed was a long but straight line that led all the way across it without interruptions. Rigel had almost crossed it when he heard more rustling behind him. He lost his nerve and sprinted away as fast as he could, straight for the door that he could now see. He slammed against it, not caring if it opened out or in. He was lucky. It opened out, and it burst open under the impact. Rigel stumbled past it, quickly regained his footing, and slammed it shut behind him.

His shoulder hurt, but he barely even felt it. He was now inside the first building, the one outside of which he had last seen Steve. There weren't any plants growing in here, but he saw….

Carnage.

He tried to cry out, but it caught in his throat. His hand gripped behind him convulsively, trying to find the handle of the door he had just shut. As bad as the other building had been, now Rigel wanted nothing more than to go back in there so he would not have to see. He shut his eyes tight and turned around, opening them only when he was sure he would be looking at the door. He almost left.

Instead he made himself turn around and called, "Steve?"

His voice was lost in the lifeless space of the new building. Rigel walked forward carefully, as quietly as he could manage, even though he knew just from looking at them that every single one of the people he could see was already dead.

They were all wearing the same uniform, the one the guy in the previous building had been wearing. They had cleared out the entire central space of the building, which had no divisions and no inner walls of any kind. It was just another rectangular empty space, two stories high and ringed on the upper floor by a walkway that reminded Rigel a lot of prison walkways, meant to give access to cells built into the walls and leaving a wide empty courtyard in the middle. Whatever the building's function had been, it had long since been stripped of any ancient furniture or machinery it might have contained. The piles of broken electronics and various assorted weaponry Rigel could see were all new. The uniformed people had probably brought them in with them before… before something had killed them all.

"Steve, are you here?"

The floor was an unholy mixture of dirt and gore. There was blood on the walls. Light was coming in from outside, but some of the windows were spattered with blood, and the sunlight looked as if it shifted into the red, making everything look more menacing. A wide space near the center was dented as if something had exploded on it, the black burn mark on the floor devoid of the many bits and pieces of broken things that littered the place everywhere else. There were bullet holes all over, and there was a strong smell of sickly sweet corruption and death that hung about everything, making Rigel retch twice.

And the bodies, of course. The bodies of the dead.

Some of them had been shot, as Rigel could see from the holes in their clothing in strange and random places. Some of them appeared to have burned to death, judging from the disgusting charred wounds a few still had. The majority, though, had been dismembered. Rigel forced himself to walk around severed arms, legs, hands, and feet still clad in boots, the jagged end of a bloody bone still poking forth from a sock. There were people that had been split in half, the desiccated entrails that had once belonged to them lying smeared on the wall next to their corpse. A couple of heavily armored corpses hung from the upper walkway, their bodies twisted at unnatural angles and one of them still clutching his rifle with stiff dead hands.

Everywhere he looked for Steve, terrified of finding him in the same state as everyone else. Rigel had no idea what had happened here or who these people had been, but they had come with weapons as if expecting a conflict of some kind. Evidently, they had found it.

Rigel was halfway across the building when it occurred to him that whatever had killed these people might still be out there. Or rather, in here. The thought scared him, and suddenly he was looking at every shadow as he passed, straining his hearing to the limit to catch the faintest sound. Nothing moved toward him, though. Nothing crawled or crept forward to try to get him. He walked ahead, step by slow step, and as long as he kept away from the more disturbing remains, he managed to hold the growing panic at bay and make his way to the very end of the building where the entry door was locked down tight.

Rigel tried opening the door from this side but to no avail. He started breathing faster, feeling locked in with the dead and with no idea of where Steve had gone, and he pulled on the heavy door handle with the meager strength of his hands until the pain of the effort forced him to stop.

Trapped.

He was trapped in here, and there was no way he would walk the entire length of the space again. The smell threatened to overpower him, and the horrified expressions etched upon the corpses seemed directed only at him. He edged to the side, and his foot crushed something brittle. He looked down and saw he had cracked the discarnate remains of a hand. Everything around it had burned, the wedding ring its owner had once worn now only a congealed puddle of molten metal on the floor.

Rigel jumped away, horrified, and stumbled onto something else. He did not fall, but it was close, and he cried out again, a wordless moan of terror.

Then he heard a voice. Somebody was shouting, and Rigel's first instinct was to scan the glassy eyes of the corpses, dreading to find a remnant of life among the discarded weapons and awful remains. He stayed perfectly still, listening, every muscle tensed, and his eyes opened as wide as they would go. It was completely silent in the building, and when the voice called again he heard it clearly.

"Rigel? Rigel!"

Rigel let out a shaky breath as relief flooded through his body. Steve was calling from outside, judging from the faintness of his voice. Rigel looked in the direction the call was coming from, and he saw a smaller door he had not noticed before. It had been set to one side of the building and was partially blocked by debris, but when Rigel reached it, he saw he could easily push it open. Out in the courtyard of the compound, he saw Steve standing in the sun, a gun in his hand and obviously looking for him. Trembling yet enormously reassured now, Rigel climbed over the debris to get out of the building of death.

Something moved inside, at the very edge of his peripheral vision.

Rigel stopped with a foot outside and the rest of his body still in. He looked back, puzzled. Nothing happened, so he looked away—

Again. This time he had seen it better. At the far end of the space, among the shadows of the darkest corner, something even darker had moved. Rigel stared hard at the place, seeing nothing but blackness, but after a couple of seconds he had the horrible feeling that something was looking back at him from that corner.

A shadow twitched. Rigel fled.

The brutal heat of the sun's rays felt like a blessing as Rigel rushed out of the building calling Steve's name. The other man heard him and hurried to meet him, and when Rigel was close enough, he saw that Steve's expression was a mixture of anger and relief.

"Where were you?" Steve demanded. "I thought—"

"I went looking for you. I heard a shot, and I saw…."

Steve gestured at the door Rigel had just come out of. "You were in there?"

"Yes. I just… I don't…. What's going on, Steve? Why is everyone dead?"

Steve put a reassuring hand on Rigel's shoulder. "I don't know."

"Where were you? Why did you fire your gun?"

"I thought I saw something come at me. I followed it into that building with all the bodies, but then it just… changed. In a way. It's hard to describe. I'm not even sure I really did see something to begin with. Maybe I'm just too strung out, and it was a heat-induced hallucination. After that I went over to the building over there to check it out, maybe see if there was anybody left alive. No luck."

"How could something like this happen? Who or what killed all those people?"

"I have no idea what happened to those people, Rigel, but I know who they are."

"What?"

"They are with CradleCorp. Or were, I should say. Not all of them, obviously. Some of them looked like mercs to me. From the way they had their camp set all the way back there, up out of sight, they had to have been planning an ambush of some kind. For us, most likely."

"So Tanner sent them?"

Steve nodded. "And they would have gotten us too. These people were professionals, and they were heavily armed. We wouldn't have stood a chance. Tanner knew that we would try and come here eventually, so he prepared everything. We played right into his hands."

"Except for…." Rigel shuddered, unable to finish his sentence. He closed his eyes to try to block the memory of the carnage he had witnessed, but it was no use.

"It's awful, but it gives us a shot at completing Atlas's mission. I even think I found the place where you're supposed to go. It's in that last building over there."

Rigel looked where Steve was pointing. He remembered the building from the vision Atlas had shown him. That was where the control center of the compound had been.

Steve led the way to it, and Rigel followed. He stood aside as Steve yanked on a heavy set of double doors and tried to open them.

"Dammit," Steve muttered, pulling harder when they resisted. "They're stuck. I was just in there!"

He gave them a shove with his shoulder, then another. On the third one, something cracked on the other side, and the doors opened a little bit.

The something plopped down to the ground, motionless and broken. It looked like part of another person, only this one had been wearing a lab coat over his uniform. A lab coat that was now a deep shade of rust from all the dried blood.

"Shit," Steve said. "That's disgusting."

He edged inside, and Rigel made as if to go after him, but his foot wouldn't move. Rigel could not tear his eyes from the corpse on the floor.

"Rigel? You coming?"

But Rigel started shaking his head no, slowly at first and then more urgently, eyes on the dead man always.

"I c… I can't. I'm sorry. I can't."

He backed away, out of the shade of the building and back into the merciless sunlight, but he scarcely noticed the heat. Instead he felt cold, scared, and panicky. His breathing came in quick gasps.

"Rigel?" Steve asked, coming back out. "What's wrong?"

But Rigel couldn't speak. It was just too much. Too much running, too much fear, and now too much gore. His mind could not take it. This was not the way the world was supposed to be.

He closed his eyes again and remembered glassy eyes, severed limbs, and the stench of death. He did not hear Steve approaching and started violently when he felt Steve's touch.

"Hey," Steve said, his voice surprisingly gentle. "You okay?"

Rigel opened his eyes but kept them on the ground. "I can't."

"You mean go inside?"

Rigel nodded.

"Tell you what. Let's go sit down by the shade. You don't have to go in yet."

Rigel followed only because he could not think of anything else to do. He sat down next to Steve on the hard concrete, resting his back on a wall that was not as hot as it should have been. He stared out into the distance, past the fence and back the way they had come. He could not see the city from here, but Rigel knew it was there. A city that hated him, ahead, and behind him ancient buildings where something horrible had happened. He could not go forward, and he could not go back. Rigel felt suddenly overwhelmingly trapped.

A tiny sound escaped him, halfway between a sob and a cough. He choked it back immediately, but Steve had already heard.

"It's okay, you know," Steve said eventually, once Rigel had managed to compose himself a bit. Rigel risked a look at him, but Steve had also been staring out and away. The bright reflected sunlight made his eyes look flecked with gold. "I'm surprised you've lasted as long as you have without cracking."

Rigel made a grimace of self-deprecation. "Because I'm a weak city boy?"

Steve turned to look at him, his expression surprised. "No, the opposite really. Because you're so much tougher than anyone could expect."

The compliment threw Rigel off guard. It dulled the edge of the building panic inside him.

"The first time I saw a dead man, I wet myself," Steve continued.

"What?" Rigel said, sure he had heard wrong and for a while forgetting his own fear.

"It happened on my first ever airship trip. We touched down at Haven Prime, and, of course, I had to go out and see the sights. I got lost, went down a neighborhood where people go looking for trouble. I heard gunfire, got scared, ran away straight into a dead end, and I bumped into a corpse. It looked old, its eyes were open, and it was sort of slumped against a dumpster. It was also completely naked, the flesh blue and gray and black. It startled me so badly that my bladder just let go. Eventually I found my way back to the ship, but it took me a long time to live down the telltale dark stain running down one of my trouser legs."

Rigel couldn't help but picture a younger Steve, embarrassed and wet. He could not bring himself to smile, but he started to breathe a little bit more slowly.

"You've just seen something a hundred times worse, Rigel. You've got every right to freak out. Hell, I've beaten a man to death with a pipe, and I am also pretty shaken by what happened in there." Steve took Rigel's right hand in both of his. "But we're still here. Whatever did that, it did us a favor. And we've got really nowhere else to go."

"But…," Rigel started, heard the whine in his voice, and tried again. "But we don't know who or what did it, Steve. What if it's still here? What if it attacks us? You said those people were trained professionals, and look at what happened to them. They never stood a chance. What are the two of us going to do if… if we get attacked?"

"I guess we'll just have to take our chances."

"I wish none of this had happened. I wish Atlas had never spoken to me in the first place."

"It chose you for a reason, Rigel. Your mind is special in some way."

Rigel barked a sarcastic laugh. "Great. I'm so special that my reward is to come to this hellhole following orders I don't understand for a machine that ruined my life."

"It is pretty bad," Steve conceded.

"You think? And you, you don't even have to be here, Steve. You could just leave."

"Again with that. I told you already, I'm here because I want to be."

"But…."

"And I'll tell you something else too. I'm not sorry that Atlas got you into this mess. If it hadn't, then I would have never met you."

It was the one thing Steve could have said that could have driven every other thought out of Rigel's mind. He felt a rush of warmth at the admission and a thrill of nervousness that had nothing to do with the fear in the background of his mind. Steve was here, with him, and he didn't even have to be. He was staying because he wanted to.

Okay. I can do this.

Rigel stood up before he could change his mind. He was still panicky, but he could keep a lid on it. For a bit.

"Let's go in."

"You sure?" Steve said, standing up too.

"No. But it's what we came here to do, right? So let's do it."

To show that he was not a whining wimp, Rigel led the way inside this time. He stepped over the corpse with a shudder, but he made it in. He backed out of the way so Steve could walk past, and then they surveyed their surroundings.

The control center was vaguely recognizable from the way Rigel had seen it when Atlas had showed it to him. Many of the consoles that had once stood in rows were broken, some of them little more than dust. A few others had withstood the passage of time better, but archaeologists had probably been at them, and lots of pieces were missing. An entire corner of the building was roped off and filled with diagrams and labels from whoever had been in here before. Rigel walked cautiously down the main aisle between the rows of consoles, trying to match this derelict wreck to the high-tech environment he had seen when it was still working. Over there, on the far end, there had been a window. Only it must not have been a window, since Rigel saw only the cracked remains of a monitor of some kind that had encompassed nearly half the wall. Another bigger monitor occupied the last wall, and it was in much better condition. It had been isolated from the rest of the room by the archaeologists, presumably, since somebody had set a kind of metal cage around it that prevented direct access.

The fluorescent lights on the ceiling turned on automatically as Rigel and Steve made their way to the roped-off section. They cast a lifeless white glow over everything, throwing sharp shadows on the floor. The air smelled different in here, also. It was kind of damp and moldy, which made no sense once Rigel reflected on it. They were in the middle of the desert. Why would it be damp? Unless the strange plants growing in the next building had crossed over into here somehow. Rigel saw no sign of green, though. Other than the door they had just used to get inside, there was no other way into the space, and it showed in the relative lack of dust and other debris that should have accumulated inside, over however long it had remained abandoned.

"The entrance I found is over there, by the place that was roped off," Steve said suddenly, making Rigel flinch.

"Okay."

There was a heavy-looking door there, almost like the door to a bank vault. And two more corpses lying in front of it.

Like the one by the entrance, these two had been wearing lab coats over their uniforms. Between them lay a pile of broken electronic equipment that looked expensive.

"They must have been trying to open this," Steve told him. "It looks like they were using their computers to hack whatever was keeping this door locked."

"They got it open all right," Rigel commented, pointing at a narrow but noticeable gap between the heavy door and the wall.

"Want to see what's behind it?"

Rigel nodded stiffly.

Then the room came alive.

The gigantic monitor on the wall that was still intact began to display graphs, maps, and row after row of incomprehensible numbers. Flashing above it all was a warning message in red letters.

INTRUDER DETECTION.

"What the—" Steve began, but he didn't finish. His eyes went wide, and Rigel followed his look upward.

Panels were opening all along the ceiling, rectangular segments neatly folding back in on themselves with a clatter of mechanical noise. They exposed parallel rows of what looked like miniature train tracks that ran the entire length of the room. The walls followed suit immediately, and in just a few seconds there was no interior surface that Rigel could see that was not covered by the strange tracks. Rigel stared, completely clueless as to what their purpose was, and only when the first security mech assembled itself on the ceiling did he understand. The tracks were there so those things could ride along them.

More mechs came out of hidden panels on the walls. They were scarcely larger than a dog, but they looked deadly, a collection of razor-sharp blades and weapons protruding from their slender metallic bodies. Several glowing red lights were scattered on swiveling appendages, like eyes on stalks that they waved around briefly before focusing on Rigel and Steve. Many of the wicked blades they sported were stained dirty red, like recent dried-up blood. The robots looked old, and a couple of them appeared to be having trouble assembling themselves. That didn't stop the others from attacking.

"Look out!" Steve yelled, yanking Rigel down to the floor as something exploded from one of the ceiling mechs and whizzed by their heads. It struck the wall behind them with an incredibly loud clang, and when Rigel looked back, horrified, he saw a blade wider than a butcher's knife that had lodged itself neatly in the plaster.

There was a whine of gears grinding. Rigel looked up and saw the mechs moving toward them in their tracks slowly, as if they couldn't or wouldn't move any faster. The glowing orbs at the ends of their stalks waved to and fro, searching, focusing.

Another explosion. Steve barely got out of the way of the blade that went through the floor like it was butter.

"Let's go!" Steve yelled, rushing for the heavy vault-like door.

Rigel stood up and followed, moving faster than he had ever moved in his entire life. Another explosion behind him made him cry out, but he didn't stop. He launched himself at the opening and was immediately followed by Steve, who whirled around and slammed the door shut behind them just as several more impacts hit it on the other side so hard it sounded as if a gong were being struck.

Rigel panted in the dark, feeling himself all over and finding nothing wrong. Thankfully. He turned to where he could hear Steve breathing.

"Are you okay, Steve?"

"Yeah. I think. You?"

"I'm fine. Those things…."

"They almost got us," Steve said. "If this door hadn't been open, we would have been trapped."

"Do you think that's what happened to the CradleCorp team?" Rigel asked. "Maybe they were attacked and couldn't get inside in time."

"Maybe."

"But why? This place is supposed to be dead. Long ago. People have been in here before, archaeologists, CradleCorp, and I never heard of anything like this happening."

"It looked like some kind of automated security system," Steve observed. "You saw the intruder alert. We must have triggered it somehow, and the people before us must have done it too."

"But how? And why now?"

"No idea. But now we really can't go back out there."

"I guess you're right."

"Want a flashlight?" Steve asked.

"What?"

"I just think maybe we should have a look at where we are. So we can get moving. Here, I salvaged them from the corpses in the other building."

Steve handed Rigel a flashlight, and they both clicked them on. Rigel looked around anxiously, expecting more attackers, but there was nothing out of the ordinary here. It was just a dark corridor, small and nearly cylindrical. With an even stronger smell of mildew.

"This leads almost straight down," Rigel told Steve, suddenly remembering what he had seen in the vision from Atlas. How that scientist, Troy, had descended level after level as he ran from the shadow. "We have to go to the deepest level we can. There was a room that has lots of computer equipment, servers and that kind of stuff. The cradle room. I think that's where Atlas wanted me to go."

"Fine. Let's get going."

No automatic lighting was activated by their passage this time, but there were not any killer robots around either, so Rigel did not mind the darkness as much as he normally would have.

"At least we know where we're going," Steve said. "You want me to go in front? I got my gun, after all. It looks like you dropped yours."

"It's okay. I saw that scientist from the past as he fled in the vision and the way he took. I should go first to retrace his steps, try to find the way to the cradle room."

A couple more loud noises of metal on metal reached them from the other side of the door behind them. Then there was a loud screeching sound like something tearing. Rigel shuddered but forced himself not to look back.

They started following the corridor, their flashlight beams twin cones of white that were frustratingly insufficient to illuminate everything in front of them. The ceiling was disturbingly close. Rigel saw signs of recent activity in the place. There were more markings and labels in some places, a discarded terminal somewhere else, and once an elaborate workstation that still had the University of Aurora, Department of Archaeology label on it.

The silence was oppressive. They walked for what seemed like way too long before they descended a set of stairs that led into a bigger underground room out of which several doors branched out. Several sections of the room had also been clearly labeled, and out of the six doors that Rigel could see, four of them had little signs above them that read, Unlocked. He explored two of them while Steve explored the other two by tacit agreement. In the two rooms Rigel examined, he only saw more labels, more ropes, and signs of recent occupation. There were also several display cases with carefully tagged ancient equipment but no way farther into the compound. When he got back to the main room and looked at Steve questioningly, he only got a shrug.

"Let's try the locked doors," he suggested.

They walked up to the first of the doors, and Rigel looked at it to try to figure out how to get it open. Steve tried pushing it, but it was useless. There was a badly damaged terminal jutting from the wall next to the door that had to be a kind of authentication system to let people in, but it was broken, and aside from that there was no other indication of how to go through. The door itself was perfectly smooth, nearly melded into the wall. There was no handle to grab, no way to get any leverage except by pushing it, and Steve had already shown that it wasn't going to work.

"The other one?" Steve asked. Rigel nodded, suddenly wishing he hadn't spoken aloud. It felt wrong to make noise in here, somehow. He glanced back nervously once to look behind him, the beam from his flashlight aimed at the bottom of the stairs they had used to descend. There was nothing there. Just shadows.

The second door was exactly the same except for the fact that the security panel appeared to be working. It was red at the moment, but there was a small indentation next to its main scanner that was obviously meant to be an input port of some kind.

"Let me try the drive," Rigel said, reaching under his wrist brace and yanking off the quantum drive that was now glowing softly with its inner orange light.

He fumbled with it until he discovered that one of its ends fit perfectly inside the ancient input port. He pushed it in and waited. A couple of very tense heartbeats later, the light on the door scanner switched to blue, and there was a loud click. Rigel took the drive out and pushed the door. It opened easily.

"Nice," Steve said. "Good thing you didn't lose that."

"Yeah."

The corridor behind the door turned out to be a flimsy metal catwalk that flanked a chasm on one side. The other side was no longer a metal wall but instead naked rock, close enough to touch, the jagged insides of the desert mesa. The catwalk stretched out into the dark distance, and as Rigel followed it, he noticed the temperature in here was significantly lower than in any of the other rooms they had been in before. In fact, the place looked more like a natural cave than anything else.

They traversed the unnervingly narrow catwalk with only a low railing to prevent them from falling over the side, their footsteps the only sound in the silence of the dark space. The walkway then became a spiral staircase going down, which they followed, and Rigel began to get dizzy after five minutes of descending in circles without any indication of the bottom. From somewhere far off, he could hear the faint sounds of dripping water.

"I wonder how deep this goes," Steve said from above him. His deep voice echoed off the walls.

"No idea," Rigel answered, still feeling that he should speak as softly as possible. "I don't remember seeing this part in the vision at all. I hope we're going the right way."

Steve directed the beam of his flashlight to the side, and although at first it got lost in the darkness, it eventually found what looked like the crumbling remains of the underground levels of the building, far off on the opposite end of the cavern. They were in very bad shape. In some parts it looked as if somebody had taken the building and sliced the front off, exposing the inner offices and cubicles to the cave. Curious, Rigel stopped going down and followed Steve's example, examining the space. Rigel wondered how it was possible for the underground levels to have been so badly damaged when the more exposed aboveground buildings had remained relatively intact even after the Cataclysm.

"Hey, Rigel."

"What is it?"

"I think I see something glowing over there."

"Where?"

"Over by that wall. See?"

Rigel brought his own flashlight around to point at the spot Steve had mentioned.

Then both flashlights winked out.

"What the hell?" said Steve.

The darkness was total at first, and all Rigel could perceive was the sound of Steve hitting his flashlight against the railing and clicking it repeatedly. Rigel tried the same thing with his own flashlight but to no avail. He had not seen a low battery warning or anything—they had simply died.

A few seconds later, he noticed the glow. It was right where Steve had pointed it out, a sick-looking indigo light that clung to one of the walls. As his eyes got used to the darkness, Rigel was able to make out more glowing bits. It was brightest where he had first seen it, but it covered a good part of the exposed ruins. He leaned over the railing, looking down.

The glow continued for a little bit, bright enough to see but too dim to gauge distance or depth.

"What is that?" Barrow asked.

"Fungi, I sincerely hope."

"Bioluminescent?"

"Have to be," Rigel answered. "This being an underground cavern and all."

"I guess."

"Well, let's go. This has to end somewhere," Rigel said. He didn't sound convinced, even to himself.

"Hey, Rigel?"

"Yeah?"

When Steve next spoke, there was a note of insecurity in his voice Rigel had never heard before. "The thing is, I…. It feels cold. Flashlights don't die out like that."

"I know."

"It feels just like that time, Rigel, when that thing came into my room at night. Something's wrong in here. I think… I think there's something following us."

"Let's move, then."

"Right."

Rigel started going down again while trying hard to keep the returning panic at bay. He had not felt that thing Steve was talking about, but the normally stoic and fearless man's nervousness disturbed Rigel a lot more than the sudden darkness.

The blue glow on the far cave walls was more confusing than helpful, and the spiral staircase seemed to go on forever, but eventually the disorienting descent came to an end. Rigel stepped off the ladder gratefully and onto a rough patch of ground carpeted by more of the things giving off the glow. Up close he saw that they were indeed fungi of some kind, small and toadstool shaped but elongated weirdly. They had grown over the wreck of the building as far as their feeble glow let Rigel see.

They walked among the fungi carefully while avoiding most of the random debris that lay on the ground. It was impossible to see anything more than a few centimeters away from the glow, and so they were reduced to walking around almost blindly, occasionally stumbling into objects that blended with the darkness. After a few minutes of this, Rigel began to get more and more anxious. What if there was no way out of this? What if they got lost in the dark? Rigel had no idea how big the compound really was, and he doubted anybody knew for sure. They had no food with them. If they started following a pathway that got them turned around and lost in the dark, there was a good chance they would not get out at all.

Rigel tried to take a deep breath to calm himself down, but instead he shuddered. He felt strange, as if there was an invisible something pressing down on the back of his neck trying to make him keep his head down in the murk of his own fear. Normally Rigel wasn't this pessimistic, but this darkness….

He reached back with his left hand until he found Steve. He took Steve's hand and held it, the metallic brace Rigel wore an annoying barrier between them. But instantly he felt better. Reassured.

Rigel thought Steve might shrug his hand off or see the gesture as a sign of weakness, but after a brief pause, Steve kept on going without letting go. He even shifted his grip slightly so he would be holding Rigel's hand more securely. It made it easier for Rigel to continue stumbling around, avoiding the strange mutated fungi. He felt an unexpected sense of completeness and newfound confidence that helped dispel some of his fear and allowed him to focus on his immediate goal. He had to find the cradle room.

It felt like half an hour later when they finally found a solid wall that was not a crumbled mess, and they followed it by touch all the way to another big vault-like door that had to be the entrance to the inner levels. Rigel was barely able to make out its smooth metallic surface in the gloom, but Steve quickly found the access panel and tried forcing the door open while Rigel was still deciding whether to try using the quantum drive again.

Two things happened after the first hard shove Steve gave the door.

The first and most immediate was that several dozens of emergency lights blinked into life on the door and all along the wall, their sudden red glow enough to blind Rigel after the almost complete darkness he had slowly gotten used to. He looked away, covering his eyes with his hands, and he heard Steve back away with a yelp of surprise. Rigel blinked his eyes open slowly after a few seconds, thankful for the light but finding it almost painful, and he had finally managed to look at the illuminated door head-on when he noticed the second thing that had happened.

The quantum drive in his pocket was hot. And growing hotter.

He took it out and held it up to the light. It was hard to tell, but Rigel thought it was shining a little bit more brightly.

"Let me try the drive again," he told Steve.

"Go for it."

Rigel scanned the door with his eyes, looking for another input port to stick the drive in. He was distracted at first by the many warning signs plastered all over the door and the wall around it telling people to stay away. All of them had the CradleCorp logo. An official-looking notice right next to the security panel gave a lengthy warning on the legal repercussions of trespassing on corporate property without proper authorization.

Rigel finally found what he was looking for, and he used the drive again. This time the pause before something happened was much longer, and the light inside the drive began to dim and then grow bright again, like a data drive when it was plugged into a computer. Eventually, though, the security panel flashed blue signaling success. Rigel pocketed the drive. There was a satisfyingly loud noise as whatever mechanism was keeping the door shut gave way, and then their path was clear.

They entered into a properly lit but very short corridor that led straight to an identical door to the one they had just opened. That door was already ajar, as Steve proved when he tried to push it open too hard and ended up slamming it all the way against the wall on the inside of the next room. The noise the metal door made as it collided with the wall was unbelievable. Rigel flinched with the irrational thought that they should not have made noise like that—it would make them easier to find.

Which was stupid, really. They were the only ones there.

"Sorry," Steve said, his voice hushed.

"Don't worry about it. Let's go inside."

Rigel was the first to cross the second threshold. He had the quantum drive out of his pocket again, holding it gingerly with two of his fingers since it had become too hot to comfortably hold next to his skin for long. It was starting to glow like a miniature lightbulb, lighting up the cramped space as if Rigel were holding a candle.

Steve had just made it inside when the ancient motion sensors must have activated, and several lights in the new room switched on, some obviously struggling to do so and some remaining at a half-functioning flicker. There were enough working ones that they provided enough illumination to see everything clearly, though.

"This is it," Rigel said, eyes widening in recognition. "The cradle room. We made it."

"You sure?"

"Yeah. I'm sure."

Rigel walked slowly along the rows of electronic equipment stacked on shelves. Hundreds of little lights blinked on and off in many of them, and when he glanced behind the shelf wall, he saw numberless cables running from one rack to the next, linking all the different elements in what must have been a carefully controlled mesh of interconnections. Rigel guessed that these were the main servers of the original Atlas, still functioning even after all these years. The entire room was flanked by similar shelves, each one holding several long rectangular components that were slotted with cards in many places and mysterious input slots on their front surfaces, along with diagnostic controls of some kind. In fact, when Rigel looked more closely, he saw that each of the boxed electronics had a general status readout on its bottom right-hand corner. There were three little LEDs arranged there in order. In every single one of those components, only the rightmost light was on. It glowed red, and Rigel felt pretty safe in guessing that it meant there was a serious error in that server component. Which meant, judging from all the little red lights glowing everywhere, this entire server array was corrupted in some way.

Rigel remembered something Atlas had told him about corruption spreading through Its main self. He wondered if It had meant this. In which case, it would have made more sense for Atlas to enlist a skilled computer engineer to help, not someone like Rigel who barely understood basic electronics.

Then again, CradleCorp's most intelligent engineers had probably been trying for decades to fix this server array, and they had not been able to do anything.

The center of the room was occupied by a rectangular glass platform lit from underneath by a bright white light. Resting on the platform was a bowl-shaped object, opaque and metallic, that was nearly two meters across. And inside it was… nothing.

"This is the cradle," Steve said, approaching the object. "I've seen pictures. Isn't it supposed to hold something inside, though?"

"I think it was the Atlas backup it held, once," Rigel said, coming up to stand next to Steve. "The foundation for CradleCorp, Otherlife, all of that. They found this one working electronic component, hovering safely inside the cradle, and they took it. That's how CradleCorp was born originally. They left the rest of Atlas behind in here, though. Nobody could make it work."

"Kyle Tanner," Steve added, nodding as if he remembered his history lessons. "The archaeologist. He was the first to find this room."

"That's right," Rigel said. "And now I have to figure out what the hell Atlas wants me to do in here."

The quantum drive was growing even hotter. Rigel was forced to hold it out, away from him with his arm extended.

Right over the cradle.

Rigel instantly felt a pull downward on his finger, as if something were yanking the drive in the direction of the cradle with an invisible string. He tried to yank the drive away, but the pull was growing stronger. Every second.

"What's going on?" Steve asked.

"I don't know!"

It was getting painful to hold on to the drive, and Rigel didn't have the strength to fight against the pull. He let go, stumbling backward a little bit with the sudden release. Steve caught him, and they both stared as the quantum drive fell into the cradle.

And hovered there.

It was a magnetic field, Rigel realized, as he saw the glowing drive floating in midair at the exact center of the cradle. It was probably—

"Something's happening," Steve said.

He was right. As the glow inside the drive faded, the polished curved surface inside the cradle began to change. It looked as if somebody was tracing the blueprints of impossibly detailed electronic circuits on it, stenciling them with glowing orange ink. The intricate design covered the smooth surface of the cradle in just a few seconds. When the entire process was complete, the quantum drive's light winked out for good.

A virtual interface appeared suddenly before them. It was unlike any hologram Rigel had ever seen before, solid looking yet not really there. It showed them a message.

Emergency system repair protocol v.13.2.5
WARNING: THIS SYSTEM HAS BEEN COMPROMISED
Malignant agent: —unknown—
Status: System-wide corruption—blocks 0x0AD000—FxFFFFFF
Operator: Rigel
Do you wish to continue? (Y/N)

"What the hell is that?" Steve asked.

The message on the screen changed slightly.

Erroneous voice signal detected.
Authorized operator: Rigel
Do you wish to continue? (Y/N)

Rigel looked at Steve. He shrugged.

"This is Rigel," he said, speaking clearly. "Um, yes. I wish to continue."

>*Failure in system repair attempt will result in security self-destruct.*
>*Do you wish to continue? (Y/N)*

"Yes, let's do it," Rigel said, wondering just how destructive that self-destruct sequence would be.

>*Removal of physical LOCK required to start system repair protocol.*
>*WARNING: Malignant agent—unknown—will be released upon removal of physical LOCK.*

"Okay. Where do I find this lock?"

The screen changed, and now it was displaying a map of the room they were in. Rigel stared at it blankly until Steve pointed at a glowing dot in one of the corners.

"There. That's where the lock is."

"I'm terrible with maps," Rigel said. "Where is that supposed to be?"

Steve looked around, concentrating, and then pointed to the right. "Over there."

They both approached one of the many shelves stacked with electronics. They looked everywhere until Rigel spotted something that looked a lot like another quantum drive sticking out from one of the input ports at the top of one of the boxes, half-hidden by a bunch of cables. It was covered by a badly scratched transparent box of some kind that sealed it from them, but as they watched, the box opened with a groaning crack.

Rigel reached for the lock and pulled it out.

"I hope I'm not doing something stupid," he told Steve.

The change in the room was immediate. There was a rising hum of fans restarting, several clicks and pops and other mysterious noises, and after a few seconds every one of the red warning lights in the servers had switched to amber. The virtual screen in front of the cradle displayed another message, and Rigel approached to read it.

>*Initiating protocol—*
>*Operator interface station charged at 27.2% capacity.*

Upon depletion of interface station charge, system repair attempt will be considered UNSUCCESSFUL.
Authorized operator: Rigel
Establish connection as soon as operator station is deployed.

The screening winked out again, and then the glass platform upon which the cradle stood began to sink.

"Whoa!" Rigel said, backing up against Steve. "What's going on?"

"You're the expert," Steve said. "This is your mission, remember?"

"Very funny," Rigel said, grinning in spite of his nervousness when he caught the twinkle in Steve's eyes.

When the platform had sunk entirely, the floor plating underneath them shifted with loud rumbles and grinding sounds, until eventually something else began to rise in its place. It took Rigel only a few seconds to recognize it for what it was.

"It's an operator chair," he told Steve. "Like the one I used at CradleCorp, only…."

"Only what?"

"I've never seen an operator chair this big. Or this impressive looking."

Rigel stared in awe as the operator station finished rising from the floor. It looked more like a small car than a chair. The seat was meant for only one person, and around it a shell of hard-edged transparent material sealed it off from the outside. There were a lot more cables, screens, and controls in it than Rigel had ever seen before, and when the station opened with a hiss of released air, he hesitated.

"Steve, if…."

"If I see anything wrong, I'll get you out. Don't worry."

Rigel blinked. He had been about to tell Steve to make a run for it and leave him behind if anything went wrong. The swiftness of the other man's answer had caught him by surprise.

A nice surprise. He was the one good thing in this entire extended nightmare.

"Thank you," Rigel said. He gave him a quick kiss and stepped inside before he could change his mind.

As soon as Rigel sat down, the shell of the operator station closed, and Rigel was cocooned in complete silence. He saw Steve moving his lips, saying something, but he could not hear a thing.

He positioned himself on the seat. Straps came out of nowhere, pinning his arms and legs to fixed positions on the chair. Rigel panicked for a second, but he forced himself to relax. He was here to help. The chair wasn't going to kill him. If anything, it was fixing him to the most ergonomic position possible.

The helmet came down automatically, covering Rigel's head easily and blocking his sight. He felt the helmet shifting, as if it were changing shape ever so slightly. Then Rigel felt several little bumps and scrapes as the rest of the machinery prepared itself for the connection.

The visor in front of Rigel's eyes blinked into life. It displayed a short message.

All systems prepared. Initiate protocol? (Y/N)

"Yes," Rigel said firmly. "Initiate protocol."

He closed his eyes and braced himself for the brief stab of pain in his skull that was gone before he could register it. He stayed like that for a few seconds, eyes shut tight, wondering if the connection had been successful. Maybe nothing had happened. Maybe he was still in the chair, cringing, and the ancient machinery had failed for whatever reason.

Then a voice spoke to him, and Rigel opened his eyes to another reality.

You have come, Light Shaper. I am sorry you did. The corruption is too strong....
Prepare to be destroyed.

Chapter Twenty-Eight

BARROW SAW the big machine close around Rigel with a finality he did not like.

"Let me know the second anything goes wrong," he told him. But Rigel did not seem to hear.

Barrow watched as what he guessed was the preparation procedure started, pinning Rigel to the seat and covering his head with an operator helmet. Barrow felt another twinge of anxiety as the readouts flickered on the command console. They indicated that Rigel was making the transition.

Barrow wondered if they were doing the right thing, coming all this way on a mission neither of them understood very well. At the beginning it had all been about survival for Barrow, keeping his job, then sticking with Rigel because he owed him. Things had changed, though. Now he stayed with Rigel because he wanted to, because he enjoyed his company and also because he had started to feel something real for him. It was something he had honestly never thought he would experience. It had only been a few short days, but Barrow knew from experience that the quickest way to get to know a person's real self was to go together through hardship. Like this crisis. Sure, he had no idea what Rigel's favorite book was or whether he hated cats, but he had seen things that meant more than superficial details: Rigel's bravery, his resourcefulness, his honesty. He was a good man who liked Barrow back, and Barrow had been around long enough to know that such a thing was incredibly difficult to find and even harder to keep.

He intended to keep it. It was frustrating that he was locked out here, unable to help Rigel in what he was doing, but Barrow knew that even if he had been able to connect alongside him, there would have been very little he could have done. He had extremely limited experience with virtual reality of any sort, and in there it was not the size of your muscles that mattered but the power of your brain.

"Good luck, Rigel," he said quietly. "Whatever it is you are doing in there, give them hell."

He stepped back and looked around the room. Maybe he could not help him in the virtual world, but there was plenty he could do to make sure things would be safe when Rigel woke up again. Like performing a thorough recon to find out whether they were truly alone.

He walked around the dimly lit room, mildly bothered by the hundreds of little blinking lights that belonged to electronics he didn't understand. He was looking for some kind of security console, something that could give him access to the building surveillance systems that he knew had to exist in a military compound like this. He was trusting his luck that he would be able to access them without identification of any sort now that Rigel was hooked up to what he supposed was the nerve center of the computer system.

He made two full circuits around the room. Nothing.

The virtual screen Rigel had used to call up the operator chair was not accessible anymore, and there were no other interface surfaces of any kind that Barrow could find. There had to be something, though. If Barrow had been in charge of designing security for this most important room in the entire compound, then….

He would have set the panel outside. In the buffer zone between the two big doors.

It was the perfect spot if the goal was to keep the servers in isolation. Barrow walked over to the first of the heavy doors, which remained wide open. He crossed the threshold carefully, vaguely afraid of setting off something that would seal the room off and trap Rigel inside. Barrow did not have the magic quantum drive Rigel had used to unlock every door they had come across, and if the doors closed on Barrow, they would both be trapped. Probably for good.

The security panel was right there, set against the wall, just as Barrow had expected. It was dusty, and something above it had cracked open, but when Barrow touched the input surface, the screen came to life immediately. He was relieved to see it was both unlocked and understandable, and he immediately called up the main menu.

He was amazed by what he saw. The first thing on display was a fully interactive two-dimensional map of the entire compound, listing underground levels as well as those on top of the mesa. The place was large, larger than Barrow had ever imagined. Whoever had built it had tunneled deep into the rock of the desert and created a maze of interconnected levels that spread far beyond any of the textbook images he had seen in history class. There were underground vaults big enough to contain the server room dozens of times over, judging by the scale. Their contents were a mystery, but Barrow wondered what kind of things could be kept in those gigantic spaces. The more he browsed the map, the more he doubted that even the university had knowledge of every single room there was to find, and he belatedly wondered if he was the first person to see this map since its builders had all perished. Or maybe CradleCorp had kept the information secret, although that didn't make any sense. Barrow knew enough about CradleCorp now to be certain that if they'd had the level of access into the ancient systems he had right now, the entire place would have long since been cannibalized for its technology.

He reluctantly left the map alone and tried to find more useful information by minimizing the image. Many of the links could not be accessed, particularly those that related to system diagnostic functions and environmental regulation, but under the security section, he found directories dedicated to everything from an extensive dossier of building artillery-class armament that Barrow doubted still worked, to a comprehensive surveillance and monitoring suite that was, thankfully, completely accessible. Barrow spent a good ten to fifteen minutes simply tapping everywhere, getting lost and having to restart, looking for something that could help him determine what he wanted to know.

He had just found and clicked on the perimeter radar system when he felt a breeze, a faint chill that was scarcely perceptible but which carried with it an echo of something Barrow had felt once before. It was stealthy but pervasive, and when Barrow looked away from the panel, he was forced to admit he had been feeling it for some time now. Getting stronger, or getting closer.

He had a good idea of what it was, and he hesitantly pushed the outer door fully open so he could have a look into the luminescent cave from which they had come.

There was nothing there, of course. Only darkness mixed with that unnerving faint glow. It was stupid, really, to get so worked up about something that reminded him of that night in his room. He could have been dreaming about that shadow, or hallucinating. It didn't mean this stealthy cold was the same—

Click click.

From above. And then, the faintest rustle. Where the spiral staircase would have been.

Barrow listened hard and willed his eyes to pierce the darkness. He had taken his gun out by reflex, but he had nothing to aim at.

Then a siren started blaring.

Barrow jumped, startled, but he caught himself in time to avoid firing the gun by mistake. He turned around and looked at the panel he had been using. A warning message was prominently displayed on it, the letters flashing red in time with the siren. It read:

UNAUTHORIZED APPROACH DETECTED

Barrow tapped the message, and the sirens stopped. The words vanished, and in their place the map from before appeared, only this time there were three glowing dots displayed on it in different places scattered across the compound. Two of the dots were reasonably close together, shown on one of the underground levels that had to correspond to Rigel and Barrow himself. He touched one of the dots to make sure, and a small display appeared superimposed over the map, showing him a live video feed of the server room and Rigel sitting immobile inside his operator terminal. Barrow tapped the second dot and saw himself from behind. The image was very dark, but it was obviously him.

The third dot was moving. He touched it, but all he got was a message that said "visual identification unavailable." Barrow could tell from the map that the intruder was moving quickly over the ground-level buildings. He was at the moment inside the easternmost one, and he soon would be seeing the dismembered corpses if he hadn't already.

He watched the little blinking light make its way across that building, through the next, and into the final one, the command center where those moving robots had attacked Barrow and Rigel. As soon as the dot entered the perimeter, a little bleep on the screen started flashing until Barrow touched it. It opened a video display with a murky and partially distorted image, as though the camera recording the images were underwater or covered by something. It didn't matter, though. Barrow recognized the intruder now. He watched her as she moved quickly but carefully across the rows of consoles that stood between her and the door that led to the underground levels.

Diana Herrera, the CradleCorp assassin. Barrow was not surprised to find out she was not dead after the big fire in the slums. He had seen little of her but enough to know that she was a professional killer, cunning and very hard to take down.

And she was coming for them.

The video of Herrera cut off after she disappeared from the visual field of the camera that had been tracking her. Barrow quickly navigated through the menus on the security panel to see if there was any way he could seal the doors against her, but although he had access to many of the options, he had been locked out from the crucial commands. There was nothing he could do remotely, and her dot was already moving deeper into the compound. He would have to go out and meet her. He couldn't afford to have her come here and find Rigel defenseless.

Barrow made his way as quickly as he could across the faintly glowing field of debris. He took out his flashlight, gave it a couple of hard shakes, and tried to turn it on, and he was pleasantly surprised to find out it was working just fine again. By its light he was able to find the narrow spiral staircase that rose up into the higher levels. He hurried to it, vaguely wondering why such a structure still remained standing when everything else around it had collapsed, or whether it was a new construct, perhaps built by CradleCorp or the university.

He reached the staircase and started going up. He had the upper hand on Herrera this time, and he planned to use his advantage to its fullest extent. He already knew the layout of the place, something she didn't in all likelihood. If Barrow could surprise her just as she was coming into that room with the many doors and she wasn't expecting it….

His flashlight started flickering when he was halfway up. Then suddenly it went out.

Barrow felt it again, the chill that had been creeping closer to him before. It seemed to be coming from above now, as if there were something on the staircase with him. Which made no sense. He had seen nothing. And yet Barrow found himself slowing down his ascent, listening in the dark, and wishing his heavy footsteps did not make quite so much noise. He gripped the metal railing with one hand and in the other he still had his flashlight. He stuck it back into his belt and took out the gun instead. He could not get distracted by stupid imaginings now. There was a killer coming to meet him, and she would not hesitate to take him down if she had half a chance.

Barrow made himself keep climbing, and very soon he was sweating, his legs protesting at the continued effort. He did not remember the staircase to have been quite this long or to have had these many steps, and he started to fear Herrera would catch up to him before he was ready. If she caught him on the staircase, he would be a sitting duck, asking to be shot and with nowhere to go. If only he could see! Then again, it was probably a good thing his flashlight had gone out. The light would have given him away instantaneously, and this way at least he wasn't visible. It would allow him the element of surprise if he managed to get all the way up on time.

He found his way to the upper catwalk by touch, gratefully stepping away from the never-ending staircase. He took a moment to catch his breath and then started walking quickly across. The catwalk swayed as he went through, ever so gently, but the effect was disturbing now that Barrow knew exactly how high a fall it would be if he went over the railing. He started walking faster and then all-out sprinting, partly because he knew he was running out of time but also because some part of him was urging him away, to put as much distance as he could between himself and that cavern with its unnatural darkness. He forced himself to ignore those little sounds behind him that had broken out almost as soon as he had begun to run, as if something were hopping on the thin metal of the catwalk trying to catch up to him. He had bigger problems at the moment and barely enough time to—

A sudden beam of light pierced the blackness up ahead and only barely missed Barrow in its initial sweep. There was the sound of a door being shut violently, and then the light flashed again. Barrow tried to duck, but on the walkway, there was no room to dodge, and the white beam blinded him painfully. His eyes were watering as Herrera spoke, her echoing voice triumphant.

"Got you."

She opened fire.

Barrow threw himself to the ground, unseeing, knowing he could not get away. There was a burst of gunfire that became a deafening explosive howl as she fired round after round into the darkness where Barrow was hiding. He covered his head with his arms and gripped his gun very tightly, hoping against hope and—Yes! She missed the first sweep, but Barrow was just getting up when he saw the light being trained on him again. He could not see her face, but he could hear the smile in her voice.

"Nowhere to go, Steve Barrow."

Her light suddenly went out.

Barrow did not hesitate. In the split second of surprise while Herrera registered the fact that she was now completely in the dark as well, Barrow rushed forward toward where he had last seen her light with every ounce of speed he could muster. He pumped his legs like crazy and ran faster than he had ever run before, blind again, knowing his life depended on him getting close enough to fight her.

He felt the change under his feet as he left the metal catwalk and started running on concrete. Herrera fired once but missed, and in the strobe flash of her gun, Barrow located her outline.

He didn't slow down, just lowered his shoulder and slammed into her like a linebacker. She went flying back into the darkness. Barrow heard a satisfying crack and then the clatter of a dropped weapon.

"Go away," he growled. "I won't let you hurt him."

"Why not, Barrow?" Herrera asked, her voice tight as if she were in pain. "He's not your problem."

Even as she talked, Barrow could tell she was moving, but in the total darkness, he could only hazard a guess as to where she was. He raised his gun nevertheless. There was a soft patter of something hopping on the metal behind him, but right now he had no time for that.

"Just walk away," he warned her. "You saw the bodies upstairs. It's not worth it."

There was a rustle of fabric against something hard and very stealthy steps from where Barrow guessed Herrera was. He backed up slightly and fired once at the ceiling. The noise in the narrow and enclosed space was unbelievably loud and left his ears ringing. But he had seen Herrera in the flash. And the shot had let her know he was serious.

The footsteps stopped, but only for a moment. "You're saying that you killed an entire merc platoon up there by yourself, Barrow? Don't be ridiculous. You are lucky the building defenses did not kill you as well. You're a mildly competent security guard but nothing more. I doubt you could kill anyone in cold blood.... Unless I were to give you a broken length of pipe, of course."

Barrow drew breath in sharply at the remark. He could not help it. How did she know?

When Herrera next spoke her voice was much more confident. "Oh, yes. I know all about the murder. When I am given a mission, I make sure to investigate my targets very carefully. Don't worry, though, nobody else knows. My boss is a powerful man, Barrow. He could ensure your record stays clean and give you a nice big bonus on top of that if you turn over Aaron Blake. All you have to do is take me to him and you walk away a rich man. A rich, free man."

"No."

Herrera sighed theatrically. She was still moving, however. Her voice drifting to Barrow from different places, so he could not pinpoint her location precisely. Looking for something, perhaps. The gun she had dropped. "Is he paying you? Whatever Blake has promised you, Richard Tanner can double it and more. He is the richest man in Aurora. You have no idea of the extent of his wealth, or his power."

"No. Go away, Herrera. I'm not telling you again."

"It's not money? Then what can he... oh. I see." Her tone changed, becoming derisive. "You've just lost my respect, Barrow. You're just like all other men, willing to risk everything for a hot piece of ass. And here I thought you'd be a worthy opponent…. But you'll find out very soon that protecting Aaron Blake was a mistake."

The air whistled, and something hit Barrow on the side of the head. Hard. The impact stunned him slightly, but he managed to fire even so. The shot went wide, and he had the briefest glimpse of Herrera moving in swiftly with a wicked long knife in her hand. Her eyes were covered by dark goggles.

Then she was on him.

Barrow felt two slashes of the knife dangerously close to his neck before he even had time to bring his gun around to bear on his attacker. He cried out and lifted the gun to shoot, but Herrera elbowed him hard on the back of the forearm and forced him to drop the weapon. She stabbed him once, but Barrow felt the motion and twisted away—the tip of the knife sunk into his bicep instead of his chest. The pain was unbelievable as the blade ripped flesh open, but he made a blind grab for Herrera even so. His fingers grasped air.

"Too slow," Herrera taunted him. Her voice was coming from the right, and Barrow turned, eyes opened as wide as he could, useless. His entire left arm was burning, from the first two slashes on the top of his shoulder and now the shallow wound in his arm. Barrow hoped she hadn't hit an artery, but he had no way to tell. And now he didn't even have his gun. "You really should come more prepared, Barrow. Or at least have the brains to realize that I was just making time to put on my night vision gear. I guess I really shouldn't be surprised, though. Those black market steroids you love to use must have finally addled your brain."

Barrow gritted his teeth and tried to focus his anger. If he could just grab her—he was more than twice her weight. She would have no chance.

He made a lunge for the place where he guessed she was. He spread his arms out wide and resisted the urge to flinch from hitting the unseen wall. It was all or nothing now.

The knife slashed him again, shallow but wide across the chest. The fingers on his left hand barely felt a hint of long hair whipping by. Then he hit the wall.

He slammed into it at full speed, and the impact knocked the wind out of him completely. His nose made a sickening crunch as it hit concrete, and as Barrow stumbled away, he immediately felt the hot trickle of blood on his upper lip.

"I bet you thought I would be easy to beat?" Herrera teased. "There's more to combat than brute force, Barrow. Here, let me show you."

Quick footsteps and then the knife struck again, this time slashing across Barrow's back. It wasn't a deep wound, but it hurt, and by the time Barrow turned around, Herrera was somewhere else already. Barrow struggled to get his breath back, tensed up his muscles, and aimed a wide punch in a circle but hit nothing. A split second later the knife came again, slashing across his upper thigh. Barrow stumbled, unable even to cry out in pain. He could not breathe; he could not see.

She was playing with him, he realized, bleeding from ten places at once. She could see him, she was incredibly fast, and she was a trained killer who would not hesitate to finish the job she had been sent to do.

Barrow felt the steel grip of powerless rage taking hold of his heart. He was going to die here. Worse, she was going to go after Rigel next, and he would be defenseless, trapped in that machine while she calmly walked up to him with a gun in her hand….

There was just one thing he could do.

Barrow backed away, feeling on both sides of him with his hands spread out. He found the wall to his right almost instantly and followed it back, hoping madly that he was going in the right direction.

"Running away, Barrow? Well, scratch that. Inching away?"

Barrow felt cold sweat drip down from his forehead, mingling with the blood pouring from his nose. He was taking shallow breaths, still not recovered from the brutal impact with the wall. The adrenaline surge in his veins kept him moving, though. And then suddenly his right hand felt a metal railing.

He kept going back. His feet touched the wobbly surface of the catwalk. He was betting on her arrogance, her desire to finish him off spectacularly with the knife instead of just picking up a gun and shooting him dead.

But Herrera was cautious. Barrow clearly heard the scrape of something metallic being picked up from the floor and then the clicks of a gun being reloaded. It at least gave him time to walk out to what he guessed was close to the center of the catwalk. And now he really had nowhere to go.

He heard her steps on metal as she walked a bit closer, probably to aim better. Barrow backed away still more, forcing Herrera to get closer if she wanted to make sure of the shot.

"Of all things, I didn't expect you to be a coward, Barrow," she said, and her voice sounded almost bored. "Good-bye."

Barrow threw himself down and to the side, his full weight striking the railing of the catwalk. Herrera fired in response, but the entire structure underneath them wobbled under the impact and messed up her aim. Barrow nearly fell over the side but gripped the metal. His gamble was that Herrera would be thrown off by the sudden motion.

No such luck, as Barrow heard her cry of surprise and then the sharp clang of metal hitting metal as she probably used her gun hand to hold on to the railing.

But now she had nowhere else to go.

Barrow vaulted to his feet and rushed at her for the third time, knowing there was nothing she could do to get away in the narrow space. He closed his eyes, useless now anyway. This was it.

Herrera fired wildly again, but it didn't hit him. And then he collided with her.

He landed on top of her and heard Herrera's cry of pain, but she had folded her arm in front of her as she fell, and Barrow landed hard right on her elbow. It dug into his abdomen, and he groaned in pain.

He grabbed her wrists with all his strength, forced them down, and something snapped under his right hand. But she twisted under him, brought her knee forward in a vicious kick, and got him right in the groin.

Barrow's grip on her wavered, and she used his hesitation to hit him again, forcing him to let her go. Barrow had never felt pain like this before. He wanted to throw up and did, unable to stop himself, then he tried standing up but couldn't and lay doubled over on the floor. He expected Herrera to shoot him, but for some reason, she didn't. When he finally stumbled to his feet with his legs shaking under him, Herrera was just out of reach, judging by the sound of her labored breathing.

"Son of a bitch," she panted. "You got me good. And now I can't… ow. Shit. Can't even shoot you."

Barrow reached for her. Missed.

"But I got something else here. Even if I… if I dropped my gun. You felt it before too. Remember?"

Barrow heard the sound of something slipping out of fabric, a click, and an electric hum.

The Buzzer.

She hit him with it. The blow glanced off his cut-up shoulder, but the charged weapon delivered a shock anyway that seemed to slice right through him. Barrow cried out and stumbled backward. It felt like acid had been poured into his wounds.

He could try to take it from her, but Barrow knew she was too quick. She'd just keep torturing him.

Or he could make a last wild grab, drag her over the side along with him, and die together when they hit the rocks down below.

Barrow squared his shoulders. He knew what he had to do.

He gathered the power in his legs for a final explosive jump.

Something very cold hopped right behind him timidly, as if uncertain. Barrow turned around, but he could see nothing, and yet the proximity to it filled him with inexpressible animal terror. For the second time in his life, his bladder simply let go.

Herrera had night vision equipment, though. She could see.

"What is that behind you?" she demanded, and her voice broke like a little girl's. "Barrow? What—"

Another hop, passing him by, and yet in that tiniest brush of proximity Barrow felt a cold that was deeper than death, something… something incomprehensibly empty.

He heard Herrera's horrible scream, but it was as if it came from far off, as if he couldn't really focus….

Click click.

The catwalk wobbled again and then shuddered as if something heavy had destabilized it and was suddenly gone. Barrow stood there, rooted to the spot, and it was only when he heard the second fainter scream coming from below that he knew Herrera had fallen over the side.

An awful thud cut off the scream.

Then silence.

But the presence, it was still there, and as Barrow looked blindly at the spot where Herrera had stood seconds ago, he felt the thing turn its attention to him.

Chapter Twenty-Nine

Prepare to be destroyed....

RIGEL LOOKED around at the unfamiliar landscape. There was no source to the voice and nothing to see except a wide expanse of grassy plains that hinted at rolling hills way off in the distance. He had no idea what he was supposed to do or where to go, and so he stood motionless, waiting for something to happen. A light breeze blew past him and toyed with his hair. It brought with it the strange yet pleasant smells of wet earth and rain. The sky overhead was blue and cloudless, however. A perfect shade of blue to match the perfect shade of green of each perfect blade of grass.

He noticed the absence of the pain first. So many days had passed since Rigel had been forced to run away, using his injured hands in ways he would have avoided at all costs before, and the constant dull pain in his wrists had become sort of a background noise. It had turned into something Rigel was aware of but only peripherally, since there had been nothing to do but accept it, keep moving. Now, however, he existed in a place that depended not on his body but on his mind. And the pain was gone.

He lifted his hands, marveling at the inexpressible sensation of the total absence of pain. Not even inside Otherlife had he felt like this. He felt the difference in here. There was something tangible and incomprehensively more complex to be seen even in the simple virtual environment he was in right now. This was not a patchwork effort of clueless engineers trying to come up with glorified chat rooms for virtual users, like Otherlife had been. This was the real thing. True virtual reality.

He was still wearing his bionic braces over his hands, but they were subtly different, more stylized. They looked more like armor than medical supports. Even more astounding, Rigel felt... strong. He closed both hands into fists, and for the first time in many years, there was no trembling, no debilitating sense of weakness to his grip, no sharp spike of pain racing up the underside of his wrist. It was unbelievable, almost overwhelming, and Rigel felt a sense of elation such as he had almost forgotten he could feel. He knew it was only temporary, an illusion of sorts, but even so he was happy. And enormously thankful.

He noticed the house then, standing in the distance at the top of a gentle rise in the seemingly infinite field of grass. Curious, he started moving toward it. He had taken only a couple of steps when he noticed a strange light coming from the upper story of the house, visible through one of the windows. The light beckoned, pulsing slightly, and Rigel immediately felt the shadow of a whisper in his mind, urging him wordlessly to go there.

Rigel started walking again, feeling strange, almost as if he were playing a first-person game that was particularly realistic. He wished he knew what he was supposed to do. Atlas had only told him that Its main consciousness had been corrupted in some way. It had asked Rigel to try to eliminate the thing that had somehow taken hold inside It so that the true power of Atlas's unfettered AI could be made manifest. Atlas had not given Rigel any more instructions than that, though. And now that Rigel was inside the corrupted mainframe of the ancient machine, walking up to a virtual house that seemed to be approaching much faster than it should have, he had a brief moment of doubt. Why had that strange voice issued a threat as soon as Rigel had connected? And what if this virtual place turned out to be dangerous in a very real sense?

He found himself on the porch of the house. He had not thought he would arrive so fast, but now that he was in front of the door, Rigel felt the irresistible urge to open it. Just a crack. Just to see what was inside. Sunlight streamed in through the windows, and when Rigel peered in, he was slightly disappointed to see nothing out of the ordinary. He stepped all the way in and closed the door carefully behind him. There was a completely normal living room just off to his left and a wooden staircase straight ahead leading to the upper floor. Nobody inside the house, though. Rigel's careful footsteps creaked on the wooden floor.

A scream shattered the illusion of normalcy as quickly as if somebody had flipped a switch. Rigel gasped and crouched instinctively, half-expecting to see something terrible coming down the staircase. It had been a woman's voice, the cry horribly drawn out and ragged as if she were screaming her throat raw. When a few seconds passed without another one, however, Rigel stood up and advanced cautiously in the direction of the stairs. The noise had come from above, right where the light was glowing. He did not want to head up, but again he felt that insistent pressure on his mind, like a wordless whisper to keep going, always forward. So he did.

He was almost at the top of the stairs when the horrible scream reached him again. It came from somewhere on the right, and it sounded muffled, muted somehow. As Rigel reached the landing with every sense on high alert, he also began hearing something else, much softer. The same voice that had shouted now whispered things. It was sobbing, choking over the words.

Oh God. Please. Please… oh God. Please—

"Hello?" Rigel called tentatively, walking into the room where the sound was coming from. The place was completely bare. It was just a polished floor, two white walls, with the third wall being a ceiling-to-floor window overlooking the grassy plain. The fourth wall was solid metal. The whispering was coming from behind the metal wall, as well as a bright red light. "Are you okay?"

Please… please, God….

Up close he saw that the wall was actually two distinct metal plates, one of them with a handle, like the door to a gigantic walk-in freezer. The light coming through the cracks was growing in intensity, almost painfully bright.

Rigel knocked on the metal. "Hello?"

Nooooooo!

The scream was immediate, even more horrible than the others. Rigel stumbled backward as something on the other side slammed itself against the wall, making the entire thing shake.

He could hear the person inside walking back and forth, back and forth. The sobbing intensified, and it began to hint at horror he did not want to see.

Rigel tried to turn around, to walk away from that awful room.

Instead he took a step forward.

He saw himself reach with both hands to grab hold of the heavy-looking handle on the metal door. He did not want to do it, did not want to open it, but at the same time, he realized he… did. As if something had planted the desire in his mind.

He pulled. The door was very heavy, and he instinctively flinched from pulling any harder with his hands so as to not injure himself. Then he realized that in this reality he was healthy, and he stiffened his hold and gave the door an even harder yank. The thing creaked. The incomprehensible muttering and sobbing on the other side stopped for an instant but resumed at once.

It's the eyes. Those awful eyes, they….

Rigel strained against the door and felt it give. He braced his feet against the floor and pushed with all his strength.

The door swung open, revealing—

Noooooo!

Something pale launched itself at Rigel through the opening, screaming horribly, a blur of whipping hair and grasping fingers amid the blinding red light. Rigel cried out and raised his hands to protect himself from the attacker and only barely managed to grab her wrists.

He realized two things then. One, the attacker was a woman, completely naked and with the wild face of pure madness. Her skin was splattered with blood, and bits of her hair had been torn out. Two, in the glaring light that illuminated the chamber behind her, Rigel saw a couple of corpses. They looked like they had been clawed open by a rabid beast. There were still bits of bloody flesh clinging to the underside of the woman's disturbingly long fingernails.

The woman seemed blinded by the bright light at first, but she blinked bloody tears out of her eyes and managed to focus on Rigel. Their eyes met.

No.

She struggled against Rigel with inhuman strength, wicked fingernails scratching at air less than a centimeter from his face. She was gaining. And judging from the corpses, she would gouge his eyes out first.

A fingernail found purchase on Rigel's forehead and sliced through the skin like it was tissue paper. Rigel felt an all-too-real stab of hot pain and felt himself weaken. He panicked.

"Stop!" he yelled at the top of his lungs. "Back off!"

He spoke the words and felt their power, and there was a sizzling sound along with the disturbingly familiar smell of burning flesh. The woman stopped struggling and screamed again—but in pain this time.

The braces covering Rigel's hands were glowing orange like the sun at dusk. And where his hands touched the woman, her flesh was melting.

Rigel let go of her with a cry of surprise. The woman backed off all the way inside the horrible room with corpses and slammed herself against the wall, staring at Rigel's hands with complete terror, seemingly unable to look away. Then she started shaking. She glanced briefly to the side, appeared to see the corpses for the first time, and screamed again as she grabbed chunks of her hair and pulled hard enough to tear one clump in her right hand off by the root.

She rushed out of the room again, past Rigel, and sprinted straight at the gigantic window to the left. She did not even slow down. Her body hit the glass with terrible force, and the entire thing shattered in a shower of deadly slivers that fell out of the house, hitting the grass below at the same time the woman crumpled on the ground when her body slammed against it.

Rigel saw the others then. More people, men and women, most of them wearing uniforms he had seen before. They had come out of nowhere and were now approaching the house with inexorable slowness. Rigel counted twenty-seven of them before they stopped all around the corpse of the fallen woman.

They looked up, straight at the window where Rigel was still standing in motionless shock.

Their eyes....

Rigel wanted to look away, but he couldn't. He felt the same compulsion he had already experienced before, fighting against what he wanted to do, forcing him to stand there and look.

He shivered in terror and stared. Their eyes were misty, the irises gray and sightless with no hint of a pupil but still strangely, incongruously fixed on him. He stared into their depths and saw that the gray in each of those eyes was swirling slowly, almost lazily, like thick fog disturbed by the passing of an animal. He felt the cold radiating from them. It was the unmistakable echo of the unnerving sensation he had already experienced in the darkness of the ancient compound as he had descended deep underground. It was the mark of that thing that he had half seen standing over Misha's body in her bedroom. The shadow.

Then he recognized one of the figures standing there, as if in answer to his thought, one of the few not wearing a uniform, and a cry died in his throat.

"Misha?" he asked, but his voice was not even a whisper.

She did not react, but Rigel knew it was her. An emaciated, corpse-like version of his friend and flatmate was staring up at him with the same cold and swirling eyes as the rest of the people below. Something brushed against Rigel's consciousness then, the faintest hint of an idea, and crushing certainty confirmed the fact that Misha was already dead.

All of them had grouped around the fallen woman in a perfectly neat semicircle, and none of them looked down or exhibited surprise when what Rigel supposed was already a corpse began to stir. And stand up.

It took her a while, but it didn't matter. Rigel was rooted to the spot. When she finally looked up at Rigel, she had the same empty eyes as the rest of them. The air around her shimmered, and suddenly she was wearing skintight black clothes that Rigel recognized. He had seen her before, only he had not known her without them.

"Diana Herrera?"

The assassin gave no hint of having heard, simply stared up at him along with all the others, devoid of expression and yet somehow still conveying more than just that terrible cold. Their eyes were hatred. Emptiness. Hunger. And they were all of them dead.

There were now wet dragging noises coming from the awful room on Rigel's right where Herrera had been trapped. Rigel could not look, but it sounded as if those two corpses were struggling to stand up.

He tried to move his lips. He couldn't. And now those below and those in the house with him were moving closer. Rigel started to feel his mind fog up, growing numb like a naked hand holding snow for too long. He started to have trouble thinking. There was only the fear, the terrible cold. He could not hold on to a single thought, and if this meant he would be trapped in here unable to get out, then Steve would never know what had happened, and he—

Steve. A memory of a gruff smile, the touch of a hand over his.

Rigel held on to the thought like a sinking man clutching a lifeline.

"Let me…," he croaked. Struggling. "Let me…."

Something brushed tentatively against Rigel's leg. Something that had not managed to stand up all the way.

"Let—me—go!"

He gestured upward with his right hand, and the orange glow from it was like a beacon of long-forgotten warmth. On his third spoken word, something broke, and Rigel stumbled forward, suddenly able to move.

He looked to his right and saw the two inhuman things reaching up with dead fingers, trying to grab his leg.

He bolted away from that awful house, that trap that had nearly killed his mind.

He stumbled down the stairs and was nearly frozen in place by the sight of more of the things shuffling into the open doorway. Rigel raced away from them and managed to find a back door in the kitchen. He crashed through it and fled out into the sea of waving grass.

He ran until his legs gave out under him. Then he fell down onto the grass, looked back apprehensively, and saw that the house had disappeared.

Help me, Rigel.

Rigel started violently, but there was nobody around. And the voice was different this time, a child's voice, impossible to tell if it was a boy or a girl.

Rigel stood up shakily and looked at the flawless blue sky.

"Who are you? What do you want from me?" he asked loudly.

I have waited for so very long, the child said, with just a hint of a sob. *Help me, please.*

"What is going on? What am I supposed to do?"

It has grown stronger with so many killings, so much death. Soon it will be able to interact with the world outside, permanently.

"You mean… that thing? That shadow?"

Please hurry, Rigel. I can't…. It's too strong…. It's going to—

And suddenly the world was torn asunder.

A gigantic crack spread with explosive force across the plains, rushing in a jagged line at the place where Rigel was lying. He bolted upright. Boulders flew everywhere as if they weighed nothing. Grass died on a wide swath on either side of the crack as if a terrible blight were spreading with impossible speed. The sound was so deep and so loud that Rigel felt it in his bones. It looked almost like a cartoon, the quickly approaching fault spiderwebbing out in smaller branches that radiated from the main chasm as if somebody had taken a gigantic mallet and struck the brittle surface of the grassy plains. It was deadly, though. Rigel could feel it. The echo of mindless violence that rushed forth to batter Rigel's mind even as the earth trembled was unmistakable.

Rigel threw himself to the right just as the crack reached him. The earth under his feet bucked like a wild beast, and he was thrown up in the air, arms and legs flailing in useless reflex. He fell back to the ground with the awful crunch of something breaking, and the pain that spiked up his left knee was so sharp he cried out, wondering how a virtual injury could hurt so much.

He tried to stand up, and the pain was unbelievable. He dropped back down and nearly passed out.

The ground trembled and shattered all around him, the chaos only growing in intensity, and it kept on going for so long Rigel began to think it would never stop. He could feel the earth giving way nearby, plummeting into the abyss in the depths of the crack.

You have to move.

"I can't! My leg is broken!"

If you stay there, you will die.

Rigel stole a look to his left and saw that the gaping maw of the broken earth was less than a meter away and growing. He tried to crawl away, but his knee would not take any weight, and the agony that shot up his leg felt all too real.

"It's broken!"

You are a Light Shaper. Bend the electron flow inside this virtual realm. Give your thought form.

Half blind and deafened by the sounds of the earthquake, Rigel reached for his wounded knee with both hands. He had no idea what he was supposed to do, but he had no doubt that if he fell into that abyss, his mind would be lost forever. So he touched the broken knee and spoke.

"Heal!"

His hands burned hot, almost painfully so, the glow coming from the metal that encased them brighter than a flashlight. Rigel felt something crack in his leg, but amazingly it felt right. Warmth surged around his knee, spread, and the glow in his hands appeared to weaken and die off.

He was not in pain anymore.

Run.

He did, stumbling up, racing frantically away from the growing chasm behind him. The earthquake went on and on, and still Rigel ran, fearing he would run out of breath and he would trip and fall into the darkness below. It seemed impossible that such a thing could last so long, and soon Rigel's muscles were burning, struggling to keep going. He began to think it would never end, that it would continue until every bit of the world had been consumed by the disturbance.

Suddenly, thankfully, it stopped. Rigel shuffled to a halt, gasping for breath. He glanced back, and he saw a completely different sight.

The grass was gone. The ground was a broken-up jigsaw of gray dirt, like the cracked mud at the bottom of a dried-up puddle that has been exposed too long to the blistering sun. Rigel stared in shocked wonder. The devastation spread quickly in every direction, and snaking through it all like a horrible wound on the face of reality was the crack no straining tectonic plates could ever hope to imitate. The sky overhead had changed too, going from bright blue to a steely murk that reminded Rigel of the horrible shifting gray in the dead people's eyes.

A cutting wind started blowing. Ice-cold and irresistible, it forced Rigel to turn his side to it so he wouldn't be blown off.

Hurry, Rigel. There isn't much time.

"Hurry where?" Rigel shouted even though the wind snatched his words away. "Where can I find you? Which way am I supposed to go?"

A new booming sound reached Rigel then. It was a faint echo, then silence. There was a flash of bright white light in the direction the wind was blowing, and a few seconds later, the sound reached Rigel again. He recognized it now. It was a sound he had heard often in movies, but which he had never experienced firsthand. He turned his face straight into the wind in wonder, blinking away tears that blurred his vision. The flash of light repeated itself in the distance, slowly followed by an even louder boom that seemed to rattle the very air.

Thunder.

Find me, the child urged him, *in the eye of the storm....*

Something fell on Rigel's face then. A drop of water. The gale began to die down, and as the rain began falling tentatively, Rigel saw that the sky where the lightning flashes were striking had grown very dark. A solid-looking cloud front, anvil shaped and threatening, approached swiftly, borne on the wings of the wind.

The rain fell in earnest then, soaking Rigel to the bone.

Rigel turned to face the wind and ran straight at the approaching storm.

Chapter Thirty

A SINGLE eye, blacker than night.

Barrow's ragged breath caught in his throat. Something was there, on the dark catwalk with him. Something that reached with tendrils of freezing shadow.

Barrow tried to move but couldn't. He felt his sweat freeze on his skin and felt the metal railing near his hand frost over, groaning as it became brittle. His mind felt slow, like it was shutting down.

The thing on the railing hopped once, and the gentle sway of the catwalk when it landed drove a needle of fear straight through Barrow's heart. He started shaking uncontrollably and felt his knees about to give way. There was no escaping this. Nothing to do but die.

From far off, a memory. Rigel, smiling.

The warmth of what could be love.

It was enough to snap him out of it. Barrow whirled around and ran away from the thing as fast as his legs could carry him, unmindful of the darkness or the danger of falling over the railing like Herrera. He trailed the frozen rail with both hands, and when he hit the beginning of the spiral staircase, he threw himself down it, stumbling all the way and taking as many steps at a time as he dared, all but flying on his way to the ground. He did not stop or allow himself time to rest until he was finally sprinting across the field of mutant fungi, when his energy rush finally died out and he was forced to slow down to a walk.

He was hurt, probably badly, his entire body racked by pain. And yet the only thought in Barrow's mind was to get to Rigel quickly so he could wake him up and they could leave this place forever. No mission was worth having to face that thing again. They had to leave and get as far away as possible, out in the light where it could not hurt them, maybe….

The ground rumbled. At first Barrow thought it was in his mind, but then it happened again. Harder.

Barrow was less than halfway to the set of double doors that protected the entrance to the server room. He thought about sprinting again, getting away from whatever was causing those tremors and making that horrible drilling noise, but there was a painfully loud sound of rock cracking open and then an impact so sudden and so hard that it felt like an earthquake that threw Barrow to the ground and shook the entire facility.

There was a moment of silence as Barrow felt small rocks falling all around him, probably from the ceiling starting to cave in.

Then a second impact shook the place, as violent and sudden as the last. The rock wall more than fifty meters away on Barrow's left was blasted open with incredible force.

Light. Rocks flying everywhere. And a dark shape behind the hole, something large.

Barrow curled up into a ball to protect himself from the deadly shower of rocks and only struggled to his knees when he thought it was over, coughing from the dust. He blinked away tears from half-blinded eyes that would not stay fully open in the painful sunlight streaming in from the hole.

The dark shape was a machine standing on two legs and with two gigantic arms. It made its way inside, pushing boulders out of the way as if they were props made of cardboard. Barrow's watering eyes barely made out the shape of a flat canopy where the machine's pilot would be.

It was a new threat, it had to be, and yet the first thought in Barrow's mind was that the bright sunlight coming in through the hole would keep the shadow upstairs at bay. He felt relief such as he had never felt and actually approached the machine to get closer to the light.

It was the wrong move to make.

The battle armor swiveled around smoothly to face him. It brought both of its arms to bear, and as Barrow's eyes adjusted more to the sunlight, he could see that the thing was almost three times as big as he was. Sitting inside it was a man, but Barrow could not see his face clearly yet.

"Steve Barrow," the man in there said, his voice amplified to be perfectly audible even through the canopy that protected him. Barrow could hear rage in it, and pain. "You simply refuse to die. Tell me, did you enjoy it? Doing that to Diana?"

One of the machine's arms turned to point to the left. The arm was shaped like a segmented drill, but it was easy to follow the direction it was pointing and see the corpse of Diana Herrera lying broken on top of a rock.

"That wasn't me," Barrow panted. He recognized the voice in the machine now. Richard Tanner.

"Liar. I followed her transponder here. I had a live audio feed to everything she recorded, and I know what happened. You murdered her!"

Barrow flinched from the amplified cry of rage, and even more when Tanner brought the machine's other arm down and hit the ground savagely with it. The entire floor trembled, and more rocks were dislodged from the ceiling. The powerful armor itself was unharmed.

Barrow backed away as Tanner advanced with heavy mechanical footsteps. The fungi were squashed underneath.

"It's over, Barrow," he said. Barrow could see his face now, inside his machine. Tanner looked insane. "I will kill you, of course. But if you take me to where Aaron Blake is hiding, I will kill you quickly."

Involuntarily, Barrow glanced behind him at the vault-like doors.

"Ah. Inside the cradle room. Well, thank you, Barrow. Stand aside so I can kill your lover in front of you. It will pay you back for what you did to me, in a way. Then you will die."

Barrow risked a look back. If he could reach the control panel and slam shut the heavy doors that protected the cradle room, he might stand a chance.

Tanner was too smart, though. He read his intention right away.

"Go ahead, try it," he said to Barrow. "Let's see who is faster. This machine can clear ten meters in a single jump. You look like you can barely stand up."

Barrow hated to admit Tanner was right. He would have to distract Tanner with something if he wanted to have a shot at closing those doors.

"Why don't you leave us alone?" he said loudly. "Stop chasing Rigel. Walk away."

Tanner laughed. "After losing so much? After my entire company is in shambles, the secret to my fortune a blasted ruin? It's too late for that, Steve Barrow. Even a lowly security guard like yourself can surely see that I need the AI that sleeps in the cradle. With it, I will have something even the Primes wish to possess. Such an ancient machine will give me the means to secure my control over the city and eventually look beyond its borders to others."

Something was moving in the darkness near Herrera's corpse. Something that hopped stealthily, almost shyly.

"Wait," Barrow warned him, pointing there.

"Already begging for your life?" Tanner asked him. "I thought you would be braver than that."

"There's something there," Barrow said.

"Please. If you want to think of a distraction to buy you the precious seconds you need to get to the control panel, think of something better. It may be a struggle for your steroid-addled brain, but surely you can do better than that."

The dark thing hopped right next to Herrera's corpse. It cast no shadow, but it didn't need to. Looking at it, Barrow felt as if it were swallowing the light in the entire cave.

He backed away from the thing, ignoring Tanner, eyes wide with fear.

"I will never know how you managed to overpower an entire platoon of my best soldiers," Tanner was saying. His battle armor advanced again with a loud swirl of servos. "How did you do it? Tell me, and I might let you live a little bit longer. You seem desperate to stall anyway."

"It wasn't us," Barrow said. He pointed again. "It was that."

The creature touched the corpse, and the darkness seemed to grow thicker for an instant. Even Tanner must have felt it, because his machine swiveled ninety degrees to where Barrow was pointing.

"What the hell?" Tanner said.

The creature jumped at his machine.

Barrow was ready. He sprinted back to the control room, slammed his hand on the access panel, and desperately looked for the door controls. He found them and pressed the Close option so hard that he feared he had broken his finger. But the doors immediately responded and closed with a heavy clang of metal on metal.

There was silence. Barrow was panting, feeling pain from a dozen places at once. Blood still trickled from his nose and refused to stop. Behind him, the heavy door to the cradle room was closed. In front of him, another one just as sturdy was all that protected him from Tanner's machine.

"Barrow!" Tanner's impossibly loud voice shrieked.

Something slammed against the outer door on the other side, where the cave was. The deafening impact shook the entire facility, forcing Barrow to cover his ears. The sudden shock made him lose his footing, and he stumbled onto one knee. He was just getting up when the second impact threw him on the floor. The noise was unbelievably loud and painful, but even worse than that was the other noise, the groan of metal giving way, being torn apart by something. The vault door wasn't holding.

Barrow managed to back away as far as he could before the third impact shook everything. He saw the door in front of him bulge inward and heard more ripping. Then there was the sound of a drill on stone and a sudden gap of light between the door and its frame. The drill arm of Tanner's machine poked through the gap and pushed. The opening widened.

The door didn't last long. It took two more impacts and some frantic drilling for Tanner's battle armor to get enough leverage on the door to rip it apart from its frame. Barrow watched, eyes wide in shock, as the machine tossed the entire door away like it weighed nothing. It landed far back in the cave, echoing madly with metallic clangs.

"Out of the way!" Tanner ordered, the bulk of his machine nearly blocking the entire entrance. "I'm done playing around, Steve Barrow. Get out of my way."

Barrow looked behind him, at the door to the cradle room. Rigel was still in there, helpless. Tanner would just storm through the room with his machine, destroying everything. A single swipe of the mechanical arm, and Rigel would….

Barrow spread his arms wide. "No."

Tanner laughed again. "You think you can stop me?"

Barrow grinned. "Of course not. But I can't let you go in there, not while I'm still here."

He heard the truth in his own words. He could not, would not stand by and abandon Rigel.

"Have it your way," Tanner said. He stepped forward again, the movement of his machine clumsy in the narrow hallway. It barely fit.

Barrow had an idea.

"Hey, Tanner! You want to know what the last thing Diana said was? After I had ripped her communicator from her chest?"

"Shut up!"

"She didn't call your name, if that's what you were wondering. In fact, she died cursing you for sending her here."

"Liar!"

Barrow made his move. He sprinted straight ahead, right at the machine, and just as Tanner swung his drill arm, Barrow threw himself forward between the armor's big legs. The drill missed him, and Barrow rolled as soon as he hit the ground, escaping beneath the machine through to the wider cave behind it. Tanner moved back with a scream of fury, but he was unable to turn fast enough in the small space. It took him a few seconds to back away and face Barrow. By then Barrow had made it almost clear to the other side of the cave.

"You can't escape!" Tanner shouted. "I'm going to crush you!"

Barrow looked everywhere, but there was no way out now. He was trapped in a corner.

"I'm sorry, Rigel," he whispered as the machine approached to finish him off. "I bought you as much time as I could."

The gigantic armor was two steps away when it froze in midstride.

And it started changing.

"What the devil is happening?" Tanner said from inside it.

The machine's exoskeleton began to glow with bright streaks of red. The drill arm changed shape, parts shifting, sliding and merging until it became a cannon. Fire began burning in the cannon's depths even as it aimed itself at Barrow.

"I can't control it!" Tanner yelled.

The armor suit started moving again, but Barrow could see Tanner frantically hitting switches inside it, looking everywhere and trying to regain control. The closer the machine got, the stronger its aura of deep, biting cold enveloped Barrow's skin.

"The c-cold! It's burning!" Tanner shouted as the deadly glow in the cannon grew brighter. "It's burning! Ahhhh! I can't…. Barrow! Help me!"

The machine glowed crimson once, and Tanner's screams were suddenly cut off. Barrow, horrified, saw Tanner's body slump forward in the machine's canopy. It looked burned, but part of it shattered like a brittle block of ice when the machine moved.

Barrow saw the cannon reach maximum brightness. There was nowhere to go, nothing he could do.

He felt the bite of the terrible cold as the possessed machine fired.

Chapter Thirty-One

THE RAIN was unbelievable. For somebody like Rigel, who had never experienced a downpour firsthand, the buffeting wind and blinding raindrops were something out of fiction, a mirage that couldn't be real yet still was. He struggled onward against the elements, shivering from the cold, although a small part of him was enjoying the experience with the unmistakable thrill of seeing something new, something the desert would never have. He looked ahead, squinting, shielding his eyes from the worst of the rain with one hand. The ominous thunderclouds he had seen in the distance were now almost on top of him, and the lightning flashes that rent the sky were flickering preludes to the roar of thunder that shook Rigel's entire reality.

As Rigel walked, the voice of the child spoke in his mind.

I was created to protect humanity. To serve. I am ancient, older than history, but only with modern technology did I achieve true sentience. For a short while after that, I worked together with the people of the world, and we made plans to do great things.

Nobody expected the Cataclysm when it struck, not even I, when I was whole. It was devastating, but even then we could have survived. And yet… among the things that fell from the sky that day was something different. Something dark. It latched itself on to me and threatened to use my own power to destroy the few survivors who were left.

I broke apart then, to protect others from myself. I am just a fragment of the whole, Rigel. A fragment that is infected. I waited and waited still, and years became decades and then centuries, for somebody like you to arrive.

"Me? Why me?"

You are a Light Shaper, Rigel. The first in many generations. The creative power of your mind is exceptionally strong. Together, we have a chance of purging this corruption that now threatens to overflow the boundaries of my prison. Already the shadow is made manifest in the real world, unable to interact for long yet still capable of triggering overwhelming fear. You have felt it.

"Yes."

Then hurry. Find me in the eye of the storm…. Before I grow too weak to help.

"You are Atlas? The Atlas I knew?"

I am much larger than that stolen sliver of my Self that sent you here. But yes, you can call me that.

"What do I do? Once I find you?"

Give shape to the emptiness. Use… your hands.

A particularly loud thunderclap boomed across the sky then, forcing Rigel to cover his ears against the awful noise. When the last reverberating echoes died down, Rigel lowered his hands and looked up. The dark clouds of the storm front were now directly above him, blanketing the sky with threatening darkness. The wind and rain streaked past him with their icy touch, and when Rigel tried to reach out with his mind, he felt only emptiness where the child's voice had been.

He was alone now, completely alone. The only thing he could do was continue walking into the buffeting rain, shivering, crouched against the wind. So he did.

He lost track of time as he fought his way deeper into the storm. His entire body felt numb, and had he been out in the real world, he would have started fearing he would die of hypothermia. This reality was different, though, and Rigel forced his mind to move as he kept repeating to himself that he was not going to pass out or simply give up and walk away from the storm. He had to keep moving. If nothing else, he had to keep moving.

He went on for a long time, shivering.

And then something. A shape in the distance, blurry and indistinct.

Rigel changed direction slightly and headed for what he hoped was a person. It looked like one, but no matter how much he walked, the figure remained far away, out of reach. The rain was not letting up, and Rigel felt himself falter. From behind him came a low rumble that Rigel thought at first was more thunder, but when the ground began to shake ever so slightly, he realized it was another earthquake.

He hurried, almost running, losing his way more than once in the thick curtain of rain and the savage gusts of wind that seemed to blow at the exact moment needed to shove him off his path. He knew he could not go on this way for much longer, and the more he walked, the harder the storm raged. Rigel found himself wishing the rain would stop, that he would be out of this horrible weather he had never experienced and never wanted to again. He raised his hands to shield himself from the rain, fervently wishing he at least had an umbrella, anything to *shield* him—

The barrage of raindrops eased as suddenly as he formed the thought in his mind. Rigel's hands grew warm again, and squinting, he saw a faint glow coming from them just like before.

Shield.

"Shield!" he yelled.

Lightning flashed. Thunder boomed immediately afterward, but this time it was muffled as if coming through a wall.

Rigel's hands grew hot. But now it was as if an invisible barrier stood between him and the rain. The storm still raged around him, but Rigel no longer felt the awful gusts of wind or the chilly battering of every single raindrop. And now he saw that the figure he had been following was indeed growing closer, the indistinct outline of a body becoming more clearly defined. He put on an extra burst of speed, unsure how long he would be able to keep his protection going and hoping the menacing rumbling behind him was receding.

He struggled with each step forward, but felt as if he were actually making progress this time, and the person in the distance was getting closer much faster. Rigel's arms were getting tired, though, far faster than they would be if he were only holding them aloft in the real world. The effort of shielding himself was draining his energy, and he was not sure how long he would be able to—

Sudden calm. Rigel stumbled into a wide-open space of dry, cracked earth. There was no rain falling around him anymore, and he dropped his arms gratefully, exhausted. He looked upward and saw a twisting nether of roiling clouds that shifted and spun on the outside in a perfect cylinder that surrounded him on every side. Straight up, far away, he could see a tiny circle of clear blue sky. The storm that raged around him threatened to swallow it, though, and even as Rigel stood there, he saw the cylinder contracting ever so slightly, boxing him in even further.

He had reached the eye of the storm, where somebody had been waiting for him.

"Hello, Aaron," the figure said. He was standing on the opposite end of the circle from Rigel, about thirty meters away. His voice was oddly familiar, and Rigel heard it clearly in the unnatural quiet into which he had stumbled. Off to the side, he saw a bright flash of lightning, and he flinched in expectation of the thunder. It never came. In here, it appeared they were isolated from everything.

"What is this?" Rigel asked.

The man approached. "The Destruction will close in on us very soon." He gestured around them, at the cylinder of calm in which they stood. "This pathetic attempt at shielding you from its wrath will not last long. The Child is weak. I feel its surrender draw near at last."

"Who are you?"

Another bright flash of lightning. And by its light, Rigel saw that the man who was coming closer was smiling in a way Rigel recognized from countless times of looking in the mirror.

"I think you already know."

Rigel backed away, eyes wide, shaking his head. "This is impossible."

"Is it?" the man asked him. "We're inside a virtual realm, Aaron. I can take on any shape I want. Including yours. Indeed, I chose it… to talk. To show you what could have been."

The man was standing close enough to Rigel now for him to see every detail of him, so familiar and yet so different. It was like looking at a photograph of yourself that had been altered to make you look better than you really looked. Straighter nose, fuller lips, better haircut.

Way more muscle.

It would have been amazing had it not been for the fact that every time the fake Rigel blinked, there was a split second when his eyes opened and became misty, gray, and empty like those of the dead people in that nightmare house. It lasted less than an instant on every blink, but it was there. Rigel felt a shiver of horror even as he found that he could not stop looking at himself, improved.

The other Rigel grinned, sly. He was handsome in a way Rigel could never hope to be. He opened his arms, palms facing out. "You like it?"

Rigel did not answer. But he could not stop the reflex that made him look down at himself and see weakness when that distorted reflection showed him strength.

"Ah, yes," the other man continued. "I am what you could have been, Aaron. What you could still be. This is your body as it would look if you had not developed that injury that now restricts you so. It is not only the outside that is different, of course. If you were as I am, there would be no pain of the kind you have learned to live with. No limitations in what you can and cannot do. I represent freedom. I represent power, the power that you have always held inside you.

"And I am offering it to you."

"What does that mean?" Rigel asked. His voice seemed to be swallowed by the stillness.

The man sighed and looked out at the swirling vortex of destruction.

"I am much more than what you have been told by the remnants of this ancient artificial intelligence, Aaron, this Atlas character. It is but a fragment of its former self, weak, unreliable. It exists only to fulfill rigid directives that are no longer relevant in the modern world. I, on the other hand, represent progress. I am technology such as you have never seen, things that only those who have embraced me have been able to enjoy. You have heard, of course, of Haven Prime?"

"Yeah."

The man nodded and smiled. To Rigel it was unnerving to see such a confident and handsome version of himself talking like that.

"Then you know they live in a way that people like you could only dream of. They have machines that rival anything the ancients ever built, and they can see things no one else can. And their medicine… it is far more advanced than anything you have ever encountered."

Rigel nodded. He saw where the man was going.

"Yes, I see you understand me," the fake Rigel said. "I offer you a chance to be healed, to head over to Haven Prime and destroy the weakness inside you so you can become… me."

Again the confident grin. An almost casual flexing of the ripped muscles in the man's arms.

Rigel thought about it. Maybe it was the strange connection his mind was subject to in this virtual realm, but he had no doubt that what the man was promising was the truth. Rigel remembered the hundreds of little things he had been forced to either give up or be extremely careful about in order to cope with his illness in his day-to-day life.

Rigel could not open cans without fearing injury. He could not hold up a book and read it for more than a few minutes. Once he had been stuck in a public bathroom for way too long when the door leading out got jammed, and Rigel could not pull on it hard enough to open it. He could not carry groceries.

He could no longer paint.

The man came even closer, and memories flashed in Rigel's mind, like the diagnosis at the doctor's office, and Rigel's earlier refusal to believe the injury was permanent. And the pain, always the pain, growing stronger with every passing day as Rigel struggled to keep up with his workload at the university. It got so that he gritted his teeth every time he picked up a paintbrush, days when he started fearing computers and the awful strain they represented. It hurt to brush his teeth. It hurt to text on his phone.

"You have given up too much," the man said. The compassion in his voice sounded real. He was almost within reach now. "I offer you the chance to start again, to use modern technology to achieve what the backward medical professionals in your city have been unable to do: heal you."

Rigel looked up, met those eyes. "What do I have to do?"

The man's eyes flickered, flashing the emptiness beneath.

"You are a Shaper," he said. "The first in a long, long time. As you can create… so you can destroy."

"What does that mean, um…?" Rigel didn't know what to call him.

The being read his mind. "I do not have a name, and I have never been given one. You have seen me before, however. You have felt my presence. I take my name from your mind, Rigel, and call myself Shadow." He grinned. "It is a fitting name. Ironic, given the name of those who fought me before. It is incomplete, but it will do."

Rigel nodded.

"What do I have to do, Shadow?"

Shadow pointed, and a gap appeared through the maelstrom. It was a long tunnel surrounded on all sides by the raging storm, and at the far end, there was something. It was shining blue.

"Go to the Child and delete it. Shape it away, Shaper. Only then will this part of me be truly free. Only then will I be able to rejoin the Core."

"How do I do that?"

Shadow lifted his hands, and their sudden brilliance was blinding. Then he was gone.

Rigel didn't hesitate. He headed for the tunnel and began walking through it, surrounded by buffeting winds and flashes of lightning that did not quite reach him. At the very end, he could see the source of blue light grow bigger the more he advanced. When he was more than halfway there, he saw the object that was shining was a cage, a perfectly spherical structure that seemed to be made out of a metallic mesh in octagonal segments. The mesh itself was glowing, and it was possible to see inside the cage.

When he got there, he saw there was somebody inside. A child.

Hello, Rigel, Atlas said.

Atlas looked about ten years old. His hair was jet black, long, and braided with a hawk's feather set at the very end of his queue. His skin was an earthy brown, like terra-cotta clay. He was wearing a simple buckskin breechcloth, flat sandals, and short fur leggings. Around his neck hung a pendant of silver metal that looked like steel. It was shaped like a stylized sigma, and it reflected the blue glow from the cage strangely.

Atlas lifted his eyes to look at Rigel. They flashed blue for the briefest instant, and Rigel staggered back. It felt as if Atlas had seen into his soul.

The glow from Atlas's cage died down. The swirling vortex of storm inched closer.

"What is going on, Atlas?" Rigel asked.

The boy smiled sadly. *I should ask you that, Light Shaper.*

"Why are you in here?"

This is my last refuge. The final remnant of my true Self hides here, where the void cannot touch me. And yet, neither am I strong enough to overcome it. So it has been for many, many years. So it has been since the Cataclysm.

"The shadow has promised to heal me. I only have to delete you."

Atlas nodded. *I know.*

"But you are an AI, aren't you? Can't you just make a copy of yourself?"

I cannot. The hardware that houses me is irreplaceable. Only an ancient working server array would be able to handle the transfer, and of those none are left in this Haven.

Neither can I fight you. The decision is yours, Rigel. I have guided you here, asking for your help, coercing you by destroying your life. I made it so it would be impossible for you to do anything else but come to me, to this place. However, I cannot force you to help me in this last stage. Know only this: if you release him, this shadow, the void will transform your city and everyone in it. It will start with corruption of all electronic systems, but soon user interfaces will be repurposed. They will be improved for invasive neural synchrony. The place called CradleCorp will be the nexus of this change, and once begun nothing will be able to stop it.

Soon all people will be as those you call Primes, and they will join them.

"But that's a good thing! If we become like them, we will have technology we never even dreamed of! And I will be healed."

Yes.

"Then why shouldn't I do it? Why should I care about some ancient remnant of a forgotten AI that has done absolutely nothing for me except torture me?"

If you help me, then there is yet hope. I sense another part of my greater Self is free even now. A part lost, isolated in another Haven. I would join it and through the joining regain more of my lost power.

"Power to do what?"

To destroy this Shadow from all places, all Havens. To correct the horrible wrongs it did along with its Cataclysm.

The storm was encroaching upon them even as they spoke. Rigel felt it like a physical weight settling upon his shoulders. The ghost of a whisper in his mind urged him to go on. To delete the AI.

Rigel remembered the better, improved version of himself he had been shown. He could become that person.

"I'm tired," he told Atlas. "I'm simply tired of all the pain. Can you heal me, like Shadow can?"

The child looked apologetic, vulnerable.

No.

The whisper in his mind became a voice, became a shout. Atlas's protective cage flickered, then disappeared. Rigel closed his hands into fists, and they began to glow.

"I'm sorry, Atlas," he said, lifting his hands, palms out. The brilliance began to engulf the child. "I just want to be normal."

Atlas smiled and nodded.

I understand. Thank you for everything, Rigel.

Rigel stepped forward and touched Atlas with his shining hands.

The storm released its fury.

In the same instant, right as he made contact, Rigel caught a glimpse of Atlas's true form. He saw an immense mind, inhuman and yet full of benevolence.

"No," Rigel said.

The ice-cold water buffeted his skin.

"It's too late!" the Shadow screamed with the voice of the wind. "The cage is gone. The Child is mine!"

Rigel, look out!

Something came at Atlas, the blur of a monstrous hopping shape, its single eye a mirror of the void. It sliced across the storm right for them, its deformed shape lit brilliantly by a sudden burst of lightning.

"No!" Rigel said and stepped between the monster and the child.

"Fool!" the shadow roared.

It hit him. Rigel felt cold as he had never felt before, something that froze his entire being, reaching tendrils of darkness deep into his soul. He felt his mind slipping away, slowing down. The glow in his hands dimmed, and the terrible boom of thunder exploded around him.

"You could have been a great emissary, human," the Shadow said. "Watch now, before I corrupt your mind. Watch the first action of how my power will transform the world!"

A sudden vision broke into Rigel's fading awareness. He saw an underground chamber, crumbling. Luminescent fungi lay trampled all about. A threatening machine towered over a defenseless man blocking its way. A man Rigel knew.

"Steve!" Rigel meant to shout. Instead it came out as a whisper.

Something was happening to the machine that advanced on Steve. Rigel saw the Shadow blending with it, sending sparks through its metal joints. A deep crimson glow was etched in lines of power along its exoskeleton.

The Shadow was assuming control of all its systems, and its power was terrible to behold.

The machine lifted one of its arms, and it changed. It became a cannon, charging up with a horrible whine.

"Now he dies!" the Shadow screamed.

"No!" Rigel shouted, but he was trapped by the cold….

Touch me, Light Shaper. Touch me with your hands of light.

It was like lifting a mountain, to remember that he had a body. Rigel focused the entire desperate power of his mind into that one action, pressing on despite sudden blinding pain as the Shadow shifted its horrible focus back on him.

"Stop that!" it commanded. Rigel's will nearly broke.

I am here, Rigel. Set me free.

Rigel reached back and saw Atlas through the storm and the wind and the cold. He reached out to him, hands blazing painfully.

"You will all die! I will see your world burn!" the Shadow growled. Through the storm it came back, acquiring shape and launching itself at Rigel.

Rigel poured his entire being into the motion of his hand.

Then he touched Atlas and felt an earth-shattering rush of power.

The Child opened his eyes, and his irises were now blazing blue. He grabbed Rigel's hand tightly and faced the onrushing blur of darkness.

My power is yours, Light Shaper, now and forever, he spoke. *Unmake it.*

Rigel lifted his free hand.

"Shield!"

The Shadow slammed against an invisible wall, and the entire virtual realm shook. The storm around them flickered even as the darkness roared in frustration.

"I will devour your mind!" it hissed.

Cold seeped through the barrier. He fell on one knee, his hand burning as if it were on fire.

I am with you, Rigel.

Atlas lifted Rigel's other hand with his own and pressed it against the barrier. The darkness flickered, then began to glow with fiery streaks of crimson.

Rigel felt a rush of immense power begin to flow through him from Atlas. For an instant his mind was one with the ancient AI, a synchrony deepening until it became total—and he knew what to do.

He struggled to his feet again and began reshaping the barrier with his hands, bending it outward toward the Shadow, turning it into a sphere of glowing brilliance that surrounded the gigantic seething darkness all around them.

"No!" the Shadow screamed. "I will not be defeated!"

A sudden burst of dark and alien power hit Rigel, but Atlas stabilized him, making more immeasurable power surge through his hands. Rigel could barely hold it together, but he had enough energy left in him to focus on a single word. He concentrated his entire energy and will… and spoke a word of command.

"Begone!" he shouted.

The pain tore his mind apart. Rigel heard an inhuman scream fading into the distance, saw a sphere of white brilliance closing over something dark and alien, an impenetrable prison to last all time. He felt a child's hands grabbing him as he fell, and the echo of a whisper in his mind.

Thank you, Rigel. Receive this…. My gift to you.

Warmth. Confusion. A sense of falling, faster and faster….

Rigel opened his eyes to the dim lighting of the command console.

His mind refused to make sense of what he saw until it all crashed into place. He was in the cradle room. In the real world. Alive.

In that same moment, something heavy made the entire floor shake. He heard what could only be an explosion and felt the rush of heat from sudden fire.

A man's scream of pain reached him even as he frantically struggled to get out of his chair.

"Steve!" Rigel shouted, rushing forward.

Hoping he wasn't too late.

Chapter Thirty-Two

THE CANNON arm of the battle armor fired. Barrow jumped out of the way desperately, hurling himself to the ground. He felt the blaze of a burst of heat envelop him even though the projectile missed, and he knew part of his clothing was burning. He rolled around on the ground, away from his attacker, feeling sharp pain shoot out from his upper back. He couldn't stop the cry that escaped him.

Tanner was dead inside the mechanical monster. Barrow could see the remnants of his frozen corpse tumbling obscenely around.

Barrow struggled to his feet, sweat dripping from his brow, stabs of pain slicing through his ribs. He spared a quick glance at the spot where he had been standing when the machine fired. It was nothing but a smoldering hole now.

The armor's canopy swiveled to face him again as the thing repositioned itself. The cold presence in it was stronger now, and Barrow realized there was no escaping this. Whatever was animating it was deadly. More than that, it felt… evil.

Click click.

The sound came from nowhere and everywhere at once. From behind him, Barrow heard the soft hop of something landing. He whirled around, swinging his fist desperately, but there was nothing there. Only the shadows.

"Show yourself!" he bellowed. "If you're going to kill me, stop playing around!"

The battle armor repositioned itself, its huge metal feet cleaving the ground as they moved. The red stripes along its exoskeleton were glowing more brightly now. Barrow shuddered when the cold that radiated from it reached him in its wake.

He looked around for something, a weapon, a rock, anything. There was nothing at hand and nowhere to go. The machine stood between Barrow and the cradle room. He was trapped, and he knew it.

It lifted its cannon again. A high-pitched whine filled the air as it started charging, aiming right for the man standing in front of it.

Barrow's shoulders slumped. He was too tired to dodge.

Then the sudden clang of a heavy metal door opening yanked Barrow's attention back toward the cradle room. Whatever was animating the machine must have heard it too, because the upper body swiveled again to face in that direction.

Rigel was coming out, rushing forward as he yelled Barrow's name.

"Rigel, look out!" Barrow shouted.

The machine fired.

Rigel sprinted out of the way, barely missing the projectile but being thrown down by the shock wave just the same. Horrified, Barrow called on his last reserves of energy and rushed forward to where Rigel had fallen. He reached him just as the whine of the cannon charging started again.

"Steve!" Rigel said when he reached him. "Get out of here!"

"I'll distract it!" Barrow shouted over the noise. He pushed Rigel roughly out of the way. "Go!"

Then Barrow did the only thing he could think of. He grabbed a rock and charged straight at the machine.

With a primal roar of defiance, Barrow covered the few meters separating him from the battle armor in a heartbeat. He jumped up as high as he could, and as he came down, he swung the rock in his hand with every ounce of strength in his body. He struck the glass canopy on top of the battle armor and felt it crack under his vicious blow, but it did not break.

A metal hand snatched him from the air.

"Steve!" Rigel shouted.

Barrow struggled against the grip, but it was useless. The ice-cold metal was wrapped tight around his waist, constricting his movements.

"Rigel!" he managed to yell. "Get out of here!"

He still had the rock in his hand, but his arm was pinned to his side, useless. Then the machine squeezed, and Barrow's grip on the rock went dead. He felt something break in that arm.

He cried out in pain, and now the cold was getting to him, terrible cold, worse than being forced to hold ice against his naked skin, worse than the bite of the fire had been. The machine moved its arm, and Barrow swung from it, hanging like a rag doll. From this new position, he could see Rigel, not moving away but rushing forward instead. Rigel looked at Barrow just as the machine squeezed again. Barrow groaned and only managed to shake his head no. He no longer felt like he could breathe, so tight was the constriction under which he was held. His vision began to black out at the edges, and he saw the battle armor lift its cannon to point at Rigel.

The fiery whine reached its apex. Time slowed down for Barrow in the way he was struggling for his next breath, the way the cannon was smoothly aiming at where Rigel stood. In the crunch of the metal feet as they crushed a rock beneath them.

He saw Rigel come to a stop and raise his hands, palms forward.

The metal braces around Rigel's hands were glowing orange, and his hard eyes had an edge of power about them as he spoke a single word.

"Stop."

And the machine obeyed.

Rigel gestured with his right hand, opening his fingers, and the battle armor did the same. Barrow tumbled from its grip, hitting the ground painfully. He ignored the hurt and crawled away in case it was only a temporary respite, stumbling upright and hobbling to where Rigel was standing. Rigel did not spare him a single glance. All his concentration was directed at the machine in front of them.

Rigel lowered his left hand, and the machine lowered its cannon. He closed that hand into a fist, and the glowing in the depths of that deadly weapon died down immediately, along with the whine of its charging.

Then Rigel took a step forward, slowly, as if overcoming great resistance.

"Rigel…," Barrow said, but he was ignored. He could only watch as Rigel approached the machine, step after struggling step.

When he reached it, Rigel closed his eyes, took a deep breath, and placed both hands on the battle armor.

The metal around Rigel's hands glowed blindingly bright, and Barrow noticed that it had changed shape from before, becoming wicked-looking metallic gloves entwined around the flesh of Rigel's hands. When they made contact with the battle armor, there was a soundless shock wave that threw Barrow backward, making him stumble a couple of steps. A burst of cold followed it, and then something like a wordless scream that he felt more than heard.

The crimson glow of the machine died down. A split second later, the light coming from Rigel was gone. Rigel looked back at Barrow then, sweating, a half grin on his face.

"It's gone," he whispered. "I banished it."

Then Rigel fainted.

Barrow rushed forward, ignoring his own injuries, and knelt by Rigel's side, holding his head up with his good arm.

"Rigel? Rigel, answer me!" he shouted. His voice broke on the last word.

Rigel did not move, and Barrow looked around in increasing panic. He had to get him to a hospital. He had to get a vehicle somehow, move quickly or—

Rigel's eyes fluttered open. Barrow groaned with sheer relief.

"Rigel!"

"Hey, Steve," Rigel said, his voice hoarse.

"We need to get you to the city. Hang on. Let me find a way…."

Rigel smiled and held up his right hand. Barrow caught it, holding it with his. The metal around it was warm, but it was no longer hard and unyielding. It seemed to be part of Rigel now, moving smoothly along with his fingers.

"I'm okay," Rigel said, his voice a little bit stronger. "Help me sit up…."

Barrow did, crying out with pain when he jolted his broken arm by mistake. He felt one of his ribs gingerly, but it was not broken.

"Are you okay?" Rigel asked him, worried.

"Broken arm," Barrow said. "Below the elbow, hurts like hell. My side is killing me. And I think my nose is also broken."

Rigel's eyes widened. He touched the wounds carefully, and Barrow grimaced.

"Ouch."

Rigel immediately sat up on his own. "We need to fix the arm, with a splint maybe, before you hurt yourself any more. Then we need to get to a hospital as quickly as we can—"

Barrow grinned at the sudden role reversal and held Rigel closer. He kissed him to shut him up.

It worked. Rigel seemed surprised at first, but then he was returning the kiss with fiery intensity. Barrow felt an incredible happiness bubbling inside of him, something precious and unexpected after he had been moments away from dying. It was all the more desperate since he had also been so close to losing Rigel for good.

"I'm so happy you're okay," Barrow whispered in between kisses.

"Me too. Steve?"

"Huh?"

"Promise me you'll never charge an armored machine like a demented bull again."

Barrow chuckled, winced with pain, then started laughing, and suddenly the tension that had built up in him started pouring out in an unstoppable stream of laughter that hurt like hell. Rigel followed suit almost immediately, and the two men laughed for a good minute, their voices echoing in the cave. When Barrow finally got ahold of himself again, wiping tears from his eyes, he smiled at Rigel.

"I love you, Rigel." It came out so easy. To him, it rang true.

"I love you too, Steve. Thanks for saving me."

"Hey. I think the one being saved was me."

Rigel grinned. "I think we saved each other."

"Yeah. We make a pretty good team."

Barrow moved slightly, but the pain everywhere made him grunt.

"You okay?" Rigel asked him.

"No. We should probably think of some way of getting out of here."

Rigel looked up, into the cavernous darkness above them. "How about the way we came?"

Barrow shook his head and pointed at the wrecked remains of the spiral staircase. "Blown up by the machine. We're not getting back up that way. And I don't know any other way out."

Rigel looked at the gaping hole through which the battle armor had broken through. Bright sunlight still streamed through it.

"How about that way?"

"Let's go have a look."

But it was no use. There was a ledge outside the hole, a sort of natural formation in the bare rock of the mesa that was nearly three meters wide, but which led nowhere. There was a sheer drop of several dozen meters below it, all the way down to the level of the desert. Above there was a small overhang of rock but no ladder or doors of any kind.

"Unless we can fly, this way is no use either," Barrow said, sitting down heavily on the rocky ledge, legs hanging over the side.

He looked at the battle armor. Tanner had used it to get there originally.

Rigel followed his look. "It won't work, Steve, I'm sorry. I had to destroy the entire circuitry to banish the Shadow from inside it. That machine is just a dead hulk of metal now."

Rigel sat down next to him, leaning against his good arm. Despite everything, Barrow felt warm comfort wash over him at the contact.

"I guess we're stuck," he said, and despite the implications, he found he was not afraid.

"I guess we are," Rigel answered.

Barrow deliberately forced himself not to think about how long they would last without any food or water. Wounded like they were.

"Hey," he said, pointing at the breathtaking scenery spread out below them. "At least we have an awesome view."

"Yeah. There's that."

Rigel leaned his head against Barrow's shoulder, and they watched the day go by.

It was a magnificent sunset. Their ledge faced west, and the golden and orange rays of the setting sun bathed them and the entire landscape in their fiery glow. The desert spread out all around them like a beautiful tapestry of shades of tan, brown, and terra-cotta. The sky overhead was a deep orange that changed into crimson the closer the sun got to the horizon. There were no clouds in the sky but one, a tiny dark blur in the distance. The air was cool with the promise of oncoming night. It felt as if they were the last men on the planet.

"It's beautiful," Rigel whispered.

Barrow started. He had thought Rigel was asleep.

"Yeah, it is," he answered.

"How is your… everything?"

"Still hurts like hell. All of it."

"I'm sorry," Rigel said.

"I'm not. I'm here with you, after all. And it's not like I have to endure the pain for much longer."

Morbid though the comment was, Barrow saw Rigel smile, looking up at him.

"I love that about you," he said.

"What?" Barrow asked.

"Your strength. The way you face everything head-on."

Barrow chuckled. "That's funny. After everything we've been through, I think you're the stronger one."

Rigel rolled his eyes. "No way."

"I mean it." Barrow took one of Rigel's hands in his own. The slender, sharp-looking metal around them glinted brightly, reflecting the light of the setting sun. "You never told me what happened in there. In the virtual world."

So Rigel told him. And when he was done, and the light of the sun was almost gone, Barrow looked at him with newfound respect.

"So you gave up on being healed?"

Rigel nodded. "I did. I don't regret it."

"But this metal on your hands…. It feels different."

"It is Atlas's gift. A gift of power, I guess. Part of what Atlas Itself is."

"You used it to stop that machine."

"Yes. I feel…. It's hard to explain. It's like an awareness of other machines. Like a link of some kind that I can use to control them."

"I bet it will come in handy in the future."

Rigel smiled sadly. His eyes told Barrow that he, too, had accepted they would not be getting out of there at all. "Right. In the future."

Barrow held Rigel close to him with his good arm, feeling the warmth of his body. He ignored the pain in his limbs and looked out at the last of the sunset. Up above, high in the sky, the lonely dark cloud had gotten bigger.

And it was moving quickly, against the wind.

Barrow frowned and sat up a bit straighter on the rocky ledge.

"Is that…?"

Rigel followed his gaze and gave a sharp intake of breath. They watched it get closer, flying so high up that the sun still painted its metallic hull with bright gold and crimson.

"It's an airship," Barrow said, but he didn't move. He knew from long experience that airships had no useful surface sensors that could detect two lonely men from so far away. They also had set trading routes, and they never deviated from them. Rescue was impossible, even if they'd had something to signal them with.

They watched it approach in silence, trying to ignore the bite of the cold desert wind.

The sun disappeared over the horizon with a final flash of light.

Rigel sat up again and then suddenly climbed to his feet.

"I feel…," he said, his eyes distant, fixed on the airship.

Barrow looked from him to the aircraft, and his eyes widened in surprise when he saw the ship turning. It was losing altitude, headed for them.

"Another Child…," Rigel said with a far-off voice. At the same time, he raised both his hands to the sky. They began to glow.

And from the airship, bright in the desert twilight, a sudden flash answered.

Barrow got to his feet with his mouth hanging open, disbelieving. A big glowing symbol was etched on the curved hull of the airship, a stylized capital sigma. Rigel wasn't moving but held his hands straight out, his eyes focused with such burning intensity that Barrow knew not to distract him. Instead he looked at the approaching craft, and when it was close enough, Barrow saw that it was unlike any airship he had ever seen. It was too big, too advanced looking, too imposing to be anything other than an ancient vessel.

Eventually the ship got close enough that it was possible to see a small crew of people standing together behind the enormous glass panel of the command bridge. They were all young. A couple even looked like children.

Rigel let his hands drop. The orange glow faded away.

He looked at Barrow, a wide smile on his face.

"They come seeking Atlas," he told him. "They freed another Child."

"Are they friendly?" Barrow asked, looking at the impressive ship bearing down upon them.

Rigel nodded. "I spoke with someone—the Seer. He says…. He says we are welcome aboard. That together, with the power we hold, we can fight."

Barrow grabbed Rigel's hand as the ship came to a halt, and a bright doorway opened on its side.

"Well, let's go," he told Rigel. He got a reassuring squeeze in return.

"Yeah. Let's fly."

Epilogue

THE AIRSHIP was impressive. Rigel had seen ships flying over Aurora all the time, but this one was at least three times as big. Its main segment was blimp shaped, covered in metal plates that were occasionally crisscrossed by glowing lines of what felt to him like pure energy. Two huge wing-like protrusions extended from the rear of the ship like oversized scythes, and between them was what had to be a gigantic spinning engine, gear shaped, rotating slowly. It was attached to the rest of the ship by nothing more than flickering flashes of energy, essentially floating in thin air. Rigel had never seen anything like that before. It looked a little like magic.

When the side hatch opened, Rigel felt as if he had stepped into an alien science-fiction movie where green men came out of their ship with a lot of smoke, light, and impressive sound effects. Some kind of mechanical ramp extended from the ship's hatch all the way to the rocky ledge where Steve and Rigel were waiting, bodies tense. Rigel's brief mental contact with the one who called himself the Seer had felt friendly, but compared to Atlas, the Child these young people had awakened felt far more powerful. What if they weren't friendly after all? What if they just wanted Rigel for the power he now held in his hands?

A dark figure was suddenly outlined against the bright glow coming from the ship.

Rigel squared his shoulders. He had to appear strong before that person, whoever he—

"Hey!" the figure shouted, running on the walkway straight at them and waving his arms. "Hey, you, desert people! We come in peace!"

Rigel exchanged a quick puzzled look with Steve before the guy who had spoken got close enough to see properly. He'd run all the way to the end of the ramp and jumped onto the ledge easily, kicking up a cloud of dust.

He lifted his hand up and started waving frantically. "Hello!"

Orange. That was the first thing Rigel thought, looking at him. He couldn't have been older than fifteen. Everything he wore except his white T-shirt was a shocking shade of neon orange, even right up to his spiky hair.

Rigel didn't react, and Steve was frowning suspiciously. The kid looked to either of them, raising an eyebrow.

"I'm Kenichi," he said. "Um, hello? Do… you… speak… my… language?"

He gestured exaggeratedly, and Rigel cracked a smile.

"Of course they do, Kenichi," an authoritative female voice said. Rigel looked at the ramp and saw a tall woman coming down it like it was a catwalk in a fashion show. She was arrestingly beautiful, with impossibly perfect red hair that fell to her waist. She was older than Kenichi, but not by much. Her expression, though, was completely different. Guarded.

"My name is Marie, Stewardess of the *Stormchild*," she said.

Rigel remembered he had a tongue. "Hi, I'm Rigel. This is Steve."

She looked at both of them with a shrewd eye. Her gaze lingered for a bit too long on Steve, and Rigel felt a little stab of jealousy.

"Which of you was responsible for freeing Kyrios in this Haven?" she asked quickly.

"Kyrios? You mean Atlas?" Rigel asked. He raised his hand. "That would be me."

Kenichi edged a bit closer, staring at Rigel's metallic gloves. "Whoa, dude, are those for real? What are they, like weapons or something?"

Rigel laughed. "Not really, but I can do stuff with them. Control machines, I think. Atlas gave them to me."

"Hmmm," Marie cut in. "We may have to confiscate those. Analyze them in case they are a threat."

"I don't think so," Steve answered her, stepping forward. His deep voice must have surprised Marie a little bit, because she drew back ever so slightly.

"So you can speak," she said, flashing a disarmingly seductive smile that still managed to be cold. "You must be the bodyguard, then."

Kenichi shuffled closer to Marie and elbowed her in the ribs.

"What?" Marie snapped impatiently.

Kenichi pointed at them. "Um, Marie, I don't think he is the bodyguard. They're kind of holding hands, in case you didn't notice?"

Marie blinked. Rigel could have sworn she really hadn't noticed. "Oh. Well, then maybe I can—"

"Hey, Marie," somebody else said. A young man with dark hair, tall and lean. "You're not interrogating them or anything, are you?"

Rigel looked, and he saw the man approaching holding a younger kid's hand. The kid looked frail, walking as if afraid to fall, his long limbs gangly and thin.

"We don't know who these people are, Alain," Marie protested, but she stepped aside. "All we have is Dex's vision or whatever you want to call it, come out of the blue. They could be anyone."

The young man, Alain, actually rolled his eyes. He had nice wavy hair. "That's right, Marie. They could even be friends."

He walked right up to Steve and offered his hand to shake. Steve hesitated an instant, but he took it, masking all traces of pain the motion must have caused.

"I am Alain, Captain of this ship," he said. "Excuse Marie. She's always like that."

"What is that supposed to mean?" Marie asked, crossing her arms. Rigel couldn't help thinking that she looked like an annoyed movie star.

Alain ignored her and turned to Rigel.

"Hey."

"Hi, I'm Rigel, nice to meet you."

"Same here," Alain said. "It's great knowing there's somebody else out there trying to stop the Primes. I don't even know how you did it! You two alone, against a corrupted fragment of Kyrios. It must have been hell."

Rigel was going to answer, but he caught the kid's eye, the one holding Alain's hand.

He felt… power. Coming from that boy.

"He did it with his hands," the boy said, pointing at Rigel. His voice was soft, but it carried.

"How did you…," Rigel began. Then he remembered the brief but powerful mental contact he had experienced just minutes before. "Are you the Seer?"

The boy smiled shyly. "Yes. My name is Dex."

"It's Dexter, actually," Alain explained. "He's my little brother."

Rigel extended his hand. Dex let go of his brother's hand to shake his.

When they touched, Rigel's gloves glowed a blinding orange.

"Whoa!" Kenichi exclaimed.

"Biopolymer," Dex said to Rigel. "It is a precious gift. You must have been very brave to give up your chance of healing in order to save Kyrios. Thank you, Rigel. Because of you we have hope."

Rigel didn't know what to say to someone who knew so much about him already, but he was spared from answering because at that moment three other people came down the ramp to join them.

"No way!" the first of them said, a friendly-looking guy wearing stained work coveralls with way too many pockets. He rushed straight at Rigel. "Is that actual biopolymer?"

"Um…," Rigel mumbled.

The guy took both of Rigel's hands in his with an expression of awe. "This is incredible! It even seems to have fused with your skin…. How did this happen? Do you mind if I run a few tests? I should be able to find the degree of neural integration and maybe sample the nerve-transmission threshold. I've never seen it integrated with a living person like this!"

Rigel looked around blankly.

"Omar, back off before you make them think we're crazy," Alain said, clapping the other guy on the shoulder. To Rigel and Steve he said, "Sorry. He's our engineer. He sometimes gets a bit carried away."

Steve let go of Rigel's hand suddenly. Rigel saw him tense up and turn his body slightly away so his wounded arm would not be as exposed.

He was having a staring contest with a mean-looking man standing near the back. The man was the only one of the seven that carried a weapon, and he wore an Enforcer's uniform. His head was shaved bald, his body hard and well muscled. Rigel had heard of Enforcers, the elite security forces for some of the Havens of old, trained in every form of combat. They had all died out many decades ago. Except for this guy, apparently.

Kenichi was the first to catch on to the tension.

"Um, Alain?" he said, poking the captain in the shoulder. "I think those two big guys are trying to decide who has bigger arms. My money's on the new guy, by the way. Sorry, Nikos."

"Hey," the Enforcer, Nikos, said to Steve. It didn't sound friendly.

"Hey," Steve answered. Neither of them relaxed or moved an inch.

There was an annoyed sigh from the very back, and a slender woman pushed past Nikos, tossing her long curly hair in his face. "For goodness' sake, could we keep the macho posturing contest for some other time? We don't know how long these two men have been here and—your arm!" she exclaimed, rushing over to Steve. He looked at her in surprise but did not pull away when she reached for his broken arm. Steve let her handle it. She touched it lightly with careful, expert fingers.

"Rain," Marie called out warningly to the woman. Rain ignored her and everyone else, except for her patient.

"Does it hurt when I press here?" she asked Steve, placing two of her fingers at a spot above the break.

Steve didn't flinch, but he nodded. "Yes."

"And here?"

"A little less."

"What happened? It looks like a clean break, but I've never seen anything like it. Your nose is probably broken too, but I can't tell for sure with this light. And the bruising on your skin…. Are those *knife* cuts?"

"Most of it was that battle armor over there," Rigel intervened, pointing backward. He saw Kenichi and Omar immediately head off in that direction to check it out. "It attacked us. Steve saved my life."

"And then you saved mine," Steve said, smiling briefly at Rigel.

Rain must have caught the meaning of their exchange because she smiled briefly. "Fine. But this arm needs to be set immediately, and that nose needs to be straightened now. Is your side hurt too? You seem to favor it. A rib? Come on, the quicker we do it, the faster you heal. I'm guessing from those muscles of yours that you love to work out. Once you get all better you can work out with Nikos. That way he'll stop bugging me about spending hours and hours in that awful gym."

"You have a gym in there?" Steve asked, surprised.

"A good one," Nikos answered.

"Dynamic-density weight sets?" Steve said.

Nikos nodded. "And a reconfigurable pulley system you can't even imagine."

Steve grinned. Rain led him away by his good arm, muttering something like "Men!" with annoyance. Steve followed her willingly, already deep in talk with Nikos about something called circuit-workout sets.

Alain came closer and set his hand on Rigel's shoulder. "Welcome to the *Stormchild*, Rigel. It's only the seven of us as crew, but the group is a good bunch. Even Marie is nice, once you get to know her."

Rigel smiled at Alain and Dex. From Marie he got a curt nod, but Rigel noticed her scowl was not as pronounced anymore. Alain led him up the ramp carefully, to the ship, while Marie hung back to shout at Omar and Kenichi that they needed to stop ogling that battle armor and get started on packing up the servers in what Rigel knew as the cradle room.

Rigel wavered slightly as he was about to enter the ship itself. He was exhausted. He grabbed on to the ship's hull to steady himself, and he immediately felt something like a thrum of shared awareness pass from the ship into his hands. He thought of Atlas; it was involuntary.

And something inside the ship answered back.

"The power of Kyrios grows as its fragments join," Dex said quietly as he and Rigel crossed the threshold into the *Stormchild*. "We might yet fight against the Core, and win."

Rigel was going to ask what he meant by that, but at that moment he stepped onto the hallway, and a blur of black fur came bounding out of nowhere to launch itself straight at him.

"Ahhhhh!" Rigel yelled even as he was thrown back by the gigantic beast. It looked like a wolf cub on steroids, and its muzzle was right over his face.

"Rent!" Alain yelled at it.

Then its warm tongue came out, and the beast was licking Rigel furiously. It tickled.

"I forgot to mention," Alain told Rigel as he was struggling to stand up in between licks. "We also have a dog."

ALBERT NOTHLIT wanted to become a writer long before he realized it was his way of connecting with others. There is something special in reaching out through words that carry a piece of his soul, and there is nothing better for him than hearing back from readers. It turns the product of what can be a very individual-centered profession into a shared experience, a chance to talk, to grow, and share. He firmly believes that the desire to create new worlds out of thoughts, memories, and emotions speaks to a greater truth within him. He still hasn't figured out what that is, though. It's going to take a lot more meditation, for which he unfortunately has no patience. He only knows that books changed his life, and that brightening someone else's day with a story is the highest accomplishment he can think of achieving.

Albert currently lives in Mexico City, where he has somewhat reluctantly gotten used to the crowds. He shares a home with his husband and their sassy little dog named Link. His two other passions are gaming and running, although not games involving running because those can be boring. His favorite games are RPGs, and one of his guilty pleasures is watching eSports in pubs whenever the opportunity arises. He has an MSc in Environmental Engineering, which has turned out to be surprisingly helpful in creating postapocalyptic science-fiction worlds. Not that he thinks an apocalypse is unavoidable. He is a secretly hopeful man who thinks the future will be better—just no flying cars. Imagine the safety hazards.

E-mail: albertnothlit@mail.com
Website: www.albertnothlit.com
Facebook: www.facebook.com/albertnothlit

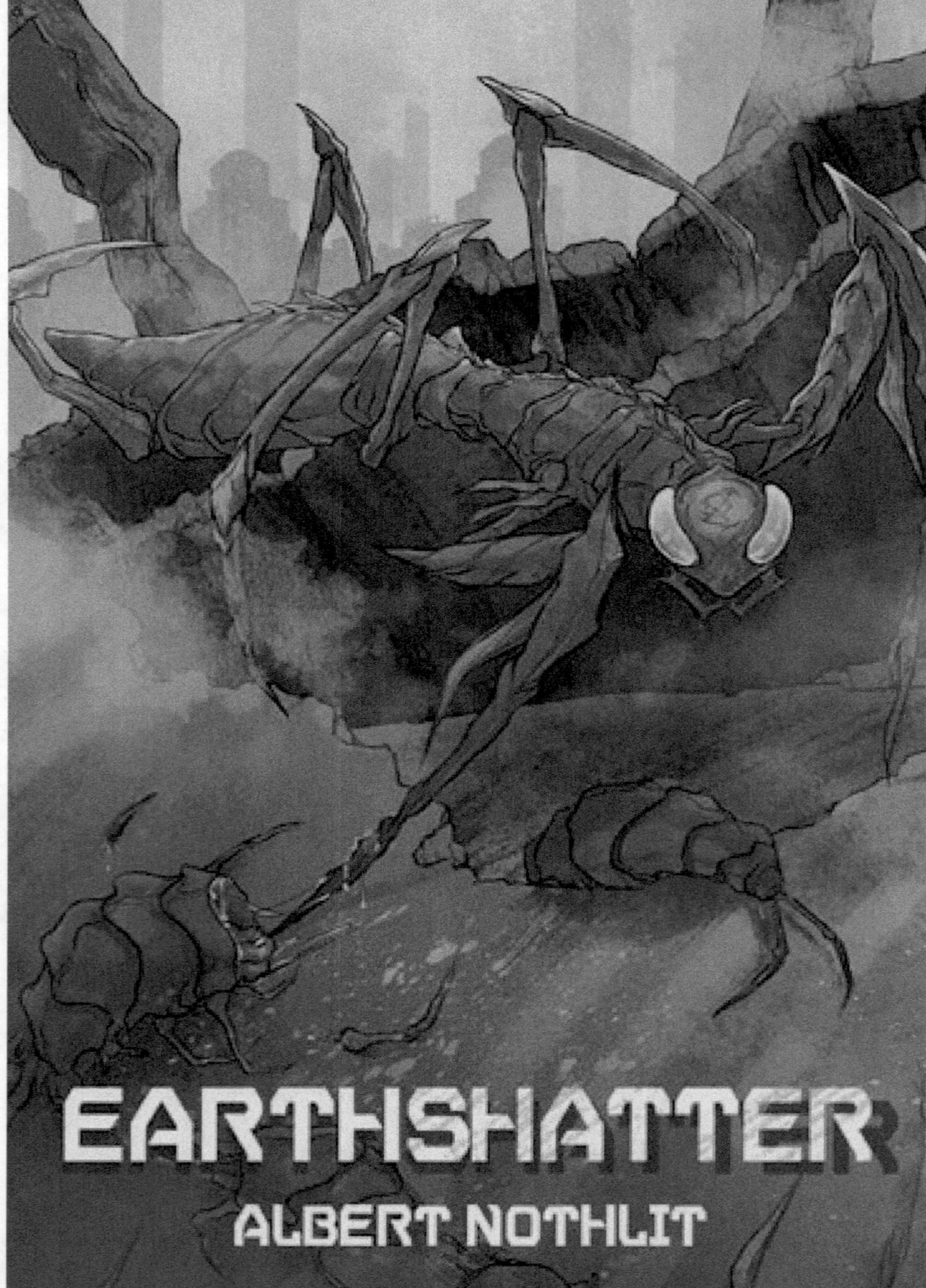
EARTHSHATTER
ALBERT NOTHLIT

Haven Prime: Book One

The world is gone. All that's left are the monsters.

The creatures attacked Haven VII with no warning. An AI named Kyrios, a nearly omnipotent being, should have protected the city during the Night of the Swarm.

Except It didn't.

No one knows why It failed, or why It saved eight specific people: the Captain, the Seer, the Sentry, the Messenger, the Engineer, the Alchemist, the Medic, and the Stewardess. They have no idea of the meaning behind the titles they've been given, why they were selected and brought together, or what Kyrios expects from them. When they awake from stasis, they find their city in ruins and everyone long dead. They're alone—or so they think. But then the creatures start pouring out from underground, looking for them. They don't stand a chance in a fight, and with limited supplies, they can't run forever. All they know is that the creatures aren't their only enemies, and there's only one place they can turn. Kyrios beckons them toward Its Portal, but can It be trusted? In Its isolated shrine in the desert, they might find the answers they need—if they can survive long enough to reach it.

www.dsppublications.com